A
Letter
from
Ireland

BOOKS BY ANN O'LOUGHLIN

The Irish House
My Only Daughter
Her Husband's Secret
Secrets of an Irish House
Escape to the Irish Village

Ann O'Loughlin

A
Letter
from
Ireland

bookouture

Published by Bookouture in 2024

An imprint of Storyfire Ltd.
Carmelite House
50 Victoria Embankment
London EC4Y 0DZ

www.bookouture.com

Storyfire Ltd's authorised representative in the EEA is Hachette Ireland
8 Castlecourt Centre
Castleknock Road
Castleknock
Dublin 15, D15 YF6A
Ireland

ISBN: 978-1-83525-525-4
eBook ISBN: 978-1-83525-524-7

To John, Roshan and Zia xxx

ONE

'We have to do it. Hell, we're obligated.'

Casey stared intently at her two friends.

Silence.

They hadn't met in so long, and here they were stuck in a windowless office with dull grey walls, with an attorney who had an annoying habit of constantly checking his phone, and they couldn't even commit to honouring the last wishes of their dear friend. Their little group had once been so tight, and now...

Casey shook herself, and eyeballed the other two women.

'Come on, let's make the best of it. Rosie has reached out, and asked the three of us. It might be an adventure, fun even,' she said, her voice high pitched with emotion.

Debbie took out her handkerchief and blew her nose.

'What was Rosie thinking? What does she expect us to do – throw up our lives on a whim? Isn't it bad enough that she's gone, leaving us all feeling like crap?' she said.

'We can manage; it's only for two months,' said the third woman, who was using one finger to straighten a framed painting on the wall.

'You would say that, Georgie. You don't have teenage kids to think about. Are you still on husband number two or have you moved to number three?' Debbie said sharply, before muttering under her breath, 'Still the same whimsical, carefree Georgie, I suppose.'

Casey rapped her knuckles on the table.

'Enough. Rosie would be furious to see us tearing strips off each other. We need to honour her memory, no matter how inconvenient it is for all of us.'

Georgie sat down, and sighed.

'I feel really bad; I hadn't talked to her in so long. Did any of us even know Rosie was ill? Are any of us even friends any more?'

Debbie dabbed the tears from her eyes.

'That's nasty and unnecessary. We hadn't seen each other, but we will always be friends. The past is irrelevant,' she said quietly.

'Let's not go there,' Casey snapped as she leaned towards the attorney, who was sitting, drumming his fat fingers on the table. 'Can we hear what she wants again, please?' she said.

Looking impatient, the attorney cleared his throat, and called for quiet, before reading from the last will of Rosie Brentwood one more time.

'Casey, Debbie and Georgie, you have been my friends forever; my family when I needed one most. How I wish it could be the four of us together again. Please, can I cash in all the friendship tokens, and ask you to scatter my ashes. Have a glass of prosecco and remember me fondly.'

'That, I don't mind,' Debbie interjected loudly.

The attorney raised his hand and Casey dug Debbie in the ribs, making her shush as he continued to read.

'I know you are all so very busy, but please block out your schedules for July and August. I want you to travel to the West Coast of Ireland. I will be there in spirit when you set foot on Scarty Island off the County Clare coast. It has been my happy *place for so many years. spending every July and August there. They are the sweetest months on the small spit of land on the Atlantic Ocean. Scarty has been my guilty secret all these years.*

'*It is my wish, dear friends, that you will travel and stay on the island. Think of it as an opportunity to be together again.*'

Debbie jumped up.

'I've heard enough; what she is asking is only days away. Rosie is dead. What is she trying to do, control us from the grave or make us feel even more guilty that we haven't been in touch in so long?'

She suddenly stopped when the attorney purposefully shut the folder on his desk.

'Any other questions?' he asked, smiling wearily at the women.

Casey looked at him.

'First off, why isn't her husband doing this? He surely must have a say,' she said.

'At the time of her death, Ms Brentwood was in the process of getting a divorce from Mr Wilding.'

Georgie sat up straight.

'Nobody mentioned divorce. What's going on here?'

The attorney sat back on his swivel chair making it squeak.

'It's not for me to speculate. Ms Brentwood was a private woman, and she wasn't fond of explaining herself. I can help with logistics, but if you're looking for answers, perhaps you'll find them if you follow her wishes. Can you come back to me in a few days with an answer on the will request, please?'

Casey placed her hands on the desk, and read the attorney's nameplate.

'Mr Silver, this is no ordinary request that is being made. It involves us leaving our families, our careers, to travel some-where unknown, to stay there for two months. You can't expect us to decide on it immediately,' she said.

'Or ever,' Debbie interrupted.

Georgie leaned forward.

'I will go, but why on earth does Rosie want us to do this? We hadn't met in two years. This is so weird,' she muttered.

Unfazed, the attorney reached into a drawer in his desk.

'I have letters here for each one of you. It may help,' he said.

'It's ridiculous to think we can cast our lives aside to go on this foolish adventure. Those days are over,' Debbie grumbled.

'I have to comply with Ms Brentwood's wishes. She insisted you give your answer within the week,' the attorney said, holding out the envelopes. 'Go home, get some rest and have a long hard think about things,' he said.

Georgie took her letter, and stuffed it in her jeans pocket.

'It's the least I can do for her. I'm in,' she said softly. Debbie shoved a manicured hand forward and snatched her envelope.

'I will read it, but I'm not promising anything,' she snarled.

Casey waited until the others had gone out the door before she took her letter.

'You surely know – please tell me why she wanted to do this?' she asked.

The attorney shrugged.

'Honestly, I have no idea. Maybe to focus on the past was a good thing when there was no future.'

Casey took a paper tissue from her handbag, and blotted the tears from her heavily made-up face.

'This is all too much. It's a huge ask; we barely know each other any more. Our lives veered off in different directions.'

She got up to leave, but lingered at the door.

'Do you know how long she was ill?'

'I probably shouldn't be telling you this, but she was diagnosed with cancer six months ago, and for the last two months, she was really bad.'

'But she never called; I would have come,' Casey said, tears streaking through her make-up.

'You may have been busy, but she was stubborn. Ms Brentwood was always so single-minded. She occupied herself, when there was a respite from the pain, with devising this island challenge. I just hope you can do it.'

Casey examined the envelope as she walked out the door. Her name was written on the front, and the handwriting was definitely Rosie's. There was the flourish of the loop at the end of Casey's name that only Rosie did. Running her finger over the script, she felt ashamed that she had not made contact with her best friend in so long, and now it was too late. She had deluded herself into thinking she had all the time in the world, but she would never see her best friend again or hear her raucous laugh.

Casey procrastinated opening the letter. Every time she saw Rosie's handwriting, a sadness crossed her heart, and guilt coursed through her that she had lost touch with such a good friend. She felt bad too that, though she wanted to go to Ireland, she was afraid to leave Manhattan and her job for two long months. She could not even remember when she had last sat down with Rosie. They had been so tight once, but in recent years had grown apart.

After two days, Casey knew she had to read the letter. Telling her secretary she was taking the morning off, she stepped out on to the penthouse terrace, a mug of coffee in one hand, Rosie's envelope in the other. The sounds of the city were far below her; the wind currents buffeting the building; the drone of air traffic a constant background. She should have ripped the letter open the day she got it, but she was afraid of what it might contain.

Part of her thought opening it would be an acknowledgement that Rosie was really gone, and she just couldn't believe it. Rosie had always been the steady one; she had a plan from the off, and wasn't shy about declaring that she wanted a husband

and a big family. She got Barry and while there weren't children, she appeared content.

Using a knife, Casey slit open the envelope. There was one typed page, which had been signed by Rosie.

My Dearest Casey,

I know you are wondering why you're sitting there with my letter in your hands, rather than with me in front of you. But that is a long story, and I can't give it to you just yet. I'm sure you have plenty of questions that will be answered in time, but first, consider this – do you ever feel like you're not really living the life you want?

Once it was all so easy. Do you remember how we laughed together? You surely don't forget the time we got purple highlights at the hair salon. Our parents were furious. We used to sneak to each other's homes, and listen to music and smoke, and sometimes swig beer.

That was one of the best times of my life.

I know you have a very glamorous life in the city now. I follow your career defending all sorts in big criminal cases. I get a thrill when I see your name in newspaper reports. I am so glad you persevered to the end to become such a great attorney. But I sometimes wonder where that mad young girl went, when I see you looking so smart and polished.

I had this crazy idea for getting us all together. and recreating the past, but cancer got in the way. I was going to bring you girls out to Scarty myself, for a retreat into nature, where we would have plenty of time to chat, drink bubbly, and set the world to rights. Cancer had a different plan.

Now, I ask you to carry out this idea, the three of you; renew the friendships, and spend time away from your usual lives. Please recharge. Make it like old times.

You may be surprised that I'm asking you to go to such a

remote place. But Scarty Island has my whole heart. Everybody thought I was escaping each year to an island off the Maine coast, but all this time I have holed away on a small dot in the Atlantic Ocean. Scarty Island is perfect and for me, holds special memories. It is tiny, but there is a small farmhouse, and while it's nothing glamorous, it's felt like more of a home to me than my house in New York ever has.

I have included here all sorts of details on how to get to there. I don't need to tell you how special the place is; you will see soon enough.

You will know too, in time, where is the best place to scatter my ashes, across land and sea. I trust you more than anyone, and I know you'll put me where I'm meant to be.

My gift to you three is the island for the next two months. How I wish I could be part of the group, but think of me as being with you in spirit. Casey, don't, like me, leave everything until it is too late. Make time for yourself, and make time for the friends you once knew so well.

Take my hand, Casey, and dance with me to Scarty Island. This group will be nothing without all its parts. Let's put all the differences aside. I hope we can have this last adventure together on Scarty Island.

All my love forever,

Rosie xx

In tears, Casey let the letter drop on the table. She still did not understand why Rosie hadn't called or met her, hadn't wanted to say goodbye, and instead left so much unsaid.

Casey yearned now to go to Scarty to somehow make up for the lost time with Rosie; the need to do the right thing lay heavy on her shoulders, but she had no idea how she was going to manage to get eight weeks' vacation.

Googling Scarty Island, she noted it covered sixty-six acres, whatever that meant, and there was a small farmhouse and a separate old ruin. There were two spits of land and two sandy beaches. It ranged from beach to jagged cliffs which had a huge bird population, and was just about quarter of a mile out to sea from the mainland. In winter, it was often cut off for weeks on end, because the sea between the mainland and island could get very rough and the currents were notorious. Casey shivered; she wasn't even good when they visited Hudson Highlands State Park.

Just as she was picturing Rosie huddled in a boat, on her way to the island in secret, she heard her husband, Gary, make coffee in the kitchen, and she pushed the letter under her diary on the table.

'You never sit out here. What's up?' he called out.

She pretended not to hear, cringing when he followed her out onto the deck, scratching his belly as he talked.

'Something wrong?' he asked, sitting down beside her.

'I have to go away for a while.'

Casey stopped abruptly; she had said it out loud.

'What? Where?'

'Ireland. Rosie has asked me along with Debbie and Georgie. We have to go there to scatter her ashes.'

'Why? I didn't think you were all still buddies.'

'We've always been friends; we just lost touch in the last few years.'

'And now you are going on vacation together?'

'Not exactly; like I said, we have to scatter Rosie's ashes.'

'What did the partners say?'

'I haven't talked to anyone yet.'

'How many days?'

'Weeks – eight weeks.'

'Hell, Casey, we go to trial very soon. It's going to be big news.'

'You can handle it without me.'

'Of course I can, but do you really want that?'

'Gary, I have to do this. It was her dying wish.'

'But you hardly know those people any more.'

Casey got up, and walked across the balcony. She stood gazing at the Chrysler Building crown. This was her favourite building in the world. Gary had proposed to her on this balcony with that backdrop; the crown golden in a New York sunset.

That was ten years ago, and they had been so happy. The happiness had faded, and when his string of affairs started, she wanted to walk out on Gary. She had been waiting for the right moment, constantly coming up with excuses why it wasn't the ideal time. Rosie's invitation might just have offered her that chance to finally break free. Gary, she thought, had some cheek sounding so concerned about her all of a sudden.

'I need to go. I will talk to the partners tomorrow; it's my story to tell. I expect you to keep quiet; I need time to decide on my approach. I have given a lot to the firm. I need this time,' Casey said firmly.

Gary grunted that he was off to work, and she knew by the set of his jaw, he wanted her to suffer and to worry. He would blab, she knew that, but maybe a little notice to her boss would not be a bad thing. Gary kissed her goodbye, and whispered 'See you later', but she had seen him drop his leather holdall by the front door, and she knew he planned to be away from home for days. She was so tired of Gary and his lame excuses, and so annoyed at herself that she was letting this situation continue unchecked. She suspected she didn't want to rock the boat because work and home were so welded together. She needed to go far away, and clear her head so she could make the right decision for the future.

Scarty sounded far enough away.

TWO

Casey texted Debbie and Georgie and invited them around to her apartment for a late-afternoon get together. She put two bottles of white wine in the fridge, and ordered a cold platter from Katz's Delicatessen. Chardonnay used to be their favourite tipple, and she hoped it would help smooth things over with the others.

Debbie, wearing a bright blue jumpsuit with gold strappy sandals, her long hair piled into a messy bun, arrived first, calling loudly for a glass of wine. Once she got the wine, she announced she was off out to the deck for a smoke.

'You haven't changed much,' Casey remarked light-heartedly.

'I have changed a lot, but I still smoke and drink. It's no big deal,' Debbie retorted.

Casey was glad when the doorman rang to say Georgie Hunt was on her way up. She came in carrying a small parcel and a bottle of prosecco. Slipping out of her black silk kimono-type jacket, she pulled off her big sunglasses, and nervously looked around, all the time tugging at her long blonde hair.

'I remembered I painted this building when it was a

construction site, and I thought you might like it,' she said, pushing the package towards Casey. 'It's a watercolour. I was experimenting with the use of soft lines to portray an almost ethereal quality to what was the harsh environment of a building site.'

'You really know your stuff. Georgie, this is beautiful,' Casey said, taking in the brown steel girders and the hints of dark spikes pushing out of the ground which now underpinned the building. At one corner, two men were standing, pointing to the patch of intense blue that was the sky. Casey scanned the wall looking for a place to hang the painting. Taking down one of Gary's favourite works of art, she stuffed it behind the sofa, and put Georgie's painting on the wall.

'Won't Gary mind?' Georgie asked.

'He won't be home for days, and I hope to be on the way to Ireland by then.'

'Thank goodness you're coming along; we must travel together.'

Debbie, as if summoned, appeared in the doorway between the sitting room and the outside terrace.

'You two aren't seriously doing this thing?' she said, gesturing that she needed a refill.

'Someone has to. And I want to know why that island was so important to Rosie,' Casey said.

'It's nuts, hauling us all to that place to scatter her ashes. We can do it in my garden, say a few nice words. Rosie won't know.' Debbie sighed, topping up her wine glass to almost over-flowing.

'But we would know. I think what she wants us to do is incredibly romantic. We have to do it; Rosie has asked us,' Georgie said, helping herself to salami from the platter.

'All of a sudden, Georgie Hunt is so co-operative and willing to do what Rosie wants. Easy, I suppose, now that she's dead.'

'Quit it, Debs. That's not fair,' Georgie said, putting some of the salami back on the plate.

Debbie sighed loudly.

'It might not be fair... both of you were at fault, but it managed to bust up our little group.'

'I am not doing this now, not when Rosie isn't around to defend herself,' Georgie said, before gulping down her wine.

'Debs, Rosie is dead. Can you just be a little kinder and can you stop going on about the past? None of us wants to go back to bad times,' Casey said, her voice agitated.

'Hell, strike me down with lightning! I was only saying,' Debbie said.

She turned to stare at Casey.

'It's not just that. I have two fifteen-year-old boys and a lazy husband. I can't go traipsing across to an island off the Irish coast. I have responsibilities.'

'Won't the boys be at summer camp?' Georgie said.

'And what if they are? I don't just sit around all day when they're gone. Besides, I can't justify the time and money. Also, how can I leave my husband for so long.'

'What are you afraid of, that he will run off with a younger model?' Georgie sniggered.

Casey got a spoon, and clinked her glass as if she were calling a meeting to attention.

'Ladies, can we at least be civilised? Can't we talk about this? We used to be able to sit around and chat for hours.'

Debbie snorted loudly.

'Casey, we are grown women, all in our forties; we know our own minds at this stage. Just let it be.'

'Rosie wants us to do this. That's the bottom line here, and maybe it will be good to rekindle the old bonds,' Casey said.

'You two are all for it, so go, do it. But Marvin has started up another business. I need to help out.' Debbie said.

'Are you sure?'

Debbie lit up another cigarette, and blew a puff of smoke up to the ceiling.

'If I were you, Casey, I wouldn't risk my career, and maybe my marriage for a dead woman's stupid idea.'

A silence hung in the air between them. For a moment even Debbie looked a little surprised by what she had uttered.

'That's so harsh,' Georgie said.

Debbie swung around.

'Who does Rosie think she is or was, anyway? Do any of us have time for this palaver, for goodness' sake? I am sorry she's dead, but I have no more tears left.'

Casey took the cigarette from Debbie, and stubbed it on a small plate on the island worktop.

'From the get go, you have been so confrontational. If you don't want to come along that's fine, but let those of us who loved Rosie honour her memory.'

Debbie swept her hands in front of her as if she were showing off the room.

'It's so easy for you, Casey,' she said, 'we don't all have the advantage of a high-power career and lots of money. Some of us have to work bloody hard for what we can get.'

'That's so unfair,' Georgie said.

Debbie swung around to look Georgie in the eye.

'From the woman who never did an honest day's work in her life. Pardon me, if I don't think arts and crafts is the real deal.'

Casey jumped in between the two of them, afraid Georgie would lash out at Debbie.

'I apologise for inviting you here, Debbie, and I'm very sorry you can't come with us, but we are going to Ireland, with or without you,' Casey said.

'Is that supposed to mean something to me?' Debbie asked as she took her purse and pushed it under her arm.

Casey walked her to the elevator.

'I hope you will change your mind,' she said quietly.

'I won't,' Debbie declared as she stepped into the elevator, and pushed the button so the doors closed.

Disappointed, Casey returned to her apartment.

'Did you really expect any other outcome?' Georgie said.

'I guess not, but I hoped she had changed. She always was the one who started and continued the rows.'

Georgie took out her phone, and scrolled, calling out dates and times for flights.

'Could you be ready in two days?' she asked.

'Yes, I think so,' Casey said.

'Good, because if we go on Wednesday, we get the flight much cheaper.'

'Wednesday, it is,' Casey said, trying to hide the trembling in her voice.

'Have you told Gary?'

'Yeah, but he's away at the moment; it's no big deal. How about you, do you have anyone to leave behind?'

Georgie filled a roll with salami.

'Me? I'm easy and free, like Debbie says. I just need to organise the tools of my trade; I will paint out there.'

'I hadn't thought of that. Maybe I can work a little as well. It will make it easier broaching the subject of a vacation if I can propose a work schedule. I don't even know what I will do on this island. I have never even considered such a long vacation before.'

'It's a shame Debbie won't come; she would surely give you enough to do with all of her arguing and bossing about.'

'I won't miss the tension,' Casey said.

Georgie stood up. 'She is still so sore with me.'

'You two need to talk it out.'

'Fat chance of that if she isn't coming with us. What I do know is... maybe she is right. I was a selfish brat back then.'

'You did what you thought was right. Nobody can fault you for that.'

'Nobody, except Debbie, and I don't know, probably Rosie too,' Georgie said despondently.

Casey put her arm around Georgie.

'Let's go to the island, just the two of us.'

'Don't forget – Rosie's ashes too.'

'Three out of four aint bad,' Casey said.

'Still, how will we get on?'

'Don't say you're going to pull out next?'

'Would you go on your own?'

Casey walked to the long window, and stood for a moment, her eyes fixed on the Chrysler Building crown.

'Rosie wants us to do this; so yes, even if I have to go solo, I will honour her request,' she said.

Georgie laughed.

'Don't worry, I wouldn't miss it. Rosie is right, in a weird way, it's an opportunity, but it will be better if Debbie gets over herself and comes too.'

Casey shook her head

'This is not like trying to persuade her to go to a nightclub on a Saturday night. If she can't leave her family, she can't.'

'She's just a loud scaredy cat, and she doesn't want to be around me,' Georgie said. Casey gave her a stern look.

'That may be so, but there's nothing we can do about it. Now, go home, I have a lot of administration to get through, if I am to get that flight. I'll be in first class, how about you?'

'Of course you will. No, I'm good paying substantially less, but we can meet at the airport for a drink beforehand,' Georgie said as she made for the door. 'That is, if you will drink anywhere besides a first class lounge,' she said, peeking over her shades.

'Don't be silly. I travel first class because I want more leg room, and I have a bad back,' Casey said, defensively.

'I believe you,' Georgie laughed as she made her way to the elevator.

After Casey closed her apartment door behind Georgie, she didn't move for a few moments. It was as if she were rooted to the spot. In the space of just a few hours, she had prepared herself to turn her back on her career, and commit herself to this trip to a small island, where she didn't even know if there was sanitation.

It was late when her secretary called. She knew Gary had already told the partners she intended to step back from the trial.

'Casey, you have got to get in here as soon as possible. A lot of things are being said.'

'Tell them I will Zoom them.'

'I really think you should show your face in the office. They are saying you're going away for two whole months.'

'I see Gary has been very happy to tell my news. OK, I'll be there first thing tomorrow.'

Once she'd finished her call, she stood shaking. What had she done? She was almost too scared to consider it.

The next morning it was still dark when Casey walked into her dressing room. There were rows and rows of black jackets and skirts, neat trousers with razor-sharp pleats and white blouses in cotton and silk. On another wall, there were the same clothes in grey and bottle green, because she thought the colour went well with her reddish-brown hair.

Picking a dark green jacket and black trousers, she teamed them with a silk green blouse. She never usually went to work in a two-tone outfit, but today was different.

Sweeping her hair into a ponytail, she dabbed on enough make-up to look presentable. How she looked today was not going to make a difference. She was going on vacation, and the company either accepted that or they didn't, but she hoped her past record of wins could persuade the partners to give her some leeway, and they would agree to keep her job open until she was ready to come back.

Her secretary was waiting in the lobby when she got to headquarters.

'Harry says to go directly to his office. He didn't sound happy,' she said.

Taking a deep breath, Casey took the elevator to the tenth floor.

Harry, the senior partner, was in his glass corner office as always. When he saw her approach he gestured to Casey to sit opposite him as he finished the call he was on.

She watched him gently replacing the receiver, then sit silently for a moment before looking Casey directly in the eye.

'What's going on? Why am I losing my best lawyer when the biggest case for the practice starts in a few short weeks?'

'Harry, something has come up. My best friend died, and she has requested I bring her ashes to scatter in Ireland.'

'So take a few days.'

'Her request stipulates that I spend eight weeks there. This is something I have to do. I have to honour my dear friend's wishes.'

'Hell, Casey, do you really have to do this?'

'Yes, I do.'

'Can you defer for a while? The dead don't have anywhere to be,' Harry said, throwing his hands in the air.

'Much as I would like to, I'm afraid I can't.'

'You can't do this to us, Casey; you're the only one who can handle the client,' Harry said, slapping his hands down on the desk.

'I'm sure that's not true, but I can check in over Zoom, as often as you like.'

'Which sounds nice in theory, but what about the time difference?'

'That can be my problem.'

Harry shifted in his chair, and shook his head.

'I think you want it both ways, Casey Freeman.'

She straightened, and exhaled slowly.

'Harry, I can do this. I have given the company everything over the years. I need a return now. I need to go to Ireland. I can check in and jump on Zoom when required.'

'Don't make promises you can't keep, Casey. I won't be able to protect you.'

Casey got up and paced the room.

'The corner office is pretty neat,' she said.

'You're in line for one – you know you're putting all that at risk.'

Casey sighed heavily, looking at the window washer on the building across the way.

'I don't have a choice, Harry; I have to do this for Rosie. We were super close once. I owe her and can't not fulfil her wishes.'

She sat back down.

'Gary is well able to take the lead on the case. You know he wants to.'

'Wanting doesn't mean he should, Casey.'

'All the hard work is done. It shouldn't be that difficult for him.'

Harry rocked from side to side on his swivel chair.

'I was told to fire you on the spot if you decided to go through with this, but I don't want to do that. The Romney trial doesn't begin for five weeks. Take a month; go wherever you like and recharge, but be back here and ready to work after the four weeks. We can Zoom in the meantime.'

Casey leaned forward in her chair.

'I need eight weeks; that is what the will stipulates.'

'You're killing me, Casey. You can't do it in four weeks?'

'I didn't say that. I want to honour her wishes, and I want to do it right. I have not taken any significant vacations in the five years I have been with the company.'

'So?'

'So I'm doing this, and you respond whatever way you feel you have to.'

Harry got up from his desk, and paced up and down the room. After a few minutes had elapsed, he sat down and spoke slowly and firmly.

'I don't want to lose you, Casey. How about you go for your eight weeks and after four, we will review. Maybe increase the Zoom consultations?'

'I am not sure of the internet connection there; the island where we will be staying, nobody else lives there.'

'Jesus Christ, Casey, could it be any worse?'

'I understand, if you have to let me go...'

Harry sat back down, and shuffled the documents on his desk.

'You're forcing my hand, Casey, and with the firing will be a non-compete clause for two years which means after your eight weeks, that's it, in this town.'

Casey straightened up on her seat. She should be upset; she should be fighting for her job, but something was holding her back. Maybe this was the one last time she had to kick out, to do something different. It would be dumb to let it pass. Rosie must have had her reasons for setting everything up this way, and she needed to follow through. She loved being an attorney, and while she loved this job, there would be other opportunities. She knew in her heart she had to go to Scarty.

'You do what you have to do,' she said flatly.

Harry shook his head.

'I won't implement it for four weeks. I will tell the partners you have agreed to the one-month sabbatical without pay, and you will soon come to your senses, and you'll be ready to resume work.'

'You don't have to do this,' Casey said quietly.

'I know I don't, and believe me I'm not doing it for you. You have four weeks to get back to me on whether you are resuming work or not, and not a word to anybody else about our arrangement.'

Casey stood up.

'Don't worry, the wildlife on the island won't be interested in the goings-on in a Manhattan law firm.'

'Very funny. What about Gary?'

'What about him?'

Harry shook his head.

'OK, I am staying out of it. Just be careful, and come back to me in four weeks, please.'

Casey quickly left the office and the building in case she ran into anybody she knew.

She was on the pavement when her secretary caught up with her.

'Casey, I heard you're going away for several weeks. Will I send you daily updates?'

'Hell, no, but thank you.'

'Is there something wrong?'

'No.'

'Are you dying?'

'Why do you ask?'

The other woman looked uncomfortable.

'Why? Tell me,' Casey said, her tone exasperated.

'You said thank you.'

'What?' Casey said.

'You have never said thank you before.'

'How long have you worked for me...?'

'Celine, my name is Celine and I have worked for you for four years.'

'Shit.'

'What about updates?'

Casey looked up to find the sky. She could hardly breathe. The skyscrapers all of a sudden made her feel hemmed in.

'No weekly updates please, Celine, but if it makes Harry keep you on, you can tell him you're doing it.'

'I might do that to buy myself some time to find another position, just in case you don't come back.'

Casey took Celine's hand and squeezed it.

'Thank you, and good luck,' she said.

Casey smartly walked away. She wasn't going to look back. She couldn't explain it, but she suddenly felt free. She could do this – keep in contact with work, and honour her commitment to Rosie.

She wanted to walk faster, but her high heels wouldn't let her. On impulse, she kicked off her stilettos, and threw them in a bin. She tripped down Fifth Avenue, and she didn't care that people were looking at her. She ran into a store, and pulled out her wallet. Taking off her fitted jacket, and throwing it in the bin, she called the shop assistant to assemble her new wardrobe. It was time to embrace this new life on an island, even if she wasn't even sure exactly where it was, or how long she was going to stay.

THREE

At JFK, Casey paced up and down at the gate for the flight to Shannon Airport, but there was no sign of Georgie. Casey should have boarded, but she wanted to wait. She texted her a number of times, but there was no reply. Casey loitered until the last minute, scanning all the passengers, but there was no sign of her friend. She expected her to race to the gate, her blonde hair bouncing around her and full of stupid excuses. She asked if Georgie had checked in, but they wouldn't tell her.

By the time she took her seat on the plane, Casey was cross and upset. Was Georgie seriously ghosting her? She decided not to think about Georgie or Debbie, and if she had to go to the island by herself, then so be it. She downed a glass of champagne, and tried to sleep for the rest of the flight. Tossing and turning, she couldn't get comfortable. She wondered when Gary would see the note she'd left him, because she had no idea when he'd eventually come home.

Unable to sleep, she called for another glass of champagne. There was no point worrying about Georgie or Gary. She had to start looking after herself.

When the announcement came to fasten the seat belts for

landing at Shannon Airport, Casey clenched her hands tight, and prayed she would have the strength to go through with this alone, along with a bag of dust that was once her friend, Rosie.

Casey was at the baggage carousel when she heard her name being called.

'They wouldn't let me into first class to tell you I was on board, and the snooty hostess refused to pass on a message,' said Georgie, who looked upset.

'What happened – you didn't answer your texts?'

'My stupid phone died and I forgot my charger. But I'm here now, and ready to take on whatever this brings. Do you know where we go next?'

'We have to go to a place called Ballymurphy, and from there a boat will take us to Scarty Island.'

'I am so tired. Can we stay overnight at Ballymurphy? We can't go to the island without supplies, right?'

'We'll see when we get there.'

The taxi driver told them to make themselves comfortable; it was a fifty-mile ride to Ballymurphy.

'What's the interest in the place? It's not a huge tourist spot, just a small harbour village,' he said.

'We're going to Scarty Island.'

'Why would anyone go there? There's nothing, not even a tree to protect you from the wind.'

Casey was relieved when Georgie made the excuse that they were jet lagged, asking if they could get some sleep, and his questions stopped altogether.

Casey was so glad they were on a motorway, but panic seeped through her when they turned off onto a secondary road, which was so narrow two cars could barely pass. Everywhere she looked there were stone walls, small cottages and fields interspersed with newly built grand homes that would fit better into the landscape back home.

She had nodded off when the taxi driver said they were pulling into Ballymurphy.

There was a wide main street and various shops including a small supermarket, a public house and a ladies' boutique, the façade painted in black with a pattern of gold flowers.

'Ye can enquire in Kennedys about a boat to bring you out to Scarty. They have bed and breakfast rooms, too, if you want to rest,' the taxi driver said kindly as he pulled in front of a large house, then got out and took their luggage from the boot.

Casey looked at the imposing building with traditional sash windows overlooking the harbour and bay. Painted a deep blue colour with the windows and door picked out in white, it was clear this was one of the premier properties in the town. There was a large deck to one side where tables and chairs had been placed, and a conservatory to the other side with picture windows, which she thought must offer a panoramic view of the bay. She was reading the sign over the door when a tall man, his black hair scooped into a small ponytail, wearing jeans and a brightly coloured T-shirt, came out of the pub door, and grabbed Georgie's bag.

'Sir, please, don't touch the luggage,' Casey instructed.

'Sorry, but we're the only accommodation around the place that has vacancies. Are you looking for bed and breakfast?' he asked.

'We want to go to Scarty Island.'

The man laughed, and Casey noticed the warmth in his hazel eyes.'

'Why would you want to go there?'

'We intend to stay there for the next two months,' she said, her tone firm.

The man looked at them oddly.

'You're American?'

'Yes, our friend owns the island.'

'You're friends of Rosie?'

'Yes, did you get to know her? She has been here a few summers.'

Before Casey had time to answer, he called out to an older man, who was clipping a hedge on the deck.

'They're Rosie's friends from the US. Come and meet them.'

Casey dithered as he snatched up the cases, and told them to follow him up the steps. Halfway up he stopped, and turned around.

'I'm forgetting my manners. I am Shay Kennedy and here is my dad, the original Dan Kennedy; the name on the sign above the door.'

Dan walked towards them, his hand extended in welcome.

'Any friend of Rosie's is a friend of ours. Come in, and have a cup of tea. Ye must be shattered after that taxi journey, never mind the flight.'

Tongue-tied, Casey smiled meekly, and followed Shay into the bar as Georgie ambled behind.

'Rosie is not with you, then? She is usually here in the first few days of July,' Shay said as he balanced the small rucksack on Casey's luggage.

'We were expecting her this week. She should be here by now,' Dan said, ushering the visitors to sit down on a comfortable couch by the window.

Casey looked oddly at the two men.

'You haven't heard the news?'

Dan sat opposite in an armchair while Shay stood nearby.

'What news? Has something happened?' Dan asked.

Georgie put her head in her hands as Casey straightened up in her seat.

'I am very sorry to tell you Rosie has died,' she said quietly.

Shay stamped his foot on the wooden floor, while Dan took a long, deep breath.

'Mother of God, not Rosie. What happened?' Dan whispered.

'Cancer,' Casey said, the word echoing around the pub.

Shay dipped his head, and she could see he was crying. 'She was getting tired all the time when she was here last summer,' he said.

'You knew her well?' Georgie asked.

'Yes, we all loved her. Rosie wasn't the usual type of American tourist, no offence.'

'None taken. Rosie has asked us to stay on the island for the next two months,' Casey said.

Nobody spoke for a moment until Georgie piped up.

'We have Rosie here with us; her ashes, I mean,' she said, pointing to the small rucksack.

Shay stepped back.

'Whoa, not sure I want somebody so vibrant and bright to be reduced to being carried around in a rucksack,' he said.

Dan stood up.

'It's a bad day when this sort of news comes to us. Rosie was a fine woman and a great friend to us and all in Ballymurphy. She will be sorely missed around here. Can I ask why have you brought her ashes this far?'

'She wants us to stay on the island, and at some stage scatter her ashes there,' Casey mumbled.

Dan nodded, 'She definitely loved the island. Everybody thought she was half mad to be staying out there. We thought she wouldn't last a night once darkness drew in, but she proved us wrong.'

Shay went behind the bar, and took a bottle of Midleton whiskey from the shelf.

'She liked her prosecco but here at the bar, this was a rare treat for Rosie,' he said, pouring a generous measure into four glasses on a tray.

Casey watched as he carried the tray over to them, and she thought he was trying too hard to compose himself.

'Isn't it a bit early for alcohol?' she said.

Dan put his hand up to stop her talking.

'Whist, it's important to remember the dead,'

He handed a glass to Casey and Georgie, and held up his own.

'To Rosie, our very dear friend, who will be forever missed, and remembered here at Ballymurphy and Scarty,' he said, his voice towards the end shaking.

Shay put his hand on his shoulder, and gripped it tight as they all sipped their drinks.

After a few moments Casey placed her glass on the table.

'We are hoping to go to Scarty Island today. Maybe you know somebody with a boat who could drop us there?'

'Usually Rosie called ahead and we had the house aired out, and the cupboards stocked. If you go out there now, it could be a bit of a shock. You have water from a spring on the island, but there's no electricity. Best let us out to clean the place up before ye set foot in it.'

'We can clean it up ourselves, and bring out the supplies,' Casey said.

'I don't mind putting ye up here for tonight, free to any friends of Rosie, and we can see about travelling out to the island tomorrow morning after ye have had some rest.'

Georgie, who had wandered across to the big picture window overlooking the harbour, shouted that she could see the island.

'That's Scarty all right,' Shay said.

'Maybe you can put me in touch with a ferry or boat operator, so we can book ahead,' Casey said.

'That's me: the pub, restaurant, guesthouse and island tour operator.'

'Does anybody else live or carry out business in the village?' Casey said, her voice strained.

Shay laughed.

'You will soon find out that the only way to survive around here is to have a number of jobs to fall back on,' he said.

'Stay here tonight,' Dan said. 'We have the room; and it's the least we may do until the house is sorted for ye out there.'

'If you are both sure,' Casey said.

'It will be nice having the American accent around us while we get to grips with the loss of our dear friend Rosie,' Dan replied, swiping tears from his face.

Shay led the way upstairs to their rooms overlooking the bay. After he had gone back downstairs, Georgie whistled.

'At least we know there's one good-looking man in the area. You're married, Casey, so he's mine.'

'You don't know anything about him!'

'I like what I see.'

'You haven't changed a bit, Georgie.'

'Come on, Casey, you have to admit he's rather cute.'

'I guess, in a rugged sort of way.'

Georgie was still laughing when Shay came back in with a tray of coffee and sandwiches piled high on the plate, along with two slices of lemon drizzle cake.

'Rosie loved our lemon drizzle cake,' he said. Casey thought he was going to say more, but he hesitated, then added, 'I'll let you get settled. I'd better get back to work.'

As he backed out of the doorway, Casey followed him.

'Wait! Are you sure you can take us to the island tomorrow? We don't want to inconvenience you.'

'It's no bother, if the weather stays like this. I can bring you over to the island in the morning; you can look at the place, and decide if you want to stay,' he said.

'That suits us fine, though I promise we'll want to stay. It's for Rosie.'

He looked at her linen trousers, silk shirt and white Converse shoes doubtfully. 'If you're sure.'

Casey relayed the information to Georgie, who had already been happily tucking into the food. Halfway through the ginormous sandwich she pushed the plate away, and announced she had to rest.

While Georgie slept, Casey decided to go for a stroll. Downstairs, she tried to slip out the front door unnoticed, but Shay spotted her.

'How were the sandwiches? My usual assistant is on a day off, so I had to rustle them up myself.'

'They were good, thank you.'

'You didn't have any, did you?'

'I don't have an appetite.'

'Nervous about the move to the island? Try not to worry. It's not far away and we will all keep an eye on you.'

'I appreciate that.' Casey said uneasily, not sure how she felt about the idea of the locals observing them from across the water.

'If you're going for a walk, go up the cliffs – you will get a good view of the island,' he said, reaching for his binoculars. 'Take these, and you should be able to see the house.'

Timidly, she took the binoculars. She didn't know what to say, but luckily a large group entered the pub, and Shay had to rush off.

Casey wandered down the street. There was a small post office and a newsagent's, and the fashion boutique. She stopped to look in the window. The woman behind the counter waved to her, and Casey felt she should go inside.

'Are you looking for anything in particular?' the woman, who was wearing a pink gingham summer dress, asked as she patted her grey hair, which was cut in a stylish bob.

'I'm just browsing,' Casey said, fingering a crochet dress in a deep blue colour.

'Are you brave enough to wear it? I have made a silk slip to go underneath, because nobody in these parts would be bold enough to wear it without one. It would go so well with your beautiful copper hair.'

'Where I am going, I won't need a beautiful dress like that.'

'Are you off to prison?'

Casey giggled.

'Scarty Island, for the next while.'

'By yourself?'

'No there are two of us planning to stay there.'

'Wow, brave.'

'Why do you say that?'

'No electricity, and the water depends on what the spring well lets you have. You can't even get a phone signal out there.'

'Oh.'

'Anyway, I shouldn't be putting you off before you go. You can find some way of signalling, if you need help. We'll all keep an eye out.'

Casey held the dress to her, before putting it back on the rack.

'I don't think it's for my life right now.'

'Nonsense, girl, you won't even need to wear the slip out on the island, and God knows you will need a bit of luxury.'

'OK, I suppose, thank you.'

'Call me May. You'll get to know me. I run the post office as well, but we only open certain mornings,' she said as she folded the dress into a big paper bag.

A mobile phone rang, and May rushed to answer it, telling the caller to hold on.

'Dear, I will drop the bag over to Kennedys; you don't want to be carrying it around with you now,' she said, and Casey, who had tapped her credit card, took her cue to leave.

Casey continued on her way, walking up the headland and away from the village. She turned onto a path that ran near the edge of the cliff, stopping to take in the view of the grey- blue sea. In the distance she saw a long ship ploughing through the waves. On the shore, children were playing in the water; surfers lounging about, hoping for a change in weather and a higher tide.

She could see the island. It looked further away than a quarter of a mile, so she took out the binoculars to see better. Scanning the horizon, she waited until the island came into view. Her heart skipped a beat when she saw the pristine white sand beach, the jagged cliff edges, the rocks piled all around as if they had been arranged by some greater being. Birds were flying back and forth on the high cliffs at one side of the island. Casey followed the lines of the stone walls enclosing the green fields until her gaze fell on the old whitewashed farmhouse with small windows and a door, which somebody had painted pink.

All of a sudden, she felt weak. What were they doing here, and how could they live on that island for weeks on end? Anxiety took over, and she wanted to run from the headland and hail a cab, if there was such a thing in these parts, and rush back to the airport. She felt very far away from Manhattan, the sound of the city and the comfort of having a lot of people around her. Maybe Debbie was right after all, and this was a crazy mission.

She missed Rosie so much. They had not spoken in two years, but they had emailed. When she read her friend's words, she heard her voice, and there was a comfort in knowing that in the vastness out there, there was somebody on her side. She wouldn't be where she was today but for Rosie. When Casey's dad had died suddenly during her last year of college, and she thought she would have to drop out, Rosie stepped in to help her. While the fees had been paid, Casey needed money to live and eat, and she couldn't ask her mother, who was over-whelmed with grief, and by the debt her father had left behind. Rosie took on extra work for her friend, and paid all her bills until Casey was able to pick herself off the floor, and graduate with honours.

Casey needed no-nonsense Debbie here to tell her to pull herself together. She wished Debs had got over her indignation and travelled to Ballymurphy. She would have bossed everybody, and they might even be running an electricity cable to the island by now.

Feeling sad, Casey sat on a seat near the edge of the cliff. The soft breeze circled around, caressing her cheeks, and gently lifting her hair. Closing her eyes, she let the sunshine pass over her face. Somewhere above her, she heard a bird cry. She tried to glimpse it, but the sunlight blinded her.

Getting up, she wandered back down the path to the street.

Shay called out to Casey as she slipped upstairs to her room.

'The weather forecast is very good for tomorrow, so if you want to leave after breakfast, that's fine by me.'

'Are you sure you have time? Isn't there anyone else we can ring?'

'It's not a bother; I have to check on my lobster pots anyway, so I might as well do it all in the one go. Go out have a look at the island and the house, and see what ye need, and come back to shore to order your supplies. The supermarket will have the basics, but if you are looking for anything fancy, it will have to be the next big town Kilkee, about five miles away or further afield.'

'I suppose you run a cab service to Kilkee too.'

'Now, you're getting the hang of things around here,' he laughed as he turned back to pull a pint at the bar.

Georgie was awake when Casey got back to the room.

'I'm afraid I have run up a telephone bill. I rang Debbie.'

'And?'

'She was furious. I forgot they are five hours behind and she thought when her phone rang so early that somebody was dead.'

'But did you persuade her to come here?'

Georgie got up and walked to the window.

'She wouldn't even listen to me. She is never going to let go of the past, that one. How many times do I have to apologise? It was so long ago.'

'I told you, you two need to talk things through.'

'Fat chance of that considering she hasn't bothered to come here. She is still so sore. She didn't even ask why I was ringing. She had the cheek to say I had ruined her day; that her schedule would be upside down because of me.'

'She's very busy with her interior design business as well as running a family, I suppose.'

'Keeping herself busy more like, because she's afraid of the sound of silence. If anyone needed to spend time on an island and have the warmth of friendship all around her, it's Debbie.'

Casey sighed. 'We can only ask her; she has to make her own decision.'

When there was a gentle tapping on the door, Georgie opened it.

'Look, Casey, it's the man who makes really big sandwiches,' she said.

Shay gave a half-smile.

'Lucky for you, the dinner menu is available. You can come downstairs to the lounge bar, or we can give you a tray at the table by the window in your room.'

'After gorging myself on those sandwiches, I couldn't eat another bite,' Georgie said.

Shay looked at Casey.

'Don't eat on your own up here; come downstairs,' he said.

'I may do in a while,' she said, taking a menu.

When he had retreated, Georgie whistled long and low.

'Pity he can't come to the island with us.'

'Georgie, stop it,' Casey said a bit too sternly, and her friend chortled happily.

FOUR

The next day, Casey was up shortly after dawn, and she walked down to the little harbour. Everything was quiet except for a man loading boxes and what looked like mesh cages onto his boat. As she got closer, she saw that it was Shay.

'You're an early riser,' he said as he lifted a number of boxes together, and placed them on board.

'What time are you thinking of going to the island?'

'Soon I hope, so I can get ye back to get supplies after that. I imagine, though, your friend wants to sleep late.'

'She certainly likes her sleep.'

'I have to open up by noon, so the earlier we leave the better.'

Casey smiled, and he stopped what he was doing.

'I know you didn't come downstairs for dinner last night, but I am a trained chef, and I am told that my dishes are quite tasty. I admit I am not good at sandwiches, however.'

Casey tittered. Shay looked at her.

'If your friend doesn't mind, we could take a spin out to Scarty now; open up the house and windows, and let you have a look around. It will give you time to assess what you need.'

'I haven't had breakfast.'

'If you're game, I've a nice pot of coffee brewing and a few homemade muffins. They are a day old, but they're pretty tasty.'

Casey agreed and he held out his hand to help her on board.

After pouring the hot coffee into a small tin mug, he handed it to her, and pushed a box containing homemade blueberry muffins towards her.

'I'm told it's a recipe from Jordan Marsh, Boston. I hope you like it.'

She picked one up, and took a tiny bite.

'How do you know about the Jordan Marsh muffin? You even have the crunch top.'

'Rosie insisted if I had to bake a breakfast muffin, it had to be the right one.'

'I had forgotten she was so good at baking,' Casey said, her voice sad. She was transported back to the long nights she had spent studying in the college library then coming home to the smell of baking in the apartment, and trays of different cookies cooling on the counter. She and Rosie had been such good friends back then.

As Shay started up the engine he touched an ornate silver frame which was secured on a shelf directly under the wheel-house window.

'For luck; you need it every time you go to sea,' he said shyly.

She noticed the frame contained a photograph of a woman with long black hair standing beside the boat and smiling. It was obvious this woman was an important part of Shay's life. Strange she had not come across her yet, she thought.

Casey moved to a seat at the back, as the boat chugged slowly out of the harbour, before building up speed, heading out past the headland into the open sea. The wind was cold even though it was a sunny morning, and she pulled up her hood. After ten minutes, Shay waved to her and pointed to the island.

It sat in the middle of the sea, a huge imposing piece of land, the cliffs at one side high, birds flying in and out of their cliffside nests. The boat pulled over towards the jetty which was tucked into a sheltered spot, looking towards the mainland.

She could see the grey rocks sticking up from the water and the white strand beach, where two seals were basking. There were no trees on the island, but there were green fields and stone walls running here and there. As they neared the jetty, there was a blur of purple and white, which she later found out were foxgloves and oxeye daisies.

The farmhouse, surrounded on one side by stone outhouses, was tucked on the mainland side of the island. Excitement tinged with sorrow soaked through Casey that Rosie wasn't here with her.

Shay pointed to a school of dolphins, swimming close by but seemingly unconcerned about the nearness of the boat.

'They always come out to see us safely into shore,' he said, gesturing to Casey to join him at the wheelhouse.

'It is so...' Casey said.

'Magical,' Shay interrupted.

'Yes,' she said softly.

Shay laughed.

'That's it today and most of the summer, to be fair. In a storm, there's no real shelter. In winter the driving wind, rain and sea are fierce. It was only ever an island for lazy summer days. A farmer put a few sheep out here one winter, but it was even too tough for them. He came out a day or so after a particularly bad storm and the poor creatures were all huddled beside the farmhouse walls. He moved them back to the mainland after that.

'Are there any summer storms?' Casey asked nervously.

'Sometimes, but never as bad as in winter and we get plenty of notice. Don't worry, we don't expect two New Yorkers to stay on the island during an Atlantic storm.'

He pulled the boat into the jetty before instructing Casey to take the wheel, while he jumped out with the rope and secured it to a post. She turned off the engine when instructed, before joining him on the pier.

'It's a bit of a walk, but you'll get a nice feel for the place on a day like today,' he said.

The kittiwakes overhead screeched and cormorants stood still on rocks as they made their way along the small jetty and onto the coastal path.

'How did Rosie get anyone to do the renovation work on the farmhouse?' Casey asked.

Shay turned around, a grin on his face.

'I forgot to say, building and renovation – another of my hidden talents.' He took a good look at the house. 'I'd do it all again for Rosie.'

The path brought them up to a small headland where they could see to the far side of the island. Casey gasped as she saw the dolphins surface from the water as they headed further out to sea.

Shay pointed to the seals on the beach.

'Those seals loved Rosie; she'd swim in the sea beside them. She had no fear, but then they knew she was a friend.'

'You were good friends?'

'I was the first person to meet her, but everyone around here got to know her over the years. She ran a little tearoom out of the farmhouse, and ploughed half her profits into projects in the community. You would be surprised how many people want to have afternoon tea on an island. I ran the boat trips. It worked well for us.'

He continued, 'She donated and arranged for a local child to go to the US for life-saving surgery, and there were other things like funding a wheelchair ramp at the church and the community centre. She always paid for the senior citizens' Christmas dinner at my place. There were other projects too that all add up when there is so little money in the community.'

He stopped to pick up an arrow sign which said farmhouse and tearooms.

'I guess we won't be needing that any more,' he sighed.

Casey looked all around her. She could see the little strand where one seal was still basking in the sunshine, and further on the rocks, where the cormorants were standing perfectly still. She scanned as far as the horizon where the sea and sky seemed to meld together. A feeling of freedom came over her, but also a sadness that Rosie would never get to visit here again.

'We had better check the house,' Shay said, tapping her gently on the shoulder to follow him.

She tramped behind him as they made their way single file to the old farmhouse, which stood solid against the cloudless sky. Shay made his way past the outhouses to the back door, and unlocked it. Light filled the large kitchen as Casey stepped inside.

There was a dresser with crockery against one wall and a rectangular wooden table in the centre of the room. Under the back window was a sink with cupboards and shelving along the wall for tinned goods and small items.

The floor was tiled with slate slabs. Casey walked over to the big open fireplace which had a stove set into the hearth and a high mantelpiece. She reached for a framed photograph. It was the four of them, when they were much younger and wearing their party dresses.

Casey traced her finger over the glass, her heart breaking. 'I never really knew how much she thought of us all,' she said.

'She spoke about your group non-stop; said ye had been friends since schooldays.'

Casey felt a stab of guilt, and she turned away, walking to the other room which had once been a front parlour. The air was chilly, and but for a new window and plaster on the walls, little else had been done with the room.

Shay called out that he was going back to the boat to bring up a gas canister for the cooker.

'Have a look upstairs; there are two bedrooms and lovely views,' he said.

'What about the bathroom?' Casey asked.

Shay pointed to an outhouse.

'Rosie had it put out there but she never got round to continuing the work. She intended an extension to link everything to the house.'

'We have to go outside? You're kidding?'

'Afraid not.'

'I'm glad the third person in our party didn't come. Debbie would have freaked and, to be frank, I am not sure how Georgie will take it either,' she said.

He set off down the path to get the canister. Casey opened the front door. Breathing in the clear fresh air, she looked towards the mainland. She could make out the bar and the quay, where she thought people were walking; small figures at this distance. Further along was the headland which she had explored the day before. For a moment she didn't want the wide expanse of sky and sea, but the tall buildings and the skyscrapers crowding in around her; the bustle, the buzz and the swift way people had of walking in Manhattan. She wondered if Gary had even noticed she was gone. What had brought Rosie here year after year? She wished she knew.

She saw Shay struggle up the path with a heavy bottle of gas, and she ducked back into the kitchen.

'The place isn't looking bad at all,' he said as he pulled out the cooker, and hooked up the canister.

He checked the rings were working before washing his hands.

'We thought Rosie might make it over this Easter. May and

a few ladies from the village came over, and gave the place a
good spring clean. All it needs now is a thorough dusting and
airing out.'

'It feels further from the mainland than I thought. What do
we do if something goes badly wrong?' she asked.

'I know it looks a long way away but we had a system with
Rosie all these years, and it worked. If something was wrong,
she put out the Irish flag. We checked through the binoculars
morning, afternoon and evening. If we saw the flag, and it was
safe to put the boat to sea, we would tip out here straight away
or I would be out in the boat at the next available opportunity.
She had a flare if there was an emergency, but we never had to
go down that road.'

He stopped suddenly, and Casey thought he was trying to
hold back tears.

'We don't know why she didn't tell us how bad things were.
She emailed two months ago, and she was so upbeat and full of
plans for the summer. We sent her silly things from Ireland like
crisps and chocolate that she loved. We feel so damn stupid
now.'

'She didn't tell us either.' Casey made to reach out to Shay,
but something stopped her. 'Maybe we didn't deserve it, and
Rosie knew that,' she said, her voice shaky with emotion.

'Why not? You were friends.'

'Since we were nineteen years old, but I guess life got in
the way; busy city lives. It seems so silly and inconsequential
now, but I was building my career; I felt if I took a day off,
my boss would find an excuse to make my life miserable, or
worse, fire me altogether. Imagine! Rosie came to the city so
many times and I never made the time to see her. I thought
there'd be plenty of days for that when I secured the next
promotion, then the next. But look at us now. That time is
gone.'

Casey sat down at the table, and put her head in her hands.

'I didn't really know Rosie at all; not the way you guys did. I didn't allow myself to know her, I guess,' she sniffed.

'You shouldn't torture yourself like this. You flew over an entire ocean for her, because it's what she wanted,' Shay said.

'I'm not so sure we know what we are supposed to be doing. We have to scatter her ashes, but we don't even know where on the island.'

'You have weeks to worry about that. Stop looking for answers so fast and give it time,' Shay said as they walked out to the yard, and down the path to the jetty. 'We had better get back, I have to get ready for the lunchtime rush.'

Casey smiled.

'You get that out here?'

'It's the tourist fast track in Ballymurphy, didn't you know?' he said, jumping on the deck, and starting up the engine.

She took over at the wheel while he pulled in the rope, before he manoeuvred the boat out to sea.

Drifting down to the far end of the boat, she sat, the sun in her face, the breeze tangling her hair. As they approached the harbour, she returned to Shay's side.

'Are you really expecting to be busy?'

He shrugged.

'I have lunch done. There are two coachloads of tourists due in. A group from America wants to visit the island. Rosie and I, we had a system; I advertised the trips, and she provided home-made scones and tea in the farmhouse and on the benches outside. It was a flyer in July and August, and we both did well out of it.'

'You have bookings, but had no idea she wouldn't be here?'

'Something like that.'

'So what are you going to do?'

'Lunch for the French group just needs to be served. I was going to ask you, could I at least bring the Americans out to the island? They can have the afternoon tea in the pub afterwards.'

'Just for a visit?'

'I do a walking tour of the island with them. May is doing a few trays of plain and fruit scones with homemade jam and cream.'

Casey stayed quiet for a minute, then she said, 'It won't be the same, though. The farmhouse is looking good and the benches are already there.'

'What are you saying?'

'I can do it with you; it will be fun.'

'What about your friend?'

'Georgie – don't worry about her; she will join in, if she ever gets out of bed.'

When they got back to shore it was already 11 a.m.

'How are you going to manage everything?' Casey asked.

'It will be stressful, but we should be able to do it. May and my father will serve the French and talk to them. I have done all the cooking, so it won't be that difficult. It's a party of thirty.'

'Were you up all night cooking?'

'Up since before the crack of dawn. May should have the scones made, and if you don't mind ye can come out to the island with the American group, and serve the afternoon tea.'

'Your boat isn't going to fit so many.'

He laughed.

'I don't run charters. It's a small party of ten, but we will divide everybody between two boats. Going to be manic for a while. The French group arrive at Ballymurphy quay at 12.30 p.m., and the Americans at 1 p.m.,' Shay said.

Georgie walked down to the quay to meet them.

'Hey, you guys! Why didn't you wake me?'

Casey jumped off the boat, and tried to think of an answer that would appease her friend.

'It just sort of happened. Shay was going out to the island to check it out, and I hopped on.'

'I have been hanging around waiting for you, but I have done a nice sketch of the bar,' Georgie said, holding up her charcoal drawing. 'And would you believe, I have already been offered money for it.'

Shay, who was tying the knot on the rope, looked over Georgie's shoulder.

'I bet that was my dad. Dan has a good eye for a work of art, and he loves it when anyone does anything with the Kennedy name on it,' he said

'You're not going to charge Mr Kennedy, are you?' Casey asked anxiously.

'We have an arrangement that suits us both fine,' Georgie said mysteriously.

Shay chuckled.

'That's my dad, I bet he wouldn't take it for free. He loves a little wheeling and dealing.'

'He promised to tell the whole story of us Kennedys, Scarty Island, and how Rosie found it years ago,' Georgie said, taking her sketch pad back from Casey.

When Casey looked at Shay, his face had clouded over.

'Is there something wrong?' she asked.

'No, busy morning into afternoon ahead,' he said a little too quickly.

Casey didn't feel she could push for an answer, and they followed him slowly up to the pub. Somehow, this trip didn't seem as easy or as free as she had first imagined.

FIVE

The next few hours passed in a blur of activity. Georgie helped out as a waitress while Casey offered to give May a hand moving catering to the island.

'Rosie ordered some nice oilcloths for those outside benches. She said there wouldn't be time to paint them as she didn't expect to get here until the start of the season on 1 July,' May said, pulling a big box out from under her counter.

Casey lifted one of the tablecloths from the box.

'Wow, beautiful; she always did have an eye for detail,' she said running her hand over the smooth oilcloth which was predominantly blue, like a summer sky. Delicate blurs of pink and white flowers fringed the edge.

'It shouts lazy summer days. I hope the weather on Scarty lives up to the expectation,' May said.

'Nothing wrong with having something beautiful,' Casey replied.

May snorted loudly.

'I told her, don't bother spending money on them; they never last beyond the season and that is just three months at most. Once the wind and rain starts to hit, the oilcloths are ruined, and if there was a summer storm, you could lose it all in one night, but Rosie insisted.'

'You knew her well.'

'I never thought of it, but I suppose I did. She was one stubborn woman. When she bought that island, we thought she would let everything go to rack and ruin, but she put Scarty on the map. She made TikTok videos of the island, called Scarty Reels. Even I wanted to go there, they were so atmospheric, and she was just filming the sea and the wildlife. July, August and September, there were boatloads going over every day. It's all thanks to Rosie. Shay was even thinking of getting another boat, but that's a big investment, and he would have to employ somebody.'

'I never knew Rosie was such a businesswoman.'

May pointed to a framed photograph in her window.

'She got me into selling photographs of the island. It's been a good earner too. She was always coming up with ideas for us. It's bloody amazing what she did out there. That farmhouse was only four walls when she bought the place. I don't know how she managed it all, but she had a way about her,' May said.

'She seems such a different person to the Rosie we knew,' Casey said.

'The Rosie we loved was so kind and generous with her time but very driven, not for herself but for others. Shay would never have built on the deck and the conservatory extension and turned the place into a full-blown restaurant, but for Rosie,' May said.

Casey sat down.

'I never knew any of this.'

May went through to the back to her little kitchen behind the shop and took the last tray of scones from the oven.

'It's terrible to think we didn't even know she had died. Hard not having said goodbye; I hope she knew we loved her for what she did. I always looked forward to her arrival. She really was like a breath of fresh air.'

Casey placed the scones in a tin. Shay stuck his head around the boutique door and said the Americans had arrived and they would gather at the quay in ten minutes.

'We're all ready – a well-oiled machine, even if we have lost the rudder,' May said sadly.

Casey helped get the oilcloth back in the box, and she carried it, while May followed with a little cart carrying flasks of hot water for tea and coffee, a tower of takeaway cups along with the scones, jam, butter, cream, sugar and two big cartons of milk.

Shay at the quayside took the supplies, and stored them in a special spot on the boat.

'May, can you travel with Dan on Peter Kelly's boat, and Casey can come with me,' he said. May clicked her tongue impatiently.

'I can swap over,' Casey said.

May put her hand up.

'It's too early to inflict Peter 'the storyteller' Kelly on you, but those other Yanks will love all his talk,' she said as she moved to the other boat.

Shay said he had to check something at the pub and would be back in a few minutes. Casey watched as he walked quickly up the quayside to meet his father, who was chatting with the French visitors. She saw the two men move to one side, and it looked as if they were having some sort of argument. They kept looking at the boat and the island, and Casey suspected that she and Georgie were somehow the cause of a row between the two. The discussion came to an abrupt halt when Shay threw his hands in the air, and walked quickly back to the boat.

He shouted welcome to the Americans as he checked their tickets, and helped each one on board. When he got to the wheelhouse, Casey noticed he still looked upset.

'Is everything OK?' she asked.

'You saw that with my father?'

'I couldn't hear but...'

'He's a stubborn old man, who never knows when to keep his nose out of it.'

'I'm not sure what you mean.'

Shay shrugged.

'Let's leave it, there's work to be done,' he said as he took the microphone, and began his commentary for the tourists.

Casey sat beside the small group from Minnesota. It was strangely comforting to hear the American accent. She didn't speak, not wanting yet to be drawn into awkward conversations. At the island jetty, they waited for Peter's boat to pull in behind them, and Shay took the group on a hike while Peter, May and Casey brought the supplies up the path to the farmhouse.

Casey was given the job of getting each table ready, and she stood outside spreading the oilcloths on the tables and benches. They all fitted perfectly, but then everybody knew that if Rosie had ordered them, they would.

After she had arranged the tables and put out the plates of scones, she picked a number of daisies, and sat down to make a daisy chain. Using her long nails, she pressed a hole in a daisy stem, and threaded through a long-stemmed daisy before starting all over again, the slow rhythmic movement strangely comforting. She kept going until she had a long daisy chain.

She remembered the first time she had met Rosie. Rosie was the new girl on the block. She was sitting on a grass patch as she waited for a bus. She was weaving a daisy chain then. When some boys started to mock her, she ignored them. Casey was so impressed by Rosie and her quiet strength that she sat down beside her, and began to make her own chain. Rosie didn't talk at first, but Casey didn't mind. When the bus came, they got on, and got off together six blocks further on. Rosie had only moved into the area, and lived four doors away and so, when just nineteen years old and in the first year of college, they became friends. It wasn't long before Georgie and Debbie, who lived in the next street along, teamed up with them and they became the best of pals.

'What is with you New Yorkers, always making daisy chains?' Shay said as he came up behind Casey.

Immediately, she scrunched up her chain.

'I was just killing time until the group came back,' she said nervously.

The American tourists took over most of the tables outside. May served the tea and coffee and answered questions about the farmhouse.

Shay tipped Casey on the elbow.

'We won't be heading back for another hour; would you like to walk to the strand? I saw the seals there earlier.'

'I would so like to get away,' she said, and they set off around the back of the house, down the path which curled past the bank of tall purple-pink foxgloves to the sparkling white strand.

Shay kicked off his runners and socks, and rolled up his trouser legs before walking into the water.

'Paddle, it helps relieve the stress,' he said.

'How do you know I am stressed?' she asked, kicking off her sandals, and joining him in the water.

'The daisy chain, some of the holes were too big. Rosie was always making daisy chains.'

Casey let the water flow around her legs, enjoying the coolness as her feet sank into the sand.

'What were you and Dan arguing about?' she asked.

'Why do you want to know?'

'Back home I am a lawyer, and it's my job to notice things. Both of you glanced over at the quay where I was standing, and at the deck where Georgie was clearing the tables. It just felt that we were the problem.'

Shay shook his head, and laughed.

'You're reading too much into it,' he said hurriedly.

Casey looked at him oddly, and wondered if Shay had meant something special to Rosie.

He turned, and looked at her directly. 'Honestly, it was no big deal, my dad wanted to tell Georgie a lot of things about us and Rosie, but I told him to stay out of it; it is too early for all that. I don't know what Rosie would want you guys to know, but I guess it's not our business. She was such an organised person, she will have found a way to tell you anything she wanted to share.'

'What are you saying – that Rosie had a total second life here that nobody knew about? Even her husband?'

Shay kicked at a wave which collapsed around him.

'Can we drop it now? I just don't think it's our story to tell, and maybe that is why Rosie wanted ye here to live her life for eight weeks, so that her best friends would have some understanding.'

Casey strode out of the water, pushing the waves apart, and hurried up the beach.

She heard Shay call her, but she ignored him. By the time he caught up with her, he was out of breath.

'Casey, what is it?'

'Were you having an affair with Rosie?' she shouted.

'God, no. Why do you think that?'

'Because nobody wants to tell me anything. What is the big secret? Rosie is dead. I am only a friend, not family. Why keep hiding things from me?' she said, feeling angry that tears were rolling down her face.

Shay bunched his fists in his pockets and stood, his head bowed. After a moment, he looked at Casey.

'There is no big secret. I think our Rosie was different to the Rosie you knew. She and my wife, Anna, were best friends. Anna died in August last year. Rosie was devastated. She supported us so much afterwards. It is my awful regret that none of us could be by Rosie's side in her time of need.'

Casey kicked herself that she had pushed this kind stranger. He didn't know her or Georgie, and she had tried to force his hand. This trip was off to a very bad start, and it was all her fault. Turning around, she moved closer to Shay who was standing looking out to sea.

'I feel I have overstepped the mark, I apologise,' she said.

'You weren't to know,' he said, pulling a foxglove petal, and bruising it between his fingers.

Before she had a chance to say anything, he had turned to walk back to the boat. He was halfway down the path when he turned around.

'We will move you and Georgie over early in the morning. There's a box of Rosie's things in our attic. Every year she gathered all the bits that were dear to her, and stored them at ours. She said they were only worth something to her, but she would be awfully upset if anything happened to them. Maybe you should have them.'

Casey could only nod, but she wanted to shout that she wanted the box straight away in the hope that it would help her unlock this secret life of Rosie, who had once been such a good friend. She hoped that the box would reveal some of her dear friend's secrets, and help unravel the mystery of Rosie and Scarty Island.

SIX

The next day Shay had the boat ready bright and early to move Casey and Georgie to Scarty, but Georgie, who had persuaded Dan to drive her to the local big town, still had not returned.

'What is she doing there, buying up the place?' Shay complained, but Casey pretended not to hear. May called Casey to the small local supermarket.

'Rosie had a standing order at the grocery store, so we always had her boxes of groceries ready. Have a look through before you go buying anything else. Remember you don't have a fridge out there, though Rosie had one shipped out in the hope she could get the electricity hooked up.'

'So how did she keep things cold?' Casey asked.

'She was mainly worried about her white wine and Prosecco, but there's a cave where she stored it. It's a good spot, but you have to make your choice before high tide cuts off access.'

Casey stared at May.

'You're kidding me?'

'No. Shay will show you, if you like.'

Casey rifled through the boxes of groceries.

'Everything is covered here. What do I owe you?'

May shook her head.

'Rosie paid months in advance. You will get a box of groceries once a week, and fresh bread every two days, and you can chop and change all you like. Rosie left more than enough to pay for everything.'

Casey snuffled, trying to hide her upset.

'I don't understand any of it. It's like this was her home, and not back in the States.'

May put her arm around Casey's shoulders.

'This was her happy place, maybe that's why she didn't come here to die. The memory of all the happy times was better than struggling on the island as her life was ebbing away.'

Casey began to sob.

'Oh, don't mind me. I can be maudlin at times,' May said.

Shay stuck his head around the door, and said he was going back to the pub, and to call him when Georgie arrived.

'He seems so annoyed,' Casey whispered.

'Not at you, darling, but your friend is a bit difficult. She insisted last night that he re-do her burger because it wasn't right. Would you go into to a top-reviewed restaurant in Manhattan and send back a burger, because it was not incinerated to your personal taste?'

'I didn't know she did that. I went to bed early, I was beat.'

'She is not exactly his favourite as a result.'

Casey shook her head.

'Georgie is the arty type, and her people skills aren't the best. I just hope she hasn't bullied Dan into driving her further than Kilkee.'

'We'll know soon enough, look at the whip of Shay coming back,' May said.

When Shay arrived at the boat, he looked angry.

'I rang my dad. She only had him drive her all the way to Ennis town looking for a particular type of paint. It will be hours before they are back.'

'I apologise... do we cancel? I will of course pay you for your time anyway,' Casey said.

'We won't bloody cancel. Let's get the supplies across to the island,' he snapped as he headed down the quay. When Casey got as far as the boat with May following in the car behind with the boxes, Shay had calmed down a little.

'I am sorry, I didn't ask. Maybe you don't want to be out on Scarty without your friend,' he said.

'To be honest, a break from Georgie would be a good thing. She is incredibly intense about her painting. I want to go, if you don't mind taking me.'

He turned on the engine, and told May to untie the ropes and throw them on board.

Casey walked to the back of the boat, and sat down.

She felt disappointed. She had wanted this crossing to the island to be special, friends arriving and settling into the farmhouse together, and now she was on her own with Shay, who seemed upset and impatient.

Closing her eyes, she let the sun stream onto her face. The light breeze lifted her hair as the boat nudged slowly out of the harbour before picking up speed.

She stayed like this for a while until she realised the engine had been cut, and they weren't moving any more. The boat was drifting. When she opened her eyes, she saw Shay lean over the side, and pull on a rope to bring in a big pot. Inside were two lobsters.

'What are you going to do with them?' she asked.

'I thought for your first official day on Scarty, you would like to cook, and eat lobster at the shore.'

Casey looked at the two lobsters huddled together.

'You boil them alive, don't you?'

'You haven't had lobster before, then?'

'No.'

'Well, there is always a first time. We will get you settled in the house, then set up a fire on the beach.'

Casey didn't answer, but she turned away from the cage. She couldn't look them in the eye if she was going to be there when they were cooked.

Shay started the engine back up, and they continued to the island. Scarty sat like a beached whale; the sea glistening in the late-morning sunshine. It was strange but as the boat neared the island and she could see the farmhouse, she felt like she was coming home. If Georgie didn't make it back to spend the night on the island, Casey was quite happy to be on her own, she thought.

At the jetty, she jumped out of the moving boat and caught the ropes, and tied each one to the post. Shay checked her knot when he got off.

'Not bad at all. You have tied knots like this before,' he said.

'When we were young, my family always had a house beside a lake in Virginia. There was a jetty like that, and we had a little rowing boat that always had to be tied up well. I learned that the hard way from my two brothers. I was the youngest, and agitating to be given more responsibility. Milo said I could tie up the boat when they were finished fishing one evening.'

'And you did, like a little girl would. What happened?'

Casey smiled.

'Next morning, my father was up at the crack of dawn to go fishing. I can still hear his shouts; the rowing boat was bobbing on the water in the middle of the lake with our golden retriever on board barking and whining. The dog liked to sleep on the boat at night to stay cool.'

Shay laughed heartily.

'It wasn't funny then. My dad had to ask the neighbours for help. He didn't like them; they had a lot of money and looked down on us, but they helped that morning.'

'And what happened?'

'The dog was so relieved to be rescued, he greeted Mr Philpotts by jumping up on him, and knocked him in the water.'

'A good childhood memory to have,' Shay said.

'Yes, especially as my parents had to sell the lake house soon after.'

Shay lifted the boxes from the boat and slipped the lobsters into another container.

'It's a happy memory to draw on. That is all we can do, draw on the memories,' he said leading the way up the path to the house.

She followed slowly behind, wondering about what Shay had said, and what was in his past that made him want to draw on the memories, and why was he so afraid of the future? She felt nervous too, that there were over seven weeks stretching ahead, and she wasn't sure that Georgie would stay the course.

Walking past a bank of green leaves with yellow flowers, a kaleidoscope of small intense-blue butterflies rose up from the plants into the air. Casey stepped back in surprise, watching the butterflies with wings like gossamer flutter about. As they got higher she lost sight of them against the blue sky.

'Aren't they beautiful? Not so many of those butterflies on the mainland any more, but there are plenty out here in Scarty,' Shay said.

Casey looked at the plant.

'Is it a particular favourite?'

'Must be. But I don't know where they all were when I brought a group of German tourists two weeks ago. They came looking for them, and it was like I was telling them lies. They weren't going to put on a performance for my party, but they have no bother doing it for you,' he said, before pointing above them. 'Look, they are dropping back down.'

They stood side by side watching the dainty butterflies flutter past them once again, and Casey felt glad he was there to share this moment with her. She felt oddly comfortable here beside this man, watching the sky like it was the most important thing in the world.

'Let's get the stuff in the house, and we can head to the beach for our lobster lunch,' he said quietly, 'You take the smaller box of Rosie's stuff.'

She picked up the mid-size box. Rosie was just ashes in a tin, and now her most treasured possessions were in a brown cardboard box, which wasn't even heavy to carry. Casey felt very sad for her friend who had once been so dear to her. She followed Shay up the path, past the bank of foxgloves and the gorse which had spread out around the outhouses giving a good wall of shelter.

'Do you have the key?' he asked, and she handed it to him to open the back door.

'Best to get the windows and doors open, then I will bring the rest of the boxes from the boat,' he said.

Casey left Rosie's box on the table, and moved to the hall, pulling back the bolts on the front door to open it.

It was probably her favourite view, looking across the channel to the mainland. It reminded her that for a short time she was here and had left the world she knew. It reminded her that she should grab every opportunity. For that reason, she would not object to Shay boiling the lobsters, and she would try to eat them.

She heard him plonk a few boxes on the kitchen table, and she ducked back inside the house.

'I am off to light the fire. Will you bring the big pot stored under the sink down to the beach? Maybe some plates and cups too,' he said as he pulled a bottle of wine out of a bag slung over his shoulder.

'A light white wine, and I have some nice fresh brown bread; we don't need anything else,' he said.

Shivering at the thought of watching the lobsters cook, Casey opened the cupboard door under the sink, and pulled out the pot and lid. She pushed the packet of butter into the saucepan along with the cups, forks and knives and small plates. She placed the saucepan on the table beside the box. Shay wouldn't need her help setting up.

Getting a knife from the drawer, she carefully sliced through the tape that sealed the box. Opening back the flaps, she reached inside. There were a few bulky items and what looked like a diary or notebook at the bottom. Casey picked up an ornate silver frame, which seemed to match the wheelhouse frame.

Her heart jerked when she saw Rosie wearing a big straw hat, and that smile they all loved; her arm around the woman with the long black hair. Casey thought the two women looked such good friends, and were so easy together, laughing and smiling for the camera. She felt a stab of jealousy as she examined the photograph. There was a time she was Rosie's bestie, but that changed somewhere along the line. She wasn't even sure that Rosie would have let her into the secret of Scarty if they had stayed in touch.

Quickly, she put the frame back in the box, and picking up the saucepan, headed off down the path to the sea. At the foxglove bank, she stood and watched the smoke curl upwards from the makeshift fire Shay had set up. He saw her, and waved as she continued down the path, walking more slowly than usual, struggling with the weight of the pot.

'Do we really have to boil them?' she asked, watching the lobsters squirm in the box.

'If we're going to eat them, yeah.'

Shay picked up the pot, wandered down to the water line, and filled it with seawater.

'You're in for a treat,' he said as he cut a lemon in half, and threw it in the water, before placing the pot on the fire.

'I once went to a fancy restaurant in Chicago, and my boyfriend at the time ordered quail for both of us. I couldn't touch it when it came out on a plate on a bed of fresh herbs. It looked like a helpless, dead bird. The maître d' came and asked me was there something wrong with my food, and when I said I couldn't touch the helpless bird, they laughed, and took it away. They gave me a chicken breast, and I ate that, which I know makes me a hypocrite. My boyfriend was furious. He broke up with me soon after.'

'You have no worries like that here,' Shay said, chuckling as he lifted first one lobster, then another head first into the hot water.

Casey shivered as he put on the lid, and stoked up the fire.

'We will get it to boiling point, then turn it down.'

Casey concentrated on the waves, anything to take her mind off what was happening. When she heard a strange hissing noise, she turned to Shay in alarm.

'What is that?'

'Not what you think; it's the release of gas from under the shell.'

'Oh.'

She couldn't take any more, and jumped up, rushing to the sea, to paddle in the water.

'It will be about another five minutes or so, they're small lobster,' Shay called out.

She saw him drop some butter in a bowl, and melt it over the heat.

After a while, he called her to where he had a blanket laid out on the ground. A plate of bread soaked in olive oil, some salad and cups filled with wine were arranged on the blue check rug.

'I know you're a little nervous, but let me show you how to eat this. You will never taste any meat so sweet,' Shay said, taking a red lobster, and slapping it on a wooden chopping board. He split the tail in half with a knife before rotating it until the tail snapped off. Reaching in, he pulled the fleshy tail right out. Cutting some off, he dipped it in the butter, and offered it to Casey.

Tentatively, she accepted it.

'If you don't like it, it's fine,' he said.

She took a small bite. It tasted sweet and light, and she felt that she was tasting the sea. When he handed her more, she took it, and ate it without hesitation.

Shay next cracked the claws.

'Thank you for making me try; it's delicious,' she said.

'Good, wash it down with the olive oil bread and the wine, and you could be on a beach in Portugal or Greece,' he said.

Casey did as she was told. They sat back on the blanket, sometimes eating or drinking the wine, watching the waves move in and out of the shore.

'What happens if Georgie does not make it back in time to bring her across to the island?' he asked.

'Then I stay here with Rosie and drink my bottle of prosecco, eat my bread and cheese and the chocolate cake May insisted she bake for me.'

'You won't be nervous?'

'Considering I come from a city that can have as many as thirty homicides in a single month, I think I will do OK with just myself for company.

'I don't know how you live in New York.'

'Have you been?'

'My wife, Anna, loved it, and we spent our honeymoon there. I don't think I have ever walked so much,' he said, keeping his gaze out to sea.

'How long were you married?'

'Nine years. Sounds long, but in terms of marriage only baby steps.'

She saw his face cloud over, and she worried that she should not have asked him any questions. She wanted to reach out to rub away the frown which had formed across his forehead, but she wasn't sure if she should. For such a tall, strong man, she thought he suddenly looked vulnerable, and she liked him all the more for it. He began to pack up, and she helped him, laughing as they kicked sand onto the fire to put it out.

'I didn't think it was allowed to set a fire on a beach,' she said.

Shay looked all around him.

'I won't tell, if you don't,' he said and gathered up everything into a holdall bag. 'If Georgie is back from her shopping spree, I will try to get her over to you,' he said as he wandered off towards the jetty.

She walked up the hill to the farmhouse, stopping to watch his boat pull away from the pier and cross the channel to the mainland.

She was finally alone. It felt good.

SEVEN

Casey didn't bother getting the house ready, and instead set off for a walk around the island. She followed a path across the centre, through fields which were divided by grey stone walls. She could feel the strain on her legs as she made her way up the hill to what must have been a lookout point for the island. Back home, she would never dream of walking anywhere. The dull concrete pavements were hard and unforgiving, and she hailed cabs like they cost nothing.

A helicopter flew overhead, and she waved enthusiastically like a child. She was continuing on her way when she saw something slink through the grass. She stopped, and waited. The stoat popped its head up, sniffing at the air, looking at her. Casey was rooted to the spot as the animal stood tall on its hind legs, observing her. If it were a competition to see who moved first, she was ready for the challenge. Channelling all her energy into staring the stoat down, she didn't relax until it appeared to hesitate before turning away, and padding off to the left. She wondered where it could possibly be going, and she attempted to follow, but it was nowhere to be seen. It was as if the stoat had disappeared and may never even have been there. She suddenly felt very foolish.

The stoat could almost put on as good a disappearing act as Gary, she thought. Funny, when he came to mind, she wasn't angry any more. It was as if she didn't care enough for Gary to bother too deeply. It was disconcerting.

They had adored each other for so long. There had been an instant attraction, and a whirlwind romance. Gary joined her company soon after they had moved in together. It seemed as if they were totally in tune, and life was perfect until one day she woke up, and he wasn't beside her. When he eventually tumbled into the apartment, Gary was still drunk, and could barely hide his excitement to have been clubbing all night. There was the pong of cheap perfume from him, and she ordered him to take the bed in the spare room.

And so the second phase of their life together began. That was when Casey's heart hardened to Gary.

Sometimes, he stayed away for days on end, and she became satisfied with her own company, and the life she led apart from him. When he came back, it was as if they lived separate lives under the one roof, but they joined together to show a united front at work. She technically was his boss, but Gary never kept those boundaries.

He took privileges and she had indulged him for too long. She didn't have a marriage, she thought, she had a business partnership, and that was now as good as dissolved.

Casey sat on a stone wall. Everything suddenly went quiet and still. She had not realised the cacophony of sound around her until it ceased. The birdsong which had been a constant backdrop had stopped, the butterflies fluttering low, and the bees she thought weren't humming as they used to. Looking all around her, she began to feel uncomfortable and nervous. When the hawk swooped, and scooped a dormouse from the grass not far from her, Casey screamed; the sound echoing across the island, and joining the last plaintive squeals of the mouse as it was transported to the clouds, and far away.

Casey felt cold. The sun was shining, sparkling across the sea, striking her back, but she was shivering. All of a sudden, she felt a stranger on this island. She retraced her steps; her stride longer now as she was anxious to make it back to the farmhouse. As she reached the front door, she heard the familiar chug of Shay's boat on the sea. She stopped to listen to the sound of the boat before going into the kitchen. She found herself hoping that he would soon turn in for the Scarty jetty.

Looking for a distraction from the wildness of Scarty, and her memories of Gary, she pulled Rosie's box to her. Digging down, she took out the purple notebook. She hesitated, wondering should she open it. Was it OK to read a dead woman's musings?

Tentatively, she opened the book, and looked at the first page. She was disappointed it was a shopping list and phone numbers of building suppliers who would deliver to Bally-murphy and Scarty.

Flicking through the pages there was a list of TTBD which she figured was things to be done. Rosie always did like her lists. Top of the list was a note.

Make contact with C, D and G and persuade them to be friends again. I miss them.

Casey snapped the book shut.

It was such a simple statement, and it broke her heart. Flop-ping down on the chair, she let the tears flow. She had been such an idiot to let her career get in the way of a friendship which had already survived decades. And what did she have to show for it? A large apartment that was always empty? A job working her to an early grave? A husband who wouldn't hesitate to take both from her to save his own hide?

When she heard Georgie on the path, she hurriedly wiped her face, and made to put the notebook back in the box. A line of passport-like photos fell out of the notebook pages, along with a letter addressed to somebody else. Casey quickly gathered them, and pushed them all in the box, stuffing it to the side of the dresser before going outside to greet her friend.

'Isn't this the most fantastic place ever?' Georgie said, her eyes wide.

She pulled Casey into a big hug.

'We're going to have such an adventure, and I have bought loads of paint. I'm going to work and paint so much. It's going to be amazing.'

Casey pulled out of her grip.

'Calm down, Georgie, I just saw a stoat.'

'Oh, you lucky thing, I was reading all about the stoats on the island, and I am jealous you got to see one first.'

'Where were you reading that?'

'There was a book at Kennedys, and Dan let me borrow it.'

'I probably will never come across one again anyway. We need to sort out this house. Like where we are sleeping, for one,' Casey said.

'I want the front bedroom. The view is better, and I can paint there as well,' Georgie said. 'I think the light should be best at the front. Oh, Shay says he will need help carrying the boxes.'

'And you left him down there; why didn't you say it earlier?'

Georgie, ignoring her, ran upstairs. Just then, Casey heard Shay walk across the backyard.

'I have to get back to the bar, I need some help getting all the stuff up to the house,' he said unhappily as he stepped into the kitchen.

Casey rushed to take a box from him.

'Georgie is like every artist I know, selfish,' she said. 'She has disappeared to set up her Scarty studio.'

'I thought as much. She had my father gallivanting around the country to get the exact blue of the sky. She had the man demented. He told her except for these few weeks, the sky is only ever grey in these parts.'

They walked together to the boat, and collected the last of the boxes. Casey spotted a cage with three hens.

'Going to eat those next?' she quipped.

'May sent them over, said you will be glad of them if the boat can't make it out any day.'

'We're not killing, and plucking chickens.'

Shay guffawed out loud.

'I'm sure May was thinking of eggs.'

'Oh,' Casey said.

She was a little put out that he was laughing at her, but Shay didn't notice, and said he would check up on them the next day.

'I have a big birthday group in at seven, and I still have to perfect one of the desserts,' he said.

'How do you do it all?' Casey asked.

'What do you mean?'

'Wearing all these different hats; isn't it stressful?'

'Of course it's stressful, but isn't life?'

'It's just you make it look so easy.'

Shay shook his head.

'My commute is not difficult. I make my own hours, but I still have to pay the bills and taxes. I guess after what happened last year with Anna, nothing much throws me any more.'

'Of course,' Casey said stepping back among the suitcases still on the jetty. She noted there was a softness to his voice when he said Anna's name. Anna, she thought even in death was a lucky woman.

'Do you need a hand with the last bits?' he asked.

'I'll get Georgie to pitch in,' she said, gesturing back to the house.

'Good luck with that,' he said as he started up the engine.

Casey untied the rope, and threw it on the boat before hurrying up the path, calling Georgie's name.

Georgie stuck her head out the back window.

'Is there something wrong?'

'I could do with some help.'

'Coming.' Georgie arrived downstairs wearing denim shorts and a skimpy top.

'Can we get a move on? I want to go to the strand, and do some initial sketches.'

'We need to get the hens out of the cage and the sun first.'

'Why do we need them anyway?'

'May says we will get eggs.'

'Gross, why can't we get them from the grocery store?'

'Silly, these are the real thing; free range, just for us.'

They each grabbed an end of the cage, and heaved it up the path, stopping by the foxgloves to take a break.

'I'm going to sketch here first; I just have to work out how to get that exact purple-pink colour; and the faint spots on the petals, exquisite,' Georgie said, but Casey wasn't sure if she were talking to herself.

'Come on, let's get going,' she said gently.

Georgie reluctantly picked up her side of the cage.

'What's the rush?' she grumbled.

They were near the farmhouse outhouses when Georgie let her end of the cage drop to the ground.

'Damn it, oh no. Oh no. I'm so sorry. I completely forgot,' she shrieked.

'Forgot what?'

Georgie stormed down the hill to the quay, shouting and waving at the disappearing boat. Casey dropped her end of the cage on the ground, and ran after her.

'Georgie, for heaven's sake, what's wrong?'

Georgie turned to Casey, her face pale and her eyes staring.

'I was supposed to tell you your law firm rang Kennedys looking for you. They are expecting a Zoom meeting with you this evening at five our time. They said it's important.'

Casey slumped against the bank where nettles and grasses were fighting for space.

'Why, why didn't you tell me before Shay left?'

Georgie sat down on the ground, shaking her head.

'I don't know. I got so caught up in my own silly world, I guess. I got excited about being here, and making sure I got the room at the front for my studio cum bedroom. Selfish Georgie strikes again.'

Casey was too angry and upset to reply, but she stomped back to the farmhouse.

She banged the kettle on the stove, and lit the gas. She was finding it hard to contain her anger, and she badly needed caffeine.

Georgie came, and stood in the door.

'I am so, so sorry, Casey. I have messed things up big time, and I want to make it up to you.'

'How am I going to make the meeting? What do you suggest I do – swim the channel?'

'We have a few hours, they said they will be calling you into a Zoom conference for 5 p.m. Irish time?'

'And what am I going to wear? Look at me. This is a business conference.'

'You're on vacation. Why does it matter how you look?'

Casey flopped into a chair at the table as Georgie poured boiling water into a mug.

'It's not going to matter anyway; how am I going to get to the mainland for 5 p.m.? I never thought they would look for me so soon. I emailed from the mainland, and there was no indication there was anything wrong. If they are looking for me, something big is up.'

'Shay's dad said there is a signalling system, maybe we could raise the flag?' Georgie said.

Casey shook her head.

'It's too late; Shay said he would keep a lookout morning, afternoon – that is, after lunch – and evening. He won't check again until 5 p.m.,' she said flatly.

'We could throw up a flare. It's an emergency,' Georgie ventured.

'No, they would never forgive us,' Casey said firmly.

Georgie dashed out the front door, and started to hoist the flag.

Casey wanted to run after her, and scream at her to stop, but instead she stayed at the table breathing deeply in an effort to calm down.

She stopped when she heard Georgie shouting.

'Get the binoculars on my bed. Quickly,' she commanded.

Casey ran upstairs for the binoculars, so new they still had the sales tag attached.

'I think I saw somebody standing and waving,' Georgie said, grabbing the binoculars from Casey's hands.

When she looked through, she punched the air with her fist.

'It's Shay's dad, and he's making funny signals.'

Casey snatched the binoculars, and peered through them.

She counted one, two, three, four, five fingers.

'Oh no, I think they are signalling they are coming to collect us at five. That's too late,' she said.

Georgie grabbed her writing pad, and drew a huge number 3 on it.

'Do you think they will see it?' Casey said.

'We will know soon enough if we see the boat coming out of the harbour.

They stood together on a bench for a better view; Georgie clenching and unclenching her fists; Casey practising her deep breathing. They saw Dan go inside, and ten minutes later the two men came back out of the pub. One man quickly walked down the quay to the boat.

When they saw the boat turn out of the harbour, they cheered.

Georgie began to dance, and twirled Casey about. Casey pulled away.

'Shay is going to be cross, and what am I going to do? I look a mess.'

'It's a Zoom meeting, all you need is just a little make-up, and you can tie back your hair.'

'But I need a jacket; I need to look professional.'

'Don't be silly, maybe a nice blouse will carry you through,' Georgie said.

'I am a mess,' Casey said despairingly. Georgie jumped off the bench.

'Stop worrying; let's get your make-up done and you will just have to touch up before the meeting.'

'Aren't you coming back with me?'

'If you want, but I thought I was the last person you would like to be around right now.'

Casey shrugged.

'Maybe, but I don't fancy having to explain everything to Shay on my own.'

'It's good, he will forgive you anything; you're his favourite.' Georgie laughed.

Casey opened her case, and took out a royal blue blouse.

'This might work if I put my hair up and wear earrings.'

'Girl, you're on vacation. Why are you so worried?'

'Gary is going to be on the call; it's stupid, but I don't want him to think I have let myself go.'

Georgie hooted with laughter.

'I think he'll see a healthy glow in your cheeks and a sparkle in your eyes, which is as yet unexplained.'

Casey ignored the last comment, and took out her make-up bag. She hadn't even put on lipstick since she arrived here.

Georgie caught her by the shoulders, and steered her to the kitchen table.

'One thing I'm an expert on is a quick makeover,' she said.

Casey knew she hadn't long before she needed to be on the jetty, so she agreed to accept Georgie's help. She only stopped her when she picked a siren red lipstick and instead, Casey chose a deep pink.

'What about my nails?' she said.

'No time, girl; just sit on your hands so you don't wave them about.'

Casey changed into the blue blouse, and put on her mother of pearl earrings, before tying her hair up in a messy bun.

She left her jeans on because nobody would see them. Before she left, Georgie hugged her tight.

'I really am sorry, Casey,' she whispered in her ear.

'It's OK,' Casey said, and made her way to the jetty.

Shay looked worried as he pulled into Scarty.

'What's up?' he said.

'I am so sorry to drag you out here, and I will of course pay you for the trip, but I have a work Zoom meeting and if I don't attend my job will be seriously at risk.'

'No bother, but I'm not sure our own internet connection will be trustworthy enough for Zoom.'

'What do you mean?'

'It's enough for email and internet bookings, but you could never look at a full movie with it; Ballymurphy is in a bit of a blackspot.'

Casey got on the boat. Her stomach felt sick, and she didn't know what to do.

She sat on her own at the back, trying to keep her hair in place. She felt slightly idiotic wearing make-up and dressed city style.

At the harbour, Shay phoned his father, and told him to bring the car around.

'Anyone who needs a good internet connection has to go to the church in the next village.'

'Excuse me?'

'It's on a hill and the car park there has the best service.'

'But—'

'Don't worry, everybody uses it, and the priests sell teas, coffee and cakes, and make a few bob. God is happy about it,' he said in a fake serious voice.

'But it's a Zoom meeting. I can't do it from a car.'

'That can be sorted too. There's an old trailer there and a mountain and sea backdrop installed which everybody says works well. You can sit at a desk, and nobody will be any the wiser.'

Casey didn't know what to say.

Dan pulled up in the car.

'It's four already, so we need to get you there, and set up,' he said.

They drove across small roads, past fields and grey stone walls until Casey saw the church in the distance.

'Is this for real?' she asked.

'We may not be as fancy as anything in New York, but we're good at making do,' Dan said.

'I need a paper and pen, I forgot that,' Casey said, panic rising inside her.

'You might want a jacket too. The fathers will have a few in different colours to choose from, along with the stationery. People get very excited about the Zoom calls, especially if they don't want bosses knowing where they really are.'

'My office knows where I am,' Casey said stiffly.

The church was a big modern building with a large tarmac car park.

Dan pulled up, and a man opened the car door for Casey.

'Your trailer awaits, I hear it's a time sensitive situation,' he said.

Casey was shown to a desk where she set up her laptop. The man offered her a choice of three different jackets in black, cream and navy. She picked the navy, and touched up her make-up before joining her business call.

Gary took the lead, and said the client was going to plead guilty, and there was a half-decent offer from the State Attorney on the table. When Casey asked for details, he said it wasn't necessary; the offer had already been accepted.

A legal assistant asked to pass on a message of congratulations from Harry to the team.

The group clapped, and Gary said they were going to celebrate to kick off the weekend.

'Harry wanted this case done and dusted, and that is what we have achieved,' he said to a loud whoop from the group.

Casey felt as if she had been called to the meeting so that Gary could gloat, and bask in the glow of a case finalised in her absence.

'I am not sure why you called me to be here,' she said.

'We didn't, but Harry insisted we keep you in the loop,' Gary snapped.

'Let me add my congratulations,' Casey replied, her voice stiff and formal before abruptly leaving the call.

She was cross but in a bizarre way, she also felt happy. This guilty plea might mean the pressure was off for her to return after four weeks. She was smiling as she went back to the car.

'How did it go?' Dan asked.

'The client has decided to plead guilty; I don't know why they needed me.'

'But you didn't tell them that,' Dan laughed.

'Not exactly, everybody was celebrating.'.

'It's good to see you happy, girl,' Dan said as he turned the car for Ballymurphy. 'Shay says come back for a bite, and he will drop you to the island later,' he said.

She leaned back in the car seat. For the first time in a long time, she felt at home. There was nothing about the call to the law firm in Manhattan which made her want to leave Ballymurphy and Scarty Island. The truth was it made her so glad she was here, going for supper at Kennedys, before being dropped home to the island. Despite all the idiosyncrasies of this place, and the lack of proper Wi-Fi as well as the eccentric locals, the island and Ballymurphy already felt less complicated than her life in Manhattan.

Opening the car window, she breathed in the clear air with a hint of sea salt. What was really nagging her was why Rosie had had kept this place secret all these years.

EIGHT

Shay was already in the boat waiting for Casey, when Dan drove into Ballymurphy.

'I reckon Georgie won't be happy being on the island on her own, so can we shift dinner plans to Scarty, if it is OK with you?' he said.

'You must think we are a terrible nuisance?' she said.

'Not at all. May is hosting a small gathering and a bite to eat for Dan for his birthday. It would make it very special to have it on Scarty.'

'Oh my gosh; I would never have bothered you all if I had known. Happy birthday,' Casey said, turning to Dan.

He smiled broadly before going off to collect May, who had everything prepared.

'Scarty is our favourite place in the world. We were so glad when Rosie opened it up to all of us,' Shay, said.

Perplexed, Casey stared at him.

'Surely, you could go to Scarty anytime you liked.'

'Before Rosie took over the place, we were warned against trespassing on the island. The family who owned it didn't want anybody out there, and they were very direct about what would happen if anybody was caught. There were lots of warning signs too; they were the first thing Rosie got rid of.'

'Seems a pity, it being so close to the mainland,' Casey said as May and Dan drove down the quay to the boat. It took a few minutes to transfer everything over, including deck chairs which May insisted on bringing.

'Anyway,' Casey said, 'we are just visitors on the island, like yourselves.'

'That's true, we should enjoy as many days as we can on Scarty,' Shay said as he manoeuvred the boat out of the harbour.

Georgie was on the jetty, pacing up and down. Her shoulders were hunched with her arms folded.

'We have a problem,' she shouted as soon as the boat aligned itself to the jetty.

'What's wrong now?' Casey asked, taking in the anguished look on Georgie's face.

'Two of the hens are dead, I couldn't stop it. It was horrible. There's one left, the poor thing. I have it in a box in the kitchen.'

'Oh my lord, that pen was secure; what on earth happened?' May said.

'What pen? They were still in the cage,' Georgie said.

Casey ran her hands down her face.

'This is my fault. I'm so sorry, but when I got news of the New York Zoom meeting, everything else went out of my head.'

'No, it's my fault; I caused all the frenzy about your meeting, and now two hens have been butchered. I can never get anything right. An animal of some sort attacked them. There was pandemonium; it was horrible. It shook one hen, and left it outside the back door, and tore off with the other chicken in its mouth; the poor thing was still squawking as that thing ran across the field.'

'Probably a stoat,' Shay said.

'I have left a big rock by the back door; I am going to be ready if it ever comes back again. Poor Number Three is not going to end up in a stoat's mouth,' Georgie said as she led the way up the path. The cage had been pushed onto rocks, the lock broken.

'The stoat turned it over and managed somehow to break the lock. Number Three came squawking into the kitchen. It was terrifying,' Georgie said.

Casey, Dan, Shay and May took in the scene. Feathers were stuck on the cage rungs, and balls of bloody feathers were all over the rocks.

'You should have put them in the pen straight away. I told you to do that,' May shouted at Casey.

Casey put her hands over her ears and began to cry. Georgie stepped forward.

'Shout at me. This is not Casey's fault. You don't know what it was like, May; I thought I was going to have to fire flares, but I couldn't leave Number Three.'

May clicked her teeth in exasperation.

'You daft girl, at least you didn't launch that flare; we would have been the laughing stock of the county. All you have done is give a nice feast to a stoat. Where exactly is the other hen? Because he'll come back for her.'

'I never thought a stoat would do that. I saw one earlier and he was so cute. He stood on the path and looked at me,' Georgie said.

'Did he sit while you did a sketch? I hear the stoats on Scarty love to pose,' Dan laughed, and May gave him a fierce look.

Shay stepped forward.

'Do you even know what a stoat is?'

Georgie threw her eyes to the sky.

'Yes, but I didn't think we were out in the wilderness here.'

'Why don't I put the cage in the boat, and you lot find the other hen before our four-legged friend does?' Shay said.

Casey stayed back with him.

'I apologise. We know nothing; we don't know the rural life anywhere.'

'It is May you should apologise to; she loves her hens, even gives them a name. She had promised Rosie three hens while she was on the island this year.'

'I feel terrible, but I don't know what to do.'

'Carry on, and just don't make the mistake again. That is all you can do,' he said as he took the boxes off the boat, and onto the jetty.

'Are we still going to celebrate the birthday on the island?'

Shay shrugged. 'In the countryside, if you stopped every time something dies, you wouldn't get anything done,' he said.

They heard a lot of squawking coming from the area of the farmhouse, and they rushed up the path. Dan was standing holding the remaining hen, while May opened up the pen.

'Prunella is going to be very lonely on her own. But you'll have to show me you can look after this beauty right, before I allow any more on the island,' she said.

Georgie said she had a quick charcoal sketch of the three in the cage, and she would be happy to work on it, and give it to May when it was finished.

'No, I don't want a reminder of their terrible fate, but thank you, anyway,' May said in her marbles-in-the-mouth voice.

Shay said they had better get a move on down to the beach, if they were to cook supper.

'Before you go, can you put the pen in the kitchen? I don't like to think of Prunella having to live outside,' Georgie said.

'Girl, you don't want to do that; she will smell the place out. It's not hygienic, and a hen can't be trained to use a litter tray,' May said.

'I'm not going to risk losing our last hen. We will work something out,' Georgie said.

'You're such a silly. God bless your poor head,' May laughed.

'Oh, does this mean we are forgiven?' Georgie asked, and May turned to stare severely at her.

'It means you get a second chance, so don't mess up this time,' she said sternly, before leading the way past the foxglove bank, and down the steep path to the beach.

The group split up; Dan and May drifting off for a walk hand in hand across the strand; Georgie said she had to finish a painting, but would join them later. Casey and Shay picked a spot, and got to work building up a fire to cook the fresh salmon Shay had brought.

'I guess when you were on Zoom, you didn't expect to be dining al fresco at Scarty on the chef's fish special,' he said.

She sat watching him as he worked, wrapping the fish in tin foil bags full of butter and fresh herbs before placing them on a grill over the fire. She had never before met a man like Shay. He worked so hard, and felt everything so deeply. She wondered what his wife was like. All she knew was he was bereft without Anna.

'I didn't know you're a criminal lawyer,' he said.

She shook her thoughts away.

'Yes, we were defending a man charged with killing his wife, cutting her into several pieces and storing her in a fridge.'

'Charming – and you can't take a little bit of rural living.'

'It's different; I am out of my depth here.'

'I know if you put me in the middle of Manhattan, I wouldn't be so comfortable either,' he said.

She sat on the sand looking out to sea, watching the waves curl towards the shore.

'I could stay watching the sea forever,' she said quietly.

'So why, if you're on holiday, are you taking Zoom calls? Are you one of those people who insist that the office can't go on without her?'

'I hope not, but my boss demanded it, if I am to keep my job.

I'm not sure what I should be doing, because they don't need me. They are on top of everything.'

'So don't do the Zoom meetings; tell them you're only available if they run into a glitch.'

She laughed. 'I wish it worked like that.'

'I think it will work whatever way you insist,' Shay said as he pulled Casey to her feet.

'We have time to walk across to the cave where Rosie kept her stash of prosecco,' he said.

'For real? I thought you were all kidding.'

'There may be a bottle or two chilling there still,' he said.

She followed Shay as he strode across the beach as if he owned it. Every now and again, he stopped to check that she was still holding up the rear.

At the bottom of the cliff, he disappeared before she caught up with him.

Cautiously, she approached the entrance to the cave, the kittiwakes and gannets were squealing overhead.

'In here,' he said, lighting her way with his phone.

The cave was still dark, but she could see where she was going.

Shay reached up high where there was a makeshift door. He pulled it back. Something flew low over their heads, and Casey screamed.

'It's only a bat,' Shay said, reaching up to take one of the four bottles of prosecco there.

'How did Rosie ever find this?'

'A woman desperate for a chilled glass of bubbly will do anything,' he said smiling. 'Seriously, it has always been here. When I was a teenager we stole over to Scarty, and we kept our stash of beer here. We felt as if we were fooling the world,' he laughed.

'Doesn't the sea ruin everything?'

'Maybe in a bad storm with the wind coming in from the south-west but we have only ever lost a few beers.'

'Rosie's bottles were probably never there long enough to be in danger,' Georgie said from behind them, making Casey jump again.

'Christ, Georgie, why would you sneak up on me like that?'

'I had to follow you; Casey, can I talk to you?' she said.

Shay, sensing the seriousness in Georgie's tone, said he had better get back to check the fish.

'What's up?' Casey asked as she and Georgie walked to sit down on the sand.

'Debbie has raised old ghosts. I can't forget what she said to me the other day. And now this whole business with May's birds, I feel like I just ruin everything. Casey, please tell me, I know I can be selfish, but did I do the right thing with Rosie, all those years ago?'

'I think you did what you thought was right at the time, and that is all that matters.'

'Why is Debbie so sore with me? Do you really think I broke up the group?'

Casey sighed.

'Rosie was upset because you would not agree to be her surrogate, and she had no right. It's a big deal, and no one can make you do something like that unless you're all in.'

'She offered me a lot of money. I guess that is why she asked me; she thought I would be lured by the bucks, but I wasn't ready to have a baby; I could barely look after myself. I still can't.'

'Debbie stood by Rosie, even though she knew it wasn't something you should be forced to do.'

Georgie kept her eyes on the waves rolling in to shore.

'Rosie was so desperate to have a child, and I took that dream from her. After that, we all seemed to drift apart.'

Casey rubbed Georgie's shoulder.

'This is not on you, and Debbie is wrong to pretend it is. Rosie was desperate. They had been trying so long for a baby. She asked you to be her surrogate, and you weren't able to do it, but for some reason, instead of looking for another surrogate mother, she decided to stay upset at you, and pull Debbie into the argument.'

'Where do you come in all this?' Georgie asked.

'I told them they were wrong to be so cross at you. We stayed in touch, but like you said, things drifted. It's not your fault; in fact, I don't think it is anybody's fault.'

They sat in silence for a few moments, each lost in her own thoughts. After a short while, Georgie reached over, and took Casey's hand. 'Are we good?' she asked.

'I made the stupid Zoom meeting, didn't I? Of course we're good. Let's go back to the others now,' Casey said firmly.

The two women held hands as they walked across the beach.

Dan and May had the picnic laid out when they got back.

'We got Rosie's prosecco for a toast,' Georgie said, holding the bottle aloft, and fiddling with the cork to open it.

May stood beside her with plastic cups ready to catch the flow of bubbly.

'We don't want to waste a drop; Rosie always bought the expensive stuff,' she said as the cork flew off with a pop, and Georgie poured the prosecco in the cups.

'To Mr Kennedy, a wonderful man and friend, and the most patient person I know,' Georgie shouted.

May stepped forward.

'After those kind words by Georgie, can I say to Dan, my best friend, happy birthday,' she said.

Dan put his arm around May, and kissed her gently on the lips as the others clapped.

'Now let's eat, and enjoy this beautiful place,' he said.

They all tucked in to the fish and fresh salad, and used the crusty bread to wipe their plates clean. The waves fell lightly on the shore as they relaxed, and chatted happily.

After they had packed away the dinner plates, Casey asked the others to wait while she ran back to the farmhouse. She had a ridiculously expensive box of handmade chocolates she had bought in Duty Free. Snatching it from her case, she ran down the path too fast and nearly slipped, but got up again giggling, buoyed by the bubbly.

'We'll have these chocolates for dessert,' she said, slightly out of breath, when she arrived back on the beach.

Dan stood up, and kissed Casey on the cheek.

'It's easy to see why you two were friends with Rosie; all of you are such lovely, generous people,' he said as he opened the box of chocolates, and handed it around.

They stayed for a good while longer talking and laughing, until Shay said they had better head for the mainland, before the sun sank.

'Will you two be all right here on your own?' Dan asked.

'As long as that stoat doesn't come back,' Georgie said.

'Go after it with a sweeping brush,' May advised. 'Show it who's boss.'

They tidied up the picnic before strolling back to the jetty.

After the boat had turned out to sea, Casey and Georgie linked arms, and wandered back to the farmhouse.

'It's nice when we have the island to ourselves,' Georgie said, and Casey nodded her head in agreement.

'May says Prunella might not lay an egg for a while because of the stress of the attack. We have to look after her well,' Georgie said picking up the hen, and stroking her gently.

Casey nodded, too tired to argue.

· · ·

The next morning the sun was high in the sky when Casey woke up. Georgie had already left, but there was a note on the kitchen table.

We need a lead to walk Prunella about outside, otherwise she will get cabin fever. I have let her roam free in the kitchen, so don't forget to put her in her pen if you have to open the door. Off on a hike with my gear to the end of the island; see you later. G.

Casey looked all around the room.

'How do you call a hen?' she muttered.

Making a clicking noise with her tongue, she looked under the table and chairs, and checked the sink. She got a slice of bread, and crumbed it with her fingers, tossing the small bits on the floor. There was a clucking sound from overhead on the mantelpiece and the hen took off into the air, whooshing past Casey, and onto the floor.

Nervously, she pulled out a chair, and sat down at the table to watch the hen. Prunella was going to be a big headache. She knew what Georgie was like when she became obsessed about something and right now, she was caught up with this bird who did not even know what a litter tray was. Hurriedly she caught up with the hen, and pushed her back in the pen with a bowl of water.

She wanted this time to be on her own. She didn't need to be babysitting a hen. Casey brewed a pot of coffee, and brought it and a mug out onto a bench at the front. Georgie's binoculars were still on the tabletop, and Casey idly looked through them.

She could see Shay, or maybe it was Dan, sweeping the pub deck. She wanted to call out and wave, until she realised they didn't know she was watching them.

She was rarely alone; she didn't know what to do; how to enjoy her own company. She was forty-one years of age, and

counted on work to fill her time; without it, she wasn't sure
what to do with herself.

Pouring out her coffee, she walked across the grass in her
bare feet. When had she last felt fronds of real grass between
her toes? It tickled, and she smiled. Still wearing her long silk
nightdress she wandered around the farmhouse, and down the
path to the sea.

There were stones in places and in her bare feet, she had to
zigzag along the path. She felt young and free, and even silly
again. Her silk night gown was more like an evening dress.
When she purchased it on a whim at Saks, Fifth Avenue, in the
January sale, she had no idea the first time she would wear it
was by the sea at Scarty on a July day. Casey didn't care if
anybody was watching her. She scanned the horizon; there
were no ships or boats on the sea. She sneakily checked through
her binoculars, but it was all quiet at Kennedys bar.

Casey knew what she wanted to do. She and Rosie had said
that one day they would run together naked into the sea and
swim, not caring if anybody could see them. What age had they
been then? Probably in their twenties, she thought. They never
did, and then they weren't living near each other any more.
Somewhere along the line, they became sensible women, who
would never dream of running into the sea naked.

Grief engulfed Casey for all the years lost, when she barely
talked to Rosie; for all the secrets that were never divulged; for
the friendship that was let go dry.

She walked past the spot where they had their small gathering the night before, and went down to the sea.

Slipping off her nightgown, she let it fall down to the sand
in a tumble of silk. Stepping over it, she walked in purposeful
strides down to the water, paddling at first, before wading in,
letting the waves break around her.

Dipping down, she let the water cover her breasts and
splash against her face. She swam out a few strokes until the

shore was no longer under her feet, and she stood treading water watching the horizon, and not caring if any boat or anyone appeared.

She must have spent a while, because she began to feel tired, and turned to swim back to shore. It was then she spotted the seal, floating on the water between herself and the shore.

She didn't panic, she stayed calm and watched it as it bobbed along, enjoying the water as much as she was. She saw its whiskers and its funny face, which seemed at odds with the bulk of its body. All of a sudden, the seal twisted its heavy frame, and gazed at her before dipping under the water.

Unsure of what to do, she moved slowly towards the shore. The seal popped its head up further away.

They eyed each other. Slowly, she reached out with her feet to feel the strand, and began to walk through the water. The seal dived and disappeared. Casey stood uncertain for a while, before running up the beach to scoop up her nightgown and pull it on.

She was squeezing out her hair, when Georgie called from the path.

'There you are, I thought you had gone to the mainland without me. Let's have breakfast together,' she said, turning back to the farmhouse.

'Sure,' Casey replied, but as Georgie scrambled up the path, Casey turned one last time towards the sea, trying to convince herself she hadn't imagined the whole thing.

NINE

Georgie and Casey settled in well to a routine, enjoying the peace of the island and long lazy summer days. Georgie got up early every morning to spend time with Prunella, tying a scarf around her so she could walk her on the grass outside. Sometimes, too, she brought her on short sketching trips, the hen tucked up on Georgie's lap as she worked furiously on charcoal drawings.

A week had passed when Casey one morning watched Shay's boat move slowly out of the harbour. She wasn't expecting any visitors or a delivery, so she continued down to the small cove for her morning swim.

She may be the only inhabitant of the island along with Georgie, but her morning dip was the one time she felt she had completely to herself. Sometimes the seal came close to shore to watch her. Casey thought it was mocking her, and the way she tentatively got in the water, and attempted to take long strokes parallel to shore.

She wasn't afraid of the seal, who always stayed in the shadow of the big shore rocks, resting in the water observing her. Georgie had come down to the beach just once since they arrived, but she had screamed when she saw the seal treading water, eyeing her curiously. It had dipped below the water line before going into a deep dive and setting out to sea.

Casey didn't think she would see it ever again, and she had sulked for the whole of that day, not saying a word to Georgie.

She laughed to think of it now. Floating on her back, she gazed at the sky; the white clouds appeared to be almost bustling about, but never colliding. It was hard to believe that bad weather was expected in a few days. It seemed like summer would stretch on forever in their little slice of paradise.

The chugging sound of the boat got louder. She swam to shore and threw on a long dress over her swimsuit. Gathering up her flip-flops, she wandered across the rocks watching the line of the boat from shore. She wasn't expecting a stop at Scarty today, but the boat was making for the mooring jetty; she was sure of it.

Shay hooted the horn, and waved as he manoeuvred the boat closer. Wandering down to the jetty, she was surprised that she felt so happy that he was making an unplanned visit. By the time she got onto the wooden pier, he had jumped out and tied up the boat.

'I have a delivery for you, and I didn't want to leave it until later,'

'Oh?' she said, embarrassed and surprised at the same time.

'It's from Rosie,' he said, jumping back on board to pick up a letter.

'Pardon me, did you say Rosie?'

'Yes, I got a package from her attorney today. It should have arrived earlier in the week, but it got held up at customs...'

Casey suddenly felt faint, and stumbled to lean against the old stone wall. Shay put his hand out to steady her.

'I'm sorry I could have broken that news a bit better,' he said, helping Casey to a grassy bank where she sat down.

'I don't understand – what package did you get?'

'I reckon it was expected that it would be delivered before you lot arrived. It was from her attorney in New York acting on her instructions, telling us about her passing and—' Shay stopped to swallow hard.

'There are letters for you, Casey. She said you would be the leader of the group, and she asked me to deliver one out to Scarty at different times.'

'She what?'

'She wrote a letter to me and my dad, and she included several letters for you guys, but she warned you were only to get them at specific times.'

Casey pulled away.

'I don't understand any of this. Why such a palaver? We are here to scatter her ashes, and sample island life. Isn't that it?'

Casey felt cross at Rosie. She was just getting used to life here, when Rosie was interfering from beyond the grave.

'I shouldn't have come over; Dad advised to wait until you were back on the mainland rather than spring this on you two, and maybe he was right,' Shay said.

Casey got up and set off to the farmhouse. She was glad when she heard Shay walking quickly behind her.

At the house, he didn't follow her in, but knocked on the back door.

'It's open, you can come in,' she snapped. She didn't know why, but she was angry at Shay and furious at Rosie.

'Would it help if I show you the letter she wrote us?' he asked gently.

'I'm sorry, I just don't understand any of this,' she said, pulling out a chair and sitting down at the table. 'Why the secrecy? Why the games?'

Shay handed over the letter, but she pushed it back across the table to him, and told him to read it aloud.

He didn't argue, and cleared his throat before starting.

My dearest Shay and Dan,

It is so strange to write to you, my friends, knowing when you read it, I will have departed this world. Words can't really express what I feel right now. Let me first apologise that I did not keep you or anybody in Ballymurphy in the loop in relation to my terminal cancer diagnosis. This was a battle I chose to fight apart from those I loved most. Since I met you all those years ago, I have been considerably enriched by your wonderful warm company, and felt the warm embrace of your friendship. I have truly cherished every moment I have spent on Scarty Island, and every moment I have spent in Ballymurphy. It had been my intention to move to the area long term, but you know what they say about the best laid plans.

My love to you all, and I hope you continue to enjoy Scarty Island and please, Shay, continue to bring your tour groups there. Tell May, too, I will miss her so much.

There are times as I sit here, covered in soft blankets to keep out a cold that I think actually emanates from inside my body, that I close my eyes, and I am back in Ballymurphy and crossing the sea to Scarty. There is no place I would rather be at this moment. I have some energy still which I devote to my letters, but how I wish I was sitting on a bench outside the farmhouse at Scarty and looking across to Ballymurphy. The memory of my beautiful island, and you my mainland family, is what gives me strength for what is to come.

But before I go all maudlin as May says, and make everyone cry, I want to ask you a favour. My three best US friends – all the way back to college days – I hope will honour my request to scatter my ashes at Scarty Island. I have asked Casey, Georgie and Debbie to live on the island over July and August, so they may rekindle the bond of friendship which has slipped in recent years. I have included here dated letters; I was

*hoping Shay would bring across to Scarty by boat once a week,
so I may in some way connect with them.*

*Call it an extended wake if you like; these letters will help
me be part of the group, and hopefully my friends will grow to
understand why I asked them to stay at Scarty.*

*Thank you, Shay and Dan, for your unwavering friendship.
It has meant so much to me, and I know that my letters and
request are in good hands.*

All my love,

Rosie xx

Casey slapped her hand on the table in frustration.

'I just don't understand all the organisation she put into this.
She could have picked up the phone, and called. We would all
have come.'

'Maybe she didn't want you to see her the way she was, and
she wanted to be remembered as whole, rather than somebody
diminished by disease.'

'Wow, this is heavy talk for a sunny summer's day,'
Georgie said, walking in and plonking her art box on the
table. When Casey turned her face away, Georgie looked
agitated.

'What's wrong, has something happened?' she asked,
looking from Shay to Casey.

Casey held up an envelope.

'From Rosie, I don't know if I want to open it. There are
more on the way too.'

'Good old Rosie, she always wanted to be in the middle of
everything,' Georgie said, reaching for the letter.

Casey snapped it away.

'Just when we were beginning to settle here; it's not fair.'

Shay got up, and said he had to get back to the mainland.

'Maybe Rosie just wanted you guys to talk about her, and exchange stories while you're here. She said it was her way of somehow feeling included,' he said.

Georgie laughed, and pointed to the biscuit tin on the mantelpiece.

'She's here with us every day,' she said, taking back the letter.

This time Casey didn't resist. She was annoyed at Georgie for making light of the ashes of their dear friend. She didn't say anything but got up, and accompanied Shay outside.

'Thanks for making the journey over; it was good of you,' she said.

'I felt bad that it had arrived late.' He was going to finish, but Georgie ran out the door.

'It says here, there are more letters, why don't you give us the rest?' she called out.

Shay stared at the two women.

'I have to honour Rosie's request, I'm sorry,' he said as he turned to walk away.

Casey put her hand out to stop Georgie following him.

'Let him do what he has to do; I think one letter at a time is probably all I can take anyway.'

Georgie pushed the opened letter into Casey's hand.

'Read it, it's just typical Rosie. I scanned through it,' she said, her voice full of emotion.

Casey walked around to the front of the house and sat on a bench. Shay had pulled out of the jetty and she could hear the chug of the boat, which she found strangely comforting as she began to read.

My dearest ones,

How are you settling in? Not a word please about the lack of amenities. Scarty Island is my home, and I hope you too will enjoy its embrace. I love the island so much; there is nowhere else on this earth that I have felt so at peace. There is a magic in the stillness here. On Scarty, it's almost as if time stops still and waits for me.

I am hoping that all three of you made it to the island but if that is not the case, it's OK. We have been out of touch so long, and I know what I asked was a big imposition on your time.

I have entrusted Shay to hand over my letters to you and, I hope, in the course of the two months, we will begin to get to know each other again.

Scarty Island has been my wonderful secret. All Barry knew was I was gone to an island for alone time. He only wanted me to be happy, and he never enquired further. I guess we were both guilty in our relationship of never confronting our unhappiness. We pretended to each other, and to the outside world. Poor Barry, he probably still believes my island was somewhere off the Maine coast.

There was such a delight and freedom being here and nobody knew where I was. On Scarty, there have been so many magical moments, but now as I battle through my own cancer darkness, I remember and take comfort from the awe-inspiring beauty of standing alone on Scarty under a starry sky, the sound of the waves on shore my backdrop. There is no greater balm for the soul.

I wanted to share all this with you, but you know what they say, life happens when you are busy making plans.

I fought it at first. I was so angry; I was dejected, and I was depressed, and then I stopped fighting the inevitable, and began planning our grand reunion. It doesn't matter that I am not physically with you, planning and anticipating this time has been so uplifting.

I close my eyes now, and I think of you all at Scarty.

Today, indulge me by walking to the far end of the beach where, if you are lucky, the sea pink flowers, cushions of delicate blossoms, will still be in bud at the base of the cliffs. Little pillows of pink can be spotted between the rocks.

These tiny, but strong flowers are a reminder to all of us, that just as these beautiful blooms can withstand the harshness of their environment, so too can we weather all storms.

Go now and enjoy the sunshine. My birthday is round the corner, and I look forward to sharing it with you all. Go, and have some fun for me.

All my love,

Rosie x

Georgie came out of the house carrying a backpack.

'I have thrown together a few bits and pieces so we can have a picnic.'

Casey folded the letter.

'I was afraid she was going to be cross we had been out of touch, but instead it was...'

'So damn touching? I don't know about you, but it still made me feel guilty.' Georgie shook her head. 'But you heard Rosie, let's get going; I'm going to paint these clusters of pink flowers.'

Casey thought Georgie seemed happier as they set off down the path together. Casey helped carry the paint equipment as they tramped across the sand to the far cliffs. Georgie ran ahead like a kid, squealing with delight when the water came in around them, and splashed over the rock pools.

They moved inland a little until Georgie shouted, pointing at the tufts of pink flowers swaying as if suspended over the grey rock.

'I will do a few quick sketches and then we will eat,' Georgie said as Casey peered inside the rucksack.

'You packed prosecco and three glasses?'

'Of course, we will pour a glass for Rosie too.'

Casey giggled, and picked a large flat rock they could use as a table for their simple lunch of brown bread and cheese with prosecco for three.

'To Rosie,' Casey said, and Georgie raised two glasses to the glittering sea.

TEN

The next morning Casey slept late. Tucking Rosie's letter behind the biscuit tin on the mantelpiece, she smiled happily as her hand brushed the shells they had collected on their expedition the day before. They had been like kids on a picnic adventure, she and Georgie, pouncing on long razor shells and common whelks and tiny periwinkle shells that Casey thought looked so pretty. They had chatted, and laughed like they never had before, the stress of what was expected of them on this trip magically lifted.

She made some coffee, and placed a cover on the cafétière so that it would keep warm for Georgie for when she came back from her early morning painting trip. She was making her way onto the beach, when she saw Shay's boat run into Scarty Island. Tying her long hair into a ponytail, she set off across the rocks to the mooring point. She had climbed three large boulders, and jumped between two flat slabs of granite, when the boat horn sounded, and somebody on deck waved enthusiastically.

Casey waved back, and the person on board seemed to shout something, but the words were lost in the space across the water. Casey scrambled over the rest of the rocks to the mooring.

As the boat neared the shore, she saw the visitor was wearing a wide straw hat and a long kaftan-style dress. The person looked ridiculous jumping up and down, and waving as if she knew Casey.

Georgie, who had set up her easel in the nearby field, wandered over to find out who was arriving.

'I couldn't paint with all the noise,' she said.

'I told Shay not to bring anyone over on a whim either because a storm is due, and we don't want anyone stranded here.'

They heard the distinctive American twang of the accent as their names were called.

'Don't tell me that is Debbie,' Georgie squealed, running down to the jetty.

Casey followed as Debbie was helped off the boat, and scurried towards them, her hands outstretched.

'Girls, I'm here. I can't believe I have made it,' she shouted, almost tripping over her long rainbow-coloured kaftan, her hat flying off, and landing on the wooden jetty planks. Shay followed behind, and scooped up the hat.

'Anything else you ladies need?' he asked as he handed it to Casey.

'We're good,' Casey said.

'You heard about the storm that's expected on Thursday. We don't often get storms in July, but any bad weather rolling in across the Atlantic can be fierce. I can collect you all tomorrow, and you can stay on the mainland. There's no shelter on the island, and the Atlantic storms are fierce.'

'We have the house; we want to stay,' Casey said.

'Is that wise?' Debbie asked anxiously.

'We've weathered fierce storms in Manhattan including big

snowfalls; we can get through a day-long storm here,' Georgie said dismissively.

Shay shook his head. 'I don't think you realise that a storm at sea is very different. There are no skyscrapers for shelter or emergency services immediately at hand.'

Casey patted him on the shoulder.

'If we change our minds, we'll let you know. We have enough supplies in, and we should be fine,' she said.

'Signal before lunch tomorrow if you change your mind,' he called out as he walked back down the jetty and hopped on the boat.

'What does he mean "signal"?' Debbie asked.

'We have no cell reception here, so we put up a flag up, if we need Shay to come out, and he usually throws some staple supplies in the boat. If he doesn't bring the right things, he runs us back to the mainland to do a shop,' Casey said.

'He has learned pretty quickly wine and prosecco are top of our list,' Georgie laughed. Casey grasped Debbie by both hands and took her in.

'Why are you here? I thought you couldn't make time.'

Debbie told Georgie to get her bag, and she would tell all after she had a glass of bubbly.

Casey gave her a funny look, but led the way up the narrow path that wound through the grassy headland until they turned towards the island centre, and the whitewashed farmhouse.

Debbie appeared to hesitate, but Casey pulled her along and led her through the half door into the kitchen.

'Sit down, I want to hear all about your change of heart,' Casey said, stopping to wipe the crystal glasses with a paper towel, before setting them on the table. Georgie opened the cupboard under the sink, where there were two bottles of prosecco. She took one and quickly popped the cork, before pouring the bubbly into the glasses, splashing a little onto the wooden table.

Debbie took a glass and a held it aloft.

'To the women of Scarty Island. I am so happy to be here,' she said.

They clinked glasses, like farmers meeting over a pint.

There was a whoosh of air, and Prunella flew down from her perch on the mantelpiece and landed on the table.

'What the heck is that?' Debbie shouted, jumping out of her chair.

Georgie giggled.

'Keep your hair on; that's just Prunella.'

'Well, if this is the level of hygiene around here, I am glad I came. You guys need help,' Debbie said pushing the hen off the table.

'Hey, careful!' Georgie snapped, scooping up the bird, 'How about you tell us why are you really here?'

'You never did beat about the bush, G, and I don't blame you. I was so set against the idea, and this island. Where is Rosie, by the way?'

Casey pointed to the fireplace with the high mantelpiece, where the old biscuit tin had been placed with a candle beside it.

Debbie raised her glass to the box.

'Rosie, I'm sorry it took me so long,' she said, before turning to the other women.

'I had committed myself to my husband, and our two boys. Marvin, believe me, won't even notice I'm gone, and my boys are like teenagers everywhere: selfish; they insisted on attending a very expensive summer camp. So I found myself sitting at home, watching the housekeeper do her work, and my assistant quite ably running my interior design company, so I packed my bags and came here.'

'Just like that,' Georgie said.

Debbie swung around to face Georgie.

'What is your problem? I was invited here, too, you know.'

'Yes, and you left us in the lurch, and let us come here on our own. Now that we have the place cleaned up, and have some routine, you just waltz in.'

'I really don't see what the problem is; I'm prepared to pay my way,' Debbie snapped.

Casey got up and put the kettle on the gas ring.

'You two need to talk, and sort things out,' Casey said.

Debbie, her cheeks puffed, turned to Georgie.

'She's right; I should have said it earlier. Georgie, I owe you an apology. I stuck my nose in when it wasn't welcome or required. I deeply regret my actions. I ended up losing you as a friend, and Rosie was furious at me for interfering. She was my one true friend, and I pushed her away. Casey, you tried to stay friends with all of us, and for that I am very grateful. Do you think there is any chance we could start over?' she said, reaching out to the others.

Casey stepped into Debbie's embrace, and they hugged tightly until they had to stop to catch their breaths. Georgie hung back.

'Just so you know, there are only two bedrooms, and I'm not sharing,' she said.

Casey took some mugs from the shelf and put them down hard on the table.

'You've the biggest room, and there is a second single bed in it.'

'I need room for my easels and my artwork.'

'I can sleep anywhere; maybe we can move the single bed,' Debbie suggested.

'There is a room at the front, but it's not in great shape and there's no furniture there,' Casey said.

'Let me have a look. After all, interior design is my job; I'm sure I can pull it around,' Debbie laughed, winking at Casey.

'What about your job?' Casey asked.

'It's my own business. I can oversee things from here.'

Georgie sniggered.

'No Wi-Fi and no cell reception, good luck with that,' she said as she picked up a box of her paints and slipped out the back door.

Debbie stretched her legs under the table.

'That suits me fine. All I want to do is stop. Are you tired, Casey, tired of life?'

'Not as much now, but when I came here, yes.'

'So what do you do all day?'

'Swim, read, walk, and sometimes Shay brings over some visitors. I give them an afternoon tea of sorts after their tour of the island. It breaks up the monotony.'

'It's pretty blissful here from what I can see,' Debbie said.

'It was so hot last week that we brought the table down to the beach, and sat and had our meals as the waves came in around our ankles. That's not something I have ever done before.'

The hen ran around the kitchen pecking at the floor. Debbie quickly tucked her legs underneath her chair.

'May, who has the boutique at the harbour, gave us three hens. She says we will never be without if we have hens, but a stoat snatched the other two,' Casey said.

'How does a stoat live out here?'

'Obviously, our hens made it a feast day for it. Now Prunella stays in the house most of the time.'

'Gross,' Debbie said, making a face.

'If you need to rest, you can use my bed,' Casey said, desperate to change the subject.

'No need, I flew in yesterday, and stayed in the rooms over Shay's pub last night.'

'What? Shay never said anything when he dropped by yesterday evening.'

'I told him not to tell. I wanted to surprise you this morning.'

'Well, you definitely did that,' Casey said, her voice betraying her annoyance.

She told Debbie to follow her to the front room.

'We aired out the room but it's bare. We can move a bed down here for you, and there's a desk and chair you can have as well. We will have to ask Shay to set up a rail for your clothes,' Casey said.

'Any chance he would know where to get four-hundred-thread Egyptian cotton sheets or maybe linen?'

'You may have to travel some distance to get your exact specifications.'

'Shay told me you found an old linen cupboard and you have washed and dried them all. I can make do with them, if you like.'

'You've really got to know Shay, if you were talking to him about the island linen cupboard,' Casey said, her tone stiff.

Debbie guffawed with laughter.

'I can see I have upset the balance by coming here, but I assure you I have no interest in Shay Kennedy. I am here to get away from family life, and to scatter my friend's ashes.'

Walking over to the small window, Debbie pulled at the old frame before she managed to open it.

'Once I get this room sorted, I might even start to love this place,' she said as she pulled a long cerise silk scarf from her voluminous handbag.

Throwing the scarf over the window, she bunched it at one side using a piece of cord she found on the floor to secure it to the wall.

'Doesn't the place look better already? I can help dismantle the single bed in Georgie's room, if you like.'

Casey led the way upstairs.

When they walked into Georgie's room, it was a mess, clothes thrown everywhere and her paints laid out on the spare bed.

'We can put her stuff on the floor,' Casey said.

Debbie didn't answer; she was too busy looking out the bedroom window.

'What a pity to waste this room as a bedroom. I can see all the way to the mainland from here, and look at the sun sparkling across the water. Is it really true a storm is on its way?'

'That's what everybody keeps telling us,' Casey said as she started to clear Georgie's art gear from the spare bed.

'If one was staying full time, a sitting room up here would be lovely.'

'You can tell Georgie that,' Casey laughed.

'Please don't tell me the beds have been here forever,' Debbie said.

'No, Rosie completely renovated and brought in all new furniture. Shay says she spent every summer here.'

Debbie sat down on the other bed.

'It so darn sad. Do you know why she travelled so far away, and bought an island? I would have thought Barry would have had something to say about that too. She must have forked out big bucks for a whole island.'

'God knows, I think she just wanted somewhere she could go to get away from life.'

'Weird, but it's a beautiful place.'

'We didn't think you would come,' Casey said, looking directly at Debbie.

'I didn't think I would come either.'

They had lifted off the mattress, and were looking at the old-fashioned base, when Georgie came up the stairs.

'You're going to need a hammer to take the bed apart,' she said.

Debbie beamed a wide smile.

'I knew you would come around, eventually.'

'OK, but I don't want you lot messing my space,' Georgie said as she got to work with the hammer.

It took another twenty minutes before they had the mattress and the heavy iron frame down the stairs, and up against the walls in the old sitting room.

Georgie directed operations, and they put the bed together.

'I washed and folded all the linen; it's in that cupboard by the fireplace,' she said.

Debbie sifted through the pile of bed linen and pulled out two white sheets.

'Pure linen – were these in the house when Rosie bought it?'

'Around these parts they don't have much time for linen sheets; they say it takes forever to dry them,' Georgie said.

'I guess there isn't a dryer, then.' Debbie laughed, and the others shook their heads.

Debbie put her arm around Georgie's shoulders.

'We can be friends again, I'm sorry if I caused you upset.'

Georgie curled into Debbie's arms.

'I didn't think I could come here without you; you always were the organiser of our little group.'

'Well, this time round, I was the one who got a wee bit dramatic,' she chuckled.

'Let's get out in the sunshine,' Debbie added.

Georgie got the last bottle of prosecco and a few glasses from the kitchen table, and they walked together across the fields until they came to a little spot where Casey had, a few days earlier, set up a wooden table and chairs.

'Definitely better than a dryer; I see you have your priorities right,' Debbie said, flopping into a chair. They sat listening to the birdsong, and in the distance the sound of the waves rolling into shore. Nobody said anything, but each one of them in that moment felt happy that the group was back together again.

ELEVEN

The next morning Debbie was in the kitchen and had coffee made when the others surfaced.

'It's raining, and I can hardly see the sea. Maybe Shay was right after all,' she said glumly.

'We just have to get through one day and night,' Casey said.

'Do you think we should go back to the mainland?' Georgie asked.

Both Casey and Debbie answered at the same time, and said no.

'All the locals are going to be watching to see if we chicken out. They already call us the clueless city slickers.'

'Who the hell cares? I don't need to prove anything,' Georgie said, her voice cracking.

'If we stick together, we'll be fine, and it's Rosie's birthday tomorrow. She specifically asked us to celebrate it on Scarty,' Casey said, her voice tense.

'But she wouldn't expect us to put ourselves in danger. We can have dinner at Shay's restaurant. Celebrate properly,' Georgie said, slapping down the chopping board on the worktop before swinging around to the other two.

'I don't want to stay here. May said the people who lived here used to board up the windows because when the wind was from a certain direction, the sea swept around this part of the island, throwing up rocks, and breaking the glass.

'That sounds a bit extreme,' Debbie said.

'I went out early, and put up the flag. I am leaving this morning,' Georgie said.

'Goodness, Georgie, you're such a baby. Why can't we all see it as part of the adventure?' Debbie grumbled.

Casey took down three glasses, and poured in a small measure of whiskey in each.

'Sounds like you're serious, Georgie, so let's toast Rosie together now,' she said.

'Not the way Rosie would have imagined the celebration of her birthday,' Debbie sniffed.

'Let's make the best of it,' Georgie snapped, holding up her glass towards the biscuit tin on the mantelpiece, and calling out loud: 'Happy birthday dear Rosie.'

Debbie sighed and clinked Georgie's glass while Casey waited a moment before speaking.

'To our dear friend, thank you for bringing us to Scarty,' she said, lightly touching the biscuit tin with her glass so that it shook a little.

'Enough, I'm going to cry; I need to get off this island,' Georgie said, knocking back the rest of her whiskey. Casey and Debbie did the same.

'I guess it's better than not marking her birthday,' Debbie muttered as Casey handed Georgie a list.

'Our shopping list for when you come back. We will have run out of white wine by then as well.'

'There are three bottles left.'

'So?' Casey said, and Debbie chuckled.

'Sounds like you're going to miss a party, girl,' she said.

When there was a loud tap on the kitchen back door, there

was a flurry of activity, as both Debbie and Casey grabbed shawls to throw over their PJs.

Georgie flung the door open for Shay.

'Come in, have some coffee. I will be ready in a few minutes,' she said.

Shay, who was wearing a raincoat, said he didn't want to wet the kitchen floor, but Debbie told him not to be silly.

When he sat down Debbie took his coat, and hung it on the back door where the water flowed down the door jamb, and onto the floor.

'I am hoping that ye are all coming back with me,' he said as he spooned sugar into his coffee.

'Only Georgie,' Casey said.

'It promises to be pretty wild. I wish ye would take advice, because once the storm hits, there's not a boat around that can launch,' he said.

Debbie sat opposite him.

'Do you think we're crazy to stay?'

He slurped his coffee, and carefully placed his mug on the table.

'I think you've no idea what you're letting yourself in for. I think you should take the advice of those who know. Nobody ever stayed on Scarty during a storm.'

'But won't it just be a big blow for one night; it's not as if we will be cut off for days,' Casey said as she buttered some brown bread.

'I can't make ye leave, no matter how much I wish I could. If you insist on staying, make sure you have enough logs in for the stove to last days, because once the wind rises, you won't get out the back door, and best to stay upstairs in case the windows get blown in down here.'

'You don't seriously expect that to happen,' Casey said.

'Anything can happen in a storm, and it's best to be

prepared for the worst,' Shay said, and Casey saw Debbie's face go pale.

'I can stay with the house; you go if you want,' she said to her gently.

'No, I have weathered a lot in my life, including tornados and hurricanes. I hardly think a storm off the Irish coast is going to put me off.' Debbie spoke with such determination that Casey did not question her further.

When Georgie came downstairs, she had her box of paints and an easel under her arm.

'Do you mind if I bring Prunella as well?' she asked. Shay shrugged, and picked up the steel pen where the hen was sleeping. 'I thought you're going for one night only,' Debbie said.

'I'm not taking any chances. These oil paints are precious to me and so is Prunella. They go where I go,' Georgie said, before pulling on a big cardigan, and wrapping it tightly around herself. When they got out of the house, Casey watched as Shay held her by the arm as he guided her down the jetty to the boat.

'Decision made,' Debbie said, and she shivered.

Casey, feeling nervous, felt like running down the pier after Shay, but instead she concentrated on heating up her coffee in a saucepan.

'How can you do that? Rank,' Debbie said.

'It's all about taking it off the heat at the right time. Here, I find I never have time to sit and finish a cup of coffee.'

'What an odd thing to say; and you call this the good life,' Debbie said as she took a sip of her coffee and grimaced.

'Give me that saucepan and let me heat up my damn coffee,' she said, pulling out a packet of cigarettes.

'When did you start smoking?'

'Once I had teenage children, I had to start smoking. Everybody said get a dog, but then how would I leave it, and boy, have I dreamed of leaving. Smoking is an easy way out.'

Casey took Debbie's coffee, and put it in the saucepan.

'I would prefer a fresh cup, even if it is instant,' Debbie mumbled.

'We have to be careful not to waste anything.'

'For pity's sake, Casey, we might be on the ocean, but the mainland is only a quarter of a mile away, and I have a feeling Shay will be back and forth even more,' Debbie laughed, standing at the gas cooker and watching her coffee begin to bubble slightly at the saucepan's rim.

Casey prised open a box of shortbread biscuits. 'So are you going to tell me the truth about you coming here?' she said.

'If you want to know that story, I need a whiskey on the side.'

Casey pulled open the door of the cabinet under the sink, and produced a bottle of whiskey.

'Now, you're talking,' Debbie said.

Casey stretched, and pulled two glass tumblers off the work-top, and poured a measure of whiskey in each. Debbie tipped the coffee in the saucepan into her mug and sat opposite Casey.

'They don't know where I am.'

'Who? What do you mean?'

'Marvin and the kids; I didn't tell anyone what I was doing.'

Casey, who was stirring sugar into her coffee, stopped. 'You told no one?'

'There was no one to tell.'

'But won't Marvin worry? Won't he call the cops or something?'

'Like I said, even if he notices I'm gone.'

'You're a right Shirley Valentine.'

'I did talk to the wall, just like Shirley,' Debbie giggled.

Casey looked at her friend, and took in her strained face, the wrinkles around her eyes accentuated by the fact that she had her hair scraped back in a bun.

'Why do you wear your hair like that?'

'It's easy, I guess.'

Casey reached over, and pulled at Debbie's hair until the bun gave way, letting her tresses tumble around her face and across her eyes.

'That's the old Debbie I knew,' she said, smiling.

Debbie ran her fingers through her hair.

'The truth is I have not felt like that Debbie in a long time. Casey, I have a successful interior design business, my sons are good boys, and they are off to college in the fall. I don't know who the hell I am, and Marvin – well, that stopped being fun a long time ago.'

'It happens.'

'I just wish it didn't,' Debbie said, wiping away a tear. She got up, and paced the room, knocking back the whiskey as she went. 'It's why I came here. I want to live again; I rather imagined white sand beaches, crystal clear water and time to think; I wasn't planning on rain, wind and storms, but that's OK.'

'You should have told Marvin.'

'He needed a wake-up call; maybe this will be it. I like it here. My business practically runs itself, I have such a good team. Casey, let's love it here.'

'Rosie knew we needed a break; it's time to recharge.'

Debbie grabbed her by the shoulders.

'But it's more than that. This is our survival course; this is our chance to prove to ourselves that we are not going to age gracefully, but splendidly and disgracefully.'

'I'm not sure anyone will take much notice of us on a remote island. Why were you so set against the idea in the first place?'

'Because I was so goddamn afraid to confront all the things wrong in my life. That whole thing between Rosie and Georgie and my involvement... that made me afraid, too, that me and my big mouth would spoil things all over again. But when I said to Marvin you guys were going to do it, he said you were silly broads. I decided there and then, I wanted to be a silly broad too.'

Casey clinked Debbie's glass.

'Let's be silly broads, together.'

Debbie sighed deeply.

'I think I have forgotten how to be silly, Casey. I work so hard; I look after my family. I know today is Tuesday, and they like to have meatloaf, but Marvin always complains it is not like his mother's. I lay on that uncomfortable mattress we pulled down the stairs to the front room, and I was thinking, maybe I can get horsehair and get it restuffed. And why can't we move the sitting room to upstairs, just while we're here.'

Casey opened a packet of biscuits and pushed it across the table.

'Double chocolate; it really helps.'

Debbie shoved the packet further down the table.

'Don't we have to prepare for this storm?'

'Shay said we should get the candles out as it'll be so dark during the day once the window shutters are in place.'

'Well, we had better get that done, then.'

'We don't have coats, I never thought there would be rain in summer.'

'There's always rain in this country. Didn't you read up on the place?' Casey said.

'I was too busy trying to leave my life.'

Casey looked directly at Debbie.

'I suppose we should just get on with it. The shutters are in the shed, we have to haul them around to the windows.'

Debbie tied a shawl around her head.

'Thank goodness nobody can see me now,' she said as she followed Casey out the back door. Strong gusts of wind pushed against them, the rain drenching their hair, and beating on their backs as they pulled and pushed the shutters to the front. With one great heave, they hauled each shutter onto the windowsills and shoved them into place.

Drenched, they were making their way to the back door when Debbie pulled Casey's hand.

'Let's run and look at the sea.'

'But we are soaked through.'

'So, what does it matter? Even looking through their binoculars they won't be able to see us.' She swept her hand across the rain-soaked land in the general direction of where the mainland was no longer visible.

Casey gripped Debbie's hand, and they ran down the path together to the beach. The gorse bushes whipped at their bare legs, and in places it was slippy where the rain had washed away the sand path. They stopped short of the cliffs. The surf which had been flung up in the air by the wind clung to their hair, and hit their cheeks. The waves were beginning to crash into shore, and they could not go further.

A squall of wind pushed them and they grabbed each other, so they didn't fall over.

Debbie held her face up to the sky as Casey stood watching the waves hit the shore with a loud noise.

'I am so glad I came to Scarty,' Debbie shouted above the din of the wind.

'Me too,' Casey said, and they ran, hand in hand, back to the farmhouse, buffeted off course by strong squalls of wind.

Once they got inside, they scrabbled around until Casey found the candles and matches, and lit two, before balancing them in old jam jars on the table, while Debbie produced towels so they could dry off a little. They changed together in front of the stove, which Casey lit before making hot whiskeys.

'It's summer, and yet it feels like winter,' Debbie said.

'I hope we will be all right. Those waves will be huge by this evening,' she added.

Debbie ran to her bag and produced a box of Baileys Irish Cream truffles.

'I am going to eat and drink, and the wind can howl and howl, I don't care,' she said.

Casey held her glass up to Debbie's, and they clinked like two girls on a night out.

Later on, Casey got the biscuit tin holding Rosie's ashes, and she set it down on the kitchen table.

'She was right about this place. She would have loved this trip,' Debbie said, her voice teary.

'I just wish I knew exactly why she wants her ashes scattered here,' Casey said.

'Maybe she felt happiest here; that it's as simple as that,' Debbie replied as she topped up their glasses once more.

'To Rosie and the mystery island,' she said, and Casey lifted her glass higher.

Debbie downed her whiskey in one, then Casey topped up their glasses.

'Eternal birthday to our dear friend, Rosie. I don't know why you brought us all here, girl, but I am glad you did,' Casey said, and they clinked glasses again.

'Hear, hear,' Debbie said, sipping this drink slowly. 'Do you think anyone in the States will try to find us?' she asked.

Casey didn't answer at first.

'My Gary is not going to bother. Could you see him on Shay's boat?'

Debbie cackled. 'I have more chance of the man in the moon finding me than Marvin,' she said quietly.

They busied themselves, Casey reading and Debbie beside the fire rifling through the many magazines she had brought with her. The wind continued to howl, and screech down the chimney in the front sitting room. When they heard a thud against the front door, they both froze.

'What was that?' Casey asked.

Debbie put up her hand and they both fell silent. There were smaller thuds against the front room shutter and the door.

'I think the sea is throwing things at us,' Casey said.

'We're not afraid,' Debbie shouted, gripping Casey's hand so tight it hurt.

'Maybe we should stay upstairs, just in case the wind pulls the shutters off,' Casey said.

Wearily, they tramped upstairs.

Feeling scared and clutching each other tight, they decided to sit on the bed against the far wall, and tell silly stories, to keep their minds off the wind, rain and the sound of the sea, which was so loud it was as if an army of banshees was trying to get in.

'I don't know how we're going to sleep through this,' Debbie said.

'If we get through this, we can do anything,' Casey whispered, and Debbie, who was practising her deep breathing exercises, nodded fiercely. At one stage, it was as if the whole house shook, and the window glass rattled violently in the frames.

Debbie gripped Casey's arm, digging her nails in, but Casey, who was paralysed with fear, hardly noticed.

'We should have gone with Georgie,' Casey whispered.

Debbie held a candle near Casey's face.

'We never admit we were scared. We never tell her. We tell nobody,' Debbie said, reaching for the whiskey bottle, and taking a swig from it, before passing it to Casey.

Pressing the on button of the old fashioned tape recorder, Casey waited to hear some music, before turning the volume up high so it blared over the sound of the wind and the sea. They settled under the covers, and prayed they would get through the night.

TWELVE

They must have fallen asleep, because when Casey opened her eyes there was a soft light filtering in through the curtains and the raging sound was gone. The house was silent except for a creaking noise, which after a few moments she realised was coming from a front-of-house shutter which had come off one of its hinges. Slowly, she made her way to the window, and pulled back the curtains. The sea was sparkling, the sunshine dancing across the calm ripples of waves. She could see a school of dolphins dipping in and out of the water, the rhythmic movement making her stand mesmerised by this place, and this island.

Debbie moaned, and rolled out of bed.

'I have not had so much to drink in a very long time. This reminds me of when we had that two-bed apartment in the Lower East Side... Gosh, I forgot, is the house still standing?' she asked.

'It's like it never happened,' Casey said.

Debbie made her way to the window, and peered out.

'Look at the grass and flowers pounded into the ground. Did the wind do that?'

'It couldn't have been the sea, could it?' Casey said.

'Shit, did it come near the house? We could have been swept away.'

'But we weren't,' Casey shouted triumphantly, punching the air.

Debbie stood back, her face pale and her hands trembling.

'Let's inspect the damage,' she said, stepping in to her slippers, before leading the way downstairs.

Casey pulled back the bolts of the back door, and they walked around the house to the front. A shutter had been ripped off the front sitting-room window, the glass shattered across Debbie's bed, her pink silk scarf ripped to shreds, but still hanging from a pole over the window.

The flower pots Georgie had placed at the front door had been smashed into little bits, sand, pebbles and rocks strewn around the grass, where in the days before they had walked barefoot.

'I can see the drag back from the waves, like this was the beach,' Casey said excitedly.

Debbie leaned against the windowsill.

'We did it; we survived it,' she hollered.

Casey took her hands, and together they danced over the flattened grass, kicking the bits of terracotta pots out of the way.

Suddenly, Casey stopped.

'They will be looking out for us through the binoculars. Let's pretend it was no biggie,' she said.

Debbie laughed.

'Let's get these shutters off,' she said as she began to tug at the other shutter at the front to dislodge it.

The shutter came away in her hands, and she fell back laughing.

'I have a better idea. Let's go for a walk around the island, and see what the sea has thrown up,' Casey said.

They went inside to change into their runners. Casey made a flask of coffee and grabbed some blueberry muffins from a tin.

'Georgie is going to be jealous when she comes back that we had one heck of an adventure,' she said.

'Georgie likes to be jealous,' Debbie mumbled.

Casey swung around. 'A bit harsh, Debs.'

'I don't think so; Georgie is the youngest, was always the most beautiful by far but look at her life; barely scraping it together with her artwork. She always acts jealous of our success and our lives, like we succeeded to spite her.'

'Hardly. My life is nothing to be jealous about.'

'Maybe not, but mine looked spectacular from the outside, and Rosie's appeared amazing,' Debbie declared.

'Yeah, so good she fled to an island on the other side of the world,' Casey said quietly.

They set off on the path across the island, rushing along to the highest point where the light breeze ruffled at their cheeks, and made the flowers bow down.

Debbie threw her hands in the air, and twirled until she became dizzy. Casey laughed and did the same; the two of them lurching against each other like two drunks.

'I have not felt so free in a long, long time,' Debbie shouted.

'If I did something like this with Marvin, he would frown and disapprove. How I'd love not to have the disapproving eye on me all the time.'

'We really are pushing the boat out, trekking across a small island on the Atlantic Ocean.' Casey snorted.

'OK, it's not a rave, but it's mine; it's ours, and nobody can take that from us.'

Casey stopped to pick up a gnarled piece of driftwood.

'It must have been thrown up by the tide.'

'The Atlantic Ocean threw itself at the island, and at our little house, and we survived,' Debbie said.

'You like it here after just two days.'

'Didn't you?'

'Yes, I'm not sure Georgie likes it, though; she prefers to be on the mainland.'

'There may be an added attraction in those quarters,' Debbie sniffed.

They saw Shay's boat pull out of the harbour. Casey tracked it, her head beginning to throb, and she wondered why she was reacting this way.

She turned to Debbie. 'Let's continue on our walk; if they want us, they can find us,' she said.

'Isn't it a bit childish?'

Casey, still smarting at the idea that Georgie and Shay might be getting together, walked on, her stride purposeful and long. What did it matter to her anyway? Shay could do as he liked, and she was, for now at least, a married woman.

Debbie scurried after her, trying to keep up.

After a while, Casey slowed down and they walked, and foraged together not bothering to talk, but enjoying the sun on their backs and the stillness that remained after a bad storm. The far side of the island was Casey's favourite. She led the way to the headland, where they were surrounded by the Atlantic Ocean, and sat watching as the waves made their way to shore, this time stopping short of the small cliff, and gathering at the bottom.

'May says this is the last stop before America,' Casey said.

'And a world away from anything we know,' Debbie said, lying down on the grass, and closing her eyes.

'How did Rosie find this place, do you know?' she asked.

'I hadn't talked to her in nearly two years. Sent birthday cards and holiday greetings, but we hadn't been part of each other's lives for so long. After the whole surrogacy thing, I think she cut down contact with everyone, but especially me. It drifted, and suddenly it was too late.'

'I didn't think she ever left upstate New York; for heaven's sake, I invited her to a Broadway show once, and she was too afraid to come into the city at night.'

'Remember, she always said we should go on holiday together, just us, somewhere lovely.'

'Hardly a place like this. I think she was imagining cocktail bars and night clubs back then.'

'Maybe.'

Casey heard her name being called. The shouted word danced through the air, and she smiled, thinking Shay was looking for her.

Debbie sat up. 'Did you hear that in the wind? I'm sure I heard our names being called.'

Casey got the flask and poured the coffee into two takeaway cups, and opened the tin with the tiny muffins.

When Shay and Georgie came closer, Casey waved to them. Georgie rushed over, her face red from exertion.

'We thought something terrible had happened to you two,' she shouted.

'Nonsense, we thought we would like a little walk to inspect the storm damage, but this place is so beautiful we had to linger and have our coffee,' Debbie said.

'I'm afraid I don't have enough mugs to go around, other-wise I would offer you one,' Casey said.

Georgie sat down beside them.

'I thought I was the only one who knew about this lovely spot. Shay, it would be perfect the next time we have dinner on a beach.'

Casey looked oddly between the two of them. Catching her gaze, Shay said he had better get back to the boat.

'I'm glad you got through the storm. It was quite a blow,' he said.

Casey thought he looked a little odd.

'I will walk back to the house with you,' she said, throwing away most of her coffee and packing up her flask.

He didn't say anything, but started back across the fields and past the old ruin.

She had to walk fast to catch up with him.

'I apologise if we gave you a fright,' she said.

'Ye left the farmhouse wide open, and we were worried when we saw the damage to the front window. Georgie was very upset.'

For a moment Casey thought he had been worried about her. It hurt her so much to think he only cared she'd upset Georgie.

'Of course, we should have cleaned up, but to tell the truth, we were so relieved it was over. There was a lot of alcohol imbibed.'

Shay smiled at her.

'It's one way of sitting out a storm,' he said.

'I am ashamed to say we slept through most of it.'

'We were worried for ye because it was even stronger than we predicted, and when it changed direction we knew the house was in danger.'

Once they got back to the farmhouse, she thought his face brightened.

'You don't like that part of the island, do you?' she asked gently.

'I'm not good at hiding anything.'

'Any particular reason?'

Shay sat down at the kitchen table, and she made some tea.

'I think if you have any whiskey left, it might be a better choice this time,' he said.

Surprised, Casey pulled an unopened bottle of whiskey from the cupboard under the kitchen sink, and poured measures into two tumblers.

'Spill,' she said.

Shay took the whiskey, and appeared to consider it before holding the glass to his lips, and taking a long slug.

'I'm surprised it hasn't come up until now, to be honest, but we try to avoid that beach.'

'You should have told us; is it dangerous to swim there? Because Georgie likes it down that side of the island,' Casey said, but Shay put up his hand to stop her talking.

Taking in his face which had a grey tint to it, she sat back on her chair. They both remained silent; the only sound in the kitchen was of the sea hitting the shore. After a few minutes, Casey spoke.

'You need to tell me, considering we are living out here on our own on this island,' she said, her voice high-pitched because she was nervous.

Shay put his glass down, and rolled up his shirt sleeves as if he were trying to buy time before telling his story.

Impatient, Casey drummed the table with her fingers.

'There is no need to be worried, it was a long time ago. But my brother, many years ago, drowned, and his body was washed up on that beach.'

Casey put her hands to her face.

'Oh, Christ, I had no idea. I am so sorry.'

Shay looked all around him.

'It was a tough time for the family. Andrew was the youngest...'

'You don't have to talk about it, if you don't want.'

'It's all right. It was decades ago, though it feels like it was yesterday. The pain never goes away, you just learn to manage it.'

She caught hold of his hand, and squeezed it.

'Is that the real reason you didn't come to the island before?'

'Yes, and no; Dad took it so hard, and Mum never recovered; she died a year later. There was no specific cause of death, but we all knew it was a broken heart.'

He took away his hand.

'Why do you think I stayed in Ballymurphy? I couldn't leave Dad to run the pub on his own. We're lucky we get on.'

'Your brother, was he caught in a storm?'

'We don't even know why he was out on the sound; there was a high wind due, and it can make the section between the island and the mainland like a wind tunnel. Andrew would have known that. It is the question we kept asking, but there was no answer.

'He was missing and the rowing boat was found in pieces on the rocks further down the shore from Ballymurphy. A girl from the next village who was with him managed to swim to safety, and raise the alarm, but it was too late for Andy.'

'This is terrible. I am so sorry,' Casey said.

They heard Debbie and Georgie chatting as they came up the path to the farmhouse.

Shay knocked back the last of his whiskey.

'I had better get along. The old man wants to go into Kilkee; there's a new organic store, and he has heard so many raving about it.'

'I didn't know he was so into his food.'

'He was the chef until he took me in hand, and insisted I learn how to cook if I was going to take over the pub. He said we weren't going to be just a pub at the side of the road, but a foodie destination. It gave us something to aim for, and he was right. It has gone very well.'

'There are nights here I wish I could order takeaway,' Casey said.

'We can do that one night. Dad would love to come back with May.'

'Doesn't it hurt coming to Scarty?'

'He knows Andy loved this island for some reason, and funnily this is where he feels closest to him.'

'Not you, though?' Casey paused. 'We must arrange for a meet-up soon,' she said as the others came into the kitchen.

'I hope you are arranging a party; we need to liven things up around here,' Georgie said, twirling across the room.

Shay pulled a letter from his pocket.

'From Rosie. We can get back on track from next week,' he said, before quickly ducking out the door. Casey followed him, wondering if she had overstepped with his brother.

'Thanks for remembering the letter. Don't mind the other two; they are either up or down,' she said.

'They were not to know.'

'Can I tell them?'

'It's common knowledge in these parts; I'm surprised ye didn't hear it before now.'

'Being stuck out on an island helps.'

'Tell them as long as they realise that it's a no-go subject with Dad. If he brings it up, fair enough, but no touchy-feely stuff, if he doesn't.'

'Give us some credit, Shay.'

'I do... I just don't want any unnecessary upset being caused, and ghosts being pulled up when it has taken so long to claw back some of our lives.'

'Is that why your dad dissuaded Georgie from looking for a rowing boat to rent?'

'Probably, and the fact that rowing on the sea may look easy, but it never is. Andy was an experienced fisherman and sailor.'

He stopped at the foxglove bank.

'No need to walk down the jetty; I'm good from here.'

She watched him go; a lonely figure steering his boat out onto the sea. Why was it every time she saw Shay in his small boat tackle the Atlantic Ocean on his way back to Ballymurphy, her heart burst, wanting him to return to her and Scarty?

Wandering slowly back to the house, she could hear music coming from the kitchen.

'We can party on our own,' Georgie said, handing a glass of prosecco to Casey.

Debbie sashayed over beside her.

'Come on, Casey, don't leave me dancing with the tin,' she said pointing to Rosie's ashes on the mantelpiece.

THIRTEEN

They danced and drank, falling into bed much later in the evening when the sun had set and the island was dark. But at dawn, Casey woke up with a start to the sound of Georgie's shrieks.

Casey fell out of bed, and thundered down the stairs.

'What's wrong?'

Debbie, rubbing her eyes, put her head around her bedroom door.

'This better be life and death,' she snarled.

'It's Prunella, she's not moving.'

'She's probably asleep after being kept awake most of the night,' Debbie said, stepping into the room.

Casey and Georgie stood staring into the hen's pen, as Debbie pushed past them.

'For goodness' sake, what could have happened?' she said, reaching down, and prodding the hen with her nail.

'Hell, she's not moving,' Casey said.

Georgie opened the door, and gently lifted out the hen.

'Look at its eyes,' Debbie said authoritatively.

'I don't need to; Prunella is dead,' Casey said, turning away.

'That can't be; the poor thing,' Debbie said, prodding the bird with her manicured finger.

Georgie began to sob.

'Oh shit, May is going to kill us,' Casey said.

'We don't have to tell her, do we?' Debbie asked anxiously.

'She's going to want to know. Poor Prunella couldn't handle the stress of life after the stoat attack. What are we going to do with her body?' Georgie said, her voice shaking.

Tenderly, she placed the dead hen back in the cage, all the time stroking her feathers as if soothing her.

'How are we going to tell the others? We can't afford to lose them as friends. They are our lifeline,' Casey said, her voice high-pitched.

'You two are OK; they will blame me, they think I am the ditsy one, but I loved Prunella,' Georgie said.

Debbie grabbed Georgie in a hug.

'Prunella had a short but interesting life, and that is all down to you, Georgie. You did good, girl, and this is not your fault,' she said, stroking Georgie's hair.

'We need to bury her,' Casey said, unlocking the back door, and grabbing a shovel from the yard.

'Marvellous, we get to dig a grave. Exactly what I imagined life on an island in the sun would be like,' Debbie said.

Ignoring her, Casey picked up the pen, and went out the front door. She walked across the field, the others following.

'What if they are looking through the binoculars?' Georgie said.

Casey rested the shovel on the grass.

'Do you really think they spend their time spying on us?'

Suddenly, feeling uncomfortable, she changed her course to the back of the farmhouse with Debbie and Georgie in tow.

They took turns digging the hard earth, using all their strength to get the tough grass to lift.

'Why does it look so easy in the movies?' Debbie said. 'And this is only for a hen.'

When they judged the hole was big enough, they stood back.

'What now?' Debbie said, wiping sweat from her brow.

'Wait, don't do anything. I have something in the house we can use,' Georgie called out as she ran back into the farmhouse.

'She's taking it hard,' Casey said.

'I am going to miss Pru, too; she was a good listener,' Debbie sniffed.

Georgie appeared at the doorway, carrying a purple and pink silk scarf.

'We could wrap her in this; it's so soft.'

Debbie made to say something, but Casey lightly stood on her toe to stop her.

'Good idea; you hold the scarf, and I will get Prunella,' Casey said kindly as she reached into the pen for the hen. Georgie tucked the silk scarf around Prunella, before bending down to place her in the grave.

'Do you think we should say a few words?' Debbie asked.

'What do you say about a chicken?' Casey muttered.

'Prunella, the finest of hens and a friend,' Georgie said quietly, and the others stood silently with her for a few moments, until Casey said she had better fill in the grave.

'Come on, let's have coffee and those doughnuts you brought from Kilkee, if they are still edible,' Debbie said.

The two of them walked arm in arm back into the farm-house as Casey hurriedly filled in the grave.

They sat at the table, and took a doughnut each as Debbie poured out the coffee.

'We should get out of the house, go for a walk. How about the island perimeter? I won't do it on my own, but I would, if there was company,' Debbie said.

'I have to paint; I have to keep up with my plan,' Georgie said.

'But you're on vacation, darling.'

Georgie got up from the table, and as she stormed up the stairs, yelled back, 'It's all right for you two. You both have money behind you, but the rest of us need to work to keep the dollars coming in.'

She banged her bedroom door so hard, tremors were felt across the downstairs rooms. Debbie shrugged her shoulders, and went out the front to sit in the sun with a cup of coffee.

Casey poured a fresh cup and brought it upstairs. They had sorted out the tension with Debbie, but somehow Georgie remained on edge. She knocked gently on the door, but when there was no answer, she pushed it open.

'Thought you could do with another coffee before you head off painting for the day,' she said.

Georgie, who was packing up her paints into her rucksack, didn't say anything.

'We are worried about you; you don't seem the carefree Georgie we expected on this trip.'

Georgie sat on the bed. 'Apologies if I am not fun enough for you guys, but there is a lot of shit in my life.'

Casey sat down beside her. 'Maybe that's why you need this break, to recharge.'

Georgie stood up and began packing again, feverishly pushing her brushes into her rucksack, before moving to her easel, and dismantling it so she could carry it.

When Casey put a hand out to stop her, Georgie began to sob.

'Don't you see, this is my last chance? I have to get a collection of work together; I have so many debts. I had to get out of Manhattan.'

'What do you mean?'

'I mean I owe thousands of dollars, Casey. Thousands! The

lease on my studio and apartment is up, and I don't have anywhere to live when I return to the city.'

'Why didn't you tell us this before?'

Georgie moved to the window, and stared at the mainland.

'I love it here; I feel so far away from all the everyday shit. You can all pick up where you left off, but I don't have anything back there in New York, only crap piled on crap.'

'Surely, we can help you out?'

Georgie swivelled around.

'I can't keep asking for your help. Remember our first year in college, and I lost my monthly stipend from my mom over something stupid? You two shared yours with me. And when I was married the first time, and he lost his job, Rosie paid my rent for three months. I'm the sad case of the four; I'm fed up of messing up, and I have messed up big time.'

'When we get back, you can bunk with me, and if we put our heads together, we may be able to come up with something that will put you back in business,' Casey said.

'I don't need your help. I need to stand on my own two feet.'

Casey put her arm around Georgie.

'There are times in all our lives when we need help. You may think Debbie and I have it all together, but we have our own shit.'

'I know, I just wish mine wasn't always to do with the lack of money.'

Casey picked up a sketch of the cove at the far side of the island.

'This is so beautiful; are you doing a painting?'

Georgie pulled a cover off a canvas on the easel. Casey stood in front of it; the sea was sparkling, the sand, a stoat idling in the grass. She stood back; there was such a sadness now looking at the scene, knowing the loss it represented.

'Is there something not right?' Georgie asked anxiously.

'The opposite. It's like I'm standing looking at the cove. I always feel there is something about that place. I don't know what it is, but you have captured it.'

They heard Debbie on the stairs. Georgie went to cover the painting.

'Darling, I want to be included in the conversation. I want to help. All right, I confess I was eavesdropping,' Debbie said, grabbing Georgie in a large hug.

Georgie pulled away. 'You have always bailed me out one way or another. I need to do this on my own.'

'Continue to paint like that, you're going to do it. Why don't you headline an exhibition in New York after showing on the mainland here? Call it "With Love from Scarty Island, two months off the Irish coast.'

'I will never have enough pieces.'

'Do all the groundwork now, and show this time next year.'

'And I live on fresh air in the meantime, I suppose.'

'Darling, every good artist has a patron. I can be yours. All I ask is that I get my pick of the canvases when they are ready.'

'But even if I work day and night, I won't have fifteen or twenty pieces; not enough for an exhibition.'

'You come stay with me in my place. There is a studio you can have; I set it up when I had this grand idea of becoming a novelist. That lasted one whole week, I didn't like being holed up on my own,' Debbie said.

Georgie walked back to the window.

'Why do I resent you two, when you are so willing to help me?'

'Cos you see all the outside veneer everybody else does, but darling, we are as messed up as you; it's just we're messed up and have money,' Casey said.

She hugged Georgie tight.

'Let's go for a picnic; you can sketch, and we can swim,' Debbie said.

They went downstairs together.

'We don't have any eggs left. How are we going to get any now? May will know if we buy them,' Debbie asked as they stepped over stray feathers on the kitchen floor.

'We could say Pru is stressed-out still. Dan likes to drive me to Kilkee. I can smuggle some back,' Georgie said.

Casey laughed out loud.

'Artist, interior designer to the stars and lawyer, and we are afraid of May Buckley of Ballymurphy.'

'Damn right we are,' Debbie said.

They packed a hamper basket, which they knew Rosie must have bought. 'Let's go to our strand and we can take a bottle of prosecco from the cave,' Casey said.

They agreed, and set off down the path.

'We can go skinny dipping, nobody is about,' Casey said.

'Yeah, and the whole main street at Ballymurphy will be eyeing us up through the binoculars,' Debbie said.

'Don't be silly,' Casey laughed.

Georgie ran ahead into the sea in her sundress.

'Now, that looks a better alternative,' Debbie said, dropping the picnic basket, and following her into the water.

Casey threw off her blue sundress, and sprinted into the water, splashing the others. They joined forces and water-bombed her so she ran away through the waves; feeling the freedom of the sand between her toes. Waves hit up against her knees, but she kept going, even when the water became higher. She heard the others call out to her, but she didn't stop. Something had possessed her. She wanted to beat the sea; the sea that could take you down, tumble you around, and throw you back up on a beach far from home.

She would have gone further out but for the seal. It swam in front of her, crossing her path, and stayed in the water between her and the cave where the water line was so high; it was almost at the entrance to the prosecco store.

She stood, her eyes never leaving the seal as she edged her way out of the water. When she stepped onto the sand, the seal dipped and dived, and was gone.

Debbie and Georgie were out of breath when they reached her.

'What has got into you? You could have drowned,' Debbie said.

'We don't want the prosecco that much,' Georgie said, leading Casey onto the sand.

Suddenly, Casey was shivering. The story about Shay's brother had spooked her. She felt as though she needed a break, to get off the island. The quiet was playing with her brain. She needed the city, the anonymity, where nobody cared about what anybody else was doing. She was on an island in the Atlantic Ocean, and away from the mainland, and yet she felt more under the microscope than at any time in her life.

Tears flowed down her face. She felt foolish and vulnerable all of a sudden. Flopping down to the sand, she could not stop shivering.

'I miss her; I miss Rosie. I didn't talk to her for two years, but I knew she was there; I knew you guys were there if things got out of control, if they got bad.'

'Of course; we are always here,' Debbie said.

'Yes, even me; the one who causes all the trouble,' Georgie said, sitting beside Casey, and leaning into her.

'She is so missed by all of us,' Debbie said.

'What does that mean? We were shit friends. We always thought she went to Maine on holidays. She never told us about this place,' Casey said.

'No point going over old ground. She is dead, and we are here to honour her memory now,' Debbie said, kicking sand like she was trying to dislodge something.

'But what are we doing here, hanging around a very nice island doing nothing? I want to know why,' Georgie said.

Casey stood up.

'Georgie is right, Rosie is playing with us, but there must be a reason,' Casey said.

'I thought it was just to get us back together,' Debbie said despondently.

'If she wanted that she could have arranged an evening in Manhattan.'

Debbie shrugged. 'And no doubt one was of us would not have been available.'

Casey said it was time to open the second letter. They wandered back to where they had dumped their clothes, and Casey pulled on her sundress before taking the letter from the front patch pocket.

She handed it to Debbie.

'You read it out,' she said.

Debbie slowly opened the envelope, and took out one hand-written page.

My darlings,

I have been tired for so many days, so forgive me if this is a short note. You must have so many questions, and I am hoping my letters will answer some of them.

Let me take a guess. Why bring you all the way to an island off the Irish coast? Well, I answer, why not? It is my favourite place in the entire world. Do you guys remember the promise we made to each other on each of our twenty-first birthdays?

Debbie stopped reading, and dropped the letter. 'I can't,' she gasped, her voice full of tears.

Casey took the letter and continued.

We promised that no matter what, we would always be there for each other. I know if I had told you about my diagnosis you would have come. But I didn't want those busy women with busy lives; I wanted my friends. I know it is my friends who are reading this letter. Those are the girls, I know; my forever friends.

Darlings, this week, trust one another more, talk, laugh, drink wine and prosecco. Swim in the sea, and remember a dear friend, who would so love to be there giving you all grief.

All my love,

Rosie xx

'It's terrible we weren't there for Rosie,' Georgie said.

'How could we? She deliberately blocked us from her life,' Debbie snapped as she grabbed a few pebbles, and pelted them across the water.

'It's done; we can only respect her wishes now,' Casey said, getting up and heading off to the water's edge.

She let the sea water curl around her, and closed her eyes; listening to the sound of the sea washing over her. It never ceased to calm her brain, and even after a short time on the island, she wondered how she would ever manage not being able to hear the sound of the waves every day, whether they rippled or crashed to shore.

She called out to the others.

'Let's paddle together,' she shouted, and she smiled as she saw them run hand in hand into the sea to get as far as her.

Debbie, the tears still running down her face, grabbed the other two in a big hug.

'How I wish Rosie was here,' she said.

Casey was the first to pull away, wading into deeper water. Debbie followed with Georgie staying in the shallow water.

'Debbie, you're so emotional,' Casey said.

'Rosie is dead, why wouldn't I be?' Debbie said, moving further away.

'You miss Marvin,' Georgie said.

'My Marvin, I wonder has he copped on yet that I have left?'

'Of course, he has,' Casey said.

'I feel like the faded old wallpaper nobody wants to get rid of, but everybody has an opinion on how to improve. At home, I am the old wallpaper; at work, I am Debbie, interior designer, but really I haven't a clue who I am,' Debbie said sadly.

Casey jumped through the waves.

'Come on, let's have fun and cheer up,' she shouted.

Georgie joined in, and the two of them danced through the water, coming back to bow in front of Debbie.

'Casey Freeman, attorney at law and lonely heart, whose husband has slept with every legal secretary in the building and probably the district,' Casey said quickly.

Debbie gasped. 'What are you going to do?'

'Divorce him, the minute I get back.'

'How long have you known about this?'

Casey looked away. 'Don't; I am a coward. I liked the life we had, and I was too afraid to step out on my own. I have been a fool for far too long.'

'Love does that to us,' Debbie said, reaching out, and taking Casey's hand. Georgie stepped forward.

'Georgie Hunt. You all know plenty about my failings, but what you don't know is that I nearly did not get on the flight to Ireland.'

She faltered, tears, streaming down her face.

'But why?' Casey asked.

Georgie shook her head.

'For another time... I'm glad I came, I missed you guys.'

They hugged and ran through the water like children until

they collapsed on the sand laughing and sighing. Opening the picnic basket, they felt like kids on a day out to the sea, munching on sandwiches where sand had crept into the filling.

Afterwards, they strolled back to the house where Casey and Debbie watched as Georgie did a quick sketch in charcoal of the three of them skipping through the water. Casey propped it up beside the biscuit tin on the mantelpiece.

FOURTEEN

It wasn't long before Debbie tried to organise everybody's day. She got up early, and brewed the coffee to make sure Georgie had some breakfast before the two of them headed off to find a good spot for her morning sketching.

Debbie had taken Georgie in hand, and devised a schedule where morning was for sketches, and the afternoon was for working on canvas. Georgie objected that she was an artist, and creativity did not fit into time slots, but Debbie was having none of it. She bullied Georgie, but Casey thought it was in a good way that forced her to apply some discipline to her craft.

Casey had stayed back in the farmhouse this morning as the other two set off across the fields on a painting exhibition. Shay was due to drop over a box of supplies, and collect her to bring her back for another work Zoom meeting. Casey didn't know why, but she paid extra attention to her appearance, and fussed over whether she should have her hair up or down. She tried to persuade herself that she was dressing up for work because she was moving towards the four-week deadline, though she wasn't even sure it existed any more. She heard the familiar chug of the boat on the water, but she miscalculated how long the journey would take, and was surprised when she heard the knock on the kitchen door.

When she came downstairs, Shay had placed the box of groceries on the kitchen table.

'I was afraid I was going to have to walk the island looking for you,' he said.

She blushed, and she hoped he hadn't noticed.

'I have a favour to ask,' he said.

'Oh.'

'Remember, I told you about Rosie opening up the farm-house to groups in the summer, and serving afternoon tea? Well, there is a full schedule of island visits for tourist groups already booked. I hate to ask, but it has already been advertised as after-noon tea on the island. If you can't take it on, maybe May could come over.'

Casey gasped. 'I enjoyed helping out before, but May can't come.'

'Why, has there been a falling out?'

Casey fiddled with the packet of coffee at the top of the box of groceries.

'Prunella died. May doesn't know.'

He laughed. 'Right, you guys are in trouble because when your time is up here, she's going to want that hen back.'

'Hell, I didn't think of that; there are still a few weeks to get something sorted.'

'If you can find a hen that looks like Prunella, I suppose.'

Casey stared at Shay. 'Hens are hens, aren't they?'

He shook his head. 'Dad might be able to help. He can't bear it when May gets upset. What do you think about the tea and coffee? I can bring over the scones, unless you want to try baking them yourself.'

'Do I look do like the sort of woman who knows how to make a batch of scones for tourists? It will have to be after my Zoom work meeting anyway.'

'Do you need to go to the church?'

'No, I am going to give it a go on Ballymurphy Wi-Fi,' she said.

He was about to say something else when Debbie rushed in, and plonked her straw bag on the table.

'We can do it, but best bring the scones. However, we'll need something from you, in return,'she said.

Casey elbowed her in the ribs, but Debbie ignored her. She opened the bag, and pulled out a number of sketches in charcoal. Unrolling one, she handed it to Shay.

'Your boat coming across the channel this morning.'

'Impressive, is this Georgie's work?'

'Yes, and that one too,' Casey said, pointing to the mantelpiece.

He walked over, and took the sketch down for a closer look.

'Wonderful movement and suggestion,' he said.

Georgie stood in the doorway. 'Not just a pretty face, I guess.'

Debbie took the sketch from Shay, and told Georgie to sit down.

'I have a brilliant idea. Shay, you have your busloads of tourists, and we will serve the afternoon tea, but Georgie here needs to sell her sketches, so you will talk her and her landscapes up, and the tourists can watch the artist at work.'

'I will be more than happy, but Georgie, do you think you can do it? It will be a ton of work,' he said.

Georgie shook her head. 'Fine in theory, but what if everyone wants a sketch? I am not a machine.'

Exasperated, Debbie said they had to work out the finer details, but it was the ideal way for Georgie to start earning, before she had to return to Manhattan.

Georgie paced the kitchen floor. 'Debbie, you don't know what you're talking about. This is too much pressure,' she said.

'Well, darling, think of a compromise, because you need the bucks,' Debbie snapped.

Shay got up, and said he had to get back to the mainland. He said he would have the first group of twenty on the island at 2 p.m. and the next at 5 p.m.

As he passed Georgie, he placed a hand on her shoulder.

'That sketch of the boat on the water is beautiful. You have a gift; maybe you can do a limited number, and show the tourists how you work?'

Debbie whooped loudly.

'And we can charge more; you do ten, and then show one you are working on. Shay, I didn't realise you were such a businessman.'

'I was only remarking, it's up to Georgie,' he said.

Casey accompanied him on the walk down to the jetty, but they didn't speak until he had untied the rope.

'Do you think Debbie is pushing Georgie too much?' he asked.

Casey thought Shay was always looking out for Georgie.

'Probably, but Georgie does need to start selling her work; she's skint. We will look after her,' she replied. Casey wasn't as sure as she sounded, but she waved off Shay while in her heart she worried that Debbie was too much, always looking to make the bucks.

In the office at the back of Kennedys pub, Casey managed a quick Zoom meeting with New York until the connection failed. She wasn't worried as everything had been covered. Shay brought her back in the boat to Scarty, and she jumped off at the jetty as he got ready to turn back out to sea.

When she got as far as the farmhouse , Georgie was working feverishly as Debbie tidied around her, but making sure to peer over her shoulder every now and again to give encouragement.

Backing away before the others saw her, Casey headed to the high point on the island where she had the vastness of sea on all sides. She twirled around, letting the sky and sea merge, and surround her, until she flopped down dizzy. She needed to think.

The work meeting had been so short; she wondered, yet again, why she had been invited to attend. Harry had come on to tell her that the case was finally closed; the client in prison had taken his own life, and that was the end of that. She wasn't sure how to answer, but Harry didn't give her a chance, and said the firm was down on thousands of dollars on what had been the expenditure on the preparation of the defence of the case, and now they would have to wait to claim off the estate, which could take years. Harry didn't say it, but Casey felt that somehow she was being blamed for the strange turn of events.

She wanted to be back in Manhattan where she could effectively fight her corner. She was torn between her busy city life and the quiet of Scarty Island. There were pluses and minuses to both. She missed her city life, too: the cut and thrust of negotiation; working late into the night looking for information which could help her client. Here, she felt as if she never got it right, and her skills were useless.

Her eyes caught movement in the grass, and she stopped. Two small rabbits were sniffing about a patch of clover, so busy eating the creamy flower heads that they hadn't noticed her.

She wished she could be like them, satisfied with her lot. She heard the familiar chug of Shay's boat engine, but it felt close to the island rather than travelling away. Scanning the water, she saw it had not gone back to Ballymurphy, but the boat had rounded the headland to the waters opposite the far strand. Crouching down so she would not be seen, she watched as the boat came as close as it could to the shore, and Shay cut the engine. Casey craned to see as he took a bunch of flowers and one by one he threw each flower into the sea.

Afterwards, he stood, head bowed as if in prayer. She turned away, worried that she was spying on a man who wanted a solitary moment. The rabbits bobbed off, the flowerheads eaten. The boat engine started up, and she turned to look out to sea. Shay waved to her, and she burned with embarrassment. What would he think of her hiding in the grass and spying on him?

Flustered, she rushed back to the farmhouse. Georgie and Debbie were sitting at the kitchen table laughing.

'We are smashing it with the sketches; we're going to make so much money,' Debbie said.

Georgie took Casey in. 'What's up? You look strange,' she said.

'I am just not feeling very well,' Casey said as she made her way upstairs.

What was it about Shay Kennedy that bothered her so much? She did not want him to think any the less of her, and she didn't know if she could face him this evening. She lay on the bed and sank her head into the pillow. Tears came quickly, and she gave in to them; tears for everything and everyone; but mostly for herself and her stupid city life which was so busy, she did not even have the energy to confront Gary or the time to lie in bed, and sob her heart out.

After over an hour, Debbie marched into the room without knocking.

'Darling, whatever is eating you, we still need to get ready for the tourists. I can't do it all on my own.'

'I'm not feeling well,' Casey said turning to the wall.

'Are you in pain?'

'No.'

'Have you a fever?'

'No.'

'Up you get, then,' Debbie said severely.

'Please don't treat me like a teenager; I am telling you I need some time out,' Casey snapped.

'And I need this aggravation like a hole in the head,' Debbie said, pulling the duvet off Casey.

Casey made to retrieve it, but Debbie slapped her hand.

'Quit feeling sorry for yourself, and let's get to work,' she said brusquely.

Casey sat up. 'Well, maybe I don't want your words of wisdom.'

Debbie sat down, and caught Casey by the shoulders.

'Do I have to slap you across the face or are you going to get out of that bed?'

Next, Debbie gently rubbed Casey's hair.

'I don't know why Rosie brought us here,' Casey blurted out. 'What I am doing here? Before this, I knew exactly where I was in life. I was so busy, but I knew what I should be doing every day and night. Now, if I went back to the city I don't even know how I would fit in or even if I would still have my job.'

'I get it, I really do; you've hit a wall. Stuck on this island makes you confront all your demons. But yours are not so bad.'

'I am not even sure I want to be a lawyer any more.'

'You're a brilliant lawyer. Being on this island is changing us all, but it's not going to change that basic fact. But just maybe, by the time we leave here, we're all going to be looking for different things. Isn't that the whole point of this odyssey?' Debbie said.

'Couldn't we just scatter her ashes in the next few days and leave?'

Debbie snorted. 'You don't mean that, but we could flush them down the loo, if we had one.'

Casey looked at Debbie. 'You're not serious?'

'Girl, we're not giving in. I bet Rosie didn't think we'd have the staying power. Well this woman is sticking it out, and if I am, you fricking are,' Debbie said.

Casey sighed. 'I am feeling stressed right now; for all I know the partners will call me back to the Manhattan office.'

'But that big case is done,' Debbie said.

'I am hoping that means I can slip under the radar and stay here but...' Casey faltered. 'I have been stupid; I spied on Shay out on the boat.'

'What was he doing – sunbathing or swimming in the nude?'

'He was remembering someone he lost at sea.'

'Hardly your fault. Now, get yourself downstairs, Georgie needs our support. She has done so many sketches, her wrist hurts.'

Debbie waited until Casey got out of the bed, brushed some make-up on her face, and made her go down the stairs first. Georgie had made a pot of coffee and poured three mugs.

'Shay will be here soon, I saw the boats leave Ballymurphy,' she said.

'Oh, they can't see us like this; time to clean up, girls,' Debbie said reaching for her make-up bag, and rushing off to the mirror in her room. Georgie went upstairs to change while Casey tidied up the kitchen, and wiped down the outside tables. After a while, Debbie called everyone together in the kitchen. She had three glasses of bubbly to hand out.

'I want to propose a toast to friendship, and the new debut of our wonderful artist, Georgie,' she said.

Before anyone had a chance to reply, she pulled a home-made sign from behind the dresser.

'I am no artist, and this was all done in a rush, but here we go.'

She held up a sign. GEORGIE HUNT. UNIQUE LIMITED-EDITION WORKS OF ART. SEE THE ARTIST AT WORK.

Georgie giggled. 'So sweet, Debbie, but next time let me make the sign.'

Casey took it, and put it outside the front door.

'It will do for today,' she said.

They heard the chatter of the group as they walked up the path, and they stepped outside to greet them. Georgie began one of her sketches. Shay called everyone to go for a walk, but some stayed back to watch Georgie sketch a beach scene.

Casey and Debbie heated up May's scones, and got the tea and coffee ready. When the tour group returned from the walk, the farmhouse was a hive of activity as the tourists took pictures, and fought over Georgie's sketches. By the time they returned to the boat, Georgie had sold all her charcoal drawings, and was holding a wad of bank notes.

'Now, you just have to do it all over again,' Debbie said.

Georgie looked at the clock.

'In what world do you expect me to produce ten sketches in less than two hours?'

'In a world where you want another fistful of notes, darling. This is why you never have money; you don't sell your talent enough.'

'Creativity is what is important,' Georgie said, stamping up the stairs and banging her bedroom door.

Debbie turned to Casey, and shrugged her shoulders. 'It's obvious why she has never succeeded.'

Casey went upstairs, and knocked on the bedroom door. When there was no answer, she walked in anyway. Georgie was sketching at the bedroom window.

'I can work better and faster without her in my ear all the time with her stupid ideas,' she said.

Casey backed out of the room. Debbie was waiting at the bottom of the stairs.

'What's up?' she asked.

'Let her work at her own pace. Take a break,' Casey said.

'We can both take a break. Handling Georgie is hard work,' Debbie said as they made their way outside to sit in the sunshine. Casey shoved in beside Debbie. They didn't need to talk; they sat, their eyes closed, listening to the sea, and letting the sun warm their faces.

'This place is beautiful, but for Rosie, it was something else; there must have been another pull,' Casey said.

The previous night she had stolen into the attic in the hope of finding clues, but it was empty. She knew they all loved being here, but equally they needed answers, and the letters so far had not yielded anything. Rosie, every year, had left her home to come to this island. Casey wondered if Shay knew more than he was making out.

'What I wouldn't give for a bagel from Bagel Boss right now,' Debbie said.

'I could just do with a regular fries and Coke.'

'Oh, yes to that too. Aren't we so sad?' Debbie said.

'I think we are missing home; especially after seeing all those US tourists.'

'I wanted to tag along behind them, maybe nobody would have noticed,' Debbie said.

'We're not prisoners, you can go home anytime you like.'

'I suppose, but I am not a quitter,' Debbie said, getting up to wash the cups and mugs before the next round of visitors arrived.

'What's in the box beside the dresser? I nearly tripped over it,' she called out from the kitchen.

Casey went back inside the house. 'I forgot about it. it was Rosie's; Shay brought it over. There isn't that much in it; a notebook, a photograph, and some bits and bobs she wanted kept safe.'

Debbie picked up the box, and peered into it. Taking out the notebook, she shook it out, the strip of passport-type photographs floating to the ground, the letter landing on the slates with a plop.

Casey picked the two of them up.

'Go on, open the letter,' Debbie said impatiently.

'It's addressed to someone else, not Rosie.'

Debbie snatched it from Casey's hand.

'Let me do it. I want to have a look before the tourists come this way.' Carefully, she opened the letter.

'It is so sweet. Listen to this.'

My love, Marian,

There are not enough stars in the sky to say how much I love you. All I want is to be with you, and for us to live a life together. Soon, my love, we will be able to spend all our time together. We can grow old, you and me beside each other, every step of the way.

A xxx

Casey sighed.

'Would that it were that simple, but what was so important about this that Rosie kept it?'

'Maybe she found it in the house, and was trying to unravel the mystery of Marian?' Debbie said as she hurriedly tidied everything away.

'Or maybe it was a reminder,' Casey replied, turning it over in her hands, 'of what's really important.'

FIFTEEN

Another week had passed, and Casey hadn't received any word from Manhattan which she had decided was good news for the rest of her time on Scarty. She walked downstairs, and stood at the front door, listening to the sound of the sea as it rolled into shore. She thought Georgie was away painting on the other side of the island until she heard Shay's boat pull in at the jetty. A few moments later Georgie, with a letter in her hand, walked into the kitchen.

'I didn't know you had left the island,' Casey said, sounding a little put out.

'I was in Ballymurphy for an hour or two. Shay sent over one of Rosie's letters.'

Debbie, who had not bothered to get out of her pyjamas all day, wandered into the kitchen.

'You shot off without telling me; I would have gone along – it would have been nice to have a break from the island,' she said, her voice low and sad.

Casey, who had begun heating up a pasta carbonara, looked at Georgie.

'You're going on a lot of secret trips to Ballymurphy. Is there something you want to tell us?'

'What do you mean? I'm doing a series looking at the island from the mainland; of course I am going to venture across more often,' Georgie said defensively.

'So where are your paints?' Debbie said, peering behind Georgie.

'What's this, the Spanish Inquisition?' Georgie said, throwing the letter on the table before she stomped upstairs.

'She's up to something,' Debbie sniffed.

Casey served the pasta onto two plates. She wasn't happy with the answers, and she was worried that Georgie and Shay were enjoying too much time together.

'So what if she is? Give her a break, Debbie; you're not her mother,' she said tartly.

'Georgie always has an aura of trouble about her. I can't help it,' Debbie said.

'Quit it, Debs, please.'

Debbie swung around. 'It has always been the same with Georgie; she keeps so much from us.'

'She is entitled to her own life.'

Casey carried the plates to the table and they sat down to eat. Debbie, after a few moments pushed her plate away.

'I'm sorry; this island life is getting to me. I normally love home-cooked food, but I could do with a hefty injection of city living right now,' she said.

'Just because Georgie went to Ballymurphy, that hardly qualifies as even town living,' Casey giggled.

'You can laugh all you like, but this island gig is hard going. I miss my boys and even Marvin. I was so anxious to get away and now...'

'Give him a call next time you're in Ballymurphy.'

'And say that I ran away, and now I want to come home. I'm

way too proud to do anything like that. I'm not going to crawl back.'

Casey didn't reply, because she knew Debbie was looking for a fight. She wanted an argument because she needed to win; she needed to feel as if she had the upper hand.

When there was a knock at the front door, they froze.

'I didn't think anyone was on the island,' Casey said.

'Maybe they came back with Georgie, but it's after 6 p.m., I hope they are not expecting to stay,' Debbie said.

Georgie came running down the stairs. 'I looked out the top window, and it's a man. He's carrying some sort of container.'

There was another knock, this time it was a little louder.

Casey walked to the door but Debbie made to stop her.

'He might go away, just leave it.'

'And he will walk around to the back door, and see us all huddled into the kitchen. I don't think so.'

Casey smartly opened the front door as Georgie and Debbie stepped in behind her. The man, wearing shorts and a T-shirt, stood in the doorway holding a large plastic container.

'Hi, is Rosie about?' he said casually, looking in surprise at the three women.

'No, I'm afraid, she's not,' Casey said.

'You'll have to excuse me. I'm Jeff; I have pulled into the jetty. I usually visit Rosie and top up on the fresh water.'

'We can give you the water,' Debbie said.

'Will Rosie be back? I can hang around the area for a day or so.'

Casey stepped back. 'You had better come in.'

He ducked his head to come through the doorway, and walked into the kitchen.

'I met Rosie a few summers ago; we hit it off straight away. Isn't it her time of year to be here?' he said, but his voice trailed off. 'Is there something wrong?'

'Did you know Rosie well?' Debbie asked, her tone almost accusatory.

'I would like to think we were good friends,' he said.

Casey took the man in; his weather-beaten face and his curly golden hair.

'We didn't know Rosie entertained anybody while she was on the island. We thought it was very much a personal getaway,' Debbie said.

The man extended his hand first to Casey, and then Debbie and Georgie.

'Let me introduce myself, Jeff Barclay; I got to know Rosie over the years, and I always dropped by when she was on the island. She liked to come sailing with me.'

'Sounds nice,' Georgie said, but there was a suspicious edge to her voice.

Casey pulled out a chair at the table, and invited Jeff to sit down. He looked from one woman to the other, but stayed standing

'There's something wrong, isn't there?' he asked.

Debbie sighed heavily and Georgie said she had work to do upstairs. Casey shuffled, not sure what to say. Finally she spoke. 'I'm afraid it's bad news. Rosie has passed away. We're here to honour her memory.'

Jeff staggered back, and Casey caught him, leading him to the chair to sit down.

Debbie produced the bottle of whiskey, and poured some into a glass and pushed it towards Jeff.

He gulped down the measure in one, coughing and spluttering as he did.

'Pardon me, but this news is so unexpected and so devastating. How did it happen – was there an accident?'

'Maybe you tell us what you really were to Rosie, first,' Casey said.

He shifted on his chair, making it creak as he began to talk.

'I met Rosie four years ago; we became friends, good friends in the last two years. We sailed along the Irish coast together, and sometimes I stayed on the island, though she liked to keep Scarty special to herself. The last two weeks in July was always ours.'

'Good friends, but you didn't know she was ill,' Debbie said.

Casey gave Debbie a dagger look.

'Debbie, we didn't know either, so drop it.'

Jeff stood up, and said he should leave, but Casey told him to sit down.

'We haven't filled your canister.'

'Ah, I don't care... it was always only a convenient excuse to meet up with Rosie. She was such a lovely woman. I would have gone over to visit her if I had known.'

'You can pay your respects here; she's on the mantelpiece. Rosie is a lovely lady in a metal tin now. We brought her ashes here.'

Jeff glanced at the mantelpiece, but as quickly looked away.

'How can a box so small carry all that made up such a beautiful woman?' he sighed.

'It's not easy,' Debbie said stiffly, as Casey put an extra bowl of pasta on the table.

'You might as well eat with us before you go back to the boat,' she said.

'Yacht, it's a yacht,' he paused, 'You know, Rosie told me about the three of you.'

'That's us, the bad friends,' Debbie said.

Everybody fell silent, and Casey pushed the pasta around her bowl. Jeff was the first to speak.

'Rosie was so impressed by all of you; she was very proud of you. Said she wished she could have achieved even some of the things you all had done.'

Casey got a bottle of red wine, and uncorked it. She poured out three glasses and handed one to Jeff.

'Can I propose a toast?' he said.

'By all means.'

'To Rosie, a beautiful woman and friend, taken too early,' he said, his voice emotional.

They clinked glasses.

'What happens next?' Jeff asked.

'We are here until the end of August,' Casey said.

'No, I mean with the island.'

Casey stared at Jeff. 'That is not any of our business.'

'I didn't mean to offend; it's just that land and property in these parts are worth a lot.'

Debbie stood up. 'We will fill the canister for you, so you can get back to your boat before dark,' she said.

Casey filled the plastic can three quarters of the way full, and placed it on the table. Jeff knocked back the last of his wine, and stood up.

'I hope I didn't offend any of you ladies.'

Casey stared at him.

'Rosie is dead, but you're only thinking of the real estate. No, we're not offended at all,' Debbie snapped as she opened the back door.

He stopped after he stepped out the door.

'I don't like to leave on bad terms. I suppose I couldn't interest in any of you ladies in a sailing trip down the coast tomorrow?'

Casey laughed out loud. 'You know the answer to that one. Make sure you are off the island before dark.'

They watched him leave. Debbie was shaking with rage.

'Do you think she had an affair with that guy?' Georgie said.

'Maybe she was bored. I might have nothing to do here; but I'm not that desperate,' Debbie guffawed.

Casey reached for the envelope, Georgie had earlier left in the middle of the table. Without asking the others, she ripped it open and began to read.

My dearest ones,

Are you still in the sunshine stage or do you think I am abso-lutely mad to have brought you to Scarty Island?

Debbie, if she took the plunge, is trying to figure how I ever managed to buy the place, I'm sure. Well, the best day of my life was when I inherited Scarty Island. I had no idea until an attorney located me, and told me I was the owner of the land. A few months later I took a flight over to Ireland to visit.

From the moment I stepped onto the rickety jetty, I knew I wanted to be part of Scarty. I knew I was at home.

There are matters that will become clearer, but know this: sometimes there is a connection that is so deep, it hurts. That is the connection I have to Scarty. When I am here, I am wrapped in contentment, and I feel safe; when I am away from Scarty, I am lost, and I yearn so much to return...

I want you to feel the rhythm of the waves as they break on shore; let the sound of the sea comfort you, and the bright stars at night light the way for you. In these simple pleasures, I hope you find peace of mind.

Remember when we used to cycle out to the lake, and sit on the pier, our feet dangling in the water? Georgie was always the only one who would strip to her underwear, and jump in. I wish now I had been that brave.

Being at Scarty made me brave. I enjoyed the freedom of walking barefoot everywhere, the grass like silk under my feet, and the sand warm. It was fun, too, tiptoeing over the parts of the beach that were stony.

Sitting in the farmhouse at night, I was never afraid being on my own. In truth I never felt alone; the ghosts on the island embraced me, and I freely let them sit with me. Often on a warm night I left the front and back doors open to allow free movement of air through the house.

I read once there was a tradition on the islands off the Irish coast to open the door and leave a chair empty at the table so the ghost of a loved one could come in and sit.

I did that, and I was happy to do it.

From my spot at the far end of the table, if I sat up very straight, I saw the lights of Ballymurphy twinkling, a reminder that life carried on in the mainland, even if on the island, I sat with the ghosts.

As I write this, I am sitting in my springtime garden, a thick blanket around my knees, and I am smiling, because in reality I am sitting at the old wooden table at Scarty Island listening to the waves thud against the shore.

I wanted you to come here, so you could understand your one-time friend a little better, and that you too may benefit from the beauty and the magic that is Scarty Island.

All my love

Rosie xx

Debbie snapped the letter from Casey, and scrunched it into a little ball, and threw it across the room.

'Does she think we are fools? Herself and her fancy man lived it up here, and on the yacht. She hasn't told us about that. Is that what we are honouring – an affair?'

Georgie picked up the paper ball, and tried to flatten out the sheets of paper.

'So what if she had a good time while she was on the island, she didn't hurt anyone. Her husband didn't even know she was here.'

Debbie, her cheeks red with frustration, banged the table.

'Rosie this and Rosie that, I am fed up of it. And all these letters, she is just presenting the life she wanted us to see.'

Casey could see that Debbie was near tears.

'Why is all this making you so upset?' she asked.

'I am not upset, I'm angry. Angry at Rosie goody-two-shoes; she was no saint and that man arriving at the door proves it. I don't like strange people prowling about.'

Georgie caught Debbie in a hug. 'You're overreacting because you need a break from the island.'

'It seems silly, but I am so stressed by all this silence and wildness,' Debbie said.

'Let's plan a day out; let's go somewhere tomorrow,' Georgie said.

'How do we do that?' Debbie asked, tears streaming down her face.

'It's an emergency of sorts; we can raise the flag, and when Shay comes we will be ready for a bit of time out,' Casey said.

'Won't he get cross at making a wasted journey?' Debbie asked.

'So what if he does,' Casey said, her voice firm. A small part of her, though, was thrilled at the idea of seeing him again.

SIXTEEN

By the time Shay's boat had pulled out to sea the next morning, Casey was not feeling so brave about their decision. She had got up at 6 a.m. with the intention of taking the flag down, but when she looked though the binoculars, she saw that Shay was doing the same and giving her a thumbs-up. She rushed to wake the others, but they barely stirred in their beds.

Walking down to the jetty, she went over and over in her head how she would explain, but she was concerned they would come across as stupid and incredibly selfish. He would hardly understand that the island was getting to all of them. They didn't know why they were here, and they felt guilty for feeling this way.

She was halfway down to the path, when she changed her mind, and dashed back to the farmhouse to wake up the others. She didn't want to have to meet Shay on her own. Let him deal with the might of Debbie, she thought. The others were sitting having coffee when she got back.

'Where have you been? Shay is halfway to the island.'

'I was going to meet him, and tell him we made a mistake but...'

'You chickened out,' Debbie said.

Casey poured a mug of coffee. 'What if he is cross at us for wasting his time?'

'Jeez, do you hear the big hotshot lawyer, nervous that Shay Kennedy would get angry about being called out to ferry us across a channel of water. We will pay the man for his time, and he can be happy at that,' Debbie said. 'Now I'm off to the loo while we still have the island to ourselves.'

'If we ask, Dan might drive us to Ennis. I'm desperate for a day out in the city, what do you think?' Georgie asked excitedly.

'Hardly a city, but good idea,' Debbie called out as she walked across the courtyard.

'I think we'd better hurry, because I can't hear Shay's boat any more. He's almost here.' Casey said, swatting Georgie to go upstairs to get dressed.

After a little while she called out to Debbie, who had stopped on her return to the house to pick a bunch of daisies.

'I thought I would put it beside the tin box; cheer up the mantelpiece,' she said.

'Get dressed, the least we can do is be on the jetty so Shay does not have to wait around for us,' Casey snapped as she quickly tidied up the kitchen.

When Debbie went to her room, Casey realised she was all alone. Carefully, she took the tin box from the mantelpiece. It was so light. Jeff had been right – who would have thought it carried all of Rosie?

There was a film of fine dust, and she wiped the box clean before putting it back, and placing the daisies in a little jug of water at an angle beside it.

When Georgie came downstairs, she was wearing a flowing purple dress, and had teamed it with a wide-brimmed straw hat.

'I didn't know you'd brought a hat to the island,' Casey said.

'I didn't, I found it upstairs, it must be Rosie's.'

The hat, which had a pink and white gingham trim, was

beautiful, and Casey was disappointed she had not found it herself. Debbie clicked her teeth, and said the hat looked a bit much for strolling around an Irish town.

'We will only draw attention to ourselves,' she said.

'As if we don't anyway with our accents,' Georgie said, sweeping out the door, and leading the party down the path to the jetty.

Shay was already off the boat, and rushing towards the house.

'What's wrong?' he asked.

Casey was glad she was at the back of the group, and she let Debbie step forward.

'Now Shay, don't get all hot and bothered. We need to get off the island; and not having any phone reception there was no time to fully explain.'

Shay stared at the three of them. If he was going to say anything, Casey saw he stopped when he saw Georgie's hat.

'Did you get that hat in the house?' he stuttered.

Georgie, not picking up on the emotion in his voice, did a twirl.

'Wonderful, isn't it? It must have been Rosie's.'

Shay turned on his heel, and walked back to the boat.

'Where do you want me to drop you all?' he asked Casey.

There was a haunted faraway look in his eyes, she thought, and he seemed somehow to be so distant; he sounded cold.

'Ballymurphy is fine, thank you.'

'We're sorry to have inconvenienced you, Shay, but we were desperate to get off the island. I think we just hit a wall as we moved further into August,' Debbie said, her tone matter of fact.

He didn't reply, but untied the boat, and asked the women to get on board.

Casey lingered on the jetty as the others faffed about getting comfortable in the back of the boat.

'We are grateful that you came across for us. We do appreciate it,' she said.

'It's OK; I am glad everybody is all right,' he replied, holding out his hand to help her on board.

Casey joined the others when she realised Shay was not going to talk during the crossing. Her head hurt, and she was glad to be leaving Scarty, if only for a little while.

She closed her eyes, and tried to block out the excited chatter of Debbie and Georgie as the boat cut through the calm seawater on its way back to Ballymurphy.

At the small village harbour, Shay chugged slowly in, waving to the fishermen who were returning with their catch from the night before.

Georgie and Debbie said they were going off to arrange a cab through Dan, but Casey hung back to talk to Shay. She lingered on the quay as he fussed about in the wheelhouse.

Eventually, she called out to him. 'We have upset you, haven't we?'

He stared at Casey. 'It's OK. I just didn't expect to see that hat again.'

'Georgie's hat?'

Shay stepped onto the quay. 'That was Anna's straw hat.'

Casey felt a stab of pain through her heart.

'Oh, no. I had no idea, and I am sure Georgie doesn't either. I will run after her, tell her to take it off.'

Shay put his hand up to stop her flow of words.

'No need, nobody around here is going to recognise it. It's just a straw hat. It gave me a land, that's all.'

They began walking up the quay, stepping around the boxes of fish which had been thrown onto the pier.

'What are your plans for the day?' he asked. 'Debbie and

Georgie want to go to Ennis town; I think we are all missing the city life.'

'I'm not sure you will find it in an Irish town, but I'm imagine Dad can drop you in.'

She dithered. 'Can I ask about the hat?'

He shook his head. 'I don't think so,' he said as they crossed the road to the pub, where Debbie and Georgie were chatting to Dan on the deck.

Debbie swung around.

'A bit of a conundrum, Dan is already doing a run to Ennis, but with his other passengers he can only fit two of us.'

'We can draw lots?' Georgie said.

Casey looked back at Shay, and took a deep breath.

'Don't worry, I'll stay back. I can help Shay out here; it's the least I can do.'

'Are you sure? You're going to miss the big metropolis of Ennis.' Debbie laughed, her voice full of relief that she wasn't going to be left behind.

At that very moment, Casey really needed to take a break from her friends. She turned to Shay.

'Do you need any help in the restaurant?'

'With Dad gone for the day, that would be great. We don't have any guests for breakfast, but there are twenty for lunch.'

'Sounds like a really fun day for you,' Georgie said, but Casey ignored her.

May called out as she walked up the street with her young niece.

'We are off to pick nice fabric for Lydia's debs dress. Debbie and Georgie can help us,' she said.

Casey did her best to contain a giggle as she saw Debbie's face sour, and Georgie look towards the sky.

'I think you might have got off lightly only having to help out at the pub,' Shay muttered.

· · ·

Casey followed Shay into the kitchen where he poured out coffee.

'We have some time before the lunch preparation...'

'I felt we overstepped the mark, calling you out to the island,' Casey interrupted, 'I'm so sorry, Shay.'

He seemed caught off-guard, placing the coffee mug back down again, and giving Casey a peculiar look.

'Or I overreacted.'

'I don't know the full details, but you don't strike me as a person who usually overreacts.'

Shay pushed a plate of mini blueberry muffins towards her.

'These are still warm; yummy,' she said.

'Yes, I took them out of the oven, just before I checked on the island flagpole.'

Casey took a small bite from one, savouring the sweet berries.

'Things just got on top of us. There can only be so much silence, sweet fresh air and female friendship a person can take.'

'Why do I get the impression it might have been the female friendship was the crunch factor?'

Ignoring his comment, Casey got up and walked across the kitchen to look out the window towards the sea. She cared about her friends deeply, but it was normal to need a break. She wasn't going to talk about Debbie and Georgie behind their backs, even if he was right in his assessment. 'Scarty looks so beautiful from here,' she said, watching the cormorants dive into the sea before flying off towards the high point of the island, where she knew they would land on a sheltered cliff edge to eat their catch.

'You sound as if you're on day release from prison.'

Casey swung around. 'No, I don't. It's probably the most amazing place I have stayed. But it's like something is hanging over us; we still don't know why we are here.'

'Maybe you expect too much too fast. Rosie had time to plan this. I imagine it's going to be a slow reveal.'

'What I don't understand is why she didn't get us together before she died, if not at Scarty, then in Upstate New York, and we could have talked everything through.'

Shay laughed. 'From what I know of Rosie, she liked her drama. You're probably reacting exactly as she suspected.'

'But drama isn't satisfying if you don't have a ringside seat to watch.'

'Who says she hasn't? It probably gave her such comfort to think of you all at Scarty.'

Casey huffed, and took another muffin, chewing it thoughtfully.

'We had a visitor last night.'

'Jeff, I saw his yacht in the bay. I guess he didn't know Rosie had passed either.'

'Do you know what they were to each other?'

'They were an item, for the summer anyway.'

'An item?'

'You know, together. He spent a lot July here, and always came back the last week in August. He made her happy. Poor guy, I saw him pull out of the jetty this morning, and he looked pretty cut-up.'

Casey stopped to examine the lemon tree growing on the windowsill.

'It was a surprise; I just never expected Rosie to have a secret lover.'

'Maybe that is what she is trying to tell you all – that she had a quiet, but interesting life.'

'But why would she need to persuade us of that?'

Shay guffawed out loud.

'A high-flying lawyer, an artist and an astute business-woman, and Rosie who was a homemaker, but didn't have any kids. It's not hard to think why she felt she had to prove herself.'

'Maybe I should have gone shopping,' Casey said, turning away.

Shay tipped her on the shoulder and said he had a better idea.

'If we walk up the headland, the view is fantastic. We can do it before we have to get ready for lunch.'

'But when are you going to cook the food?'

'Most of the prep is done. I just have to pull the salads together. We have two hours.'

Shay locked up the pub, and they set off down the street, before turning up the lane which led to the headland. They walked past stone cottages, where the windows and doors were open to let in the cool sea breeze. She stopped at one front garden where roses fought for space with tall purple and pink hollyhocks.

'I walked along here that first day,' Casey said.

'I know; Dad was following you through the binoculars,' Shay laughed.

'Doesn't sound creepy at all.'

Shay shrugged. 'He was always protective of Rosie, and when you two said you were going to Scarty and you were her good friends, he was on the lookout for you as well.'

They had reached the seat, and Casey sat down.

'That first day I was so worried about living on the island.'

'And now?'

'I do love it there, but in some way it has also made me feel dissatisfied. If I had known how screwed-up inside this whole business would make me feel, I may not have been in such a rush to come here.'

'What do you mean?'

'I don't know where I fit any more. Is it Manhattan and the constant grind of work, and the husband who doesn't love me any more? Why has this island got under my skin so much?'

'Because you were looking for change, and being on Scarty has brought it to a head.'

Casey shifted on the wooden bench, looking at Shay's gentle expression. He couldn't be any more different to Gary if he tried.

'Are you ready to talk about the straw hat?' she said.

Shay shifted uncomfortably on the seat.

'It was Anna's, but she gave it to Rosie when she was complaining of hot days on the island.'

'You weren't happy about that?'

'It's so silly now, but I was upset at the time.'

Casey stepped closer to Shay. She wanted to reach out, but she didn't know how he would react. Shay kicked at a tuft of grass on the pavement.

'I bought the hat for Anna to match a dress May had made for her. Anna didn't think giving Rosie the hat was a big deal. She teased me that I was being silly, and how could she walk down Main Street, Ballymurphy wearing a wide-brimmed straw hat with a ribbon?'

'Did Rosie wear it in Ballymurphy?'

'No, she confined herself to the island.'

'I can get Georgie to give it back to you.'

Shay shook his head. 'It shouldn't matter any more.'

Casey put her hand on his arm. 'It hurts; there's nothing wrong with that.'

'Are you going to tell me it makes me more human?'

Casey laughed. 'I wouldn't dream of it.'

'We need to get the lunch ready,' Shay said, giving Casey a quizzical look.

Casey was weary. She lost her best friend Rosie a long time ago, and then cancer stole her away again. She had thrown herself into work and a hopeless marriage, but Rosie, it seemed, had forged a strong new friendship with Anna. That name kept coming up, and Casey felt jealous of this woman who was dead, but still so much loved by Shay.

SEVENTEEN

Casey and Shay worked side by side, not needing to talk much, but concentrating on the lunch orders, and maintaining the flow of plates from the kitchen. When the rush had died down, Shay said Casey could take the rest of the day off.

'I am not open tonight; even in summer, the evening restaurant is only Wednesday to Sunday, so you're free.'

Casey lingered, not sure whether he wanted her to leave or not.

'I think I will go for a wander, and hang around and wait for the others to come back from Ennis,' she said.

Shay laughed as he stacked the dishwasher.

'Do you really think that lot will be back before midnight?'

'What do you mean?'

'I reckon they have persuaded Dad to bring them to Galway; more shops and better choice there. Georgie has him wrapped around her little finger.'

'Oh.'

'Do you want me to take you back out to the island?'

Casey suddenly felt put out to be left behind when the

others were going to a city. She didn't want to go back to the island on her own, and she didn't want to hang around here like a spare part waiting for the others to come back either.

'I suppose going back to the island might be the most sensible thing to do, though it sounds like they won't be back on Scarty until morning.'

'I think with that lot, you could safely predict tomorrow afternoon.'

Casey's face fell, and Shay hesitated.

'You're welcome to stay here in one of the guest rooms. No charge.'

'I couldn't do that; we seem to lean on you and your family so much, and I am not sure my friends are cognisant enough of that fact.

'You're using your lawyer words now,' he said.

She blushed, and he caught her hand.

'You're welcome here anytime. If the truth be told, of all the American friends – and I include Rosie in that group – you are my firm favourite.'

Her cheeks burned as she gently pulled her hand away.

'Thank you for saying that, but I still don't want to impose.

'Would it make you feel better if I asked you to help me with something I have been putting off for a very long time?'

'Yes, I suppose so.'

He shook his head. 'I shouldn't ask you, and please feel free to say no, but I would be grateful if you could help with...'

She saw him swallow hard, and she interjected softly, 'I can help.'

'It's Anna's studio and shop. I need to go in there, and clear it. I have to pick the canvases I am going to keep, and I thought of giving some to friends. I would be very grateful; I can't face it on my own.'

'I didn't know Anna was an artist.'

'Yes, the building to the right of the bar was her little shop and gallery. I really should do something with it now, but I haven't been in it for a long time. Dad wants to have her paintings on the walls of the restaurant and pub, and we were thinking of letting out the space.'

'You don't have any of her paintings hanging already?'

'I did, but after she died, I couldn't bear to look at them.'

'Georgie is probably the best one to pick which painting is suited for which spot.'

Shay plucked a bunch of keys from a drawer, and asked Casey to follow him.

'Wouldn't you rather wait for Dan or a closer friend?' she asked.

He stood to look at Casey directly, and she saw his eyes were moist with tears.

'I can't think of anyone else I want to share this moment with,' he said, pushing the key in the lock, and turning it quickly. Casey felt nervous as Shay pushed back the door, and they both stood peering into the darkness. The room smelled damp and musty.

'It's been so long; I'm surprised it doesn't smell worse,' Shay said, stepping into the gallery.

She dithered, and he told her to wait until he got some light into the room. She heard him tug fiercely at something, and then the sound of wood giving way. Daylight spilled across the room as if somebody had just trained a searchlight on it.

Dust particles danced through the air, and she saw spiders scuttle to darker corners as Shay called her to come in. He lifted more sheets of plywood from in front of the big window facing the street.

Sunshine beamed across the room, flashing off the paintings, and falling across the desk in the middle which was covered in sheets of paper and boxes of pastels and charcoal crayons. Everything was under a layer of dust. A chair had been pushed back as if the person who had been sitting at the desk had left for just a few moments.

Shay stood at the desk; he picked a silk scarf from the chair, and buried his face in it. Casey looked away, not sure if she should step outside. When he recovered, Shay pushed the scarf into his pocket.

'It's bizarre, it still smells of her perfume,' he said, his voice so low Casey could barely hear him.

Casey stepped back against the wall, not knowing if she should advance further into the room. When she saw Shay slump, she placed a hand on his shoulder. He grasped it, and she heard his breathing regulate.

'I don't know where to start; it seems insurmountable right now,' he whispered.

'Let's open the windows and the back door to get a draught of fresh air through, and let the light penetrate the dark corners,' she said, leading him over to the big windows at the front.

'When I was young, my mother ran a farm shop out of here. Then, in time, this studio became Anna's pride and joy. She did not sell that much, but she loved the idea of displaying her artwork, and that of local artists. She said it was bringing a little bit of culture to Ballymurphy. She really thought if we could invest in the culture, that everything else would follow.'

He stopped to run his hand over a small painting that had been propped up at the window.

'She so wanted us to make a go of it here. The irony was after she died, the restaurant really took off, and the island tours filled the summer calendar. She never really got to enjoy any of it. It was all Rosie's doing; she said that she and Anna had so many plans for here and the island, and she wanted to honour Anna's memory by implementing as many of their ideas as possible.'

'They seem to have been such good friends,' Casey said.

'Anna loved the summer months when Rosie came over. They were inseparable. We called them the A team,' Shay said, his voice soft.

Casey picked a small, framed charcoal drawing which had been left on a table.

'I am sorry about Anna, and now Rosie.'

'I know,' he said, wiping a tear away.

'I'm here to help, just tell me what to do,' she said gently.

'I was thinking of taking the paintings from the wall, and bringing them through to the house where we can have a proper look at them. There are items belonging to other artists, which I will need to return,' Shay said quickly.

She watched as Shay walked up to a large canvas of Scarty Island; the island sitting surrounded by a silver speckled sea. The painting had a red sticker on it.

'Anna couldn't bear to part with it. She said she put her heart and soul into the painting, and she couldn't imagine it hanging on any wall except here at Kennedys.'

He took the frame off the wall, and pointed at the red sticker. 'Everybody who came into the restaurant asked about it, and she always pointed to the sticker and said it was taken,' he said, his voice shaky.

'She has captured the island so well. The light shining on the farmhouse, the sea...' Casey's voice trailed off when she saw Shay bend over.

'What's wrong?'

'Maybe this wasn't such a good idea.'

'It will never be a good idea, but maybe it's necessary.'

'You have a very practical streak.'

'It's the lawyer in me.'

She picked up a sketch from the desk. 'Is this Anna's work?'

Shay took it from her hands. 'She was sketching all the time;

she never thought much of them. She said they were merely an aid for the final work of art, but I loved them.'

'Did she have any formal training?'

'Anna and I met at college; she studied the history of art, but after my brother's death we came here to run the pub, and set up the restaurant. I guess her art took second place, until three years ago, she said she wanted to open a gallery. I think it was Rosie's influence, she encouraged her to sell her work.'

'Rosie was good at motivating others. It's almost as if she got as much pleasure from the success of others as her own.'

'She wanted me to continue the gallery in Anna's name; said there were enough sketches to last years, and we could supplement them with selected works from local artists.'

'Is that what you are going to do now?'

Shay walked over to where the Scarty painting was leaning against a wall.

'I wouldn't know where to start, and I couldn't bear to let go of any of Anna's work. No, I was thinking of a café space, something like that, but Dad says best to make easy money and lease the place.'

Casey looked around the room with the big windows overlooking the bay.

'It would make a beautiful gallery, and an even more beautiful café.'

Shay purposefully walked across the room, and picked up the plywood.

'It was a bad idea. Who am I kidding? I don't know what to do with any of this stuff,' he said, pushing a sheet of plywood against the front window, instantly dimming the room. 'I am overrun with work already. August is the height of the tourist season; I'm mad to think I can do it. We can barely run the pub and restaurant as it is.'

'It could just be a summer gallery and café.'

'Easy to say, but a lot of work goes in to running a place like this, and I'm not sure I can handle it,' he said, closing the windows. 'Walk out now. I will close the front door and meet you in the pub,' he instructed.

Casey didn't move, but pushed against the plywood. A beam of light fell across the centre of the room.

'I didn't think you were somebody who gave up so easily.'

'I'm not giving up; I'm being practical. This will cost too much, and the time isn't right.'

Casey eased the plywood further back.

'The time will never be right, so it might as well be now. Think what would Anna want you to do.'

Shay shook his head. 'This change is so hard; this was Anna's special space.'

Casey stood in front of him, and put her hands on his shoulders. 'You can do this to honour Anna's memory,' she said firmly.

Shay nodded. 'Maybe now, I understand why you are such a winner in court,' he said.

'What do you want me to do?' Casey asked, smiling broadly at Shay.

'Let's concentrate on clearing the place today, and if you don't mind, you can help me sort out how exactly we can use the space.'

'I have all these weeks stretching ahead, so it would be good to lose myself in a project.'

They started taking the artwork from the wall, and placing it in a storeroom at the back of the pub. They worked quietly together until Shay sat down at Anna's desk.

'Could I ask you another favour?' he said to Casey. 'If I give you a box, can you pack everything on the desk into it. I don't think I can face handling any of it now.'

Casey nodded, and took his place at the desk. Picking up the charcoal sketch, she realised it was a drawing of Scarty from that very seat. There were barely any lines on the page, but she felt the sense of place as the island rose up from the charcoal wash of the bay water.

She held it up and called out to Shay, 'You should frame it; it shows how brilliant an artist Anna was.'

Shay took it and sat down. 'That was the last drawing she ever did. She was sitting here sketching because there weren't a lot of customers. It was a glorious day, the sun baking, the sea sprinkled with silver. I told her that I wanted the sketch, and when the painting was done, it wasn't leaving Kennedys. We would hang it in the restaurant.'

Casey watched as he took out a handkerchief, and dabbed his eyes.

'I was behind the bar ten minutes later, when there was a crash and a shout from the gallery. Anna had collapsed. We found her lying on the floor. I tried CPR, but there was nothing I could do. By the time the ambulance had arrived, she was dead.'

Casey wiped away tears. 'I am so sorry.'

'Thank you,' he whispered.

'How long were you together?'

'Decades, over twenty years, until the brain bleed took her so suddenly from us.'

'It is so sad.'

'I know,' he muttered, before turning away because she knew he was crying.

'You're right, I should frame the sketch because it shows when Anna died she was doing exactly what she wanted to be doing, and in the place she loved most. There is some comfort in that.'

He pushed a box towards Casey.

'Pack everything in there or we will never get the place cleared,' he said.

Casey carefully took all the sketching materials and loose pages and put them in the box.

She was finishing clearing out a small drawer on the desk which held pastel crayons, when she came across an envelope which was addressed to Rosie in New York. Not sure what to do with it, she saw it was unsealed.

Shay had dragged the plywood out on to the backyard, and was stacking it against the wall. He called out, and said he needed to get some tools from May's but he wouldn't be long. Casey turned the envelope over in her hands.

Gently, she pulled a piece of paper from the envelope, and peeked inside. It was a printout of an email.

Hi Rosie,

Things are much the same as they always were here... quiet. The gallery café is my piece of heaven, but it doesn't bring in many pennies, so Shay is complaining. I have a number of sketches ready to send you, and I hope you can find a buyer for them. It would make such a difference, and it is so exciting to think my humble drawings could be hanging on a wall some-where in New York! Talk soon,

Love, Anna.

Casey immediately felt bad that she had invaded a dead woman's privacy. Quickly, she placed the envelope in the box, and closed it. Carrying it to the backyard, she handed it to Shay, who was sorting through a box of tools.

'Thanks for doing that, Casey,' he said, placing the box in a cupboard.

She wandered back to gallery. 'Are you going to paint it?' she asked.

'Yes, blue to reflect the sea. I have tables and chairs, and I know some artists who would be happy to hang their work here.'

'What about Anna's paintings?'

'I don't know if I can let go of them.'

'Why don't you have an Anna memory wall to display the work, and maybe tell her story.'

'Casey, a genius idea. I don't know what I will do when you go back to Manhattan.'

'There are a few weeks yet,' she said shyly.

EIGHTEEN

Casey worked hard helping clean out the café space over the next two days. Shay said he could take it from there, but she told him she was happy to be occupied. Her office the day before had asked her to take part in a Zoom meeting, but had left her on the sidelines with everybody else discussing the issues, and laughing at the in-house jokes. She asked pertinent questions but she felt her presence was resented. She felt it was a waste of time, not only for herself but for Dan, who had driven her to the churchyard and had to wait for her.

'Keep the bosses happy; that is all you can do. Now, please forget about that shower. If you don't mind me saying, they don't sound the nicest people on earth,' Dan said as he drove her home along the windy country road to Ballymurphy.

Casey had to agree with his assessment. Gary had not bothered to show up for the meeting, and the legal assistant who had been sent on his behalf had been decidedly snooty.

It was on the way back that Dan asked Casey what she thought of Shay's idea to open up a café.

'I think it's great, and the gallery is a wonderful addition,' she said.

'Do you think he's ready?'

'What do you mean?'

'Just two hours after Anna died, he got the nails and timber, and hammered those boards in place. Nobody could talk him out of it; and nobody could persuade him as time passed to even walk into the room. I don't know how you did it.'

'It was Shay's idea; maybe it was just time.'

'It was definitely that,' Dan said.

'It has been a tough few years for you all, I imagine.'

Dan nodded. 'Shay is a good man, Casey, but he hasn't been able to move on. I am hoping this new project will be the final push he needs to get his life back on track.'

'He seems to be doing OK.'

'He has been a rock of strength all his life for me; when my son drowned; when my wife died months later. But since he lost Anna, that man has just thrown himself into work. He has built up a successful business, but at what cost?'

'What do you mean?'

'It looks like we live in paradise, and we do most days, but I worry. It's like he is trapped in the past. Anna was a beautiful woman, and they loved each other. I know what it is like to lose the people you love, but one thing I have learned is that as time passes, you have to make a decision to be part of life again, not just exist in it. Shay is looking after us all and me in particular, but I am not sure he is even thinking of himself any more.'

'Maybe you need to give him permission to go out and live his life to the full.'

Dan beamed at Casey. 'Casey Freeman, you must be some lawyer in Manhattan, because you read people so well. I might just do that,' he said.

When they got back to Ballymurphy, Casey returned to work at the café. There was an old dresser to clear out. Getting down on her knees, she pulled out rolled-up sketches and paintings that must have been Anna's work. She had nearly finished the top shelf when a small box fell out onto the floor.

Prising it open, Casey gasped to see a heavy gold necklace with a small black pendant with the distinctive Chanel inter-locked Cs. There was a tag which said 'Chanel Paris. Made in France'.

Casey carefully lifted the necklace from its velvet cushion, and examined it. Holding it up, she let it swing in the light, the sunshine glinting off the gold.

Shay walked in with a box of tools in his hand.

'I am going to put up a few shelves. We can paint them at the same time as the walls.'

He stopped suddenly. 'Where did you get that?'

'It was behind all the rolled-up paintings. I'm sorry, I couldn't resist; I opened it, and took it out. It's Chanel.'

Shay dropped his box of tools on the table, making it wobble.

'You had no right to open it. Can I have it, please?'

She hastily put the necklace back in the box, fumbling when she couldn't get it to quite fit. When she held out the box, he swiped it from her hand, and stormed to the front door. Slowly, she followed him to the quay wall, where he was slumped staring at the necklace.

'Shay, what's wrong, I'm sorry if I overstepped the mark again, I was only looking at it.'

He didn't answer, but stuffed the box in his pocket.

'It's nothing, I have work to do,' he said attempting to pass by, and walk to the boat.

Casey stepped in front of him. 'Have I done something wrong?'

'I need to go out on the boat.'

'What about the shelves?'

Shay sidestepped Casey. 'What does it matter; who the hell

is going to come to a gallery in the arsehole of nowhere? This whole gallery café set-up is a bad idea.'

He stomped down the quay. Casey watched him, his back straight, but his shoulders slumped in defeat.

Dan was right; this was a man who didn't know how to live, while continuing to love the person who had died.

She ran after him, reaching him as he got to the boat.

'Shay, can't we talk about this please?'

'No.'

'I should have handed the box to you; it was my mistake to open it and take out the necklace. I am very sorry.'

Shay hesitated. 'It's not that you took it from the box; I haven't seen that since the day Anna died.'

Casey stepped back. 'I never intended to cause you pain.'

'It was a gift; I was about to give it to her, but she died. I had planned a romantic dinner for two, and I had hidden the box in the dresser. I was admiring it earlier that day, when Anna walked in on me, and I pushed it behind the stuff in that cupboard. In truth, I had forgotten about it until today.'

'I am sorry for raising ghosts.'

'It's not that I don't want to open up the gallery any more. It's just not a good business idea. I am going to spread myself too thin.'

'I disagree. It's a great idea, and you know I can help out. It will put Kennedys on the map.'

Shay walked on to the boat. 'What map, Casey? The map of Ballymurphy? Kennedys is Ballymurphy, and Ballymurphy is Kennedys; we are the biggest business here. We don't need to prove anything.'

'You know it's a good idea – that tourists and even locals will love it.'

'Work stops today; I am not continuing with it. That's my final word.'

'Shay Kennedy, will you please stop and think; you're being so dumb right now.'

'Dumb? Thanks, Casey, for pointing that out.'

'Shay, you're being childish and stupid to not continue with the work on the café and gallery. It is time to step out, take some chances.'

'Like you can talk, Casey Freeman, brilliant attorney hiding in Ballymurphy beside the Atlantic.'

'That is hardly fair, you know why I'm here,'

He jumped on the boat. 'Stop trying to change the world, and concentrate on your own life, Casey. I'm all right.'

'I just don't want you to make a mistake because you're afraid to move on.'

He turned on the boat engine. 'You can't waltz in here, and tell me how to run my life and business. You will be gone soon; you have no right.'

'I thought I was your friend.'

He revved the engine too much, making thick black smoke fill the air.

'Casey, back off, this is none of your business.'

'OK, it's not, but I care about you and your dad, and I want to help.'

'The café gallery is not happening. It is a bad idea to open up; it can never be what it was.'

'But it can be something new, if you would only let it. It's time to fully move on, Shay. Anna wouldn't want you to give up.'

'What do you know? You never even met Anna!'

'I know that you're in a rut, but if you don't work to get out of it, it will only get worse.'

'And you're not in a rut?'

'What do you mean?'

'Casey, I know you mean well, but at some stage of our lives, we are all stuck in a rut. Look at you in the most exciting city in the world, with a job which pays more than I can bring in over several years.'

'So?'

'So, don't lecture me, please.'

'OK, but your rut is going to pull you down, if you don't do something about it.'

'And yours isn't?' he snapped.

Shay stepped out of the wheelhouse and looked directly at Casey.

'Thank you for your help and ideas, but we will no longer be requiring such assistance,' he said, before steering the boat out of the harbour.

He left her stranded on the quayside looking at the boat as it headed out to sea and past Scarty. She felt foolish, and now she had no way of getting home either. She wandered back to the deck, where Dan was standing watching the boat go further out to sea.

'That boy of mine needs a kick up the arse,' he said.

'I wouldn't put it like that, but yes, he needs a jolt to put him on the right track.'

'You may have just done that.'

Casey sat down on a bench. 'It wasn't my intention.'

'Which is why it worked so effectively. Don't mind him; he'll be back when he calms down.'

'The Chanel necklace seemed to set him off. I never intended it.'

Dan rubbed his hands together.

'Casey, I'm not sure I should be telling you this, but that necklace cost a fortune. Anna fell in love with it. She saw it in a jeweller's in Dublin, and she couldn't stop talking about it. She wasn't a grasping woman; it was merely that she fell in love with it. I don't think she ever intended that Shay would go and buy it; it was a lot of money for him at the time too.'

Dan stopped to take a deep breath. Casey reached over, and held his hand.

'Just a few days before Anna collapsed and died, we were very happy here at Kennedys. They had been married so long, and Anna found out she was pregnant. I can honestly say I have never seen them so happy, and for me it was a rare, sweet moment since the death of my son and wife. I was so ready to be a grandfather.'

Casey tightened her grip on Dan's hand.

'If it was a girl, they were going to call her after Shay's mother, Dearbhla, and a boy would be Andrew, of course. Shay took an early train to Dublin the next day, and wouldn't tell anyone what he was doing. He bought the necklace, and the day she died he had planned to present her with the gift.'

'What a beautiful idea.'

'Anna never even got to know he had bought it, and never got to take it out of the box. I guess that is why he reacted so, when he saw you handle it.'

'I had no idea.'

'How could you? I am sorry you are caught in the middle of this, Casey. Shay will come around about the gallery and café, but it might take a few days.'

'I feel so bad for my part in this.'

Dan stood up. 'You shouldn't. It's the past and Shay has not been good at dealing with it. You have nothing to apologise for.'

Dan looked far out to sea. 'When he bought that necklace, neither he nor any of us were to know what was to come, but life can deal some tough blows, and what happened Anna was one of the worst. That man has had so much to contend with.'

'He is strong.'

'Strength can sometimes hide a lot of pain. He is hurting so he needs a little time to come round. You can stay here and wait, if you like.'

'I don't think that's a good idea, but I'm not sure how I can get back to Scarty.'

'Don't worry, that's easy. Shay might think he is the only one who can cross the channel to Scarty, but the fisherman cum boatman Peter Kelly down the road will run you over whenever you want.'

'It's best I go now,' she said.

Dan told her to go down the quay, and he rang Peter Kelly.

'He will bring you out in ten minutes, Casey. Please don't think less of Shay after this. Give him some time.'

'Time I have, I guess,' she said, giving Dan a hug.

Casey sat quietly as Peter Kellhy started up his boat engine and moved out of the harbour. She hoped Shay would come back. She needed this project, and she felt he did, too, to move on with his life. She was afraid he would resent her for disturbing the necklace. How he must have loved his wife to spend thousands on a Chanel necklace, just because she liked it.

Casey scanned the water hoping to see Shay's boat, but there was only a cold sea under a sky which would soon go dark.

NINETEEN

Several days had passed, and Casey had given up watching the channel between Scarty and Ballymurphy for Shay's boat. Georgie had taken to getting up early most mornings, and not returning until well into the evening. Casey knew she was painting because her paints and sketch pads were always gone from their spot by the window from early, and when she returned she had a voracious appetite as if she had been so busy she had forgotten to eat.

She was quiet, too, and Casey was worried about her, but Debbie said maybe she needed some space.

Debbie put Rosie's box on the table. 'Let's have a rummage,' she said.

Casey leaned forward, and took out the silver frame.

'I think that's Shay's wife, Anna. He has a similar frame in the boat wheelhouse; she was quite a beauty.'

'Oh, put away your green horns, girl,' Debbie teased, 'By the way, I asked Dan about Marian Murphy, that name on the envelope. He said she lived in Kilkee a long time back, and he immediately changed the subject.'

'Did you tell him about that letter?'

'No, I got the impression the conversation was closed.'

'As if that ever stopped you in the past,' Casey laughed.

Debbie threw the envelope back in the box, and shoved it under the table.

'It's none of our business anyway. Now, what about Georgie; is she OK?'

She's painting; that has to be good news,' Casey said.

'But she never lets us see anything or tells us where she is going. Georgie isn't usually this secretive.'

'Maybe she's having an affair,' Debbie giggled.

Casey stared at Debbie in alarm.

'With whom?'

'Don't worry, Shay is all yours; can't you see he only has eyes for you? Have you two sorted out things yet?'

'Don't be silly; there is nothing to sort out.'

'Could have fooled me. Both of you have been walking around as if the weight of the world is on your shoulders. Kiss and make up.'

'I don't know what you are talking about. I had ideas for the gallery and café, and he backed off. That's it.'

'If you say so,' Debbie sniggered.

'Anyway, I think I overstepped the mark. It's his property and he's still grieving; I may have pushed too far.'

'You should talk to him.'

'I have said enough already.'

'Well, you had better find the words fast,' Debbie said enigmatically as she scurried off to her bedroom.

Casey was about to ask her what she meant when there was a knock at the door. Shay stood in the doorway, an envelope in his hand.

'I was coming back from checking the lobster pots, and I thought I would pass on a Rosie letter,' he said.

Unable to find the words, Casey reluctantly took the envelope.

'Have I interrupted something?' Shay asked.

'We were just wondering about Georgie, we have no idea where she is,' Casey mumbled.

'I saw her from the boat. She likes to stay out near the old ruin at the far side of the island. I imagine she's painting out there.'

'Good to know.'

Casey went to close the door, but Shay stopped her, and stepped into the kitchen. He looked at her sheepishly.

'The letter is an excuse; I really came to apologise.'

Casey slowly put the envelope down on the table.

'No, I am the one who should apologise. I should have realised how difficult all the change is for you. I understand if you think you're not ready. I am very sorry about the necklace; I didn't know its history.'

'I overreacted,' he said, catching Casey's hand, and pulling her to the front door.

Stretching and picking up the binoculars from the bench, he handed them to her.

'Look at Kennedys now.'

Embarrassed, she peered through the binoculars.

'Do you see it?'

'You have taken the hoarding down.'

'We have done a lot more than that. Could I borrow you, bring you across, and show you what Dad and I have managed to do?'

'I guess, but I thought you were going to put it on the back burner.'

'I did for a few days, but I remembered somebody cared enough to give me a right kick up the arse, as Dad would say.'

Casey peered through the binoculars again. 'I see somebody sitting outside.'

'That's Dad thinking I can't check on him. Can you come across?'

'Of course she can; her calendar is free,' Debbie said from behind them.

'You are welcome too,' Shay said quickly.

'Three is a crowd, darling, and I have a pressing schedule; you two go out from under my feet,' Debbie said in her bossy voice.

Casey shot her a grateful look, and ran upstairs to get changed. Impulsively, she picked a long, green summer dress belonging to Georgie, and pulled it on. A green and cream flowery dress with buttons down the front, and short puff sleeves. It fitted Casey perfectly.

Twirling in front of the mirror, she liked the way the fabric spun around her. Teaming it with her cream canvas shoes, she ran downstairs.

Shay let out a low whistle when he saw her.

'I don't think I have ever seen you in a dress before.'

'It's Georgie's,' Casey said quickly, feeling slightly embarrassed at her admission.

Debbie tut-tutted from behind. 'Darling Casey, next time you are given a compliment, just say thank you. None of "this old thing I borrowed", please.'

Casey giggled, and they left.

'Is she always like that?' Shay asked.

'That was quite restrained. It's often worse.'

They chatted all the way down the path, Shay offering his hand to help Casey onto the boat. She stood by him at the wheelhouse as he pulled away from Scarty jetty, and headed for Ballymurphy.

'Is that Anna?' she asked, pointing to the silver frame.

'Yes.'

'She was very beautiful.'

He picked up the frame, and examined the photo.

'She was, inside and out,' he said.

When Casey shivered he took off his denim jacket, and

draped it over her shoulders. She was still wearing it as they tied up the boat at Ballymurphy, and strolled to Kennedys.

They were halfway up the quay when Casey stopped in her tracks.

The outside of the gallery café had been painted a duck egg blue, the large window picked out in lemon, and workmen were erecting a sign which said SCARTY GALLERY AND CAFÉ.

There were tables and chairs on the pavement outside, and somebody had pulled a bistro set over beside the quay wall.

'I don't know if we are allowed to have the tables outside, but until they tell us otherwise, we'll do it,' Shay said.

Taking her by the hand, they crossed the road, and he led her into the building.

'When did you do this? It's perfect,' she said, taking in the memory wall for Anna, and the wall opposite which had a beautiful painting of a woman and a history of Scarty Island on it. As she got closer Casey gasped. It wasn't just any woman, it was Rosie.

'I never imagined you would do this,' she said.

'It was Dad's idea, and Georgie did the Rosie painting for us.'

It was definitely Rosie; the slightly untidy blonde hair framing her face. Her delicate features had been captured so well along with the soft eyes, Casey felt as if they were searching her soul. She wanted to stroke the blonde locks which were always held back at one side with a flower clip.

Around Rosie's neck was a gold chain with a small gold heart. Rosie always wore it. Even when she became a woman of substantial means, she never swapped the gold chain and heart for anything more expensive or elaborate. Whenever she was questioned about it, she rubbed the heart between her fingers saying it was her touchstone from good times past.

They had speculated that it must have been something

given to her when she was young that held a sentimental value, but they never could prise more than that out of her.

'Georgie never mentioned she was painting a portrait of Rosie. '

'Dad asked her, but she didn't know it was for the gallery.'

Casey stepped closer to read a note about the artist.

'Georgie is going to love this.'

'She has promised me two paintings before she leaves, so I can sell them for her. She said she will come back next year, and she will spend the money in Ennis and Galway.'

'If Debbie were here, she would say, "typical Georgie, who never thinks about saving, only spending".'

'Do you like what you see?' Shay asked.

'I do, but I thought you wouldn't be able to run this as well as everything else.'

'I may have been a wee bit dramatic. We will work it out as we always do. I was hoping your offer to help out stills stands.'

'Running the gallery café every day?'

'Am I asking too much?'

'No, I would love it.'

'I can come out to Scarty, and collect you around 10 a.m. if that is not too early and we can open up the shop at 11 a.m. That is when the first tours usually pull up.'

'You have it all worked out for somebody who didn't know how he could manage.'

'To be honest, Dad and May pushed me, and they have promised to help out. May is baking two types of cakes as well as her scones, and I will do some mini quiches and salad for lunch.'

'No chips and burger at the gallery café, then.'

He laughed, and led her to the desk and chair at the window, which used to be Anna's favourite place.

'I haven't changed much here but instead of a counter, I thought we could serve people from the bar and restaurant kitchen with the old dresser as the space to display the cakes and scones, and the crockery underneath. I thought if you don't mind, you could sit at the desk and take payment there.'

He stopped, and looked at Casey. 'You don't think it is a good idea?'

'It's fine; don't worry,' she said trying hard to hide her discomfort.

'Dad said I should put in a counter, that you wouldn't want to be sitting at this desk all day.'

'Tables at the window will be at a premium.'

'That's what Dad warned too,' Shay said, picking up the chair, and calling his dad to help move the desk.

'This is all about new beginnings. I am not going to stop remembering or loving Anna, just because I move her desk to the back of house,' he said.

Dan appeared at the front door, and immediately took one end of the desk and helped Shay move it.

'The carpenter won't be coming back after today so, best this is all decided now,' Dan said.

Casey walked around the café. She no longer felt like she was treading on another woman's toes. The memory wall showed photographs of Anna through the years, the last one wearing the straw hat and stepping off the boat at Scarty. She was a tall woman with long black hair, and Casey thought she had an enigmatic smile.

She suddenly felt sad she would never meet this woman, who had left such a mark on this small place.

Just then, May bustled in, a big bundle of fabric in her arms.

'I have the curtains made; Shay doesn't think the café needs drapes, but what does he know?'

'But what about the view?' Casey asked.

'What do you take me for, an ignoramus? These drapes are to frame the window, not block out the light. I have some nice tie-backs as well.'

Casey helped May get a step ladder in place, and hang the curtains which were a deep blue with tie-backs in blue and gold.

'Aren't they stunning? Dan picked out the fabric in Galway, and he never let on to Shay. He knew you would eventually persuade that young man to move on.'

'I don't know what you mean, I never spoke to Dan about this,' Casey said, her voice squeaky because she felt uncomfortable.

'Darling, there are some things you don't have to put in words,' May said, giggling.

Casey wandered outside to clear her head.

What was she even doing here? It looked disturbingly like she was hanging around, waiting for a man to get over his dead wife. That wasn't who she was. She was glad to help with the café, but she must try to keep her distance from Shay, otherwise she could face making a show of herself, and suffer a whole lot of heartbreak.

Strange that she worried more about this than whether her husband was living it up with some young thing while she was gone. She hadn't heard from her boss for a while, either, and she didn't know what she should do. She was definitely going to stay on Scarty until the end of August, but at the moment, she wanted to keep her job. Without her work, she was nothing. This was one thing she was sure of. How sad was that? She had given so many years to her relationship with Gary but there was nothing there. If she was being honest, it had been like that for so long. Gary had used her, and would continue to use her until she shouted stop.

On an impulse, she dialled Gary's number. There was no answer. Anger coursed through her as she waited for the instruction to leave a message. She had finally decided to end this sham marriage they had, and he couldn't even answer her call. She had wasted too much time on Gary, and now she had to put it on the line.

'Hi, it's me. I won't be back for a while, but when I do return, you can take it we are separated, and I intend to file for divorce. I hope we can do this in a civilised fashion. Thank you. Goodbye.'

She might be an idiot, she thought, giving advance warning of her intention to separate, and file for divorce. Gary wouldn't care about the end of their marriage, but there was a possibility that he would have cleaned out their joint back account by the time she got back onto Scarty, never mind the United States.

She didn't hear Shay come up behind her.

'Is everything all right?' he asked, his face full of concern.

'I don't know.'

'What has happened? Have you got bad news or something?'

'I rang my husband's phone, and I left a message.'

'So?'

'I told him I intend to ask for a separation, and file for divorce.'

'Oh.'

'I have been a stupid fool.'

'I thought you wanted to divorce him.'

'I shouldn't have showed my hand.'

Shay put his arm around her.

'You don't know that. Won't assets have to be split?'

'If I can locate them.'

'Ring up an attorney – you surely know one – and make sure that Gary can't touch anything that is in joint ownership.'

'I will.'

Wandering out into the backyard, she dialled a colleague she knew she could trust, and began to give instructions over the phone. Shay waved to her from the café, and she wondered how this quiet man could have turned her heart so much in just a few weeks. When she was around him, she felt safe in the best possible sense; when she was away from him, she spent the time looking across the sea, and longing to be by his side. Hurriedly, she finished up, and joined the others in the café. May had a table set up with a lemon drizzle cake on a glass cake stand.

'Did you get yourself sorted?' Shay asked.

'Yes, I feel a bit foolish, but my colleague is serving him with papers and other legal stuff to make sure he doesn't try and hide away assets.'

'I like that word "assets". It makes you sound very rich. I wish I had assets,' May said.

Dan handed her a cake slice, and poured the coffee. Casey looked all around her, her heart swelling with pride that she had been part of something so good.

'You should have a big opening for the café, a gathering,' Casey said.

Dan beamed with delight.

'Would anyone even want to come?' Shay grumbled.

May laughed out loud. 'All the questions I have been asked about this place. Are you mad, man?'

'I suppose when you put it like that...' Shay said, biting into the cake.

'Georgie could create a flyer. I am sure she wouldn't mind doing the artwork.'

'I am sorry to rain on everyone's parade, but I intend to open up in the morning. If that is OK with you, Casey?'

'Yes, but don't you want to create a buzz about the place?'

'Of course I do, but I am more interested in getting business in and bums on seats straightaway.'

'You can have a soft opening and invite the press another time.'

'The local hack for a big fry-up, you mean,' Dan said.

'I was thinking that there may be interest in Rosie's story and Anna's talent. Magazines, things like that.'

'Let me have a think about it, but it's time now to get you back to the island,' he said, and they left May and Dan to have another slice of cake.

Casey continued to wear his denim jacket until they got to the island. When she started to take it off, he told her to hold on to it before jumping out onto the jetty beside her.

'I wanted to say something, Casey, but I don't know if I should.'

'There is only the two of us here.'

He kicked a small pebble along the jetty until it plopped into the sea.

'I wanted to explain to you that Anna will always be part of my life, but I really like spending time with you, Casey. I am not saying this right at all,' he said, pulling his hands through his hair.

For a moment she held her breath, and savoured the words. She saw he was struggling, his lips quivering, and she wanted more than anything to be with him. Pushing herself on to her tiptoes, she kissed him, barely brushing his lips.

'I know what you mean, and I am glad,' she said, before skipping up the path almost afraid to look back.

She was nearly at the farmhouse when she heard the chug of the boat's engines, and it made her smile.

As she pushed the old front door open, she could barely contain her smile. Georgie was leaning against the sink, drinking a mug of coffee.

'Where were you, and what are you doing wearing my dress?'

Casey laughed, and twirled so the skirt fanned out around her.

'The cat that got the cream, methinks,' Debbie said.

TWENTY

Georgie woke up the others at first light.

'Nobody told me there was a letter from Rosie,' she shouted up the stairs.

Debbie, rubbing her eyes, came into the kitchen asking what time it was.

'Just after six, but I can't open the letter on my own.'

'Couldn't you have waited, girl?'

Casey came rushing down the stairs. 'What's wrong?'

'This silly one wants us to open Rosie's letter, and it is only six o'clock in the morning. I never rise before seven, even back in the States,' Debbie said.

'We are all here, and that is what Rosie wants; let's do it,' Casey said.

Debbie sat down at the table, and put her head in her hands. 'Will somebody please pour me a cup of coffee?' she croaked.

Georgie placed a coffee in front of Debbie as Casey ripped open the envelope, and scanned through the letter.

'Do you want to read this one out, Georgie? It's all about you...' Casey asked.

'Gross, never.'

'Go on, don't leave me in suspense after getting me up at the crack of dawn,' Debbie interrupted.

Casey cleared her throat before reading the letter out loud.

Dear Georgie,

It is my one deep regret that I treated you so badly. I was desperate to have a baby to take care of, and to create a family with Barry. That desperation clouded my judgement and turned me into someone I hated.

I should never have asked you to be my surrogate; I should never have pressured you, and I should never have cut you out of my life. I can only say to you sincerely, I am deeply sorry.

I had become obsessed with creating a family. My selfish obsession dominated my life, and set me on a course to push away the three most beautiful friends anybody could have.

I can only ask you, Georgie, for forgiveness. More than anything, I wanted you to come to Scarty so we could connect again, and I could, in some way, make up for the past.

Over the years, I held on to a grudge and resentment, but I know now I was wrong. To my eternal shame, I dragged Debbie, my greatest defender, and Casey into this mess. I also apologise to them.

I know I should have brought us together, and told you in person, but the words failed me and courage deserted me.

Please, my dear Georgie, let me make amends.

I wanted you to come to Scarty to paint, but this time, Georgie, I want to carry it to the obvious conclusion of an exhibition.

I have arranged a space in a beautiful old brownstone in Greenwich Village. My friend Richard Knowles has rooms there he rents for exhibitions. He is a patron of the arts, and I have arranged a meeting between the two of you in September when you return. I know he is already impressed by your work. Georgie, I know you can do it.

Richard is so well connected. He is quite fussy, but when I showed him your work – and yes, I know it all, because I have been following you all your life and collecting it whenever I could – he was so blown away. He can see your pieces adorning the finest walls on the Upper East Side, and I agree with him.

I also showed him my humble photos of Scarty Island, and he was so taken by the wild ruggedness of it all. I have funds set aside for all the necessary framing, etc., so you don't have to worry about that. Think big, Georgie.

Paint here on Scarty, and learn to love your talent, and be proud of it. I know I am, and I know your little family of sisters are too.

Georgie, you feel everything so deeply. Don't ever change that, but please give yourself a break.

I know in the past you have worked towards exhibitions, but life always got in the way. There are no obstacles now; I have swept them all aside. Take time out, and paint, darling. Show the world the magic and beauty of Scarty.

I have to stop now, because while my heart wants to say more, my body and brain are too tired.

All my love,

Rosie Xx

Georgie put down her mug of coffee and inhaled deeply. The three women looked from one to another but didn't say anything for a few moments.

'This is so goddamn awesome. This is such news,' Debbie said, but Casey put her hand up to stop her talking.

Georgie jumped up from the table, and said she had work to do.

'Hey, can't we talk about this? You're going to take up the offer, I hope?' Debbie said.

Georgie picked up her easel and slung her big bag of painting materials over her shoulder, and rushed out of the farmhouse.

'What is up with her?' Debbie asked.

Casey didn't answer but ran upstairs and pulled on her jeans and a hoodie. She darted from the house, hoping to catch up with Georgie. She figured she had gone to the other side of the island where Shay had seen her the day before. Her head down against the cool breeze that was blowing across from the sea, Casey took long strides as she headed off across the fields. When, after twenty minutes, she saw Georgie, she wondered if she should run up to her or hang back.

Georgie had a canvas on the easel, and was working fever- ishly. Casey could only see a little of the painting but it looked like the cove. Slowly, she walked towards her friend, watching her, her head at times bent over the canvas, other times on her tiptoes as if she were trying to make sure she got everything exactly right. When Georgie swung around, Casey almost fell back in surprise.

'I knew you would follow me. You always were the one who looked out for all of us.'

'You don't mind, do you?'

Georgie threw down her paintbrush.

'I can't do an exhibition in a place like that.'

'Why ever not? Your work is superb, and this is your big moment.'

'You're so kind, but I just can't do it. I don't even know when I get back to the States, if I will live in New York.'

Casey reached out to Georgie, but she pulled away.

'Whatever is the matter?'

'There is nothing left for me in New York.'

'But I thought we had been through this; you can live with me.'

Georgie took two strides away, her arms wrapped tight around herself.

'Will... he left me just a few weeks before Rosie died. Cleaned out our bank account too.'

'Shit, Georgie, you never said.'

'I didn't know how to say it.'

Casey ran and took Georgie in her arms. 'Darling, you should have told us.'

'What would you have done? Debbie would have lectured, and you, Casey, would have just offered me the world. Nobody can mend a broken heart.'

'But this is a new direction for you; it won't mend your broken heart, but it will help get you back on track.'

Georgie slumped against Casey.

'You don't understand,' Georgie sobbed.

Casey caught her by the shoulders so she could look Georgie in the face.

'I have known you for decades. There is nothing you can tell me which will make me think any less of you. Now, spit it out.'

Georgie crumpled into a ball on the grass. Casey sat beside her, rubbing her back.

'You need to tell someone; its eating you up inside.'

Suddenly, Georgie stopped crying, and sat up.

'I must get back to my painting; please don't stop me; It is the only way I can keep sane these days.'

She walked back to the easel and took her brush, and began touching up the sky.

Unsure of what to do, Casey sat and watched her, hoping if she stayed there Georgie would relent, and come back. Her stance was rigid, and she looked like a robot moving only her hands until she called out, and threw her paintbrush down the field. Casey ran to her, her arms opened wide, and Georgie burrowed into her.

'Let's go down to the beach; there is a path down past the gorse bushes. Somehow, our troubles feel small beside the ocean,' Casey whispered.

Georgie allowed herself to be led across the field to the path, where they had to go single file past the bank of gorse. Casey let Georgie go first, and they walked quickly on until they reached the sandy beach.

'This beach is so much nicer than the one near the farmhouse, I don't know why we don't use it more,' Georgie said.

Casey hesitated, not wanting to start a conversation about Shay's brother, and how he died.

Georgie whooped out loud, and ran down to the sea, kicking her sandals off on the way. For a moment, Casey's heart leaped, afraid Georgie was going to try something silly, but she waded in until she was knee deep, her long dress sodden with water.

Casey walked parallel to her, paddling along the shore.

Georgie jumped the waves and laughed, at one stage twirling around until, dizzy, she staggered, and fell in the water. Forgetting that she didn't want to get wet, Casey ran to her.

Georgie was laughing and crying at the same time.

Casey gently pulled her to her feet, and led her out of the sea. On the sand she squeezed the water out of Georgie's hair, and did the same for the skirt of the dress.

'It's warm today, you will dry out in a while,' she said.

'Can you keep a secret?' Georgie asked Casey.

'Of course.'

'Even from Debbie and Shay?'

'If you ask me to keep something secret, I promise, I will.'

Georgie shook her still-wet hair onto the sand, before pushing it back from her face.

'I didn't tell you the whole story about Will.'

'No?'

'Hush, please; I'm only going to tell this story once. Don't interrupt,' Georgie said, her eyes fixed on the sea.

'Everything was so good for about four years...' Georgie stopped to take a deep breath. 'We were happy; we loved each other. Will was a really good carpenter, and he got lots of work. We had a nice apartment. I was painting, selling sometimes, and not at other times. Life was good, though, and we felt... well, I felt blessed. Then, there was such a stupid accident; Will was on his phone, and stepped out in front of a car. He recovered, but it took months, and he was in so much pain.

'He became dependent and once the opioids took hold, he didn't care about anything else. I tried to get him help, but nothing worked. He began going off with other women, but he still paid the bills, and I tried to keep going.

'About a year before he died, he met a certain woman, and she was an addict too. He didn't work any more. I kept on the apartment because I had saved money down the years.'

She turned to look at Casey. 'Wouldn't Debbie be surprised?'

Casey smiled, and told Georgie to continue.

Taking a deep breath, Georgie returned to staring out to sea.

'Then, two months ago, he didn't come home. I was worried about him until I found out he had cleaned out our bank accounts. I was left with nothing, only a stack of unpaid bills; bills he had pretended to pay.

'I was heartbroken, too, because deep down I still loved him. I stopped painting; I couldn't do a thing. I began to drink too much. When I knew I didn't have money for the following month's rent, I moved out of the apartment in the middle of the night.'

Tears rolled down Georgie's face.

'It was like the bad old days. That night I sneaked into a public park, and slept there. I was terrified, and early the next morning I walked to a shelter, and pleaded with them to take me in.

Casey took Georgie's hand and squeezed it. 'You should have got in touch with any one of us.'

'Right, and admit that my life had gone belly-up. Georgie had done it again.'

Casey pulled her friend close. 'I don't think we would have been like that,' she soothed, 'Well, maybe Debbie.'

Georgie smiled, but quickly began to sob again. Casey held her tight until Georgie pulled away.

'There is more. You might as well know.'

Casey tried to remain calm, but she was afraid of what was coming next. Georgie caught a pebble, angrily flinging it across the sand.

'I live in a small hostel in Brooklyn. To be honest, when news came of Rosie, and I know how this sounds, it was a welcome distraction.'

'I understand,' Casey said, hugging Georgie tight.

'Were you wondering why I was so late for the flight?'

'Maybe.'

'I got a friend to loan me the flight money. I had to pay her back before I left, so I had to sell my vintage clothes collection. I had to wait for the money to clear, and thankfully it did that morning, and I paid my pal back before getting out to JFK. I just made the flight, and also had a few bucks in my pocket. At least I didn't have to sell my painting materials.'

'You should have told us.'

Georgie walked towards the sea, and beckoned to Casey to follow.

'I couldn't ask you for help; I was too ashamed. Promise me, you won't tell Debbie. I couldn't face one of her lectures.'

'She means well, and she loves you.'

'I know.'

'What has this to do with the opportunity for an exhibition in New York?'

Casey trailed her toes through the water.

'I am afraid, I guess, that I can't manage without Will, and at the same time, what do I do if he suddenly turns up? I am a mess, and homeless.'

Casey laughed. 'Georgie, you are a wonderful artist, and you're not without a home any more. You come stay with me.'

'You don't mean that.'

'I do; it's decided,' Casey said firmly.

Georgie blew a kiss to Casey, and mouthed 'thank you'. Casey kicked the water, splashing Georgie. They hurled water at each other, and kicked the sea fiercely, squealing, shouting, and laughing until they were both drenched to the skin.

When they got back to the farmhouse, Debbie tutted loudly, 'You two are worse than kids,' she said.

TWENTY-ONE

It was a rare day off for Casey, and she was enjoying having nothing in particular to do. Since they had opened the doors of the café, it had been so busy, right up until closing time. Every evening she was tired out. She was surprised to see Shay's boat pull over towards Scarty. Wandering down to the jetty, she saw one passenger on board. She pretended to be checking on the bank of wildflowers, so she didn't appear too curious, but there was something vaguely familiar, and unsettling, about the stance of the figure on board.

She gasped, and anxiously looked towards the farmhouse. The man waved, and called out hello, jumping from the boat before it had aligned fully to the jetty, just bridging the wide gap between the boat and pier.

Shay leaned out of the wheelhouse, and shouted that he had brought a visitor. When he turned off the engine, he handed over a case to his passenger. Nervous and curious at the same time, Casey quickened her step on the path. The man, who was pulling up the handle on his luggage so he could wheel it along the jetty, had his back to her, but he seemed so familiar.

Shay waved to her as he prepared to pull away from the

jetty. Casey suddenly felt nervous. The man swung around, and she saw... Marvin.

Frantically glancing all around her, Casey hoped Debbie hadn't spotted him.

'Casey, I am so happy to see you guys; what a journey,' he said, pulling his case behind him as he made his way to her.

'Marvin, what are you doing here?'

'I came to see Debbie.'

'Does she know you're coming?'

He chortled happily. 'I hope not, it wouldn't be a surprise then, would it?'

Casey put her hand out to stop him moving up the jetty.

'Marvin, are you sure about this?'

'Casey, I know you're her friend, but Debbie is my wife.'

Shay stuck his head out the wheelhouse window. 'Is everything all right?'

Casey threw her hands in the air. 'You could have let us know; given Debbie some notice.'

'What was I supposed to do, signal by Morse code?'

Casey gave Shay a dagger look, and turned away to follow Marvin up the path.

'Do you want me to stay?' Shay shouted after her.

'No,' Casey snapped. 'You've done enough.'

'Signal, if you need me,' he said.

'Right, like you can be here in double quick time,' she shouted over the sound of the boat engine.

Casey ran to catch up with Marvin, and overtook him on the path.

'Marvin, you have to do this the right way. You can't just walk in on Debbie.'

She saw him hesitate, and his face grew grim.

'Casey, what am I supposed to do? She has constantly complained that I'm not spontaneous, that I overthink everything. Please don't stop me now. I have never even been to San

Francisco, and I have come across to the other side of the world to see Debbie.'

Casey heard the pain in his voice. She dithered, not sure what to do.

'Please, I want to go to my wife,' he said quietly.

She pointed to the house, and watched him walk up the hill, faltering on the last steps. She didn't know if she should call out to him, so she hung back, watching him straighten his shoulders, drop his case, and walk purposefully through the backyard and past the outhouses. She hurried up the rest of the path to the farmhouse. Debbie had her music up loud; Casey knew she was sitting smoking a cigarette and having a coffee on the front bench, because that was what she did every morning.

Georgie had been up early, and was at the far end of the island painting. Casey wondered if she should slip away quietly, but she stayed where she was, because she wasn't sure if Debbie would welcome her visitor.

Marvin knocked gently at first on the back door. Casey saw him reach into his pocket, take out a handkerchief, and mop his brow before he knocked on the door again.

Casey saw Debbie walk through the house, but stop at the far side of the kitchen table. Not sure if she should be watching, Casey clenched and unclenched her fists. Marvin stayed at the door as the sound of Debbie sobbing filled the air.

Underneath all the bluster, Casey knew Debbie was as soft as butter. When they were younger they used to rib her about it, but they were also fully aware it was one of her most endearing qualities.

She saw Debbie's hand reach out, and pull Marvin into the house. Conscious she was intruding, Casey turned away, and walked back down the path, thinking, Gary knew where she was, but he was too busy, and couldn't care less about seeking her out.

She didn't know when they'd stopped loving each other, but

it had happened. Her travelling to Ireland was proof that she didn't love him any more, and even now, she didn't really care that he didn't love her either. It hurt more that he had not reacted or been in touch immediately about the separation and divorce. His silence and withdrawal were both infuriating and insulting. He hadn't turned up to their last Zoom meeting, just sent a legal assistant to update her, and take notes.

Slipping off her shoes, Casey waded through the water, letting it flow over her toes as they sank into the sand. It was hard to imagine she had ever had a life where she didn't even have time to wander through Bryant Park or stop at one of the cafés there.

When she saw Shay walk towards her, she was surprised.

'I was turning out of Scarty, when I thought I should hang around in case that chap was not welcome,' he said.

'He's Debbie's husband; she is up in the farmhouse with him. I'm just giving them some space.'

'He has come a long way.'

'For a man who has never been to the West Coast, and definitely not outside the States, yes.'

'It must be love.'

'As long as Debbie is happy, that's good enough for me.'

Shay took off his shoes, and rolled up his trousers.

'I see you like to paddle along this stretch of beach; it's your happy place,' he said.

'It's the spot where I can get away from everybody.'

He stopped. 'Do you want me to leave?'

She laughed. 'You know, I didn't mean you.'

He smiled, and took her hand, and they walked side by side, sometimes rushing from the water when a wave fiercely pounded the shore. Every now and again, one of them leaned closer to the other. Casey liked spending time with Shay; there was a certain comfortable feeling between them, which made her feel content and happy. Shay was so different in every way to Gary, who made her feel inadequate and put her on edge. Casey and Shay fitted together like two pieces of a jigsaw.

He scooped up a flat stone. 'This one is going to hop for ten or more, I bet,' he said.

'Excuse me?'

'Don't tell me you haven't skimmed a stone over water?'

'I have seen other people do it.'

'Girl, you haven't lived,' he said, scratching around until he found another flat stone for her.

'Watch me, it's all in the way you throw it. Look, swing from the hip and throw strong and low from the elbow; you won't go far wrong.'

He fingered the flat stone, kissed it for good luck, before leaning forward, arching his shoulder, flicking his wrist and releasing the stone. It whizzed through the air, skimming across the waves, skipping above the water, lightly touching the top of the waves once, twice, and three more times before it dipped into the sea and sank.

'Not my best... now you try,' he said.

'I'm not sure that I can.'

He placed a flat stone in her hand.

'You're not going to know unless you try, and nobody but the seal and myself are witnesses if it doesn't work.'

The stone was cold to the touch, flat and light.

'I have given you the best stone. Remember, swing from the hips and flick from the wrist,' he said.

Pushing her hair back out of her eyes, she positioned herself, and taking a deep breath, she did exactly what Shay had instructed her to do. The stone spun from her hand, sliding across the water, tipping against the sea four times before it sank without trace.

Jumping up and down, Casey punched the air in victory.

'The best of three,' he said, and Casey thought Shay sounded disappointed she had done so well.

They rummaged through the pebbles where the waves had left a ridge along the shoreline. Triumphantly, she held up a small flat stone.

'You're getting the hang of this,' Shay said, continuing to root for his own stones.

Feeling the excitement of competition, she asked who should go first.

'Go for it, I feel the killer instinct of a New York lawyer may be about to surface.'

She ignored him, and maybe she pitched her first stone too fast, because it plopped into the water as if she had never intended to skim it.

'Can we call it a practice shot?' she asked, and he laughed.

'I guess I have no choice but to say yes. Go on, do your thing,' he said.

Concentrating hard, making sure her feet were in the right place, and swinging from the hips, she flicked the stone, gasping as it soared over the water plucking at the waves seven times, before disappearing.

'Not bad at all,' Shay said.

'That was awesome,' she said, but fell quiet when she saw him get ready to skim his own stone.

It flew over the water, intermittently dipping at the waves as if trying to fish, and Shay shouted until the stone sank after ten touchdowns.

'OK, I suppose,' she said, fiercely concentrating on her next throw. This time she managed a respectable seven dips before her stone disappeared. She was disappointed. She wanted to feel the win, the adrenalin flowing through her – to feel the satisfaction of knowing you were the one who came out on top. She berated herself that this was a stupid game and nothing else, but the competitive side of her wanted to win, even if it was only a stone-throwing competition.

Shay scooped up another stone, and pitched it. The two of

them tracked it as it soared across the water and plummeted with a loud 'plop' into the sea after the count of five.

Casey clapped in delight. 'Yes, I won,' she said, kicking at the sand, and doing a ridiculous dance.

'Do you always take things so seriously? It's just a waterside game,' he said.

'Of course, why do it otherwise?' she said, and kicked the water so it splashed all over him.

Not to be outdone, Shay reached down, and scooped up the seawater, hurling it at Casey, hitting her in the face. They splashed each other fiercely, Casey screaming and laughing as she held onto him, dragging him down with her; both of them now soaking wet.

For a moment he held on to her and she thought he was going to kiss her, but they saw Debbie and Marvin walk across the strand towards them.

Quickly, they got to their feet, and out of the water.

'How are we going to explain this one?' Shay asked.

'We don't have to explain anything. If you start explaining, you have already lost. Haven't you ever heard that?'

He looked into her eyes, and she wanted him to kiss her, but instead she nervously readjusted the straps of her sundress which had fallen down, and started to walk up the beach towards Debbie.

Shay waited a few moments before following behind.

Casey, her clothes sticking to her, smiled broadly at Debbie and Marvin.

'Look at you two,' she said.

Debbie shook her head. 'Darling, we are quite tame compared to the two of you. Whatever were you doing, frolicking like kids?'

'You should try it, it's good fun,' Casey said walking past the two of them.

Shay told her to wait up as he stopped, and asked Marvin if he needed a ride back to the mainland.

Casey saw Debbie blush and say Marvin was staying on Scarty.

'Go home, and change,' she said, before turning to Casey, and in her bossy voice adding, 'I knew we couldn't manage without a dryer.'

Casey and Shay made their way along the strand.

'Do you want to come and dry off a bit at the house?' Casey asked, and had to hide her disappointment when Shay said he was fine; he had clothes in the boat, and he had to get home to prepare for the lunch rush.

At the top of the path, he took her hand, and kissed it.

'I haven't had such fun in a long time. You make me laugh, and I thought I would never do that again.'

Embarrassed, Casey blushed, and said she had enjoyed it, too, even if they'd ended up in the sea.

She watched him as he made his way back to the jetty, and she waited beside the foxglove bank to wave him off.

As Shay's boat chugged across the channel to the mainland, she rubbed her hand and felt again the tingle of his gentle kiss, and she wondered what was to become of the two of them. She had not spoken properly to Gary in so long, and she didn't want to. But life as she knew it here on Scarty would come to an end soon, and she didn't know what she was going to do after that.

She wished she could have gone across to the mainland with Shay, spend time talking to him, helping out in the restaurant and be part of the mainland life. Life on an island was everything she expected, but there were times that even she wanted to escape, and her friends, who no doubt were going to quiz her about Shay.

Casey just hoped the arrival of Marvin would be enough to distract attention away from the subject of Shay and Casey.

She liked the sound of that. *Shay and Casey.*

TWENTY-TWO

Casey had changed, and was sitting trying to write in her journal when Georgie came back.

'How come Shay left so fast?' she asked.

'He had to get back for the lunchtime rush.'

'Pity, you two were getting along so well,' Georgie said, slipping in beside Casey on the outside bench. Casey held on tight to her journal because she suspected Georgie would try and take it.

'Writing about the great Shay Kennedy?' Georgie said.

'No, if you must know I was trying to make notes for an upcoming Zoom meeting with work,' Casey said frostily.

'You obviously think I came down Fifth Avenue in a bucket,' Georgie said, and Casey laughed.

'What does that mean?'

'I am just giving an American twang to May's phrase.'

'What?'

'Haven't you heard her? "Do you think I came down the River Fergus in a bucket?", which I believe is a big river in this county. Hudson didn't work for me. So I changed the context a little. You're touchy.'

'Haven't you heard, we have a visitor.'

'But there is no room, what are you talking about?'

'Debbie's Marvin?'

'No.'

'Yes,' Casey said as they heard the voices of the couple as they walked across the grass to the front of the house.

'I never even liked him,' Georgie hissed as they came near holding hands.

Debbie's smile quickly faded as she took in Georgie's put-out expression. Casey held her breath, praying Georgie would hold her tongue.

'Well, has anyone anything to say?' Debbie asked.

Georgie trounced off into the kitchen.

'She is just upset she didn't know until now,' Casey said.

'She is worse than our teenage sons. I didn't even know myself,' Debbie said.

Debbie and Marvin sat on the bench opposite Casey, blocking her view of Kennedys across the shore.

'You don't mind, do you, if Marvin stays tonight? He is booked to fly home on Friday, and we will probably stay on the mainland on Thursday night.'

'You're not leaving, are you?' Casey said.

'No, Rosie asked me to stay until the end of August, and that is what I intend to do.'

Marvin reached across and took Casey's hand. 'I have realised what an idiot I was. Maybe your Gary will do the same.'

Casey scowled, and made a face at Debbie.

Debbie pulled Marvin's hand back. 'Marvin, we talked about this; stay out of everybody else's business. We have enough to be sorting out ourselves.'

He shrugged. 'My humble apologies,' he mumbled.

Georgie stuck her head out the front door. 'Wouldn't you

guys be more comfortable on the mainland? Rosie never intended for any partner or husband to be here,' she said.

Debbie stood up, and Casey got between herself and Georgie.

'Guys, it's just one night; we can work something out,' Casey said.

'It's just meant to be us three and the tin box,' Georgie said, her voice angry.

'And it will be when Marvin goes back to the States,' Debbie said, her tone firm and her eyes staring Georgie down.

Georgie didn't move. 'I don't like this,' she said.

Casey put her arms around her. 'We can manage,' she said.

Marvin stood up, and said he was going for a walk to give them time to talk. He slipped away quietly as Debbie sat on the bench opposite Casey and Georgie.

'I had no idea he was coming; this is a man who doesn't like to go into Manhattan after 6 p.m.'

'So how did he find you?'

Debbie blushed. 'I told my boys where I was going, but I had them promise they wouldn't tell unless it was an emergency. They figured the way Marvin was acting was an emergency.'

'That was bright,' Georgie said.

'I had to leave contact details in case anything happened,' Debbie said defensively.

Casey reached over, and took her hand. 'You wanted him to find you, didn't you?'

Debbie began to cry. 'For so long we have been drifting. I wanted him to make an effort. I knew if he was upset enough one of our boys would cave in. For so long we have been drifting; I don't even know how I feel about Marvin any more. He wants to change his flight, and for us to spend some time together in Dublin.'

Georgie said she didn't want to hear any more, but Casey pulled her back from leaving.

'Don't, Georgie; we need to talk this out.'

'The decision is made; what is there to talk about?'

Debbie stood up. 'Georgie, I can move to the mainland with Marvin for tomorrow, and then on to Dublin.'

'As long as Marvin doesn't get in my way,' Georgie snapped, and whipped off the bench before the others could stop her.

'Stay, it might be nice to change the dynamic here,' Casey said.

'I would like to show him the island, and move on, and just spend days together like we used to in the first days of our marriage,' said Debbie.

Casey laughed. 'It will be more like a student dorm experience tonight in your single bed.'

'I really hope so,' Debbie guffawed loudly, before heading off to get a picnic together for herself and Marvin.

Casey followed Georgie. She didn't bother knocking, but slipped quietly into the room where Georgie was lying on the bed sobbing.

'Darling, what's wrong?' she asked.

Georgie got off the bed. 'Casey. you don't have to watch out for me. I'm fine.'

'You're not fine; I want to help.'

Georgie picked up a canvas she had finished the night before. It was a stoat lifting its head out of the long grass.

Casey looked into the eyes of the stoat, and she was back on the path; the stoat eyeballing her. She found her eyes once again locked in a competition of who was going to give in first.

'I love this painting; you have captured the stoat so well. I will buy this one.'

'Because you feel sorry for me,' Georgie said dismissively.

'No,' Casey said, turning about to face Georgie. 'Because it is a fantastic painting. What a reminder of my own encounter with the stoat. I want this picture.'

'Will you hang it in your Midtown apartment?'

Casey nodded. 'Once I get Gary out.'

'What?' Georgie said.

'I am looking for the apartment in the divorce.'

Georgie stopped what she was doing. 'You can't mean that about a divorce.'

'Scarty has allowed me to see more clearly. I don't want to be married to Gary any more, and I think he doesn't want to be married to me.'

'You can't mean that,' Georgie said.

'I mean it, and now I have said it.'

Casey walked across to the window. The sea was a dull colour today, reflecting the sudden overcast sky. It mirrored her mood. Georgie was right about one thing, though, this place had changed her. Now she saw everything more clearly.

'What will you do at work if you divorce Gary?'

'I'm his boss, I think it might just be his problem, not mine,' Casey spat out.

Georgie exhaled, as if she were surprised at the venom in Casey's voice. 'Go girl, go, be happy,' she said.

'I wish I knew how,' Casey answered, only realising when she heard herself say the words that she had spoken out loud.

Georgie joined her at the window. They watched Debbie and Marvin head off across the fields to the far side of the island; Debbie wearing a wide-brimmed sun hat, and Marvin struggling with a big picnic basket.

'Who would have thought it would be Debbie's boring old man who would travel across the world to find her?' Georgie said.

'I don't want my hotshot husband to arrive; I might just kick him in the sea,' Casey said, and they chuckled together.

Georgie shook herself. 'I don't have that luxury of thinking like that.'

Casey pulled away from the window. 'I'm sorry, I didn't mean to be insensitive.'

'It's OK, it hurts; that's all.'

'Why didn't you tell us?'

Georgie sat on the bed. 'I can't talk about it, Casey, and please don't tell Debbie; I couldn't face her cross examination.'

'I think if she knew, she would go easier on you.'

'She met Will once; she didn't approve.'

'I never met him.'

'After Debbie, he said he was not going through another cross examination.'

'I wish I had known, Georgie; I would have helped.'

'Nobody could have helped. Shit happens.'

Georgie had started to pack up her paints in her holdall bag when she suddenly let it drop to the floor.

'Do you think we could get off this bloody island for a while? I could kill for a burger and fries.'

'We could raise the flag , though Shay might think Marvin has attacked us all.'

'But it will mean he will come over.'

Casey set off down the stairs. 'Let's do it now, and we can leave a note for Debbie and Marvin. They can have the house to themselves tonight.'

They scuttled down the stairs like two kids, and raised the flag on the pole at the front of the house. Then they sat quietly, and waited, checking every few minutes through the binoculars.

After fifteen minutes, Georgie banged on the bench, and said Dan had come out to check.

'We can pack an overnight bag and get ready – he will be leaving soon,' she said.

'How do you know?' Casey asked.

'Because we have an understanding; he waves in a friendly fashion if it's OK to sail,' she said, waving vigorously back.

She ran off to get ready, and Casey opened a bottle of whiskey, and took a long swig from it. She smiled to herself that she'd ever thought life on the island might be dull. Maybe it was monotonous at times, but with these two women there was always some drama. She wanted to run to the highest point on the island, and scream at the top of her voice, but instead she sat at the table and put her head in her hands and sobbed. She cried tears over Georgie's husband whom she had never met, and for her own marriage which had died a long time ago.

She swiped away her tears when she saw Georgie come down the stairs.

'I knew I shouldn't have told you, Casey. You were always the one in the group who cared so much for everyone else.'

Casey looked at her. 'Obviously not – in the last few years I didn't even know Rosie was ill.'

'Stop beating yourself up. Let's party.'

They heard the chug of Shay's boat, and Casey ran upstairs to grab some clothes, while Georgie left a note for the others on the kitchen table.

By the time they were on the path down to the jetty, Shay was halfway across.

'What did you say in the note?' Casey asked.

'I said we had been invited to a party, and see them in a day or so?'

'You didn't?'

'I sure did; I wasn't going to admit we were off for burger and fries,' she laughed.

When Shay pulled up beside the jetty, Casey joined him in the wheelhouse.

'Giving Debbie and hubby some time on their own?' he asked.

'More like we need to escape, and see something other than island life.'

'And there was I thinking you might never leave the island,' he said.

She didn't answer, but sat watching the late sun streaks glitter across the sea, happy to be moving to the mainland, and let the breeze fall around her face, and calm her down.

At Ballymurphy, Dan was waiting at the quayside.

'We have just got a request for twenty for dinner. Can you do it?' he asked Shay.

'Tonight? It's short notice. I don't think I have the staff.'

Georgie tapped Shay on the shoulder. 'We can do it as long as you do us a burger and fries first.'

'I am not sure we would know what to do,' Casey said.

Dan took her by the elbow. 'Just follow my lead, and write down everything. Ignore Shay because he will be like a demon until he sorts out the menu.'

'Have we twenty covers spare?' Shay asked as he tied up the boat.

'We will make room. I have opened up the conservatory to take the overflow,' Dan said.

Shay turned to Casey. 'Are you sure? It will mean you will have to stay overnight, because it will be too late by the time we finish to get ye back to the island.'

Georgie thumped Shay on the back. 'Lead the way, she's going to love it,' she said.

TWENTY-THREE

It had been such a busy evening. Two busloads of American tourists pulled up, and ten people also walked in from the street for dinner. Dan took care of the wine list, and he and Georgie took the orders while Casey worked alongside Shay getting out the plates of food. At one stage he pulled her up, when she put too much mashed potato beside the bacon and cabbage.

'Small portions, please. There are a lot of plates to cover, and these are not farmers in from the field,' he said, but she detected a little irritability in his voice.

From time to time, he barked out orders to stack the dishwashers or get salad on the starter plates, but overall they worked well together until a special order came in from two in the American group.

Georgie sidled in, and whispered to Casey that two customers asked could the chef make a special order. They were craving a steak burger and fries.

'Like you can rustle that up from nowhere,' Casey said.

'What is it?' Shay snapped.

Casey took a deep breath. 'There is a lovely elderly couple

out there, and they want a good burger and fries, the thin chips like...'

'Back home?'

'Yes, Georgie said they are a pair of old dears.'

'And I bet she told them I had rustled up the same such meal for you two.'

'Maybe, I don't know.'

'Looks like I have to do burger and chips when I am trying to feed twenty-eight other people gourmet meals.'

'Yes, please.'

'And what if the others see them get preferential treatment?'

Casey slapped down a tea towel. 'Have you ever travelled far away, Shay, and just wanted a taste of home? Give them a break. They said they will pay double, for the hassle caused.'

'You buried the lead there,' he said, smiling.

'Get Georgie to explain to them it will take a while, because I have to make the burgers and chips from scratch, and ask if they want pickle and homemade ketchup.'

'Maybe we could offer them a drink or a tea to tide them over until their dinner is ready.'

'You really know how to eat into my profits,' Shay said, but his voice was kind.

Casey called Georgie, who whooped with delight.

'Tell him to do extra for me,' she laughed.

'I will not; he's already put out enough,' Casey whispered.

Georgie came back, and asked for a pot of tea for two. Casey offered to bring it out to the café, where the couple were sitting at a window seat.

The elderly man thanked Casey, and asked was she the proprietor.

'I am helping out over the summer.'

'But you're American.'

'Yes, here on holiday, and just lending a hand along with my friend.'

'We already talked to Georgie; she told us all about the paintings. Do they ship to the States?'

'I am sure it can be arranged, but let me check. Is there any painting in particular?'

'Three over there. Georgie is such a beautiful artist, and not a bad waitress either,' he laughed.

Casey rushed to the kitchen where Georgie was getting ready to serve the main course in the restaurant.

'You didn't tell me they wanted to buy your paintings.'

'I didn't know.'

'Three of them.'

Georgie squealed in delight. Shay swung around to remonstrate with her, but when he saw how happy she was, he stopped.

'Must be good news,' he said.

'The best. I feel a shopping trip to Galway coming on,' Georgie said as she pushed the kitchen door with her elbow, and headed off with three dinner plates.

Shay minced steak and made the burgers while Dan peeled the potatoes, and sliced the chips as thinly as he could.

When the food was ready, Shay came out with Casey to deliver it to the table.

He introduced himself, and thanked the couple for purchasing the paintings.

'Eat your meal, and take your time. I hope it lives up to expectation,' he said, bowing gracefully to the couple, who beamed in delight.

'You can be quite the charmer when you want to be,' Casey said.

'I couldn't have done it without you, Casey; I probably would have sent them packing. We are a good team,' he said.

He poured a whiskey each, and they clinked glasses. She held his gaze, and in that moment, she felt so happy.

'Now, time to get desserts ready,' he said, calling out to Dan to set up the coffee machine.

They all worked hard for the next two hours until Georgie summoned Shay and Casey as the couple were leaving with their tour group, and wanted to personally say goodbye.

Shay put on a clean apron before going out to the café.

The couple clapped when they saw him enter the room.

'The best meal I have had in a very long time, and that includes back in the States,' the woman said as she grabbed Shay's hand, and stuffed fresh bank notes into it.

'There is no need for that, it was a pleasure,' he said.

'You bring out these nice young women and have a drink on us; you've all worked hard enough tonight,' she said, giving Shay a wink.

The man asked for Shay's contact details, saying they had settled up for everything including the artwork with Dan, and they were looking forward to receiving the paintings in the next few weeks.

Dan, who was standing at the door of the bus, personally shook hands with all the tourists as they left.

After they had waved off the buses, he turned to the others. 'I hope I am included in that drink order,' he said.

'Unfortunately, we have to tidy and clean up first,' Shay said, and Dan grumbled that he was a slave driver.

Within an hour they had some tables set up for breakfast, and others for lunch the next day, and the industrial dishwashers had been stacked, and turned on.

Shay made a big deal of going behind the bar.

'Ooh, I would kill for a cocktail,' Georgie exclaimed.

'Do the Kennedy martini,' Dan said.

'We haven't mixed that in a long time,' Shay said.

'It was once the most popular drink in the pub,' Dan said, but his voice trailed off.

'We can have something else,' Casey said quickly.

Georgie pouted. 'But I want to try the Kennedy martini,' she said.

'How can I refuse considering all the work done here tonight?' Shay sighed, 'Four Kennedy martinis, coming up,' he said, placing martini glasses in the freezer.

'Oh, lovely. Proper martini glasses,' Georgie said.

Shay reached for the vodka, whiskey and vermouth before mixing them with the juice of fresh limes and using a sharp knife to slice the curly garnish.

Taking each glass from the freezer he made a big deal of shaking the cocktail shaker loudly, before pouring from a height, and placing the garnish on the side of each glass.

'The official taster first,' he said, setting a glass in front of Georgie.

Sitting up straight, she delicately lifted the glass, and sipped.

'Dangerous and perfect,' she said as Shay poured out the mix into the other three glasses.

He raised his glass to make a toast.

'To our dear American friends who have helped us so much, and brought such joy into our lives,' he said, and Dan replied, 'Hear hear.'

The little group were nearly too tired to talk. When Georgie said she was beat, and was going to bed, Dan also said he was off.

Shay looked at Casey. 'Being stuck in the kitchen all night means I like to go for a walk after the restaurant closes. It clears the head. Would you care to join me?'

They set off for the headland. Scarty was bathed in moon-light, the sea curling into the shore and lapping against the base of the cliffs. A blanket of stars hung low over the island, like it was resting on the roof of the farmhouse.

'I don't think I ever knew there were so many stars in the sky until I came to Scarty,' Casey said as they stood together. Shay looked pensive, and Casey placed her hand lightly on his arm.

'Was the Kennedy martini Anna's favourite drink?' she asked.

'Yes, I have not made it since....' his voice cracked, 'the night before she died we had a martini on the deck when the restaurant was closed.'

'You handled it well tonight.'

Shay gripped Casey's hands. 'The truth is without you around, Casey, I can't handle anything.'

He reached down and kissed her. She responded, but as quickly pulled back.

'Shay, I'm only here for another few weeks, and I like you very much. But as of this moment I am married, and I need to go back and sort out my life before—'

He put a finger to her mouth to stop her talking.

'It's OK, I understand, and I am here for whenever you want to come back to me. Just remember that.'

She pulled further away. She was so confused. She liked his man so much, but was it the magic of Scarty or the allure of this simple way of life that was swaying her mind? She didn't know.

'We had better get back, Debbie texted a while ago. She is off to Kilkee on the first bus in the morning, so it's an early start.'

'Before we go,' he dug in his pocket, 'you should have this. Another letter from Rosie. I should be giving it to you tomorrow really, but I figure a few hours can't hurt.'

Casey took the envelope gratefully, and held it in her trembling hands.

'Thank you.'

They walked back in silence. When they got to the guesthouse he lightly kissed Casey on the top of her head, and told her to sleep well.

There was no chance of that. Fingering the letter in her pocket she sat in her room, and wondered would the others mind very much if she read it. She needed to hear the comforting words of Rosie. The letters were a balm for her soul, and she required that right now.

My dearest Casey,

Where do I start? (And yes, Debbie, there will be a note for you too. It makes me smile to think of Debbie blustering like only she can, because of these special mentions.)

I am writing in my garden; it is where I feel closest to nature. Sometimes, the birdsong brings me back to Scarty, and if I close my eyes, I can hear the distant waves as they curl into shore, tipping against the sand before dragging back.

But I digress. Casey, are you happy? That is my question for you. Of all of us, I always thought that you needed Scarty, and I hope I have been proved right, and you have found your happy place here.

Casey, I wonder do you ever have time to stop and stare? Maybe you are asking yourself the same question now, and maybe you are examining how much your career has given you but also taken from you.

I know sitting here, my head bald and a colourful silk scarf tied in a seductive bow, I am glad I did not become subsumed by a career. There is no warmth in spreadsheets, and no comfort in box files.

Of course, I am not discounting the satisfaction you get from your job, Casey, as I'm sure Georgie does from her art, and Debbie from her interior design business. But please stop for a second, and ask yourself now, do you miss it? Do any one of you miss your previous lives?

I know from my own perspective Scarty concentrated my mind, and made me realise I had to confront the faults in my own life and marriage. Maybe Scarty has rubbed off, Casey, and you will learn to balance your wellbeing with your workload in the future. I wish that for you, and I wish that you may be sustained and fortified by the peace here.

My biggest problem has always been leaving Scarty, and trying to fit back into my more usual life. I would pine for Scarty. I feel that of the three of you, Casey, you will have a similar problem. I know you, and how much you like your peace and quiet. You will yearn for the stillness of Scarty, and I wish you luck with that.

All my love,

Rosie.

Xx

Casey lay on her bed, not bothering to even take off her clothes, but just slipped off her shoes before curling up in a ball. There was so much to think about. Rosie was right, Scarty had got under her skin, and she dreaded that this sojourn on the island would soon come to an end.

TWENTY-FOUR

Casey rubbed her eyes, and yawned as Dan drove her across the countryside to the church car park. Her boss, Harry, had insisted on a Zoom call at 6 a.m. US time. It was only 11 a.m. here in Ireland, but she had to get up very early to get across from Scarty, and to the church on time.

'You seem nervous?' Dan said.

'Harry doesn't usually jump on calls. I think he's going to fire me,' she said, her voice flat.

'Ah, it's hardly that. Sure you're brilliant,' Dan said kindly.

'I'm glad somebody thinks so,' she said, before turning away to watch the fields as Dan drove along the narrow roads. She wasn't going to agree to go back before the end of August. She was more determined than ever to see her time on Scarty out until the very end. What that meant in relation to her career was another matter.

The parish curate had a black jacket ready for her to wear, and the trailer was set up for her call.

When Harry appeared on screen, he looked worried, she thought.

'Thank you for breaking into your vacation, Casey, and I

have a busy schedule, and I will get straight to the point. I need you to come back to Manhattan now. Your team is floundering without you at the helm. I can't hold off the partners any longer. Gary has attempted to step up to the mark, but it hasn't worked out. He isn't you.'

'Thank you, Harry, but as I explained before I have to stay here until the end of August. I will return to New York then, and only then.'

'Is there any way I can persuade you to change your mind?'

'Harry, this is a promise I have to keep. I can't change my plans. It's not so far away, we are already into August.'

'You know the consequences, Casey?'

'I will have to cross that bridge when I come to it.'

'You are at the bridge now, Casey. I implore you to reconsider. We don't want to lose you.'

Casey didn't reply.

'What if I throw money at it?' Harry said.

Casey shook her head. 'Harry, I have to do what is right, and that means keeping my word to a good friend.'

'A dead good friend, Casey.'

'I know, but it's important to me.'

Harry threw his hands in the air. 'I'll see if I can perform a minor miracle to buy you more time. I will talk to the partners.'

'Thank you, Harry.'

He cut off the call, and she knew by the set of his face that he wasn't happy.

Dan was leaning against the bonnet of the car smoking a cigarette when she stepped down from the trailer.

'Well, what's the news?' he said.

'I have my job for another few days but I guess after that, I'm for the chop.'

'A lot can happen in a few days. Don't give up hope,' Dan said.

. . .

When they pulled into Ballymurphy, Debbie was standing on the quay waiting for Shay.

'What are you doing back here?' Casey asked.

'Unfinished business; I don't intend to let Rosie down,' she said a little too quickly.

'Time to go,' Shay called out, as he set off down the quay to the boat.

Quickly, they bundled Debbie's luggage on board, and jumped on deck where Casey joined him. Shay, who was in a hurry back to the restaurant to serve a late lunch to a group of tourists, helped them get the luggage off on Scarty pier, and immediately turned the boat for Ballymurphy.

At the farmhouse, Georgie was cross.

'I can't believe you read a Rosie letter without us,' she grumbled.

'I'm sorry, I was feeling a little down, and I wanted to hear her voice.'

'By reading a letter, that makes a whole lot of sense,' Debbie said.

Georgie told the two of them to shut up, and taking the envelope she pulled out the letter.

'Do we get to read privately, or do we go back to the old system?' Debbie said.

'Stop fussing; I will give it to you when I'm done, and anyway, this is all about Casey.'

'I suppose she doesn't think I am worth a letter,' Debbie said, waltzing off to her bedroom.

Casey followed her. 'There is no need to be like that; we have missed you.'

Debbie swung around, tears in her eyes. 'Did you, though? I seem to turn people against me. It's always all right for a while, and then it's not.'

'Where is this coming from? We have been friends too long.'

'It's Marvin, he's having second thoughts.'

'What do you mean?'

'What I said.'

'I don't understand... he travelled here from the States for you.'

'We went to Dublin, and he suggested we go on a cruise in a few months, and of course, I got enthusiastic, and started looking up and suggesting trips, and doing what I do best, organising everybody.'

Casey laughed. 'It is what you do best.'

'Exactly, but for some reason he took exception to it. Said I never ever let him choose anything.'

Debbie sat on her bed, and Casey joined her. 'This all sounds a bit silly.'

Debbie sighed. 'It's often the small things that show the deeper rot, and break up a marriage. We had a hell of an argument.'

'Surely he will come around; he will probably be on the next boat to Scarty.'

Debbie shook her head. 'He won't; this happened on our first night in Dublin, and he left the next morning. He even paid a whack of dollars for a flight, and flew out of the country saying he had had enough.'

'That was days ago. And you haven't heard from him since?'

Debbie took a tissue, and blew her nose.

'No, at first I stayed in the hotel hoping he would come back, but once the flight had taken off, and a few hours had passed after that, I knew he was truly gone.'

'So why didn't you come back here?'

'You know me, I am pig-headed, I didn't want to show up, and be asked a lot of questions in particular by the Kennedys, and maybe Georgie, so I stayed on in the hotel.'

'Aw, Debbie, on your own? It must have been dreadful for

you.'

Debbie snorted loudly. 'Actually, to tell the truth it was a relief not having to appease anybody else, and not having to pretend I was enjoying myself. I even met a very nice gentleman who was staying in the same hotel, and we had dinner together every evening.'

'What?'

Casey was going to say more, but Georgie burst into the room.

'I am missing something. You guys are whispering in here,' she said, pushing Casey, so she had to move up in the bed.

'Marvin has left me. Satisfied?' Debbie sniffed.

Georgie didn't say anything for a moment.

'You're kidding, aren't you?'

'No, I'm not, but it's OK, I will survive.'

Georgie moved to Debbie's side, and held her tight.

'He'll be back with his tail between his legs; he can't survive long without you.'

Debbie pulled free, and got off the bed.

'I tried to make a go of it; I really did. He had come all the way over here to find me, but you know what, I discovered he missed me all right. He missed the house being organised, the laundry being done and, having the fridge stocked with his favourite food. He had not done one round of laundry since I left. He had to deal with one problem with one of the boys all on his own, poor thing. You know what I realised: I missed home, and I missed my boys, but I sure as heck didn't miss Marvin.'

'She met another man,' Casey said.

Georgie clapped her hands. 'Let's all have prosecco, this calls for a celebration. Debbie has been bold.'

Debbie did a fake punch at Georgie as they scuttled to the kitchen.

'Let's go down to the beach; I want to get in the water,

throw off my clothes, and swim in the nude,' Debbie said.

Casey shook her head. 'Is your name Debbie Kading?'

'It is, but not for long. I am going back to my own name, Debbie Barnsley. For far too long I have been a good girl. That stopped in Dublin.'

'You and that man?' Georgie laughed.

'Patrick is a wonderful man; we intend to keep in touch after Scarty.'

Casey looked at her directly. 'Are you sure you're OK? This is not the Debbie I know.'

'Well, get used to it. I'm fed up with being the old Debbie who runs a business, a home, and never does anything for herself. I intend to have lots of fun starting now.'

'You do know you are stuck on Scarty with two other women,' Georgie giggled.

'Three, don't forget the tin,' Debbie said as they got ready to walk down to the beach.

On the way out the door, Debbie grabbed the tin.

'It must be getting pretty boring on that mantelpiece,' she said, stuffing it in her straw bag alongside the bottle of prosecco.

As they passed the bank of foxgloves and oxeyes daisies, she stopped and pulled one of each flower and stuck them in her hair with a clip.

At the beach, Casey expected Debbie to bottle out of skinny dipping, but she was first to pull off all her clothes, and run into the waves.

Shouting to the others to follow, she jumped into the waves, and swam out to sea. Casey and Georgie were at first embarrassed, but Georgie said, 'What the hell!', and tore off her clothes and Casey followed. They swam, laughed, and splashed each other.

None of them wanted to get back out of the water.

'I haven't felt this free or this good, in years,' Debbie said.

'Me neither,' Georgie piped up.

Casey was about to add her opinion when they all looked at each other in alarm.

'Was that the sound of Shay's boat coming into Scarty?' Georgie asked.

'Shit, what day is today?' Casey asked.

'Thursday.'

'Hell, it's a bunch load of tourists, and he always brings them down to this beach first,' Casey yelled.

'What will we do?' Georgie asked.

'For heaven's sake, we will get out and put our clothes on; it's nothing nobody hasn't seen before,' Debbie said, swimming towards the shore.

The others followed, racing each other to the strand.

They had just got to their bundle of clothes, when they saw Shay leading the group down the path towards the beach.

'Girls, throw on those dresses; forget the underwear,' Debbie instructed.

They hurriedly stepped into their sundresses.

'Mine is see through,' Georgie said.

'Of course it is,' Debbie said.

'Step in behind me when we skirt around the group. It's a longer trek back to the house, but we can head towards the jetty a different way,' Casey advised.

She saw Shay weaving in their direction, but she ignored him as they set off hugging the shoreline until they got as far as a steep path overrun with gorse.

Debbie swore, and said her legs were scratched to bits as they tried to hurry along the path. When they got as far as the jetty, Casey checked the boat, where Shay had left a box of May's scones.

'Have you any sketches you can sell to these people?' Debbie asked Georgie.

'You're sounding like old Debbie; I am ready, thank you very much,' Georgie replied, and Debbie said she would shut up.

They hurried back to the farmhouse. Casey ran around getting the benches set up while the others went off and changed. By the time Shay and his party arrived, everything was as it should be.

'How was the swim?' Shay asked.

'Fine,' Casey said, trying her best to sound normal, but she thought she saw his lips curl in a smile.

Teas and coffees had been served, and Georgie had sold almost twenty sketches when Debbie rushed into the kitchen.

Frantically, she checked the mantelpiece before tearing back to her room. When she returned, her face was pale, and she could barely speak.

Casey looked at her oddly, but walked out to wave the tour group off. When the last one had disappeared down the path, Debbie yanked Casey's arm.

'Where is Rosie?'

'What do you mean?'

'She's not in my straw bag.'

Georgie, humming a tune to herself wandered into the kitchen.

Casey stepped in front of her. 'Rosie is missing.'

'What are you talking about?' she said, looking at the mantelpiece.

Almost immediately, she gasped, throwing her hands in the air.

'I took her out of the bag so that she could see us being brave, skinny dipping.'

'You did what?' Debbie shouted.

'The tide, it comes in around now, doesn't it?' Casey said.

'Oh no, please no,' Georgie shouted as she pelted down the path towards the sea. Casey and Debbie followed, almost falling over where the surface of the path was uneven.

Georgie tore across the sand, shouting, and pleading for the tin box to be there and intact. The sea was rolling up the beach, circling the box, which had sunk deeper into the sand. Frantically, Georgie scanned the strand until she eventually saw it as another wave came in over it. Casey got as far as the biscuit box just as it dipped deeper into the wet sand. Lunging and grabbing it, the lid flew off, and water filled the tin.

'Is she all right, have we saved her?' Debbie squealed, panting and almost out of breath as she caught up with the others.

Casey pulled the plastic bag of ashes out of the box. 'It's still sealed, she's OK.'

'I would never have forgiven myself,' Georgie said.

Debbie shook her head. 'Look, it is just the three of us; don't we intend to put her in the sea anyway? It wouldn't have been the end of the world, not really.'

'It would have just felt like it,' Georgie said.

Casey looked at the tin box. 'We won't be able to use this any more.'

They wandered slowly back to the house, each taking turns to reverently carry the bag of ashes.

When they got to the house, Georgie found a cereal box, and they put the bag in it and back on the mantelpiece.

'I know one thing,' Debbie said. 'Rosie would have adored this; what a giggle she would have had.'

'Nobody moves the cereal box until we decide to scatter the ashes,' Casey said in a mock cross voice, and they all chortled happily.

TWENTY-FIVE

Georgie and Casey were out of the house early most mornings. Debbie complained the others were too busy, and she was expected to hang around the farmhouse doing absolutely nothing. One morning she was dressed and ready when Casey came downstairs.

'I thought I could help out at the café too. I have to set foot on the mainland or I will go barking mad,' she announced, and Casey hadn't the heart to tell her that the mainland was not going to be any different except for a lot of hard work, and busloads of demanding tourists.

Shay didn't say anything when Debbie hopped on the boat, saluted and said she was reporting for duty. He thanked her, but Casey noticed the arch of his eyebrows.

In Ballymurphy, May was making breakfast in the Kennedy kitchen.

'Debbie, there is a lot of hard work ahead today; I hope you're going to lend a hand,' she said.

'I can certainly try.'

'The two dishwashers need to be emptied for starters, there isn't a bit of clean crockery in the café.'

'I can do it, but I will need a coffee first.'

May straightened up. 'Debbie, we have our coffee and full breakfast once the café and restaurant are set up, the menus organised, the cakes baked, and the food almost prepped for lunch.'

'But I only wanted a quick cup.'

May gave her a fierce look, and Debbie set to work emptying the dishwashers.

She carried a tall stack of plates to the café, where Casey was wiping down all the tables.

'It's such hard work; I had no idea.'

'But we get the view, and the breakfast is usually good.'

'It would want to be five-star, and it still wouldn't compensate for all this graft,' Debbie grumbled.

Casey set down the chair she had taken off a table. 'You are the one who wanted to come over to the mainland.'

'But I didn't think it was going to be like this. I expected time to chat, and sip cocktails or even coffee.'

Casey got on with her work as Debbie disappeared into the kitchen.

She didn't see her again until May called them all for toasted sausage sandwiches, blueberry muffins and coffee.

'I made the muffins for you Yanks, a taste of home,' May said kindly, putting two on a plate, and pushing it towards Debbie.

'You're a slave driver, but I could get used to muffins for elevenses,' Debbie said.

Debbie first helped out in the pub, and then transferred to the café. Casey noticed she was happiest chatting to the customers, and was a dab hand at selling the artwork.

'Shay should get postcards specially made; they would be a nice little earner and maybe canvas bags with a picture of the pub or the island on them,' Debbie said.

'You can't stop, can you? You're always looking for business ideas,' Casey laughed.

By the time it came to go back to the island, Debbie said she was going straight to bed.

'You go and rest, and don't forget Shay left an envelope on the bar counter for you. It's another of those letters from Rosie,' May said as they left.

When they got back to Scarty, Debbie threw the envelope on the kitchen table, and said she was off to bed, but Georgie said they should read the letter.

Before Debbie had time to object, Casey ripped open the envelope.

'Finally, it is all about Debbie,' she said.

'What's the point, I have changed so much from the woman Rosie knew,' Debbie said.

Georgie began to read it aloud.

My darlings,

Finally, I have a few words for Debbie.

They are very simple. Don't change one bit; you're wonderful. Sometimes, you have been so single-minded, it has been frightening, but mostly we followed in your footsteps. It made it easy for us, that's why we always pushed you to the front.

Do you remember that time we were viewing an apartment in Chelsea and it was lucky enough to have a garden? When we stepped out we could see it was accessible to just about everyone in the district. I will never forget, Debbie, how you stood in front of the realtor, and demanded to see another apartment in the building. When he said it was too expensive for us, you said you didn't care, and with the discount he surely was going to give us, it was manageable.

It was on the third floor with long windows overlooking the street. Of course you got the biggest bedroom, but somehow that was OK as payback. It always seemed as if you were getting your own way, Debbie, but in fact you were the one who put yourself out there, and made it happen. That counts for something, in my book.

I am not sure how you are getting on at Scarty or even – by the time you read this –

if you are still there. Obviously, I hope you all are, and if that is the case, you, Debbie, will have thought up an ingenious way to get tourists to the island, and to part with their money. You are a born businesswoman. It is the most exciting talent, and you make it all look so easy. And you combine it all with being a mother to two boys, and running a thriving business. It all appears to come naturally to you.

What I hope happens on the island for you, Debbie, is that you step back, reconsider life, and do what is best for you.

I know you probably want me to shut up with my pontificating but before I go, I have to tell this one story, which I think Georgie and Casey do not know.

Remember, Debbie, when the two of us took a sneaky weekend away in Denver? What nobody knew was, I was struck down by altitude sickness, and mother hen Debbie looked after me for the entire weekend in our tiny hotel room. But Debbie, when we got back home, concocted such a story about our wonderful weekend that even I believed I'd had the most fantastic girls' time away. We had hair-raising stories about cocktail bars, and sneaking off to the slopes of Aspen.

Keep at it, Debbie; there is no one else like you.

Today, my doctor told me to get my affairs in order.

It means my next letter will, of necessity, be more serious. Never fear, though, sometimes I lie in my bed at night, and when I am not thinking of Scarty, I am thinking of the laughs we have had over the years. Tears, too – and remember when *we used to squabble all the time. I am not sure I even recall why we fought so much, but like any relationship, the making up was fun and for us, usually involved too much prosecco.*

What good times we had, dearest ones. Think fondly of me.

All my love,

Rosie.

Debbie walked over to the mantelpiece, and tapped on the cereal box.

'Hey, Rosie, you were really something,' she said, her voice full of tears. She turned to the others. 'I feel I have been well and truly scrutinised.'

'But by somebody who loves you,' Georgie said.

'She never got to know Marvin very well, but I imagine she might say good riddance,' Debbie sniffed.

'She never liked Gary; she told me he was using me to climb on my shoulders at work. She was right, but it took me so long to see it,' Casey said.

'It's often easier for the person on the outside to detect the faults,' Debbie said kindly.

'Is that why she brought us here, to make us look at our lives through her microscope?' Georgie asked.

'I suspect the next letters will give us a real answer. I feel she's been testing the waters with us, seeing how much we could take. In fairness, I never thought the three of us could hold out on this island for all of the eight weeks,' Casey said quietly.

Georgie put her hand up as if she were asking to speak in class, and Debbie looked at her quizzically.

'I suspect we are going to hear a guilty secret,' she said.

'I feel, in the interest of the sisterhood, I should tell you all something.'

Debbie sighed loudly. 'Oh, Georgie, what have you done?'

Georgie beamed brightly. 'I have a date with Dan.'

'Oh God, is it because he's a father figure?' Debbie said, putting her arm around Georgie's shoulders.

'Euwh, what sort of mind do you have, Debbie? No, once a week Dan and I have being going to Kilkee, where I have learned about the delights of what they call a chipper.'

'A chipper? Casey said.

'Fries, burgers and the most amazing battered onions and sausages.'

'What the hell do you mean?' Debbie said loudly.

'What I said, when he comes to collect me on Thursday at lunchtime it is to go to Kilkee. We chat a lot, and we usually stroll by the sea as well.'

'And you have been doing this for how long? Casey asked.

'Since the second week.'

'What?' both Casey and Debbie shouted together.

Georgie stood up. 'Hang on to your hair, it's not as if I have been having an affair or anything, it's just a bit of food. And you guys always thought I was painting, but a girl needs a break, you know.'

Debbie breathed in deeply. 'You have been having fries, greasy burgers and nuggets when we have had to put up with the odd meal that Shay has rustled up; fancy teeny-tiny burger buns with the best of steak beef. You are...'

'A sneak,' Casey said.

Georgie shrugged her shoulders. 'Honestly, I thought you would cop it much earlier. We're going today, if you care to tag along?'

'Wouldn't four make a crowd?' Debbie snapped.

'Don't be so sour,' Georgie replied, and Casey knocked her knuckles on the table.

'Girls, we have to get down to the jetty, there are burgers and fries waiting for us.'

'I'm not sure I want to go to the bother of going into Kilkee,' Debbie sniffed.

Casey laughed. 'Come on, don't be such a sourpuss,' she said.

Debbie answered it would take her ten minutes to get her face on.

'Who is going to be looking at us in Kilkee, for goodness' sake?' Georgie chuckled and Debbie slapped her on the shoulder.

'We haven't all weathered as well as you, darling.'

By the time they heard the familiar chug of the boat coming into the jetty, they were laughing and on their way down the path past the foxglove bank.

'This is so silly, I feel quite excited about going out for a meal,' Debbie said, and the others agreed.

If Dan was surprised to see all three women, he didn't say.

Debbie sat in the wheelhouse beside him as they set off around the headland.

'I thought we were going back to Ballymurphy, and going by road,' she said.

Dan smiled. 'This is better. Shay thinks I am out at the island.'

Debbie looked back at Georgie. 'She likes being out at sea, doesn't she? I am expecting great paintings after this.'

'Every week she has brought her sketch book, there will be great works of art,' he said.

After a while he turned off the engine, letting the boat bob on the water.

Georgie beckoned to them to join herself and Casey. 'Am I forgiven?' she asked loudly

'Maybe,' Debbie said.

'Good, because I have this,' she said, producing a bottle of prosecco.

'There's tea for Dan, because he can't be drinking and in charge of a boat,' she said.

Dan went off to make his tea, as Georgie popped the bottle of bubbly, and poured the prosecco into the three mugs.

'To our time out at the chipper and the great Atlantic Ocean,' she said, and the others cheered.

'Rosie would have loved this,' Dan said as he sat down beside them. They all fell silent for a moment thinking of their friend. 'She used to do this; come with me on the boat to Kilkee, but she wasn't into the chipper. We went to the pub for a pint of Guinness.'

'Rosie didn't drink Guinness,' Debbie said.

'She did, with a drop of blackcurrant in it; just a glass, but she loved it. She always said there's something very special about being picked up at your own island jetty, and dropped home afterwards. I often offered to stay awhile or walk her up to the farmhouse, but she was determined I get back to Ballymurphy. Once there was hint of darkness approaching, she was having none of it; she wanted us back safely on land.'

'Makes a lot of sense to me, I couldn't imagine being out here in the dark.' Debbie shivered. Dan took his cue, and threw the dregs of his tea into the sea, and headed for the wheelhouse.

Debbie, Casey and Georgie were quiet for the rest of the journey as Dan pulled the boat into the stone harbour at Kilkee. Casey thought Dan might be embarrassed to be seen with three noisy American women walking along Main Street.

'Maybe we can get takeout, and bring it back to the boat?' she suggested.

Dan seemed relieved, and they were a happy group chatting and laughing as they set off down the quiet street to the one place that was open.

They ordered burgers and chips; Dan insisted everybody have onion rings, and they bought a big bottle of Coca-Cola.

Wandering back to the boat, the aroma from the chipper

paper bags tantalised them, and the heat from the food made their hands sweat. Dan set up a makeshift table so they could sit at the back of the boat, and watch the evening sun streak across the water as they tucked into their food.

'Don't anyone please tell Shay, but this is heaven on a plate for me,' Debbie said, and the others agreed.

Afterwards, Dan said they should stay over in Ballymurphy rather than risk Scarty as night folded in.

'Won't Shay mind?' Georgie asked.

'He won't, and even if he did so what; we have the beds,' Dan said as he started up the engine, and headed out of the harbour, hugging the coastline as far as Ballymurphy.

'He definitely won't mind if you're there,' Georgie teased, nudging Casey in the ribs.

TWENTY-SIX

Casey got up early, and slipped out the front door of Kennedys. She had a lot to think about. She had got an email from Harry telling her he had a proposal for her, and she was to call him. It was not long now until August end, and she feared the worst news about her job.

When she rang, Harry sounded happy.

'Look, the partners say whatever it takes to keep you. We have a new client who has a net worth of more than forty million dollars, and he wants you to take on his legal work on behalf of the firm. He has got into a spot of bother...'

'What's the charge?'

'Possession of a small amount of cocaine, but we can fight it. There are a lot of red herrings, and dirt we can throw at the prosecution. But we can't do anything without our star lead attorney.'

'And what about my vacation?'

'Be back here on 3 September; get over the jet lag and when you come to HQ, you'll have a corner office with the partners prepared to vote you in immediately.'

'That's some offer.'

'Say yes, Casey, and come home. The partners are also throwing a lot of dollars your way too.'

'Sounds like I can't refuse.'

'That's my girl. I will email the new contract. See you soon,' he said, before ringing off.

She knew after this he was going to sit in his office with his feet on his desk, and sip a whiskey because the deal had been done.

She should be happy with the promotion and the corner office as well as the salary uplift, but in reality, she felt numb. She dreaded leaving Scarty; the job offer was a reminder that her time here was coming to an end, and she couldn't even imagine having to put on a suit, and sit at a desk in her Manhattan office.

She was walking along the street when Shay pulled up in his car.

'Hop in; I'm off to a country market. I could use the company for the drive, and I think you might like it,' he said.

She suddenly felt giddy like a young girl, and she could not stop smiling.

She got in the car, and they drove inland to the small town of Ennistymon. Shay parked just down the road from the market, and they walked there together.

'Do you mind that we stayed over last night?'

'Why would I, considering all the help you guys are giving us this summer; we owe you.'

The market was held in a large car park off the main street, and beside the river. There were three long rows of stalls, each selling food and produce. Many were offering free samples, and Casey stopped to try some homemade rhubarb and ginger jam on brown soda bread.

'Mmm, delicious,' she said, taking a second piece from the plate.

'If you want to have a look around,' Shay said, 'I am usually about an hour. We can meet up at the tearoom on the left.'

She was vaguely disappointed that he didn't ask her to tag along with him. Wandering between the market stalls, she stopped to taste some cheese and chocolate before she noticed a little path down by the river and the rapids.

Wandering past the rushing water, she liked the peace and quiet of the riverside path. Every part of her ached, but she had enjoyed working in the restaurant the day before, and when they got back from Kilkee later.

They had worked nonstop until midnight, when the last guest left, they had filled the dishwashers, and got the tables ready for breakfast.

When all the work was done, all she wanted to do was climb up the stairs to bed, but Shay had produced a bottle of chianti and his signature burger and chips for everybody. Nobody had the heart to tell him they had been to the chipper in Kilkee so they did their best to eat it.

They chatted like four old friends, and she wondered why she and Gary never sat and had a late supper and a glass of wine. Gary only wanted to eat out, but sitting up to the bar counter at Kennedys, picking at her burger and chips, she felt more at home that she had in years. If only she could be in this part of the world and keep her job, she thought.

Georgie had kept everybody amused with her stories from the world of art and Dan, who had spent many years at sea, told tales of faraway places. Shay seemed quieter than usual, and she worried that they had imposed on the Kennedys too much.

'You found my favourite place,' Shay said behind her, and she swung around, the sun blinding her so she had to scrunch her eyes to see him. He handed her a small Portuguese custard tart.

She nibbled at the tart, but Shay told her to have more.

'I was thinking of making them myself with a breakfast buffet,' he said.

She bit into the custard tart, giggling when it squelched and some plopped on to her blouse. Scooping it up with her thumb, she smiled brightly.

'Just the comfort eat I needed.'

'Better than burger and chips at midnight, I imagine.'

'I loved that food; I was so hungry after all the work in the restaurant.'

'Are you telling me it is easier being a top notch lawyer in New York?'

She laughed. 'I'm saying it is totally different.'

He sat down beside her.

'Anna and I always came to this market together, and wandered to look at the rapids afterwards.'

'I'm sorry, I didn't know.'

'How could you? And you found the river path on your own.'

'I was just looking for somewhere restful and quiet before going home to Georgie.'

'We used to walk along the path, before calling in on a friend for a bowl of mussels.'

'That sounds so lovely.'

'Would you like to do it? I have all the shopping done, and I checked my friend can rustle up a bowl of mussels each.'

She hesitated, and he looked embarrassed.

'No pressure; I thought you might enjoy it,' he said jumping up.

'I am sorry, it's just when you said you did it with Anna; I thought you wouldn't want to—'

'I can do it with an American I have come to like a lot.'

She couldn't say a word; they caught in her throat. Shay, reading the signals wrong threw his arms in the air.

'If I have overstepped the mark, I apologise,' he said, bowing to Casey.

He made to walk off, but she called him back. When he turned, she saw the frustration on his face, and she nearly backed away, but the old Casey who never let anyone get one over on her rose up, and she got up off the bench.

'I would like a bowl of mussels,' she said, continuing up the path.

She held her breath, only allowing herself to exhale when she heard Shay dash along to catch up.

She didn't acknowledge his presence, but he stepped in beside her, and they walked on, their steps in unison, their hands sometimes brushing against each other's, the river gurgling beside them, and the birds singing in the trees.

The path weaved along by the river, in places almost blotted out by overgrown ferns and tree branches laden with leaves. Every now and again, Shay stepped forward, and pushed brambles out of her way.

When they came to a makeshift seat, they sat down, watching the dragonflies flick over the water.

'Are you going to go back to New York, when this holiday is over?' Shay asked.

Surprised, Casey didn't know how to answer. 'I have to go back, my life is there – or at least it was there.'

'What do you mean?'

'I don't know. My boss has offered me a promotion when I return.'

'Lucky you,'

Casey kicked at the delicate violet-purple Veronica flowers.

'I'm not so sure. I love it here, and going back will bring its own problems, such as my husband and the divorce. Change of scenery, change of pace; it's what Scarty has given me.'

'What exactly do you mean?' Shay said.

'I have stayed in a bad relationship for too long. Coming here has made me realise it.'

'You need to go back, and live your life for a while to be sure of your decision,' he said.

She looked at him. She wanted him to ask her to stay, but she knew it was right; she needed to go back to New York to decide exactly where she wanted to be. But she was disappointed that he would let her go so easily.

'Are you ready for mussels?' he said, taking her hand.

He pulled her gently to her feet and along the path to a stile where they passed out onto the road.

A woman gathering flowers in her front garden waved to them. 'I hope you're ready to eat,' she said.

Shay introduced Casey to Miriam, and they sat out in the garden with bowls of steaming mussels.

Miriam eyed Casey up and down. 'I know a little about you. Rosie was a good friend of mine when she came here in the summer. We used to knock back gin, and have a laugh together.'

'I dread to think what she said about me,' Casey said.

'She said you were the clever one; she was very proud of your achievements.'

Casey felt disappointed. 'I'm not sure that counts for much as a friend.'

Miriam told Casey to wait a few moments, and Casey looked at Shay, bewildered. She went inside the house, and soon came back out waving an envelope.

'Rosie must have given my name and address to her attorney. A package arrived this morning with a little gift for me, which I will tell you about in a minute. Casey, there is an envelope addressed for you which she has asked you to open on the island.'

She handed the envelope across the table. Casey took it, but as quickly she dropped it. That Rosie had left yet another letter made her so cross. Why couldn't she have posted them to her instead of all this drama?

Casey wanted to run away, go back to the island, and not talk to these people any more. Instead she turned to Shay.

'You knew about this, didn't you?' she asked, her voice high-pitched with accusation.

Miriam put her hand on Casey's shoulder. 'He didn't know until this morning, when he was at the market; there isn't any plan to go behind your back.'

Casey picked up the envelope, and slapped it down again on the table.

'I don't know if I can take this. I just wish I knew why Rosie really wanted us at Scarty; and I am tired of trying to second guess it.'

Miriam reached into a large manila envelope. 'I want to show you what she sent me.'

Casey got up from the table, and walked over to the herbaceous border. Shay followed her.

'I can bring you back to Scarty tonight, and if you want me to stay while you open the letter that's fine.'

'What about the restaurant?'

'I can cook everything in advance, and leave the serving to Dad.'

She walked among the delphiniums, marvelling at the deep blue.

'I feel I should open it with Debbie and Georgie, just the three of us. You don't mind, do you?'

'Not at all.'

Miriam walked across, a heavy stone in the palm of her hand. 'She posted this all the way from the States, silly woman.' She placed it in Casey's hand. 'We used to pass it between each other. Whoever was holding the stone, which came from Scarty Island, had the floor. Anything said when holding the stone was a secret set in stone, and would never be told.'

Casey handed back the stone. 'I feel I didn't know Rosie at all,' she said, her voice shaking.

'You knew your version of her, and I knew the version she presented to me,' Miriam said.

Casey looked back at the woman, her intense gaze taking in every detail. She didn't want a version of Rosie. She wanted all of Rosie. She wanted the friend she'd always known, in front of her in flesh and blood, not in piles of letters or bags of ashes.

After a few moments Shay said they had to get back. Miriam drove them to the village market where they transferred to Shay's car.

'Are you OK?' he asked.

'I am tired of Rosie's games. I just hope this letter isn't going to turn everything on its head, yet again.'

'I doubt Rosie wanted to cause trouble.'

'Trouble, no, but I just want answers. Why go to all this bother?'

Shay was about to answer as he turned into Kennedys. Just then, Georgie ran towards them, barely dodging the front of the car.

'There has been a booking for two busloads of tourists, and they all want to come to the island too,' she said.

Dan approached. 'She's in a tizzy. They are due in an hour, but we can do it.'

'I am not so sure about that; are they looking for breakfast or lunch?'

Dan winked. 'All taken care of. Coffee and scones before a trip to the island where they will watch Georgie sketch and I will bring them on a tour. Then a return to the pub for a traditional Irish lunch.'

'And who is cooking that lunch?' Shay asked.

'The ham and beef are already roasting. The bacon and cabbage and the veg and spuds have to be done, but with Casey's help you should manage it.'

'Dad, I wish you'd consulted with me first.'

'What was to consult about? It's a hell of a lot of money to make in a few hours.'

Casey looked at Georgie. 'Are you ready for this?'

'I have about twenty sketches I can sell. Every morning I try and do a few before breakfast or before I go off across the island to paint, so I build up a reserve.'

'That's my girl,' Debbie said, before looking at Shay.

'Where do you want me?'

'We had better offer tea and coffee on the island, and have a batch of homemade biscuits, if you don't mind managing that end.'

'Sounds good, and if they want to listen to me, I might have a story or two to tell,' Debbie said.

'Exactly what I thought,' Shay said, and Casey had to turn away to hide her smile.

'Chop, chop, let's get to our stations,' Debbie said, clapping her hands, and nobody objected that she was taking over operations.

There was a frantic rush around opening up, preparing the tables and setting up the coffee machines. May walked up the road holding a tray of scones, warm out of the oven. Debbie was vaguely disappointed that the tourists were not from the States. One couple asked to stay on the mainland, and she directed them on a walk beside the headland, and the beautiful little boutique just along the street.

Casey, once tea and coffee had been served, went to the kitchen to help out Shay.

'Do you mind if I ask you to peel the spuds? It will be mash and roast potatoes for everybody.'

She tried not to show her surprise when a huge box of potatoes and two huge saucepans full of cold water were placed in front of her.

'I feel I should be in one of those black-and-white movies where the punishment is peeling potatoes,' she said.

'I know it's a dull job but it gives me a chance to get on with setting up the starters and deciding on dessert.'

'What about a crumble? I love your crumble.'

'I have those lovely apples from the market, and with a little sprinkle of cinnamon it should be delicious served with freshly whipped cream. Thank you, Casey, now I have to peel a huge vat of apples.'

'It's called getting my own back,' she laughed.

Shay put on some music, and they started peeling, Shay stopping every now and again to baste the roast beef and ham, and check on Debbie in the café.

'They are getting ready to go to the island. She doesn't speak French or German, but they all love her,' he reported back.

'Debbie would boss the King of England if he happened to come around this way.'

'And she would probably get away with it.'

Once the potatoes were put on to boil, and others in to roast, Shay asked Casey to join him on the deck for a break.

'The apple crumble pies are in the oven, and everything else is doing nicely, only the white sauce for the ham and the gravy to make, a few vegetables to prepare, and we are there.'

'To me that is a lot left to do, but yes, I would love a break.'

They sat looking out to Scarty, where the boats had already moored, and through the binoculars, they could see a crowd around the farmhouse.

'Will you miss the island when you go back to Manhattan?'

'I will miss everything and everyone. I honestly don't know how I am going survive without the sound of the sea, day and night. Sometimes, I don't even hear it now, and I have to remind myself to actively listen, because when I am far away from it, I know I am going to miss it terribly.'

He didn't answer, but went into the bar. She was wondering, had he even heard her, when he came back holding a small conch shell.

'It's not the Atlantic Ocean, but it's the sound of the sea. Listen.' He held it to her ear, and she listened, her face beaming with delight. 'Take it with you; it will help with the transition.'

'Where did you get this? I couldn't possibly take it.'

'You can bring it back when you're ready. I hope it makes you want to come back,' he said.

Casey didn't know what to say.

'Come on, back to the grindstone,' he said, tapping her gently on the back as he made his way to the kitchen.

She gathered up the conch shell, and followed him, very happy to be here helping out in the kitchen at Ballymurphy, and wondering how she could ever leave this man behind.

TWENTY-SEVEN

The last of the tourists had been waved off, and Casey was sitting with Shay on the deck when the phone in the pub rang. They heard Dan answer it, but when he called Casey, and arrived out with the handset, she immediately thought it was work.

'Go somewhere private; there's nobody in the bar,' Dan said, as he sat down beside Shay.

'Casey, what the fuck do you think you are doing instructing a divorce lawyer, starting the separation process, and getting an order telling me I cannot dissipate any of my assets? *My* assets, Casey, you were nothing before you met me,' Gary shouted.

Casey held the phone away from her ear and took a deep breath.

'Nice of you to make contact, Gary,' she said, smiling to herself that he had finally cottoned on to the fact that she was serious. The last time she was in Ballymurphy, when for once there was strong Wi-Fi, Casey had taken the opportunity to transfer huge amounts of money out of their joint account. This, she knew would speak Gary's language.

'I'm not going to talk about this over the phone. I will be back in the States at the start of September, and I suggest we leave it in the hands of our lawyers,' she said.

'We are lawyers, for fuck's sake. What is going on? You have changed. What the hell has happened to you over there? You know you're going to lose your job next.'

'May I remind you my job is none of your business, and in the workplace I am your superior.'

'Except you haven't been seen for weeks; how do you think that is going to go down with the partners?'

'Gary, did you ring for any particular reason or are you just going to threaten and shout at me?'

'Why separation and divorce? Can't we just talk things through?' he said, his voice dropping down a notch.

'What do you want to talk about – your numerous affairs?'

She waited, but he didn't say anything.

'Girls like to talk, I know about all of them. I am not going to live like that any more, Gary.'

'You are being unreasonable; all you ever do is work, work and work. What is a man supposed to do, for Christ's sake?'

'Be faithful, if you love a person.'

'Do you love me, Casey, because if you did, you wouldn't have gone on this stupid odyssey to a remote island?'

She couldn't answer. Her words strangled in her throat, and tears streamed down her face.

'What has happened; are you even coming back to the States?'

'Shut up, Gary. I don't have to discuss any of my plans with you.'

'This is not the last of it. You have some cheek doing what you've done. If you want a fight to the bitter end, you will get it, Casey.'

She stood up, anger rising in her.

'You can fight, Gary, but you will only get what is yours. My career bolstered yours for years, and I helped you get your promotion, never mind all the times I covered for you when you didn't bother to show up for work. Who the hell bought the Midtown apartment? You have not put a cent into it, and of late you have barely lived there. Scrounging off other women is what you do best. Think very carefully if you don't want your murky past put up in lights, and your name dragged through the mud, because that's what will happen.'

'You wouldn't?'

'You think because I have gone on vacation, I have lost my bottle. Take a chance on that, if your like, but I assure you any feelings I had for you died a long time ago, and this is merely tying up loose ends. Having said that, I do not intend to let you have anything you are not entitled to, and we are at war.'

'You're the one who declared it, Casey,' he said, his voice full of emotion.

'When you decided to run about the city with a young thing in a short skirt, that's when war was declared,' she bit back. 'Nobody will ever treat me like that again. You have no right to come shouting, and playing the high and mighty with me. Think of settling, Gary, or you could lose everything, and I am not just saying assets and property, but reputation as well. Think carefully before you take me on,' Casey snarled.

She ended the call, and sat on her stool at the pub counter, her head in her hands.

Shay came into the bar, poured a measure of brandy, and placed it in front of her.

'I'm sorry, did you hear any of that?'

'They may have missed it at Scarty.'

'Oh God, no, I apologise.'

'Hey, it was just me and Dad.'

She sipped the brandy, and grimaced.

'Knock it back, you need it,' he said firmly. She did, spluttering and coughing afterwards. He poured another. 'This one you can sip. Maybe, just maybe, you need to get drunk, Casey Freeman.'

'I need a separation and a divorce; how is it I could have been married to that man for all those years?'

'Well, I think he's a snake hiding in a hole right now. You can pack some punches.'

'Thanks, I think.'

'What you need is a break, some time out.'

'I am on vacation.'

'I mean a break from everything; let your mind rest.'

'I have been doing so much of that on the island, it has made me feel like I am going mad.'

'Grab your jacket. I know the perfect place, and it is not far from here. It's quite a nice drive by the coast.'

'I don't think so. I don't want to go where there are a lot of people. I know I live in a city, but I don't want to pound the concrete streets.'

'Do I look like a man who would like a trip to Ennis or Galway? As long as you are not averse to pounding limestone not concrete, we will be all right.'

'Don't you have meals to prepare?'

'It's only a pub menu mid-week for lunch, and Dad can handle it. He can call in May if he is stuck.'

'OK, then.'

'Nice to know you are so enthused by the idea.'

Casey had a thumping headache, and the brandy had made her stomach feel sick, but she needed to get away. She followed Shay to the Jeep and got in.

He rang Dan, leaving a long list of what needed to be done.

'We can do it another time, if you're busy,' she said.

'Don't be a silly goose, Dad loves to be fully in charge.'

They drove away from Ballymurphy, heading off down by the coast past villages and fields where sheep and cows grazed.

'So many stone walls,' she said almost to herself.

'Marking out individual holdings and fields; you're far away from the prairies of the United States now.'

'I live in New York,' she said, laughing.

'We're going to the Burren, the land of limestone where the fields are covered in thick slabs of stone and the wildflowers fight for the tiny bits of soil in each grike.'

'I have never heard of this place or of grikes.' she said.

'Ah grikes, the fissures between limestone blocks.'

'Awesome,' she said.

'It's where I like to go when I need to get away. It feels like a different planet. I know a spot off the beaten track, where I hike across the limestone, and wait until I can't see anything for miles, but the cold grey of the stone. Only then do I sit, and take my time,' Shay said.

He turned down a narrow road. 'There is no interruption, no social media, because there is no signal. It's a place to chill, let go or even scream as loud as you like. Nobody is going to hear except the odd pine martin.'

'Sounds so good,' Casey said.

Shay pulled in at a small village shop.

'They do the best homemade sandwiches here, and I have a flask of tea for us,' he said, hopping out of the Jeep before she had a chance to answer.

He returned just as quickly. 'I got the variety box of different sandwiches. We will surely find something for you to eat,' he said, and held up two bags of crisps.

'It's a long time since I had chips.'

'Crisps, Tayto crisps; you have to try them, and after you have walked over the rocky land and jumped all the gaps, you will be very glad of them.'

For the next part of the journey, she closed her eyes. She wasn't sleeping, but she was tired of looking, and seeing new things. Her mind was jaded, and she was so upset after Gary's phone call. What had she ever seen in him? Was it just his charm that had lured her in, and she stayed, liking the fact that they worked together? They had a lot of work wins at the start of their relationship, and that fuelled the attraction between them. It was almost as if their marriage was one of extreme convenience. Their wedding had been a huge affair with the partners in the company invited. She didn't know how they would view the separation, and at this stage she didn't really care. When she returned to New York, she wasn't sure if she wanted to stay in this job, which sucked the life out of her.

She must have nodded off, but Shay shook her gently to wake her.

'Here we are, sleepy head.'

'Sorry, I—'

'Don't apologise. Come on, you need to walk.'

'Are we leaving the car here on the side of the road?'

'It's OK, we can cross into the fields over the gate further up.'

'We're not going to get a parking ticket out here, are we?'

'I don't even think a garda car would be seen around these parts – too much to do in the big metropolis of Ennis,' he laughed.

He stuffed the sandwiches, the flask of tea and the Tayto crisps into a rucksack and swung it over his shoulder before setting of up the road.

Casey found she had to rush along to keep up with him. At the gate, he asked her was she OK to climb it.

'I may be a city girl, but I can climb an old farm gate,' she said, her voice a little cross.

They got over the gate and walked through a small glade which opened up into a wide plain of stone. It was as if somebody had come along and roughly tiled the field.

'Limestone as far as the eye can see. Careful of the gaps between the limestone slabs, nasty if your foot gets caught.'

They walked on, Casey falling behind when she stopped to

take it all in. The sheer amount of grey stone ran for miles, interspersed with green pockets, where there was some grass and brightly coloured flowers.

'How can anything grow here?' she said.

'When you look at it first, you think nothing could live here, but this is a biodiverse area where all sorts of plants thrive. My favourite is the blue spring gentian – maybe if you came back it the spring, we can find it together.'

'We'll see but how can anyone farm this land?' she asked quietly,

'It is an ancient type of farming in these parts, but it works well. The cattle are kept outside even in the winter months.'

Casey bent down to touch a red-purple cranesbill flower sticking up from a tiny patch of grass between two rocks.

'Don't pick the flowers.'

'I wasn't going to, but it is so delicate and seems to be thriving on a tiny scoop of soil.'

She dusted her hands on her jeans, leaving the flower intact. They walked on until they reached what Shay called his special luncheon table. The limestone slabs spread out as far as the eye could see.

'It's like being on another planet, if this is what Mars is like,' she said.

'It is even better in the rain; you need good footwear, but the limestone changes to a dark grey, and glimmers with a bluish tint.'

'I didn't think anywhere could beat Scarty, and here it is.'

'Just down the road.'

He began to set up their sandwiches and drinks on a slab of limestone while she wandered off to be on her own.

She wasn't sure she would have walked so far into the limestone by herself; in a new city, she would have been afraid of getting lost, and not making it back to the car, but here she knew Shay would find her, and she liked that.

There was something so reassuring and solid about him. Shay didn't care either how he appeared to others. He was who he was, and she loved that about him. Gary, in comparison, was all show and no substance. If he were in Texas, they would say big hat, no cattle. She wondered, had she ever really loved Gary, or had she persuaded herself because they worked so well together?

She heard Shay calling her name, and she turned around to walk back to him. She hurried and her toe caught a gap in the rocks and she went flying. Within minutes, Shay was beside her.

'I shouldn't have shouted out your name. Are you hurt?' he said.

'Just a few scratches and, a bruised ego,' she said as he helped her to her feet.

He continued to hold her hands, and pulled her close reaching down to kiss her.

She responded, before quickly pulling away.

'It's not a good time for me; the separation and...'

'I'm sorry, I know,' he said taking her hand, and leading her back to their limestone lunch table.

'Did you and Anna come here?' she asked.

'No, we never did. It's the classic thing, when it's your own backyard you don't ever have time to visit. But after she died, I needed to find some time for myself, and discovered this place. One day, I allowed myself to scream, and get angry, and the limestone sucked it all in. I heard the sound of my anguish echo across this land, and I realised there and then, I could continue with life or continue to scream. From that day on, I threw myself into the business, and I came to accept Anna's death in some way. The opening of the café under your guidance has been that last step.'

He opened a packet of crisps, and offered her one. The sound of them crunching the crisps seemed loud.

'Mmm... good,' she said.

When they heard a long screech, Casey froze. 'What was that?'

'A sparrowhawk scanning the countryside for prey.'

Casey shook herself.

'It's a bit too close to nature out here.'

Shay laughed. There was a flutter of noise from smaller birds before everything went silent.

'They know he is scouting, looking for lunch.'

Casey grabbed her sandwich and crisps.

'Don't worry, he won't come near us,' Shay said.

There was a loud anguished tweet.

'Looks like the sparrowhawk just got what he was looking for,' Shay said.

'Life is so tough here in the countryside,' Casey said, pushing her sandwich away. She suddenly did not feel so hungry any more.

'No worse than the city,' Shay said, as he began to pack up. 'Has it helped being out here? If you want a good old scream, feel free.'

'I don't need to scream,' she muttered, 'I just need to make sure I end up with everything that is rightfully mine.'

'That sounds like bitter thinking. Wouldn't it be better if you talk it through? My experience is that bitterness over time eats you from the inside out.'

Bitterness? She walked on, a little annoyed at his suggestion. When he called after her, she didn't respond.

He followed her.

'I am all for a long walk, but the route you are taking is away from the car,' he said. She turned back, avoiding his eyes, and rushed along to reach the road.

TWENTY-EIGHT

Debbie and Georgie were sitting on the deck when they got back to Kennedys.

'Nice of you guys to invite us for the spin,' Debbie said, gathering up her straw bag. 'Do you think you can bring us home to Scarty now?' she added.

'After I have given ye enough food to last a few days, and there may be a few bottles of prosecco,' Shay said.

'You're a charmer; but I am still annoyed we had to wait so long for the ride home,' Debbie said as she began to tramp down the quay to the boat.

Casey went with Shay to pack up the food while Georgie finished a Scarty sketch. They saw Debbie walk purposefully down the quay, and get on Shay's boat, settling herself down at the back.

'Let's get the lady home,' Shay said, packing the food in a big box before leading the way down the quay.

When he got on board, Debbie snorted as if she was tired of waiting.

Casey sat beside her. 'Is there something wrong?'

Debbie gripped Casey's hand. 'I should say there is. I want to get back to Scarty, so I can sort my head out.'

'Has something happened?' Georgie said.

'Look, I read Rosie's letter. Like Casey, I was feeling a bit down, and I wanted to hear Rosie's voice. I am finding it hard being on my own, and the boys emailed me and they are in bits at what Marvin has done.'

'But what was in the letter that has upset you so much?' Casey asked quietly.

'We will be at home shortly. Can we sit down, and read it together then? I can't do this here,' Debbie replied, tears bulging in her eyes.

Georgie made to say something but Casey told her to keep quiet.

'Let's wait; it won't be long,' she said.

When Shay pulled the boat into the jetty, Georgie jumped out and tied the rope around the concrete post. Shay offered to carry the box up the path for them, but Casey said they had got it.

'Are you sure, it's heavy?' he said.

'We're good. Thank you for a lovely day,' Casey said, gesturing for him to leave it.

Casey, Georgie and Debbie stood on the jetty, and waved him off. If Shay thought their rush to Scarty was a bit odd, he didn't comment.

'How are we going to get that box up the hill?' Casey said.

Debbie picked out a bottle of prosecco.

'This is all we need for now, follow me.'

At the house, they pulled down some mugs, and filled them with prosecco.

'Can we please get on, and read the letter?' Georgie said.

Debbie took the envelope from her pocket, pulled out a sheet of paper and began to read.

My dearest ones,

I know you must be getting quite frustrated with the letters. I imagine Debbie has blustered about, and threatened to throw my ashes out with the trash. And Georgie no doubt has all but given up on me.

I can honestly say that after all this writing to you, and talking to you, I feel that we are the old band back together again. We are mature women who know our own minds, and we realise how important our friendship has been, and will continue to be.

If that is all that has come out of this letter writing, and your visit to Scarty Island, then I think we should all be happy.

However, now that we are back as the tight friends we once were, I must finally tell you why I need to have my ashes scattered at Scarty Island, and why 30 August is the day you must do it.

Stay with me a while, and let me explain.

Straight up, I wasn't always Rosie Brentwood. I was born Marian Rosie Murphy, and my birthplace was Ennis, Co Clare in Ireland.'

Casey gasped out loud.

'That's the name on the love letter,' she shouted.

Debbie nodded, tears streaming down her face.

'You have to hear the rest,' she said, and continued to read from the letter.

My father died, and when I was a teenager, my mother moved the two of us back to the ancestral home at Kilkee. It was not the happiest of times, and I was a wild child. I didn't listen to anyone, and when I look back on it now, I was out of control. My mother and father had plans to emigrate to the US, where my aunt and uncle had set up, and were doing well. All those plans fell apart once my father died. I was eighteen years old but really, I was a child – a wild child.

My grandmother said I was uncontrollable and complained 'I was walking the roads and would not come to any good'. I was lost and adrift. Nobody knew what to do with me, and my reputation preceded me. Funny, the more I was ostracised by my peers, the worse I became, and the angrier I got at the cards I had been dealt. During that time, I met Andrew Kennedy. We were the same age. He was a lost soul like me, but a gentle, quiet type.

He loved the countryside, and particularly the sea. We took to hanging around together. We kept it secret because we knew if his family found out, they would hit the roof. We enjoyed such a lovely lazy summer throughout June, July and August together. We swam, went fishing, and lazed around together. If people saw us, they took no notice, but mostly we stayed away from others because we just wanted it to be us. We got in the habit of sneaking off in Andy's boat to Scarty.

We were very much in love, and it was on Scarty that we first made love. I adored Andrew, and I know he felt the same about me. Never have I felt the intensity of love, I felt with Andy.

My heart breaks, and I so long for that love which is not weighed down by heavy responsibility and duty.

I think that summer, we thought it would never come to an end. His parents were so busy trying to run the pub that they didn't notice Andy was never at home, and never fully enquired as to why he was always out on his boat. I think they were also giving their youngest son a bit of space.

At eighteen, we thought we had it all worked out. My mother and grandmother believed I was meeting up with a girl who worked in Ballymurphy, and I got the bus from Kilkee every morning. Andy always took out the boat from the harbour at around 11 a.m., but he pulled into shore a bit further up, so I could jump on board. We usually rowed back well before sundown, and in time for my 7 p.m. bus to Kilkee, so no one was the wiser.

The days at Scarty were magical. We felt as if the world was ours, the ocean was our friend. Scarty was our secret haven. We felt free, running through the fields, skinny dipping in the sea, and drinking beer we stored in the old cave at the beach. We knew that the summer days would disappear; we lived in the moment. The great thing about young love is the belief that it will last forever, and the good feeling will last a lifetime. I wish I could have that emotion back for just one minute.

Life changed on 30 August. There was nothing at the start of that day to say how badly it would end. We met as usual, and I slipped on to Andy's boat. I had what I thought was a great idea to bring the boat around to our favourite beach, and we could push off from there, when we wanted to go home. It was an adventure manoeuvring the boat around the headland to our strand.

We dropped anchor, and dived off the boat. It was bliss. Life was as perfect as it could get. On the beach, we skimmed stones, laughed, and played tag. We talked for a long time about the future. We both wanted to emigrate. We wanted to go to New York. I told him his father expected him to stay back and help run the pub, but Andy wanted to spread his wings. He said in the big city, nobody was going to care, who we were or where we were from. We had our whole lives ahead of us, and we were so excited.

We snuggled and held each other tight. We fell asleep. When we woke up it was late, and the sun had set. Darkness was creeping across the sky.

We should have stayed on the island, but we knew we would get into so much trouble if we didn't return home. We could see the lights of Ballymurphy. Andy said we could bring the boat out further, and instead of hugging the island shore, we could just aim in a straight line for the lights.

Everything was all right for a while, until the wind started to rise, forcing the boat to the side, shaking it fiercely. The waves got bigger. I hoped the wind would drive us to the shore, but Andy was worried.

No matter what we did, we couldn't keep control of the boat. The wind and water seemed to find us all the time. We hadn't the strength to fight it. A big wave crashed over us, and we were nearly thrown into the water. I have never been so scared in my life. I was crying, and I think Andy was really scared, too, but he was trying to get us home. You have to remember that in those days there weren't life jackets on boats.

I prayed, and the lights of Ballymurphy were getting closer. I pledged if we made it back to land safely, I would never leave Andy's side again. I know he felt the same.

The angry sea and wind were all around us, but it was inky black, and I couldn't even see Andy any more. When a wave hit the side of the boat, and tipped it over, I was thrown clear into the water. I sank and sank, but I fought it, and kicked with everything I had. When I surfaced, I couldn't see a thing. I called and called, but there was no answer. To my dying day, I will never forget the eerie sound of wind and sea, but no Andy and no boat; nothing.

By the time I made it to the shore, I was exhausted. When I felt the sand underneath my feet, I screamed non-stop for Andy, making my throat hurt.

A man heard me – I think it was May's brother; he ran to me and brought me to their house. I kept shouting that Andy was out there. They got the coast guard out and searchlights and Andy's dad went out in his big fishing boat, but they couldn't find him. May rang my grandmother in Kilkee, and my mother arrived soon afterwards. She refused to let me go in an ambulance, but brought me home. I wanted to stay; wait for them to bring Andy in, but my mother was having none of it, and bundled me into a car, and drove me to Kilkee.

I remember grandmother peeling the wet clothes off me, and putting me into bed. I tried to get out several times, but they watched over me, and told me there was nothing I could do.

When daylight came and there was no news of Andy, I knew my life had ended. I wanted to be with him. I stole to the bathroom, and swallowed my grandmother's pills. The next thing I remember was being in an ambulance.

In hospital nobody spoke to me. I heard Andy's name being mentioned, and I knew everybody blamed me for leading him astray. When my mother came in later that morning, she said we were moving to America. Our family in New York had paid for our tickets, and we would chance it on a holiday visa.

I had only just left hospital, when I got the news that Andy's body had been found on our beach at Scarty, the boat shattered into pieces, washed up at different points.

We left for America the day of Andy's funeral. I wanted to go, to talk to his family, but my mother was emphatic that wasn't happening; she said the Kennedys didn't want to see me, and they would never forgive our family for what happened.

I never got to say goodbye; I never got to say I was sorry. The pain is as deep and as searing as I write this as it was then. I still have nightmares and flashbacks. I wake up and I hear him calling me, telling me I turned the wrong way, that I could have saved him.

When we came to New York, my mother took her maiden name, and I took my second name, so Rosie Brentwood was born. Before long, my mother had married a rich man, and life *appeared good, but all I wanted was Andy. I cut my hair, and dyed it blonde; I wasn't Marian any more; she died with Andy.*

I never thought I would go back to Ballymurphy and Scarty. I never told any of you girls any of this until now, because I had left that life behind, and to be honest, I was ashamed that I was the one who survived.

Andy was the better swimmer, the sailor. He was the better person. He should have survived. But when I met you three, I began to live again. I was nineteen by then, and you lot were still eighteen. Laugh about this, I was nervous you would think I was too old, so I pretended I was eighteen too. You guys mean so much to me. You will never know how much, but in those early days when we rubbed shoulders together, you kept me alive.

Barry helped me, too, and I made the mistake of thinking it was love, when all I wanted from him was the safety net he provided. It took me years to realise that, and it wasn't fair on him. He has been so good to me though this illness, even after we decided to divorce. I can't bear to tell him that I have loved only one man all my life, and he was Andrew Kennedy of Ballymurphy, Kilkee, Co Clare, Ireland.

I am too tired to write more. That is for another time. All I ask now is that you arrange to scatter my ashes from Shay's boat at sea, so that they may travel to the shore we both loved. It has to be on 30 August, the day we went to the island; the day my Andrew drowned; the day I survived. Thank you, dear friends, for doing this for me.

Please keep all of this secret for now, but can you please call Dan and Shay to the island, and give them the enclosed letter which explains everything. I didn't want to send the letter directly to them, I couldn't bear to think of Shay and Dan reading the contents on their own.

I want them to read it on the island, where I hope they can feel in some way close to Andy.

I should have told Shay and Dan before this that I was the girl who loved Andrew, but I was a coward. With you three behind me, I now find strength to do it.

Finally, I have the courage to explain to them what I couldn't do in person all these years. I have adored the Kennedys and my friends in Ballymurphy. I pray they will forgive me.

Hug each other tight, my friends. Scatter my ashes. Wish me luck that in the afterlife, if there is one, I will reunite with my Andy.

All my love,

Rosie xx

Debbie's voice was shaking. Georgie got the cornflakes box, and put it on the table.

'I wish she were here, and I would hug her. I don't want to hug the box, but it can be near us,' she said.

Casey refilled their glasses. 'This is all wrong – prosecco is a happy drink. Why didn't she tell us? All those years when we lived in each other's pockets.'

Debbie gulped down her drink. 'That woman carried so much inside her to the end. Does anyone else find this unbearable?' she said.

'Of course we do, but right now I can't bear to think how Shay and Dan will react to this information.'

Georgie downed a glass of bubbly, and poured another.

'Do we have to do this? What is the point in raising old ghosts? Can't we just leave it? They haven't seen the letters. This will break Dan.'

Debbie clicked her tongue loudly. 'The man needs to know.'

Casey sighed. 'Dan is a strong man, and yes, we have to do

it. It would be wrong to do otherwise,' she said, and the others reluctantly agreed.

Debbie pulled Rosie's box from the side of the dresser. Dipping into it, she pulled out the love letter and the black and white photo strip.

Casey carefully scrutinised the strip of pictures.

In each tiny photo the couple were fooling around, putting hands over their faces looking through their fingers, kissing or snuggling into each other. Now she was seeing them clearly, looking beneath the girl's heavy make-up and mop of dark hair.

'That's why we didn't recognise Rosie. Her hair is dark here, and there is no clear angle on her face.'

Georgie took the letter, and began to sob. 'I never knew she had been through so much; we have to tell Dan and Shay.'

'That's the next problem we face,' Debbie said taking the letter and photo strip, and putting them beside the cereal box on the mantelpiece.

TWENTY-NINE

Casey and Georgie sat at the table, not knowing what to do. They had been so tired the night before, everybody had drifted off to bed, nobody wanting to venture how they were going to tell Dan and Shay the news.

'I have to work in the café. Shay will be here in about thirty minutes,' Casey said.

'What are we going to do?' Georgie asked, for once still hanging around the kitchen, because she hadn't the heart to set off painting.

'We do the civilised thing, invite them for a light buffet supper, and we hand them the letter to read,' Debbie said, coming out of her room.

'But won't they find it odd to be invited to the island in the late evening like that? We know now they don't like to cross the channel at night.'

'I don't want them to chance it either. We can't have tragedy on top of tragedy. That would be too much to bear,' Casey said.

Debbie opened a packet of biscuits, and took two. When she next spoke, crumbs sprayed out of her mouth.

'Afternoon tea – tell Dan and Shay they have to make it. Anyway, its mid-week so there is no restaurant service tonight.'

'We should invite May too,' Casey said.

'And what if Dan and Shay want to keep it in the family?'

'May is family.'

'I think we have to be a bit ruthless here, and only invite Andrew's dad and brother,' Debbie said. Casey relented, not wanting to start an argument, she knew she wasn't going to win.

When Shay pulled up at the jetty soon after, she was waiting for him.

She sat at the back of the boat, not wanting to engage in conversation. Every now and again, she saw Shay check on her, but she concentrated on watching the water. The light breeze teased her hair, and the seagulls screeched overhead as the boat bobbed over the still sea. That this sea had swallowed up a young man, and destroyed a young love, was hard to bear, and her heart was heavy.

When they docked at Ballymurphy, Shay asked her was she feeling all right.

'I just didn't sleep much last night,' she said.

'Was the island too quiet for you? Sometimes the quietness leaves too much room for other thoughts to occupy the brain.'

'Maybe,' she muttered.

When they got as far as the pub, Dan said he had to drop May into Galway to catch the train to Dublin, and Casey breathed a sigh of relief that that problem was so easily solved.

They had served breakfast to guests and a tour bus which pulled up on spec at the café, and were taking their break when Casey invited Shay and Dan to afternoon tea.

'Don't shoot the messenger, Debbie is insisting, and was making fancy sandwiches when I left.'

'Dad should be back by the time we are finished here, and the three of us can travel together,' he said.

She was passing later with a tray of dirty dishes for the dishwasher, when Shay tipped her lightly on the elbow.

'It is almost as if we have been summoned to the island; you would tell me if there was anything wrong?' he asked.

She dithered. 'I would if I could, but the two of you should be there. Debbie is running the operation,' she said.

'Sounds like serious stuff,' he laughed.

Casey turned away, pretending to be busy scrubbing the hotplate so he wouldn't see her face.

She thought Shay must have had a word with Dan, because she was surprised when he agreed to the afternoon tea invitation without a full cross-examination.

'Should we dress up or is this a casual affair?' he asked.

'Just come as you are,' Casey said, her voice betraying her exasperation.

Shay and Dan were all talk as they wandered up the path to the farmhouse behind Casey.

'Not long now before ye set off back to the Big Apple,' Dan said as they reached the kitchen door.

'Please try not to sound so joyful about it all,' Debbie joked, as she dried her hands and gestured to them to take a seat at the table. The two men looked at each other, before pulling out the chairs, and sitting down.

'Why do I get the impression this is more than a social call?' Shay said.

'We have something to tell you.'

Dan slapped his knee.

'You gals are staying on. Right? I knew it; I said to Shay those girls love the place too much,' he said.

Shay laughed, and turned to Casey, his eyes shining.

Debbie raised her hand to stop any further talk, and said, her voice firm, 'You both need to listen to what we have to say.'

Shay dithered. 'Is there something wrong?' he asked.

'I'm not sure, but please sit down. Would you like tea, a glass of water?' Casey said.

'A glass of something stronger might be more in order,' Dan chuckled.

Shay told him to shush.

'Casey, it sounds like you have something important to tell us,' he said gently.

She took a deep breath.

'It's another letter from Rosie, and it is addressed to you and Dan. It was included with my letter, and she asked me to call you here to the island to give it to you.'

'What's the big mystery?' Dan said loudly.

Shay turned the letter over in his hands.

'I'm sorry, but she also asked that you read it here at the house with the three of us present, and of course, Dan,' Casey said, embarrassed to be making so many demands.

'It's not as if she is going to know,' Georgie said, but Shay ripped open the letter.

'Rosie was part of the family, and if that's what she wants, then that's what she gets,' he said, but Casey noticed the blood fade from his cheeks as he scanned through the letter.

'Come on boy, read it out,' Dan said, and Shay began.

My dearest ones,

It is with great sadness I write this letter because I know that by committing these words to paper, I am resigning myself to the final position, where I will not see Scarty Island again.

It has been my great pleasure over all these years to get to know you, Shay and Dan, and everybody in Ballymurphy.

My one regret was, and I think about this often now, that I didn't reveal my true identity to you.

You have been kindness itself to me, and I hope what I am

about to tell you will not tarnish the memory of our time together.

There have been many times I have wanted to speak to you, but a trepidation in my heart stopped me.

Of course, I know now that fear will never make anything better, and it is our inner strength that helps us weather the storm. However, I have come to that realisation too late.

Bear with me, while I tell you my story.

My second name is Rosie. My first is Marian. I was born in Kilkee and my name is Marian Murphy.

My grandmother lived off Main Street...

Dan jumped up.

'I don't know what's going on here, but I have heard enough. What sort of craziness is this?'

Shay pleaded with him to sit down.

'I don't want to hear anything a member of that Murphy crowd has to say,' Dan barked.

Shay ordered his father to sit back down, and continued to read.

I think my father used to sell fish to the pub. He drowned at sea when I was young. I was a wild teenager, which probably had something to do with losing my father so suddenly, I used to hitch a ride to Ballymurphy, and that is when I met Andrew first.

Dan banged his fist on the table.

'What in the name of the Almighty is happening? What does she mean her real name was Marian Murphy? That's the name of... it was her who was with our Andrew,' he trailed off, unable to continue.

Shay placed a hand on his father's shoulder, and pressed him to sit back down before continuing to read from the letter.

Andy had been to the dentist in Kilkee. He was walking home, and we got talking. I can honestly say from the word go, we liked being with each other.

Andrew made sure he had more time to hang out with me in Kilkee, and at weekends when my mother was working, I sneaked off, and got the bus to Ballymurphy.

When the summer holidays came, we spent every moment we could together.

Andrew was the sweetest, kindest person I knew, and to this day I have not met anyone that compares to him. We loved each other.

Shay's voice wavered, and he stopped to take his breath.

'Haven't we heard enough?' Dan said wearily.

'There's more. Let me go to the finish,' Shay said, as he quickly continued.

We were young, and we thought we could conquer the world together. We had plans until the Atlantic Ocean stole Andrew from me. I feel I have to tell you about that night.

We fell asleep and left it too late to leave Scarty, but Andy was sure we could get home. Halfway across the channel, the sky turned pitch black. At the same time, a wind erupted from nowhere; the sea became choppy. The boat was pushed around a bit, but then things got really rough. We were frightened, but Andy kept everything stable. That is until a wave tipped us into the water. When I surfaced, I screamed, and shouted for Andy. There was only the wind and the waves, nothing else.

Shay stopped, letting the letter drop on the table. Casey picked it up and began to read slowly.

The day of Andrew's funeral I was at Shannon Airport getting on a flight to the States. I was numb, and if Andy was gone, I didn't care what became of me.

I wish I could have been allowed to see him to say goodbye. When I got to New York my mother said we were having a complete new start with new names and passports. I became Rosie Brentwood.

In a strange way it helped. I didn't want to be Marian Murphy any more. I felt nothing without Andrew, without the reassurance of his love.

At least as Rosie Brentwood, I could invent a past, and look to a future.

It was only in relatively recent years that I began to confront my past, and I had an opportunity to return to Scarty. I had no family left in Kilkee. No one recognised me, and I was glad of that. I remember, Shay, you brought me out to the island, and you were surprised I wanted to spend time there.

That first day I walked to all our favourite spots. I felt Andy beside me, and I felt the most peace in my heart since that awful night Andy was lost to us all.

At Scarty, the memories come flooding back, and they bring me some comfort. At Scarty, I feel so close to Andrew.

Dan put up his hand. 'Please tell me that is it; we can't listen to any more,' he said. Then he stood up, and said they had to leave. 'There is only so much a man can take,' he said, his voice cracking.

Debbie moved in front of the two men as they made for the door.

'I know we've only known each other for a few weeks, but I think and I hope we're good friends. I knew Rosie for years, and I believe her that she loved Andrew like she loved no other. Just because it was a young love does not make it anything less.'

Dan made to move around Debbie, but she shifted to block him.

'I am also a parent, and to think that my boys have experienced the heady sensation of love would be a huge comfort to me. That she still loved him all these years later has to count for something, even with the pain and hurt of what you are hearing now,' she said.

Dan, his shoulders shaking, slumped against the cooker.

'All these years, we wanted to talk to that girl, to learn something of his last hours. Her grandmother said she did not have a forwarding address. I told her Andrew's mother was heartbroken, and she needed to know anything at all that would help. If she knew something of their relationship, their last hours, his last words. You know what the bitch did?'

Casey led Dan to a chair to sit down.

'She closed the door in my goddamn face. Just months later my Dearbhla was dead, and I know it was from a broken heart. She never recovered from the death of Andrew.'

Debbie handed him a glass of water. 'Dan, they were children; do you think Rosie had any choice in the way things panned out? Don't you think she was in pain? She loved your boy beyond anything to her dying day.'

Georgie took the cereal box from the mantelpiece and held it close.

'Dan, we love you. Can't we get through this together?' she sobbed.

He reached out to Georgie, and grasped her hand.

'You are a good girl, Georgie,' he said.

He nodded to Shay, who continued to read.

So you are asking why didn't I tell you all this when you could have asked me so many questions. I couldn't. Scarty Island was my place to dream of Andrew, to feel close to him, and I was selfish enough that I didn't want to share it.

My grandmother owned the island all along. I later inherited it when my uncle died and it was one of the happiest days of my life. All I wanted was to be back on Scarty where we had been so happy.

Then, I met you all and our friendship grew. It has meant so much to me, but I was afraid to risk hurting that, because it has sustained me throughout the years. As I got to know you, Shay, I saw you had the same gentle kind qualities of Andrew – and Dan, your son was so like you, it often made me cry to see the similarities. He had your can-do attitude and your stubbornness too. The glint in your eyes, I saw in his so many times.

If you were cross at me or didn't talk to me, I honestly don't know what I would have done.

Please don't think badly of me. Please remember me kindly as the woman who loved Andrew Kennedy all her life. In death, I wish to be reunited with my Andy, for my ashes to be scattered on what we used to call our beach.

Please join my friends as they scatter me on the ocean, so that I, too, may be washed up on Scarty Island. So that in a parallel universe, Andy and I can dance together once more again.

All my love forever,

Rosie. Xx

Nobody said anything. Finally, Debbie got up, and said she was making tea. Dan said not to count them in; they were off home.

Casey watched as he got up from his chair, and carefully replaced it under the table.

'Don't go, please,' she said.

Shay got up, and stood beside his father.

'We need space to think,' he said.

'She loved Andrew and he loved her and...'

'That is not at issue; what is wrong is that she never told us, never trusted us enough to tell us.'

Debbie placed the kettle too heavy on the hob. 'For Christ's sake, it was so long ago; they were kids. What did they know?'

Dan shook his head, tears streaming down his face.

'I loved her like a daughter, and she did not see fit to tell me,' he said, before whipping out the back door, and through the yard.

Casey put her hand out to touch Shay, and he hesitated.

'Not now, it's too raw for him; for both of us,' he said.

'But the scattering of the ashes is on Thursday, and we would love you to be there as per Rosie's wishes.'

Shay shook his head. 'Let me get Dad home, give him time to mull it over. I'll be back in a day or so to let you know.'

Casey made to walk out with him, but he put his hand up to stop her.

'Best leave us be for a bit,' he said, wiping a tear from his cheek.

Casey watched him walk across the cobbled yard, and her heart broke for this man who had endured so much in the last few years.

Debbie was scrabbling under the sink. 'I knew I had a bottle of whiskey here,' she said, pouring generous measures into mugs.

'What a lot of drama. Poor Rosie, loving somebody all her life and hoping death will bring her closer,' Georgie said, her voice watery with tears.

Casey picked up the cereal box. 'It's light for a life so lived, for the yearning in one person. It is so fricking light,' she said, putting the box on the table before slumping into a chair to have a good cry.

Debbie went to the back door, and pulled their hoodies off the hooks.

'Come on, let's walk to the beach; clear our heads, and

remember our Rosie,' she said, throwing the hoodies to Casey and Georgie.

Georgie grabbed the whiskey bottle.

'I have a better way. Let's build a little fire, and sit around it, and finish the whiskey,' she said.

Debbie clapped. 'Rosie would love that, and we can toast marshmallows.'

'If we had any,' Casey said.

Georgie reached into a cupboard, and pulled out a bag.

'I included them in a shop, but we never got around to eating them. We can put them on forks maybe,' she said.

They hastily packed the whiskey bottle, mugs, the marshmallows and enough forks for a family of ten along with two blocks of wood, a box of firelighters, matches and a small bag of little bits of wood to get the fire going.

They tied their hoodies around their waists because it was warm as they tramped up the hill to the highest point on the island. Looking across the sea, they saw Shay's boat pull in at at Ballymurphy harbour.

'I think they were a little bit dramatic,' Georgie said.

'How could you say that? Losing a child never leaves a person. That was raw pain on Dan's face,' Debbie said.

They set off across the fields, and the now well-worn path to the far beach.

'It must have been so exciting to be in love, and have an island to themselves,' Georgie said.

'Why did they have to hide it? Surely Dan would have liked Rosie.'

Debbie guffawed out loud. 'Easily said when you don't have children, and I am not trying to be hurtful, but I have never met a mother or father who thinks a boyfriend or girlfriend is good enough. And the younger they are, the more severe the scrutiny.'

'Also, you're not factoring in that Rosie was a wild teenager,' Casey said.

'And our Rosie, hard as it is to believe, was a bit of a tear-away,' Georgie said.

They tramped across the beach. It was quiet except for the cries of the gannets and puffins in the far-off cliffs.

'Who knows how to get this bonfire going?' Debbie asked, dropping the wood on the sand.

'It can't be that difficult; we have matches and firelighters,' Casey said as she angled the wood in a tepee-like shape.

Georgie pushed her out of the way. 'Do you know nothing? We dig a hole first. Come on, get stuck in,' she instructed as she got down on her hands and knees. The others joined in as Georgie arranged the firelighters and smaller pieces of wood in the hole and set it alight. As the fire took hold, she added the bigger pieces of wood.

'I will stay in charge of the drinks,' Debbie said, pouring out the whiskey.

'To Marian and Andrew,' Casey said.

'And Rosie and Andy,' Georgie said as they clinked over the flames.

'I am going to miss this place,' Debbie said.

'Me too,' Georgie piped up.

Casey pulled up her knees, and hugged them tight. 'There was something else that Rosie said to tell you all.

'Oh God, haven't we heard enough?' Debbie groaned, knocking back her whiskey in one, and refilling her mug.

'When I checked my email the attorney sent on a note from Rosie. She didn't want us to know until near the end of our time at Scarty but she has left the ownership of the island to the Kennedys. There is also an important codicil that we three are allowed to have the farmhouse for all of July and August each year,' Casey said.

'Which is going to be exceedingly difficult if the relationship has broken down,' Debbie sniffed.

'Let's hope everything goes back to normal – I mean island normal,' Georgie said, and the others laughed.

'Why didn't she tell us earlier?' Debbie asked.

'She probably thought we would appreciate the news more now that we know everything,' Casey said.

'I wouldn't be so sure we know everything. We're talking about Rosie and her secrets.' Debbie sniffed.

They placed marshmallows on the forks, and attempted to toast them in the flames, each sitting quietly, twiddling the forks through their hands as they got hotter to the touch.

'Do you think they can see our fire on the mainland?' Georgie asked.

'I hope they can, and it's a reminder that we are here, and we are waiting for contact,' Casey said.

'Way too serious, let's finish the whiskey. I am only carrying back an empty bottle,' Debbie chortled ,while pouring out the dregs of the bottle into the mugs.

'Tomorrow will look after itself,' she said, holding her mug aloft, and the others joined in the toast.

They tramped across the beach when the sky was dark. Holding hands and talking non-stop because they were so nervous. When one stumbled, they helped each other. When they got back to the farmhouse, they were tired and went to bed, not wanting to talk about Rosie any more tonight.

THIRTY

Casey woke up in the early hours. Her head was thumping, and she couldn't get back to sleep. It was a warm night so she stole through the house, and slipped out to the front to sit on the bench. The lights of Ballymurphy were twinkling even as the sun started to rise, washing gold over the waves.

It had been two days and Shay and Dan had not made contact. She was supposed to have been working in the café yesterday. She got ready, went down to the jetty early, and waited for Shay's boat to move out of Ballymurphy, but it didn't arrive. She held on longer than she should, because she didn't want to believe he wouldn't turn up for her. After more than an hour, she moved from the jetty. Feeling foolish, she avoided the farmhouse, and headed across the fields. Above her, a kestrel soared. She froze, waiting for it to go in for the kill, and was relieved when it appeared to move on without incident.

She sat down on the grass still damp with dew, beside a cluster of daisies. Letting her hand glide across them, she felt the velvet touch of the flowers, and was immediately trans-ported to the first time she met Rosie. She could see her now, all those years ago, sitting there surrounded by daisies. They had nodded to each other, and started making daisy chain bracelets, picking the flowers, making sure to have very long stems, and carefully making a hole on each stem with their longest nails. When Casey was finished, she put her bracelet on, and Rosie remarked it was beautiful. They had started to chat that day, and it was like they never stopped until Rosie got married, and moved upstate. Somehow, they drifted apart as Rosie settled into her new life, and Casey began to concentrate solely on her work schedule.

How she wished now that Rosie could sit on the grass, and they could work quietly together.

There had been so much noise of late; Casey craved the peace and quiet. Quickly, she made a daisy chain bracelet and put it on, before continuing along the high field towards the ruin ,and the path down to the far cove and beach.

The sky was yellow and gold; the sun sending rays across the sand and sea. She slipped off her shoes, and wandered across the strand. When she saw Shay's boat chugging across the channel towards the beach, she didn't know whether she should leave. She knew he must have seen her, so she stayed where she was. When she came across a group of rocks, she sat on the flattest stone, and watched the boat come in as close to shore as possible.

Shay jumped from the boat, and walked to the beach.

Casey regretted her decision to stay, but she knew if she moved away now, too much could be written into the gesture.

When Shay signalled to her, she waved back. She sat, and waited for him to approach. Walking with his head down, and with the sun behind him, she thought he struck a lonely figure here on the beach, where his brother's body had once washed up. It was only then she realised he had called out to her.

She stood up.

Shay called out again, 'Can we talk?'

She shouted yes, and he changed direction to join her on the rocks.

'I was hoping to meet you.'

'I was sorry the way we left everything.'

'You were in shock, I understand.'

'I'm not sure that you do; you see, we never really knew what exactly happened to Andrew, only he was in a boat with this girl, and coming back from Scarty.'

'We are only the messengers; we can only relay what Rosie has told us in her letter.'

'There was some story in the area that Marian Murphy had persuaded him to go out in the boat after dark. My family stopped talking to the Murphys; we haven't spoken to them to this day.'

'Did nobody tell you the truth?'

'Marian's mother wouldn't let anyone interview her daughter. She said she was going to be blamed for something she didn't do, and suddenly they were gone.'

'Would your family have believed her, if she had told you exactly what happened?'

Shay shook his head. 'I don't think we would. None of us, not even me, knew about this relationship. There was no hint, and Andy and I were close.'

'They had wanted to emigrate together; it was Andy's idea.'

Shay looked at Casey. 'Did Rosie tell you that?'

'Yes, but I didn't want to say it in front of Dan.'

Shay sat on the bench beside her. 'That I do know. He told me just two nights before he died, that he intended to try his luck in New York. I begged him to reconsider, that it would kill Mam and Dad, but he was determined.'

'Dan doesn't know.'

'He lost his brother and sisters to emigration; he didn't want to lose any of his children. That is why he worked so hard to build up the business. It's why I stayed on here after Andy died.'

'Have you ever regretted it?'

Shay didn't answer for a few moments.

'Regrets build into bitterness, so best not to let any of it take root. I make the best of my life; I hope I do. Since I lost Anna, it has got more difficult.'

'And now?'

Casey straightened up. Shay took her hand, kissing it gently.

'These last few weeks, you have been a balm to my tired soul, Casey Freeman. If I had my wish, you would not be leaving after scattering Rosie's ashes.'

'It's time to go, but I dread leaving on bad terms.'

'I don't think that would ever be possible,'

'This whole thing between Rosie and your brother; I hope it is not going to spoil everything between us.'

'I hope not. Dad will come over in the morning for the scattering of the ashes. He said he will bring May as well. It's hard on him, because my mother never recovered from losing Andrew. Dad was so devastated by her death.'

Casey pulled away and walked across the sand.

'That is so unbelievably sad; poor Dan.'

'He will be fine; he has May now, and he's happy. What happened yesterday opened up old wounds in all of us, and it wasn't made easier by the fact that he was so fond of Rosie.'

'She never told any of us; we never knew.'

'He knows that and he likes you all so much, but...'

Casey sighed loudly. 'I loved Rosie but she has left us in a mess. When we came here it was for a break on an island. We could never have guessed this in our wildest dreams.'

Shay walked across to her, and put his arms around her. 'I don't want you to leave.'

When she tried to pull away, he held her tighter.

'Come back to the farmhouse,' she whispered.

They walked single file along the gorse path, but they held hands as they crossed the fields. As they approached the farmhouse, Shay dropped her hand, and she didn't mind.

Debbie, when she saw them, opened her window and said they had better come in and have coffee.

'Georgie, you owe me ten bucks; it's happened,' Debbie shouted up the stairs.

'I'm not going to ask about that one,' Casey said.

'And neither will we, but it makes us so happy,' Debbie sniggered, busily clearing out the kitchen cupboards. 'Shay, are we good?' she called out.

'I think so.'

'Can we load supplies on to your boat soon? Best get it done now, and we can leave after the scattering of the ashes.'

Shay said he would go back and collect his boat, and come around to the jetty in a while.

Debbie disappeared to her room while Casey took the photo strip and the letter which were on the mantelpiece.

'We all had a chat, and we agreed that you and Dan should have these,' she said, pushing them into Shay's hand.

He took the photo strip, and walked to the front door to look at it in the full light.

'We have so few photographs of Andy; he looks so happy here.'

'We thought it might help, and the letter too.'

'Is that really Rosie?' he asked.

'We didn't recognise her either.'

Shay opened the letter, and quickly scanned it, then he bunched it up, his hand clenched tightly around it.

'Why didn't anybody tell us at the time? It would have made a difference to know in the last months and weeks of his life, he had somebody who loved him.'

Shay sat down. 'I honestly don't know if this will help Dad.'

Casey gently placed her hand on his shoulder.

'It might hurt at first, but I think it may be a comfort to know this side of his son; to know he was loved, and that love lasted a lifetime.'

'I hope you're right,' Shay said.

At that moment, Georgie wandered through the kitchen.

'Is Dan coming over for the ceremony?' she asked.

'Yes, it took until this morning but he wants to do it.'

'I knew he would come around, Dan is a sweetheart,' she said.

Shay said he had to get back and Casey, who still wanted to say so much, walked down the path with him.

'Thank you for giving me the letter and photos. It means a lot,' he said, reaching over to kiss her lightly on the cheek.

Once Shay had left, Casey continued to the beach.

Slipping off her shoes, she walked along the shoreline barefoot, luxuriating in the cool of the sea as it puddled around her. She scanned the horizon, hoping the seal would raise its head.

When it popped up, a sadness welled up in her that all of this would soon be a distant memory.

As if it sensed her mood, the seal came closer to the shore and onto the beach, sitting watching her as she stood looking at its gleaming skin, before it shuffled back into the water.

'I envy the seal being able to swim with you every day,' Shay said as he came across the strand to her.

'What are you doing back here?' she asked.

'I wanted to... I guess I am not going to get another chance to be alone with you, and I...'

He faltered, took a deep breath and began to talk again.

'I wanted to say... this place, Scarty, Ballymurphy, will always be here for you. Please think hard on whether you want to return to your old life.'

She stared at him. 'I have to go back. Anyway, with all that has happened here, I need some breathing space.'

'I probably should not have come back, but after I started up the boat, I saw you heading this way, and I needed to be beside you again, to tell you how much you will be missed; how much I will miss you.'

'Sometimes, one has to return to their old life to make sure that decisions taken on the other side of the world are the right ones,' she said, and he pulled her into his arms.

'Will you come back to me when you have had your breathing space?'

'I hope so,' she said, 'but can I ask you something?'

'Of course.'

'Why didn't you come for me yesterday?'

Shay dug his hands in his pockets. 'I found it hard to understand why you hadn't warned me. I was sulking, I guess.'

'It wasn't my story to tell. Hard as it was, it was important that you both heard it from Rosie.'

'Dad said that too. He was annoyed at me; he said you have done so much for us.'

'It was my pleasure.'

He took her two hands.

'You're a good person, Casey Freeman. Please come back to us.'

'I will try.'

'And in the meantime, we can Zoom from the church car park,' he said, making her laugh.

She stood and watched Shay run back across the sand, and she wondered for the umpteenth time why she ever wanted to go back to her minimalist apartment in the sky, and a job that drained the life from her.

Kicking the water as she walked by the sea, she found it hard to imagine that in a few days she would be pounding the pavements of Manhattan, and ordering a chai latte from the stand at Bryant Park on the way to the office.

. . .

The next morning Casey, Georgia and Debbie were up and dressed early. Debbie was wearing a hat because she said it was an occasion for such attire.

Georgie sniggered, and said it looked ridiculous.

'So what? Rosie would appreciate it,' Debbie snapped.

They locked up the house because they did not intend to go back after the ceremony, but to Ballymurphy and on to the airport.

'What are you going to do – wear the hat on the flight?' Casey asked,

'Very funny, ha, ha, ha; don't you guys want to know?' she said, leading the way down the path, past what was once the foxglove bank, but was now just a grassy mound to the jetty.

They were early so they sat on the edge of the pier letting their feet dangle in the water as they watched Shay's boat pull out of Ballymurphy harbour.

'They should build a bridge and then we could have a car here, and come and go as we please,' Debbie said.

'Don't say that to Dan or there will be another big freeze,' Georgie said.

'I am going to miss this place, but not the midges that come at night, and bite my ankles,' Debbie said, standing up, and slipping her sandals back on.

Casey was quiet; she could barely put into words how much she loved Scarty, and how the idea of leaving today was breaking her heart.

She let the tears fall when Georgie, sensing her upset, gave her a big hug. Debbie joined in, and they ended up laughing as Debbie leaned over to embrace the others, nearly tipping them all into the sea.

By the time Shay's boat turned for Scarty, they were standing quietly, Casey clutching the cereal box containing

Rosie's ashes.

When he arrived on the island Dan was wearing his best suit, and May looked beautiful in a blue silk dress with long sleeves. She was first off the boat, and she caught Casey in a tight hug.

'This is all a right mess, but Dan has come round, don't you be worrying,' she whispered in Casey's ear.

Casey latched on to May tightly for a few seconds before the other woman pulled free.

Dan made a big deal of helping Shay tie up the boat before he walked over to Casey.

'I apologise, Casey, to you and all three of you, but the shock and the new information after all these years left me severely rattled. May and Shay have persuaded me that Rosie was a victim too. We all are, of this terrible accident and the uncaring attitude of Rosie's family. It should not take from celebrating her life here on Scarty, and scattering her ashes in the one place she will be at peace.'

'Shay can bring the boat around to the far beach, but Rosie wanted the rest of us to walk to the strand so she can have a final walk across the island,' Debbie said, leading the way up the path, past the locked farmhouse and across the fields.

Beside Casey, May tugged at the cereal box. 'Dear, why in the name of God are you carrying an old cereal box?' she asked.

Casey opened the box, and pulled out the plastic bag containing Rosie's ashes.

'Meet Rosie.'

May blessed herself, and looked away. 'May God forgive you, couldn't you find anything better?'

'We had a biscuit tin, but it's a long story.'

'I bet it is,' May said, her face showing her disapproval.

· · ·

When they got to the beach, they stood around, nobody knowing exactly what to do.

Dan stepped forward. 'Would anyone mind if I said a few words?'

'Please, go ahead,' Casey said, and the others nodded.

Dan stepped on a rock and began to speak.

'Friends, we are gathered here today to remember the loveliest people I have ever had the privilege of knowing. My son, Andrew Kennedy, and the girl he fell in love with, Marian, the woman we know as Rosie Brentwood. Andrew and Rosie both loved each other and Scarty beyond anything.

'It was easy for me to feel angry and let down when Rosie's letter was read out to us, but in the last two days I have realised how much that woman did for all of us over the years, and especially the Kennedys.

'She shall not be judged by the sins of her grandmother. Rosie – or Marian – was just a slip of a girl at the time and had lost the man she loved in the most terrible circumstances. Of course, she looked to her family to help and protect her.

'I still don't understand why, when she came to Scarty, she didn't tell us. Maybe the grief inside her was so big that and she could not discuss it with anyone, she just didn't know how to start.

'I think Rosie lived with the memory of her Andrew, and to have to tell us and face the opposition and inquisition that would surely follow would have in some way destroyed what gave her the most comfort.

'That Andrew was loved and remembered for all those years by someone other than the Kennedys means a whole lot to me. To be frank, this has not been easy, but the Rosie I knew was an honourable, honest woman, and if she felt she could not tell us face to face, then she must have had her reasons.

'Let us scatter the ashes of our good friend Rosie with full and good hearts. I can only hope that her spirit will be at rest here at Scarty, and that if there is a God, she may meet Andrew in the next world.'

Shay pulled up the boat near the beach, and waved to the group.

'How do we get out there?' Debbie asked.

'No drama, we walk,' Georgie said.

Debbie hitched up her dress, and she and May, grumbling together, headed into the sea. Dan rolled his trousers up to his knees, and followed them. Georgie and Casey didn't bother rolling up their jeans, and waded through the water, carefully holding the cereal box.

Georgie pointed at Debbie and May. 'Rosie would love that, and Dan with his suit on.' She took a picture with her phone. 'There is a painting in that someday.'

'Debbie will buy it to make sure nobody else can see her from behind with her dress hitched like that.'

Casey giggled. Debbie swung around to stare at her and Georgie.

'Come on, you two, you are slowing us down,' she snapped, making Casey and Georgie laugh even more.

Shay helped everyone on board. 'We're going to head down to the middle of the channel. The current there will bring the ashes into shore like it brought our Andrew.'

They all sat down and waited for Shay to turn the boat, and manoeuvre into the perfect spot.

'How are we going to do this?' Debbie asked.

May produced a big bunch of red roses from a box on the boat, and handed a rose to each person.

Casey took out the bag of ashes, and handed it to Shay with a scoop.

'You go first, then Dan and May,' she said.

Shay gave the scoop to his father.

Dan, who had unfurled his trousers legs, and was standing as if he were waiting in church, stepped forward, and took a scoop of the ashes. Walking to the side, he threw the dust in the water as May dropped a red rose.

'Goodbye, sweet Rosie,' he whispered.

Shay followed next, and then May. When it came for Debbie's turn, she looked at Casey and Georgie.

'I feel we should do it together – hold the bag, and let all of it go at once. Maybe then she has more of a chance of reaching the island?'

Casey and Georgie stepped forward, and the three of them went to the side of the boat.

'Are we ready?' Casey said.

Each placed a hand on the plastic bag, and shook out the rest of the ashes; the dust was whipped by a light breeze into the air, before falling into a wave, to be carried to shore. May tipped the last of the roses in the sea.

Dan called for a moment's silence, and they stood, their arms wound around each other, watching the waves make towards the shore.

'May their spirits rest in peace together,' May said, and everybody nodded.

After a few moments, Shay started up the engines, and the boat moved towards Ballymurphy harbour.

Casey, Debbie and Georgie stood on the deck watching the island beach, the farmhouse and the fields as they moved further and further away from Scarty Island.

'Rosie got her way on one thing,' Debbie said.

'What was that?' Georgie asked.

'We are all friends again, like she wanted,' Casey said quietly, and they huddled together for the last part of the journey into Ballymurphy harbour, where a car was waiting to bring them to Shannon Airport.

When the boat pulled into Ballymurphy, Shay was the first to jump out onto the pier to tie up the ropes. Casey watched him as he expertly secured the knots, before turning to the others.

'Folks, I have to run. Let's do it all again next year,' Shay called out a little too brightly, before sprinting up the pier to his car.

'Where is he off to in such a hurry? He could have waited to see us off properly,' Debbie sniffed.

Casey concentrated on helping Dan lift the luggage off the boat.

'He's gone to walk the rocks of the Burren,' Dan said quietly.

Casey, holding back her tears pretended she had not heard.

'Stay here, I will get the cab to reverse down,' Dan said.

May stood with the three women on the quay. For once, nobody had anything to say.

'Shay is not good at goodbyes,' May whispered, touching Casey on the shoulder.

'So what? It's still bad form. Casey deserves better,' Debbie said, but Georgie warned her to hush.

Casey wandered up the quay towards the car.

She didn't blame Shay; if she could, she would run away to tramp across the flat rocks of the Burren as well. Anything, rather than go back to Manhattan with this hole in her heart for Shay and Scarty. The bit that was left of her heart was hurting so much, she could barely think straight. She had no idea what was ahead, but none of it really mattered without him.

THIRTY-ONE

'The car has arrived,' Georgie called out as Casey finished getting ready. It had been several weeks since they had left Scarty, and she could barely think about it or Shay, her heart hurt so much.

She looked at herself in the mirror. The couture vintage Dior dress was a real find. A sumptuous silk satin with splashes of cobalt blue cornflowers, when she saw it in a small vintage shop in Philadelphia the previous week, she knew she had to have it. She didn't care about the price; when she tried it on, she felt she could do anything. A 1950s dress with a fitted bodice and a sweetheart neckline, it was cinched at the waist leading to a full skirt which fell just to her mid-calf. The short sleeves meant she had to team it with a black wrap, but the colour complimented her red hair and hazel eyes. It had been two months since she'd left Scarty, but when she closed her eyes, she could still smell the sea. When she held the conch shell to her ear, she could hear the waves, and it made her both sad and happy at the same time.

When Casey stepped out in the living area, Georgie beamed at her.

'Wow, are you trying to take the spotlight from me?'

Casey took Georgie in. Her hair was swept up, and she was wearing a figure-hugging ruched red dress that only somebody of her personality could carry off.

'Do a twirl,' Casey said.

'OK; but I don't know why, this dress is stuck to me,' Georgie said, but obliged by doing a pirouette on her high heels, ending with a small curtsy. 'Is it a bit too much?' she asked.

'Nothing is ever too much for a woman who is launching her very own art exhibition in Manhattan. Before the madness begins, I have something for you.'

Casey handed a small gift box to Georgie. Her eyes sparkling in delight, Georgie pulled up the top from the box to reveal a thick gold bangle.

'This is too much. So exquisite,' she said, lightly rubbing her fingers along the curve of the bangle which was embossed with a design that looked like waves.

'I am back beside the sea at Scarty when I do that,' she said, slipping the bangle on her right hand.

'You haven't looked at the underside.'

Georgie took off the bangle and read the inscription inside.

'*To new beginnings,*' she read out loud, her voice full of tears. 'It's perfect,' she said, throwing herself at Casey, and hugging her tightly.

'I will never be able to thank you enough for all you have done to get me this far,' she said.

Casey, trying to hold back tears, said not to let Debbie hear her say that.

'Where is she anyway?' Georgie asked.

'She said she would definitely make it. She is just back from linking up with her new best friend Patrick in Paris. No doubt there is some of the old Debs left, and she is trying to hail a cab at Penn Station. Now, let's get along.'

'So is it serious between those two?' Georgie asked, stopping to check her lipstick in the hall mirror. Casey pulled Georgie close.

'I am not supposed to divulge anything, but let's just say those two lovebirds are fed up with clocking up the air miles. They are looking for a love nest in Midtown.'

'Ooh, this is so exciting,' Georgie squealed.

'Not a word, now let's get going,' Casey said firmly.

'You're a star, as May would say,' Georgie said.

'You are the star tonight,' Casey said, ushering her friend to the elevator.

They sat in the back of the cab, each lost in her own thoughts as the car slowly moved through the rush hour traffic. Casey knew that Georgie was deliberately not asking if Shay was coming, and she was glad she didn't, because Casey did not even want to think about it.

When they had been over at the apartment the night before, Dan and May were reluctant to get drawn into too many details about Shay, and she understood why. They had travelled to New York together, and were staying in Manhattan for a few days either side of the exhibition. Casey had offered to put them up, but they declined. She had persuaded them over for dinner last night. They chatted about everything and everyone, but Shay.

At one stage, Casey followed Dan out onto the terrace.

'Casey, you are so lucky to live here. Scarty isn't a patch on this,' he said wistfully.

'Is that what you really think?'

'Maybe not, Ballymurphy and Scarty are never far from my mind, but this place is mighty.'

Leaning against the balcony wall, she sighed deeply.

'It is, but I miss Scarty, and all that came with it.'

'And maybe all who came with it.'

'Why don't you ask me straight out? Why do we have to talk in circles?' she said.

'All right; what is going on with you and Shay? He is moping around with a face like a wet weekend, and from what I see, you're no different, though a much more beautiful wet weekend.'

'We invited him to the launch, but he said somebody had to look after Kennedys, and unfortunately he wouldn't be able to make the trip.'

'And you believed him.'

Casey trailed her hand along the top of the balcony wall, keeping her eyes on the Chrysler crown.

'He is a grown man. What could I do but believe him? If it's not true, maybe he just wanted to let me down gently.'

Dan pulled his hands down his face. 'In all my years on earth, I have never met such a silly pair. You are both talking yourselves out of happiness; almost as if you think you don't deserve it.'

'I don't think I'm doing that,' Casey said, her tone hurt.

May called out Dan's name.

'Oh, am I interrupting something?' she said, hesitating at the sitting room door.

Dan held out his hand to her, so she stepped out onto the terrace.

'May darling, tell this silly woman love doesn't come calling very often, and when it does you don't rationalise it; you don't put rules on it, and you don't make excuses, you just go with the flow,' he said.

'What he said,' May said in a mock serious voice.

Casey shrugged. 'You lived up the road from each other; it's a little different for us.'

'That is my last word on it. I don't want to be accused of interfering,' Dan said, putting his hand out, and asking May if she would like to dance under a New York sky.

Casey stepped quietly back inside, watching the two of

them move in perfect harmony around the terrace. She wasn't exactly jealous, but she felt intensely sad.

Georgie snapped her out of her thoughts.

'Look at the house; the light in every window; the house a beacon on the square. Oh my God, is this really happening?' she said, her voice full of happiness.

The brownstone house on The Row beside Washington Square Park was all lit up, and looking resplendent. Inside, in the front room, they could see a number of people had already arrived, and were closely examining the artwork on the walls, while others were clustered in small groups chatting.

Georgie got out of the cab, and skipped to the steps before suddenly skidding to a halt.

'My stomach feels sick. I don't know if I can go through with it,' she said, her voice so low, Casey almost didn't hear her.

'Of course you can,' Casey said, catching her by the elbow, marching her up the steps and pressing the buzzer.

'Too late now, here comes your Mr Knowles.'

Georgie slipped off her coat before stepping into the hall.

Casey thought it was as if there was a sea change and Georgie, her slightly scatty friend, became the artist who floated through the rooms smiling enigmatically, and talking about her paintings.

Casey dithered. She was standing looking at a painting of Ballymurphy quay when a deep desolate feeling overwhelmed her. She should have followed Shay to the Burren. She knew that now, and it was too late. Casey's head was full of what might have been, and she found she could hardly bear to look at the Scarty paintings. Afraid of memories being dragged up, and slapping her in the face, she turned and walked back down the steps.

She wandered down the street. She needed a little time to herself, and with all the people arriving at the exhibition, her presence was not going to be missed for a while yet.

Wandering into the park, she headed for the fountain. Somebody was playing a guitar and a number of youths were juggling with light-up balls at a far corner. She sat to one side of the fountain, taking in the sounds of the city, but longing for the peace and quiet of Scarty. Gazing upwards, she searched for the stars, but couldn't make out any because of the light spillage. It was a different world here, but she didn't feel part of it any more. Her heart hurt with longing for the simple Scarty life, but that seemed at this point unobtainable.

Shay would never move here. He wouldn't even travel to New York for Georgie's exhibition. There had been no contact after she left Ireland, until Georgie sent out her exhibition invitations. The exhibition invitation to Shay contained Casey's email for an RSVP. She was cross at Georgie when she found out, and disappointed when Shay sent a polite formal reply that due to work commitments, he was unable to attend.

Reading between the lines, she feared that if they ever had anything, it was over. Shay wasn't leading her on, and she was thankful for that, but it hurt so much.

Shaking the thoughts away, she walked down the side of the square to the brownstone where the sound of people enjoying themselves, and the happy hum of conversation filled the night air, even at this distance.

A cab pulled up, and Debbie, wearing a bright pink dress and an equally garish fascinator, waved out the window.

'Bonsoir, mes amis,' she called out. 'The traffic in the city is getting worse; I thought I would never get here,' she added, getting out, and bustling up the steps. At the top, she twirled around. 'I hope Georgie is here.'

'Yes, inside holding court, and I am sure selling every painting on the wall.'

'So what are we waiting for? Let's get in and party,' Debbie said, ringing the doorbell.

As they waited, Debbie stared at Casey. 'Are you still pining away for the handsome boatman?'

Casey didn't have time to answer, before Georgie bounded down the hall to them.

'Have you seen all the red stickers? Where have you two been?' she asked excitedly.

Casey was about to answer, but Georgie was swept away by Richard Knowles to meet another important buyer. Debbie helped herself to champagne and canapes, but Casey decided to walk the room to view the exhibition.

One after another, she stood in front of the framed paintings. The fields, the stoat, the foxgloves and oxeye daisies; the beach where they went skinny dipping; and Shay's boat chugging across the harbour. She giggled to think of the many lovely days by the sea with Shay, and the time she learned to skim stones across the waves, and won.

Pacing slowly along, she stopped at a marble fireplace where one large canvas had centre stage.

It was the cove at the far end of the island. The sea was sparkling silver, the strand so inviting, and yet there was a sadness about the painting which tugged at her heart.

Below was an inscription: *In memory of Rosie and Andrew, who loved each other deeply. Not for sale.*

'I asked Georgie not to sell it. I can't afford it but I asked her to give me time to pay for it,' a voice behind her said.

Casey froze. So many thoughts of Shay were flooding her brain, she was afraid she had imagined his voice. She knew how much the painting meant to him.

'I'm here,' he said softly, lightly touching her arm.

They said afterwards it was like she fainted, and maybe she did, but she fell into his arms, and when she next opened her eyes he was holding her, and looking down on her along with everyone else attending the exhibition.

'Talk about stealing the limelight,' Georgie said, and everybody laughed.

Shay led Casey to the kitchen at the back of the house, where Richard Knowles handed her a glass of water before rushing back for the speeches.

'You said you weren't coming,' she managed to say.

'I was a fool; I was afraid to take the next step, but I only realised it when everybody had already left. I couldn't get a seat so I told a big white lie that Dad had collapsed here in Manhattan, and I had to get to him, and what do you know, they found a seat on the plane for me.'

'Georgie must be thrilled.'

'I don't care about that; what about you?'

Casey closed her eyes. The last two months back at work living in the penthouse, the separation and negotiation until Gary's agreement to a divorce, had been hell without Shay. But she didn't want to reunite now to be faced with the same dilemma over the many ocean miles between them.

'I am confused; are you here for a holiday?'

'I am here for you, Casey; I can't live without you. Surely we can work it out.'

She stood up, gripping the counter because she felt a little lightheaded.

'I am so happy to see you, but unless we can sort out the distance and miles between us, what is the point?'

'Is that how you truly feel?'

'I have a life and a job here.'

'What life? On your own, living up in the sky where the clouds obliterate the view a lot of the time, and a job that eats into your soul. Come back with me, and we will be together in a place that we both love.'

'You are asking an awful lot.'

'I know, and I know you want it.'

Debbie stuck her head in the kitchen, and said they had to come for Georgie's speech.

Shay took Casey by the hand, and they went into the front drawing room, where Georgie was standing at a special podium.

'Here they are, Shay and Casey. Don't they look lovely together?' she said, and everyone in the room swivelled around to look at the pair. Casey blushed, and felt embarrassed.

'But this exhibition is named after another beautiful couple, our friend Rosie of Upstate New York, who – when she was just eighteen years of age – fell in love with Andrew, a handsome young man from the west of Ireland. Scarty Island was their favourite place. When the wind whipped up, and upturned their boat, Rosie was the only one to make it to the mainland. Andrew's body was found the next day on this beach at Scarty Island,' she said, pointing to the painting over the mantelpiece.

'I believe Rosie never stopped loving him, even when soon afterwards she and her mother emigrated to the States. All these years later she inherited Scarty Island, and spent her time there. When she died too young, we scattered her ashes on that beach at Scarty Island. I like to think that their young love would have blossomed into something even stronger and—'

Georgie faltered, only regaining her composure when Debbie reached out, and placed her hand on her shoulder.

'We can only hope that these two, who loved each other dearly, are now finally united. I dedicate this exhibition to the beautiful Scarty Island, and the two wonderful people we have lost, but who will forever be in our hearts.'

There was a respectful silence in the room, and after a few moments Shay stepped forward.

'Thank you, Georgie, for this beautiful exhibition in memory of my brother and our dear friend. Scarty Island is now in the ownership of the Kennedys of Ballymurphy, and you,

Georgie, and Casey and Debbie are welcome any time you wish.'

He turned to Casey. 'Casey Freeman, I have a question to ask.'

Casey froze as Shay got down on one knee, and the crowd gasped.

'Will you come back to Ireland with me, and give this thing between us a go? We could get to know each other better, and run the Scarty Gallery and Café. When you are ready to accept the love I feel for you, and only when you are ready, we can made it all official and be beside the Atlantic Ocean in our place together. I know it seems crazy, but I love you, Casey, and I don't want to be without you a moment longer.'

There was a collective intake of breath as Casey stood rooted on the spot. Every part of her wanted to run into his arms, and tell him she loved him. A tiny niggling part of her said she was mad, but in the end it was Debbie's dig in the back which made her react.

Taking a step forward, she saw Shay's expectant face and a sea of people she had never met in her life looking at her as if she must give an answer.

Panic rose up inside her, and her head was thumping.

'I can't do this, Shay, not here, not now,' she blurted out, before pushing through the crowd to the front door, and out onto the street. She scurried along, afraid the crowd would follow her until she came to Washington Square Park. The man was still playing the guitar. When she stopped to breathe she realised nobody was interested enough to follow her. Loitering at the fountain, she felt foolish, and stepped out onto the street, hailing a cab to go home.

When she got back to her apartment, she locked herself in her room. Not bothering to take off her dress, she lay on the bed. Curling up in a ball, she cried herself to sleep.

When Casey woke up in the middle of the night, the apartment was quiet.

Unzipping her dress, which now looked sad and wrinkled, she stepped out of it, leaving it on the floor. She pulled on a pyjamas before moving to the terrace.

She could never go back to Scarty now, not after what had happened. Her heart was in pieces. The Chrysler building stood solid, a tower of strength, and she'd never felt so small.

When she heard Georgie step onto the terrace, she turned away.

'You certainly know how to grab the headlines,' Georgie said.

'Sorry, I didn't mean to take attention from your evening.'

'Don't be silly, you didn't. The drama at the end meant the exhibition was mentioned in the newspapers.'

Casey dipped her head, and began to cry.

'However, we were trying to work out, did you actually say no to the man you love? Or did you just run scared?'

Casey shook her head. 'It doesn't matter now; Shay will never forgive me.'

Georgie got a tub of ice cream from the freezer and two spoons.

'Dig in, we have some planning to do,' she said.

Casey scooped out a big lot of ice cream, some falling on the ground.

'What's to plan? Shay is not likely to speak to me ever again, never mind bring me back and forth from Scarty Island.'

'The exhibition is sold out, and I have been invited to do it all over again in Washington in nine months' time. It means I have to go back to Scarty for inspiration, and I want you to come with me.'

'But it is already the end of September, nobody spends fall or winter in Scarty.'

'Which is exactly why I want to get there as soon as possible.'

'Georgie, are you mad?'

'Maybe I am, but I have never felt so exhilarated. Can't you imagine the work I can do?'

'I can't just up and leave my work again.'

'Casey,' Georgie looked at her sternly, 'are you happy? Because from where I'm standing, you're miserable, wearing those terribly boring suits, and representing the most abhorrent rich people.'

'It pays the bills.'

Georgie grabbed the carton of ice cream. 'I bought the ice cream, and I can pay my way now. I made a shit load of money tonight.'

'You don't need to give me anything.'

Georgie threw her hands in the air, the spoon flying from her grip, and towards the balcony wall.

'Shit, what did I just do?'

'Either caused an injury to a pedestrian on the sidewalk or it went up and a plane is in trouble,' Casey said in such a deadpan voice they both laughed, and laughed, and couldn't stop.

Georgie scooted to the balcony wall. 'Hey, what are the chances?' she called out.

As Casey looked out with her, she noticed, against all odds, the spoon perfectly balanced on the balcony rail.

'Grab it; we really don't want a lawsuit on our hands,' Casey shouted.

Georgie delicately picked up the spoon, and threw it onto the table.

'It seems like a sign, doesn't it?' Georgie said cheekily. 'We are a good team, Casey, please come with me.'

'Even if I wanted to, I don't think I would be welcome in Ballymurphy.'

'Dan and May said they love you, and we all think Shay was an idiot to ask you in public.'

'It's best left; I can't go there now. It's a mess, and I don't know how to fix it,' Casey said.

'Face to face is the only way,' Georgie said but Casey shook her head.

'Even if I did go, I wouldn't know what to say.'

Georgie guffawed out loud. 'For a highly educated woman and a fancy lawyer, you sure can be dumb, Casey Freeman. You need to fix this, girl, and fast.'

THIRTY-TWO

Within two days, Georgie had left for Ireland, and Casey was alone in her Manhattan apartment. For the first time, the space felt too big. Loneliness streaked through her. She got up every morning, and picked out her green or black suit, stopped for her chai latte en route to work, and stayed in the office until late. She worked harder and for longer than anybody else. She did all this to try to mask the pain in her heart. Gary had left the company, and at the office there were no distractions, only a stack of files she had to read.

There were times she thought of contacting Shay, but she didn't know what to say. 'Sorry I didn't even give you an answer, and humiliated you in front of all of Manhattan.' Somehow, she felt there was no way of talking her way out of that. Dan and May, before they left for Ireland, had spoken to her, and she could hear the disappointment in their voices. When Dan asked why she had run away, she answered she didn't know, and that was the truth. She had run like a frightened rabbit, and hurt the one person in the world who did not deserve it.

Georgie pushed her to throw up everything to travel back to Scarty, but when she resisted, Georgie had left anyway. She had taken to sending emails daily to Casey telling her how hard she was working, how Shay and Dan were braving the weather to get her to and from Scarty, and how Shay seemed a little lost.

He is moping, and I know you're moping. Better mope together than be apart, Georgie said in her last email. She also told her that Shay had gone straight to JFK on the exhibition night, and waited hours at the airport for a flight to Ireland. *He has never spoken about it, not even to Dan, and I know Dan would tell me if he had.*

Casey felt a knot in her stomach, and she thought it was ironic that Georgie, the least organised of them all, should have a future built around Scarty, and be the first to return.

Debbie rang Casey every day to make sure she wasn't going to do anything stupid, and in a weird way, Casey found herself looking forward to the calls. She thought she was a sad person, if the highlight of her days was an email about Scarty and a phone call from Debbie – who said she was dumb, and should hop on a plane, hang the consequences.

She had just finished one such call on a Thursday evening when her phone rang again. She answered thinking it was Debbie with another gem of advice.

'What is it now?' she snapped.

'Ms Freeman, my humble apologies for disturbing you. This is Rosie Brentwood's attorney.'

'Yes, hello, Mr Silver. What can I do for you? It is after office hours,' she said, her voice tense.

'I am afraid a situation has arisen, and I wanted to contact you as soon as possible.'

'What situation?'

'To explain, my firm are changing offices and during that, we found a letter which had slipped behind a drawer. It was a drawer in which we held Ms Brentwood's letters, which were dispatched ato you all on Scarty Island. Unfortunately, I have to inform you the last letter was not sent to you, and has been missing these last few months.'

Casey groaned. Was she ever going to escape the hold of Scarty Island?

'OK, Scarty Island was a quite a while ago, but you can send it on to me now? We are all scattered, but I will photocopy it and send it to the others. No harm done.'

The attorney at the other end of the line cleared his throat.

'I appreciate your understanding, Ms Freeman, but it is a little more complicated than that. Please allow me to explain.'

'I think you should.'

'There has been contact from a young lady, whose parents died in a car accident in recent weeks. The young woman says after her parents died she found a letter from Rosie Brentwood, which suggested she was her birth mother. The young woman wrote to my office as the name and address had been included in the letter, and she is now requesting a meeting with Rosie.'

'What? I don't understand.' Casey's heart was pounding.

'I know it is late, but do you think I could call at your home? I don't want to bring this to your office, and I know how busy you are.'

'Yes, I think so,' she said, and gave her address.

'I can be there in thirty minutes,' he said, and rang off.

Casey went out onto the terrace. The cold rush of air blasted her, and she wondered, had she dreamed all of that conversation up or was she going mad? It couldn't be true, could it? It had to be some kind of mistake, a clerical error.

She went back to her dressing room, and pulled off her sweats, and put on a green blouse and trousers.

When the doorman rang up, she directed the attorney to the elevator, and was waiting by her door for him when he got out.

'Thank you, it is good of you to see me,' he said as he bustled into the apartment. He continued to talk quickly. 'I feel awful about this. We had an intern in the office, and while tidying to fill time, she displaced what should have been the last letter to you all. Unfortunately, this letter fell from the new file where it was stored, and nobody noticed.'

'We are where we are. I want to know everything about this situation,' Casey said, directing the attorney to the dining-room table, and sitting opposite him.

He reached into his briefcase, and took out a file. Holding up an envelope, he began to speak again.

'I am not in any way trying to absolve myself from responsibility for this, but when Ms Brentwood last visited our office with this letter, I was on vacation. It was an unscheduled visit, and I was told she added a letter to the file. It explains why, when I handed over the letters, and sent them by registered post to Ireland, I thought the number was correct. I cannot emphasise enough how sorry I am.'

Casey reached over, and took the envelope.

'It is probably another one of Rosie's long letters about life, and not of great consequence.'

The attorney pursed his lips, and looked at Casey from under his eyes. 'I wish it were.'

'What do you mean?'

'I had to open the letter because it wasn't immediately clear from the envelope who was the rightful owner. Please, read it to put this in context.'

Casey nervously took the pages from the envelope.

My dearest ones,

This will be my last letter to you. I hope your time on Scarty has been what I imagined it would be, and you feel renewed and recharged for what is to come.

There is something I must get off my chest before I leave you entirely.

I have told you how much I loved Andrew. In a better

world that wind would never have overturned the boat, and we would both have got to New York to start a new life together.

As you know, my mother got me away from Kilkee and on to a flight to the States from Shannon Airport in double quick time. They were afraid I would be blamed for Andrew's death.

Four months after our arrival in Manhattan, I found out I was pregnant. I couldn't tell my mother because I knew she would go mad. It was only when I couldn't hide it any longer – when I was six months pregnant – that she copped on. The woman was working day and night to put food on the table. My pregnancy was a huge blow for her. Her brother came up with the money required, but I was shipped off to a convent in Boston, where I gave birth to my little girl. I called her Amy.

More than anything, I wanted to keep her. My mother was a kind woman, and she could see the attachment. She also knew Andrew was the father. I think if our lives had been more settled she would have brought Amy home, and brought her up as my sister. She pleaded with the nuns to let me stay and nurse her, so we could bond. She said it would help me afterwards. I suppose it did; I'm not sure, but I do know that when years later I was told that we were not able to have children, I ached for the feel of my baby girl as she pummelled me searching to feed.

They found her a good home with a couple in an expensive area of Boston, and they said the family had promised to keep Amy's first name. They promised to keep a letter I wrote to her, and give it to her when she was eighteen years old. I know it was more than a lot of young mothers got, but I was devastated.

I wrote and rewrote that letter maybe twenty times, pouring my heart out. I told her about her father, and how even though we were young, how deeply we loved each other. I told her about Scarty, and how that was our special place. I told her about our plans, and how a big wind over the sea had wrecked them all.

I don't know if she believed I loved her to the ends of the earth and back, and all I wanted was for eighteen years to pass so she could make contact. Our neighbour, Charles Silver, was an attorney, and his daughter asked him to help me, and we put his name in the letter if she ever wanted to contact me.

I also got my mother to promise if there was any contact, she would tell me. I was so excited when my Amy turned eighteen, and so disappointed when there was no attempt at contact. By then, Mr Silver's son, George had taken over the business, and I checked with him, first every month and then every six months, but still nothing.

I never told Barry, and we had come to terms with the fact that we could not have children of our own. Adoption was not an option for Barry, and I lived in hope that someday Amy would come looking for me. When I inherited Scarty, I believed it was a sign that someday she would walk onto the island looking to find the essence of her mother and father, and I would help her. She would stay in the little farmhouse and together, we would learn how to be mother and daughter.

Every summer I stayed at Scarty, I watched for Shay's boat bringing out the young girl who wanted to know about her mother and father, but it never happened. I couldn't tell the Kennedys either; it was my secret; I couldn't share it; I couldn't face their pain and their questions. I am hoping now that you will tell the Kennedys there is another member of their clan, and ask them if she ever comes looking to reach out with open arms; to please at least hear her out.

More than anything, I wanted to meet Amy, to see what of Andrew was in her. I hope it's his eyes, and his kind temperament. I wonder if she's shy like him. I have so many questions and no answers, and I leave it to you, my friends, to welcome my Amy if she comes looking.

Please – for me – bring Amy to Scarty. Go with her, if you can, because to have to travel there alone would be such a lonely endeavour. I beg you to please do this one last thing for me.

All my love,

Rosie Xx

Casey looked up from the letter. 'It is a pretty big letter to have lost.'

'I know; I can only apologise again and again.'

'At least you have brought it to me now.' Casey sighed.

The attorney shifted uncomfortably on his chair.

'While you are in such a forgiving mode, I need to appraise you of the current situation.'

Casey straightened in her seat. 'A young woman called Amy Nicholls from Boston has been in touch. Her parents were killed in a traffic pile-up on the freeway two months ago. When she opened their bank safe deposit box, she found Rosie's letter to her, and made contact with the firm looking to meet her mother. She said when she turned eighteen, she was not given the letter, and she has always wanted to connect with her birth mother.'

Tears welled up in Casey; anger coursed through her, too.

'They didn't keep their word, and Rosie never met her daughter again. How unfair is that?' she said, slapping her hand hard down on the table, before bolting out to the terrace. She wanted to scream; she wanted to be on Scarty, where she could shout loudly with only the stars in the sky to witness her anguish.

She saw the attorney loitering at the door.

'I have invited her to my office for tomorrow morning. I was hoping you could come meet her.'

Casey kicked the patio chair out of her way. 'And what if she sees me and thinks I am Rosie?'

The attorney bowed his head. 'I broke the news to her of her mother's death; she was devastated. There was little I could tell her about Rosie – the details she wanted to know, anyway. Ms Brentwood was only my client. Terrible way to find out, when she was so close.

'And now I want to make this right in some way for this young woman. I want to give her some connection. You can tell her so much about her mother, and maybe you can travel to Ireland with her.'

'This is so tragic, but now is not a good time to ask me to travel to Scarty.'

'What about your two friends?'

'This is such a shit fest, I don't know what to do.'

'May I speak?'

'Go for it.'

'If you had opened this letter on that island, you would all have wanted to meet this young woman. Why is it so different now?'

'Life has got in the way, I guess.'

'Come to the meeting. Meet the girl; maybe she won't want to travel to Ireland.'

'If she is Rosie's daughter, she will.'

'The meeting is at 9 a.m. Can you come?'

'I will have to reschedule with a client; this is not convenient.'

The attorney picked up his briefcase. 'Life is never convenient.'

'OK, I will be there,' Casey said as she accompanied him to the door.

Debbie, when Casey rang her ten minutes later, insisted on attending the meeting. Next morning, Casey got up extra early to meet Debbie at Penn Station.

Debbie arrived on to the concourse carrying a big leather bag.

'Are you staying? I thought you were only coming up for the meeting?' Casey said, her voice irritable.

'I thought Amy would like to see a few photos of her mother, and I hadn't time to take them out of the frames.'

'You could have taken a picture with your phone.'

Debbie stopped. 'I was in such a dither, I didn't think of that. What am I like? I hope she doesn't think me stupid.'

'Does it matter that I do?' Casey said as she flagged down a cab.

Debbie was quiet for a while, and seemed upset as they sat in the cab.

'Why are you so cross? It's just a silly mistake,' Debbie said.

'I'm sorry, I am not cross at you but at the situation. If her parents had given Amy the letter when they said they would, then Rosie would have met her daughter. It's just so crap it didn't happen.'

'Yes, but maybe we can make it a little easier now.'

'Tell me how. We had lost touch with Rosie; we weren't very good friends.'

'We can tell her all the old stories.'

'And that is another thing; she never told us about Amy. Why not? Did she think we'd be so judgemental?'

Debbie gave Casey a fierce look. 'Why are you making this about yourself? You need to sort your shit out, Casey, because the way you are now, you're impossible to be with.'

'What do you mean?'

'Can I speak frankly?'

'If you have to.'

Casey wanted to tell Debbie to shut up, but she was like a dog with a bone.

'You need to sort out your life, Casey. You need to make

peace with Shay. Otherwise you're going to be this angry, middle-aged woman people cross the street to avoid.'

There was silence in the back of the cab. The driver turned up the radio. A wave of tears rose inside Casey, but she concentrated on looking out the window so Debbie couldn't see. She knew Debbie was right; since Georgie's exhibition, she hadn't been herself. At work she flew off the handle so easily. Last week in the middle of negotiation talks, she had to excuse herself to go to the bathroom and cry.

She had written to Shay to explain she had been rattled by everybody there; that she couldn't cope. She had so many excuses. She should not have sent it. He didn't reply. She knew he was angry and hurt. She deserved everything he thought about her, but she didn't know how to make it right.

Georgie had emailed to say Shay was working too hard, and nobody could stop him. Often, he disappeared for hours, and nobody knew where he had got to. Casey knew where he would be. If she could, she would also go to the fields of stone to cry and scream, and scream and cry.

When they got out of the cab, Debbie ran around to Casey's side, and pulled her into a big hug.

'It will all come right, darling. at the end. Like it says the movie, we just aren't at the end yet,' she whispered in Casey's ear.

THIRTY-THREE

The attorney had set aside a special conference room for the meeting. When they were shown in, Debbie fussed about setting up the framed photographs. Casey stood looking out the window at the street below. All she could think of was herself and Rosie in their twenties, and how they had loved to stroll around Midtown and pretend they were somebody. They could barely rub two cents together, but they got their nails brightly painted, and wore thick eyeliner. She smiled to herself to think they must have looked a fright in their tight jeans and tank tops.

They told each other everything back then. Or so Casey thought.

She couldn't believe that her best friend could have neglected to tell her something so big, and yet now she was expected to pick up the pieces of her life.

When the door opened Debbie stood up, flattening her skirt. Feeling cross and stubborn, Casey stayed at the window.

'Ms Nicholls would like to meet you both,' the attorney said as he stepped back, and a young woman with long blonde hair, one part pulled to the side with a clip, stepped into the room.

Casey swung around, and gasped. She was so like Rosie: her

stance, all the bright colours she was wearing, and her smile. Casey hung back as Debbie immediately walked around the table, and hugged Amy.

'You poor darling, we are so sorry you can't meet your mother; you look so like her. Except for the eyes,' Debbie said, turning to Casey. 'This girl must have her father's eyes. Don't you think so, Casey?'

Amy approached Casey, and extended her hand.

'Thank you for agreeing to see me. It means a lot. I can't believe I just missed her,' she said.

'It is a tragedy, sweetheart, Rosie would have given anything to meet you,' Debbie said.

Amy picked up a photograph from the table. 'Is this my mother? She was so beautiful.'

'Inside and out,' Debbie said as they settled at the table, and the attorney sent out for a tray of tea and coffee.

'We wish you could have known her. Why do you think your parents didn't give you her letter?' Casey asked.

Amy shrugged her shoulders. 'Who knows? They were the best parents, but maybe they were afraid of the next steps if I wanted to meet my birth mother; I don't know. I have lost the two of them, and now I learn I have lost my birth mother too.'

Debbie reached out, and squeezed her hand. 'Darling, you will always have us.'

Amy looked directly at Casey and Debbie. 'Will you help me now to continue my search for my family in Ireland? I need to connect.'

'Of course we will. You should know your dad's family, your grandfather and uncle –

the Kennedys of Ballymurphy on the West Coast of Ireland – are the best people,' Debbie said quickly.

'Maybe you need some time to take all this in. I can write to them, tell them about you,' Casey said.

Amy sat up straight, and rubbed her hands together.

'I am not going to risk losing out again. More than anything, I want to meet my relatives, but I don't want them to have time to put up barriers. I have a grandfather and uncle; I want to travel in the next week, and I want to surprise them,' she said firmly.

'Do you think that is wise?' Casey asked.

'It is the only way I will know whether I am truly welcome or not.'

'Maybe some advance notice would be a good idea,' Casey said, but Debbie dug her in the side.

'Where is your sense of adventure, girl? If Amy wants to do it that way, then that is her right. The Kennedys are good people. I am sure they will welcome her,' Debbie said, her voice pompous.

Casey shook her head. 'Do you intend to travel alone or with friends?'

For the first time, Amy looked uncertain. 'I know it is a lot to ask, but I was hoping you guys would come along.'

Debbie immediately jumped in to say she would, though that part of Ireland in the winter months would be so different to summer.

'Georgie is already there...'

Amy reached out and took Casey's hand. 'Please,' she said softly.

Casey saw that she was so like Rosie, looking out under her eyes, and smiling so that there was no hope of denying her request. 'I can't get time from work. Debbie is the strongest person I know, and with her at your side, what could go wrong? Georgie is already in Ireland, and frankly she would be a better fit for you, Amy.'

Amy stood up. 'I know I am asking a lot. I can buy your flights. My parents have left me well provided for. However, I feel I need you around me; at the moment you are the closest thing to family I have,' she said.

She knocked on the table. 'It's all I have right now. It will only be for a few days, I am begging you.'

Casey knew she couldn't get out of the trip. Debbie would never forgive her if she continued to be so stubborn, and Georgie if she heard about it, would be disgusted.

'Thursday to Tuesday next week. I might get away with that,' she said, gathering up her handbag. 'I have to get to the office,' she added pushing her card in Amy's hand.

Debbie said she would stay to chat to Amy.

A few minutes later, Casey sank into the back of a cab, and closed her eyes. She was going back to Scarty. Maybe it was the right thing to do, but she really didn't know.

She tried to concentrate on work for the day, but she couldn't stop thinking about her return to Ireland – what would she do in Ballymurphy and what would she say to Shay? It was ridiculous, but she had to bring Rosie's daughter back to where she had relatives. Debbie was right, none of this was about her. It was about Rosie, and her lost daughter.

When Georgie emailed to say that Debbie had been in touch, and this was probably the most exciting thing to happen in Ballymurphy in a long time, Casey knew the visit was going to be very difficult. She tried not to think about Ireland over the next few days, and she let Debbie take the lead in planning the trip back to Ballymurphy.

When they arrived at Shannon Airport, a taxi driver from Ballymurphy was waiting for them.

'Georgie sent me, said you need the help,' he said loading their bags in the back.

Debbie and Amy fell asleep on the journey to Ballymurphy, but Casey stayed awake, worrying about the reaction Amy would get, but mostly whether Shay would even talk to her after what had happened the night of the Manhattan exhibition.

As they drove closer, and she began to recognise familiar streets and fields, her anxiety grew.

Georgie was waiting on the deck at Kennedys when they pulled up. Debbie was first out of the car followed by Amy. Casey hung back to pay the taxi driver, but Dan called her to join them. May ran up the road shouting out to them.

'It is so wonderful to have you all here,' she said, before turning to Amy, bewildered.

'Another young woman from America to get to know. Welcome,' she said.

Casey looked all around, but there was no Shay.

'That stupid man is gone to meet the accountant, today of all days,' May said.

Dan gave her a warning look.

Casey turned to Georgie. 'You told them we were coming?'

'I had to! They were wondering why I was making up beds; but I just told about you and Debbie,' she said pointedly.

May linked arms with Amy, and led her into the pub. 'You have a look of Rosie about you; are you a relative?'

Amy looked at Casey.

'Maybe we should wait until we get inside?' Casey said.

Dan gave her a quizzical look, but brought them to the bar, where they had the tables set.

'Let me get the scones out of the oven, and then we can have a nice chat,' May said.

Georgie helped set up the coffee machine, and Debbie poured orange juice for everybody.

When they finally sat down, nobody said anything for a few moments.

Dan poured the coffee, and waited until everybody had helped themselves to milk and sugar.

'All right, I will get the ball rolling. It's autumn, the weather is terrible. Georgie is here to paint, but Casey, Debbie and a new visitor, there's something afoot. Let's be having it.'

Amy made to talk, but Casey put a hand out to stop her.

'I will take it from here,' she whispered before looking from May to Dan.

'Amy is Rosie's daughter. She is twenty-two years of age and...'

Dan reached out and touched Amy's face. 'Your dad was our Andrew; is that right?' he said, his voice shaking.

Amy said yes, and looked into her grandfather's eyes.

'You have Andrew's soft eyes and his quiet way,' Dan's breath caught, 'but where have you been all these years?'

'I was adopted... I didn't find out about Rosie until a few weeks ago.'

'So you never met her?' May asked.

'No, but she left a letter for me which I treasure. She said I should come to Scarty.'

Dan leaned back in his chair, his breathing shallow.

'Why didn't Rosie tell us?' he said, tears flowing down his face.

'I don't know,' Amy said, her voice low.

'Oh, you poor pet,' Dan said, reaching out with both his arms.

Amy fell into his hug.

'I have a grandchild,' Dan whispered.

Debbie took out her camera to take photos, but Casey told her to leave them to it.

'Where is Shay? He should be here,' Debbie said loudly, but May told her to quieten down as she gestured at Debbie, Georgie and Casey to follow her.

They followed May to the kitchen, leaving Dan and Amy to talk together.

May pulled out a bottle of brandy, and without asking anyone poured a measure each for all four of them.

'How could Rosie not have told us? Not told me? We were such good friends,' May said.

Casey gulped her brandy. 'We can hardly believe it ourselves; Debbie will fill you in. I need to walk.'

Nobody argued with Casey as she took an old raincoat that was hanging on the back-door hook, and slipped out of Kennedys.

Walking across the road she had a clear view of Scarty Island brooding under a grey Autumn day. The village was quiet as she set off down the quay to look at Shay's boat. The sound of the sea gently pushing against the quay walls was a comfort to her tired brain; the drizzle cool on her face.

She stopped at Shay's boat. Looking around to make sure nobody could see her, she stepped into the wheelhouse.

Running her hands along the curve of the wheel, she smiled to think of the summer at Scarty and Shay's boat chugging across the channel to the island.

Reaching into her pocket, she pulled out the conch shell. Shay had given it to her, and said she could bring it back when she was ready. She wanted him to know she was ready to give it back; ready to be in Ballymurphy. In Manhattan, the first week or so after she had returned to the States she had picked up the conch shell, and listened to the sea. When loneliness gripped her, and all she could think of was Scarty, the sound of the sea helped her through.

She had come back to Ballymurphy, and she wanted Shay to know she was ready to meet. He may not want to talk to her, but she knew he would come and check the boat when he got home. She knew he could not face meeting her; he was hiding. His boat and this wheelhouse were his space.

Carefully, she put the conch shell beside his coffee cup on the wheelhouse dash. Her hope was that he could read into the gesture. She had come back, and she hoped he would understood why, and would give her a fair hearing.

Dan came out on the deck and she knew he was searching for her. She waited until he had gone back inside before she got off the boat and walked back up the quay. When she got as far as Kennedys, Dan was waiting for her.

'I rang Shay, and he is on the way back. He will be here shortly.'

'Have you told him about Amy?'

'That requires a face to face. I wanted to ask you a favour?'

'Anything.'

'I know you and Shay need to talk, but can I ask you to let me talk to him first about Amy. Maybe you guys can go for a rest, and give us a little time.'

'Of course we can. You can let us know when it is all clear. I will round up the others,' Casey said.

Dan looked back at the pub, where they could both see Amy laughing with Debbie and May.

'She is a breath of fresh air for us; a new beginning for the Kennedys. I can't believe you brought her home,' he grinned.

THIRTY-FOUR

Casey must have slept because when there was a knock on the bedroom door, she didn't know for a moment where she was. She heard Dan call her name, and she scrambled out of bed.

Opening the door a little, she saw him looking a little flustered.

'I have spoken to Shay, and he has met Amy. It's all good. Poor lamb, it has been very emotional for her. May made her a hot chocolate, and sent her to bed for a few hours.'

Pulling a cardigan on, Casey stepped out into the hall. 'Dan, where is Shay?'

'You know him, he has to process everything. He set off down to the boat. Go to him, Casey, and sort this out one way or another.'

'I will.'

'And maybe get some clothes on, or everyone in Bally-murphy will be talking,' he said.

Embarrassed, she went back into her room and got dressed quickly. Debbie stirred, and asked where she was going.

'Hopefully to talk to Shay.'

Debbie sat up. 'Christ, girl, put on some lipstick at least,' she said, reaching into her make-up bag, and throwing a tube of lipstick to Casey.

She was halfway out the door, when Debbie called after her.

'Fingers and toes crossed for both of you. Don't mess it up this time, girl.'

Casey ran down the stairs, and out the front door. She had crossed the road, and was halfway down the quay when she saw Shay duck into the boat wheelhouse. She stopped, wondering if he had seen the conch shell or had he already thrown it overboard.

Slowly she made her way down. When she got as far as the boat, she hesitated. She regretted leaving the conch shell there; it suddenly felt like such a childish thing to have done. Shay had not seen her. Her heart was thumping, and her head hurt. She should never have come here.

She was about to turn back, when Shay moved out of the wheelhouse.

When he saw Casey, he stopped. She froze. Shay stepped out of the boat and walked up to her cautiously.

'I got the shell,' he said.

'I'm sorry, it was stupid. It feels a bit silly now,' she mumbled.

'It's not, it shows me you care.'

'I should get back inside.'

'Since when does the big city lawyer walk away? Come on, I expect more from you.'

Casey dug her hands deep in her raincoat pockets.

'I can't play games, Shay, I am too tired for that.'

Immediately, he was at her side.

'I have coffee and muffins in the wheelhouse. Will you come to Scarty with me?'

'Jordan Marsh muffins?'

'Of course.'

'I would love to.'

She sat on a stool beside him as he manoeuvred the boat out of the harbour.

'It gets very cold out at sea in this weather,' he said, gently placing a thick wool rug on her shoulders.

They didn't talk again as the boat bobbed across the water, but sat in a companiable silence, the sound of the boat moving through the waves a comfort to both of them.

As Shay turned for the Scarty jetty, Casey stood beside him, the island looming large in front of them.

When they pulled up at the pier, Shay hopped up, and tied up the boat before offering his hand to Casey to help her off.

'Can we just walk to the beach, and skim stones?' he asked and she nodded, following him up the path.

When they got to the beach, he took her hand, and they walked to the water's edge.

'No paddling in this weather,' he said.

Casey scanned the horizon, hoping to see the sea, but everything was cold and grey and so different. Shay handed her a flat stone.

'We can still flick stones,' he said gently.

She took the stone, rubbing the smooth surface. Shay moved away, and fired his stone which hit off the water six times before plopping into the grey sea. Casey got in position, and threw the stone, watching it glide across the water, lightly plucking the water until it dipped down into the sea, leaving ripples to be carried away by the waves.

'You won that one,' he said.

She smiled happily.

'What do we do now?' Shay asked.

'I don't know.'

He opened his arms wide, and she stepped into his embrace.

'I am so sorry,' she said.

'I was stupid; I should never have put you in that position,' Shay said.

She buried her head in his chest, and he kissed her hair.

'We need to talk, Casey, please.'

She pulled away from him. 'I thought you wouldn't want to see me again.'

'I thought I didn't, until I saw you walking down the quay this morning.'

He kissed her, and she responded, the two of them staggering, and almost falling in the sea.

Shay pulled her up the beach, and she laughed, suddenly feeling free once again.

He pulled her to a group of rocks, and they sat down.

'Where to next?' he asked.

'I don't want to go back to Manhattan; but I will have to sort things out there.'

'Are you sure?'

Casey shook her head. 'It's like jumping off a cliff, but yes, I'm sure.'

'If we can winter together in Ballymurphy beside the Atlantic Ocean, we can do anything,' he said, holding her tight.

'I hope so.'

'So much has happened, and now with Amy...'

'Are you cool with it?'

'Of course. For us it's a big plus. It helps ease the loss.'

'It's tough on Amy; she missed out on an opportunity to meet her birth mother.'

'Yeah, it's just so difficult to get your head around the fact that Rosie never saw fit to tell us.'

'I have been thinking a lot about that, and I think she wasn't able to tell anyone. Especially when Amy, as she saw it, didn't come looking for her once she turned eighteen. It must have felt like a massive rejection to her,' Casey said.

'It is all so incredibly sad,' Shay said,

'How is Dan taking it?'

'I suggested a DNA test, and he jumped down my throat. He says he can see Andrew in her eyes. In fairness, so can I.'

Casey stood up, and wandered back to the water's edge. Far out she could see the black head of the seal in the water. She wanted to wave, and ask it to come closer, but she didn't. It was enough to see it at a distance.

She wandered back to Shay.

'All our lives have changed so much since we first came to Scarty. I wonder, did Rosie mean this, or is it all just a happy consequence of her putting pen to paper to tell her story?'

'Who knows, but it sure has shaken up all our lives,' Shay said.

'If you had asked me last year what the future held, I would have said a promotion to partner and nothing else.'

'And now?'

Casey smiled. 'A future in a place where I feel at home. Not just at Ballymurphy, but here at Scarty.'

'I hope you mean a future together,' Shay asked.

'I do,' she said and he caught her up, and twirled her around, making her scream and laugh, her happy cries drifting through the air, and across the waves.

EPILOGUE

It was a clear July morning when Debbie arrived on the island from New York hauling two large cases.

'I have just the dress for you, Casey,' she said, pulling open the case, and whipping out a white wedding dress with tiers of ruffles.

Casey stared at the frothy confection in front of her.

'This is not what I asked you to pick up. You've got to be kidding; I can't wear this.'

Georgie and Debbie chuckled.

'It was worth having to check in the extra case to see your face. What do you take us for, idiots?' Debbie said.

Georgie took a bag from the bottom of the case, and unzipped it to reveal a long blush pink silk dress which unfurled to the floor with a whoosh.

'Try it on, we'll get May to adjust it, if it doesn't fit,' Debbie said.

'May is busy enough getting ready for her own wedding. Everything should be fine,' Casey said.

Debbie handed her the dress. 'We need a rehearsal. We bridesmaids are wearing blue silk and for some reason Amy is wearing white. She is young and foolish. Who wears white to a wedding?' she said.

'Somebody young enough to know they will look amazing in white. Remember, Rosie wore white to your wedding and you made her change, and wear one of your summer dresses which was way too big for her,' Casey said.

'I don't remember that,' Debbie said, sounding a little peeved.

Casey took off her jeans and T-shirt, and slipped on the wedding dress.

She stood looking at herself in the full-length mirror. Cut on the bias, the dress hugged her body, the square neckline accentuating her long neck. Its beauty was in its simplicity.

'We will put your hair in a messy bun, and weave in some fresh flowers; you'll look stunning,' Georgie said.

Debbie went into the bathroom to change into her dress, while Georgie slipped off her clothes, and pulled on her wedding outfit.

'For somebody who went skinny dipping, she can be quite a prude at times,' Georgie laughed.

They were both wearing simple sheath dresses in blue silk with matching shawls edged in tassels.

Georgie pulled the three of them in for a group selfie.

'Who would have thought so much could change in a year for all of us?' she said.

When there was a knock on the bedroom door, and Shay asked if he could come in, there was a resounding 'No'.

'We are trying on the dress for the big day, you can't see it; it will bring back luck,' Georgie shouted.

'I just want to make sure ye want to go to Scarty tonight.'

'We do and everything is packed and boarded on the boat. We just have to wrap up our dresses; we'll be there in a jiffy,' Debbie said, opening the door a little and shooing Shay away.

'You do realise this is his room,' Casey said.

'So what? A man has to respect tradition. Let's get the dresses covered up and get back to Scarty,' Debbie said, her tone as bossy as always.

On the quay, May waved to them. Casey scuttled over to her, and asked if she wanted to spend the night with them on Scarty.

'Are you mad? Not on the eve of my own wedding to Dan Kennedy. I am going to have a nice deep bubble bath, and Amy is going to do my nails and eyebrows. A blow-dry is booked for the morning for Amy and myself. No, thank you, I will get ready at home. Myself and Amy will travel out to the island with Dan and Shay in the morning. I don't believe all that nonsense of not seeing each other before the wedding; I'm too old for that,' she said.

'What a pity; we could have had such a lovely girls' night,' Debbie said, but May only laughed.

'Don't be telling fibs, woman; there will be more prosecco to go around,' May laughed.

'That was a close one,' Debbie whispered as May turned for home.

'Why? May can be such fun,' Casey said.

'We want it just to be the three of us for one last night,' Debbie snorted.

When they got to Scarty, Shay carried the cases and boxes of flowers to the farmhouse, where he had set up food and prosecco; the table set with china plates and crystal glasses.

'You're a keeper, Shay,' Debbie said approvingly, and asked was there any chance he had made the beds as well.

'May did that yesterday,' he said, gesturing to Casey to follow him as he went to the back door.

They walked hand in hand down the path. This year the foxgloves were scattered all over and the oxeye daisies were making a big show, spreading the length of the bank.

'I will see you in the morning,' he said, holding her tight, and kissing her gently on the lips.

'Don't forget,' she said.

'I won't even be late, Debbie would kill me.'

He kissed her again before jumping back on the boat. She wandered back up the path as Shay pulled away from Scarty jetty.

When she got back to the farmhouse, Debbie had balloons hanging from the corner of the mantelpiece and colourful streamers from the ceiling light.

'It's time to party,' Debbie said.

Casey accepted a glass of prosecco, and sat down.

'Can we just sit and drink, and talk about Rosie and how we ended up here?'

'A party for three is not really a party, anyway,' Debbie said.

Georgie got up and pulled another chair to the table before opening the front and back doors.

'Now we are a party of four. Let the spirit of Rosie join us,' she said.

They sat, the sound of the sea all around them, and chatted, and drank until near midnight. It was a quiet reminiscing among friends, stories told, funny moments revisited, sad times quietly acknowledged, and their friendship rejuvenated.

The next morning, Casey was up at dawn, and sitting in front of the farmhouse looking at the sun streak pink across the sky, lighting up the sea and Ballymurphy. She was sipping a coffee when Georgie bounded down the stairs, and said they had to get ready.

'Chill, I just have to put on the dress, and put the flowers in my hair.'

Georgie held up her make-up box. 'Nails, manicure and pedicure and a full bridal face – that takes time,' she said.

Debbie came out of her room and said that Casey, for once in her life, was to allow them to pamper her, and get her ready.

Casey shrugged. 'It's my wedding day. I am happy to sit and sip prosecco,' she said, leaning back on the fireside chair, and stretching out her hands towards Georgie.

Debbie sat on another chair, and propped her legs up on an old stool.

'You're the lucky one now, Casey, you have your man, and the island. Do you think Rosie planned all this?'

Casey giggled. 'Rosie was good, but she wasn't that good,' she said.

'This island will be such a goldmine for you guys. What an opportunity to open it up for tourists,' Debbie said.

Casey shook her head. 'We have decided to offer the farm-house to artists at reduced rates from March until June, and then it's for you guys and your families. We want to keep the island as it is.'

Debbie sighed. 'I should have known; there isn't an entrepreneurial bone in your bodies.'

Debbie and Georgie insisted that Casey only slip on her wedding dress at the last minute.

Georgie had picked daisies and made a daisy chain for Casey's hair and a bracelet for her wrist.

'In memory of Rosie,' she said.

Debbie had organised a gazebo to be placed on the strand, and decorated it with roses and lilies.

'I just don't understand why you want foxgloves and those big daisies for a bouquet, but what do I know?' Debbie said.

Georgie picked the flowers, and produced a pink ribbon to tie them together.

'How do I look?' Casey asked.

Debbie took Casey's hands. 'Look at you, the beautiful bride about to marry the man she adores and loves.'

'They are crossing the channel,' Georgie said, running upstairs to change.

Casey strained to listen the familiar chug of Shay's boat, and she knew he would be at the Scarty jetty very soon.

Debbie called Georgie downstairs.

'We have time for one last glass of bubbly,' she said pouring three glasses, and handing them out.

Holding hers aloft, she proposed a toast.

'To our dear friend Casey, who persuaded us to come to Scarty. You promised us an adventure and you promised us fun, and, boy, did you deliver. Wishing you and Shay every happiness,' she said.

They clinked glasses before heading out of the farmhouse, locking the door behind them.

Shay's boat was the first of three to pull into the jetty.

Dan, in a snazzy dark grey suit jumped out, and offered his hand to May, who was in a light blue chiffon skirt and deep blue jacket. She was holding a little bunch of violets.

Shay, in a cream linen suit and pink tie, tied up the boat before picking up Casey, and twirling her around.

'You look amazing,' he said.

Two more boats moored at the jetty, and the guests and the celebrant got out. Holding hands, Dan and May led the way to the beach, with Shay and Casey behind them, to where chairs had been laid out for the small group.

As Shay and Casey spoke their vows under the gazebo, the seal came close to shore as if it were listening, but dipped back under the water as the wedding guests clapped, and shouted congratulations.

Debbie handed around plastic cups with prosecco, and proposed a toast to both happy couples, and invited everybody back to Kennedys restaurant, Ballymurphy, for a celebratory lunch.

Shay and Casey, when they could, pulled away from the crowd, and walked hand in hand along the shore.

Kicking off her sandals, Casey walked barefoot, hitching up her wedding dress with one hand. Shay, who had slipped off his shoes and socks and thrown them further up the sand, rolled his trousers up before they stepped deeper into the waves.

'Debbie won't be happy if you get the dress wet,' he said.

'Who cares?' Casey smiled.

The happy chatter of the wedding group drifted across the sand. Two dolphins further out dipped in and out of the sea, the sound of their tails slapping the water floating in the air.

'Scarty Island; this is our home now, Casey,' Shay said, pulling her close.

Above them, the kittiwakes and seagulls glided effortlessly through the air.

'It doesn't get better than this,' Casey said.

A LETTER FROM ANN

Dear reader,

I want to say a huge thank you for choosing to read this novel. If you did enjoy it, and want to keep up to date with all my latest releases, just sign up at the following link. Your email address will never be shared and you can unsubscribe at any time.

www.bookouture.com/ann-oloughlin

I so loved each day sitting down to write this novel. I looked forward to escaping to Scarty Island, the small island on the Atlantic Ocean, and into the lives of Casey, Georgie, Debbie and Rosie. How I wanted to take Shay's boat from Ballymurphy village to Scarty, and stay in the old farmhouse and make friends with these wonderful women.

I am lucky to live by the sea in Ireland, and as I write early in the morning, there is not just the dawn chorus, but the sounds of the ocean as the waves crash to shore.

The Atlantic Ocean is a backdrop to everything that happens in A Letter from Ireland and the island's flora and fauna is something I loved researching.

My wish is that you all enjoy visiting Scarty Island and the story of these amazing women and how their bonds of friendship are renewed and strengthened.

I hope you love reading this novel, and if you did, I would be very grateful if you could write a review. I'd love to hear what you think, and it makes such a difference helping new readers to discover one of my books for the first time.

I love hearing from my readers – you can get in touch on my Facebook page, through Twitter, Instagram or Goodreads.

Thanks,

Ann

facebook.com/annoloughlinbooks

x.com/annolwriter

instagram.com/authorannoloughlin

tiktok.com/@authorannoloughlin

ACKNOWLEDGMENTS

There are occasions when the writing comes easy, and times when every sentence seems like a battle.

It is during those difficult days that I appreciate the unwavering support of my husband and family. Words of encouragement are whispered, and cups of tea magically appear at my elbow when they are needed most. The home team knows that easy reading makes hard writing.

And so does my Bookouture editor, Ruth Jones, who, with her gentle nudges, encouragement and wise advice, helped get this novel over the line.

Bringing a book to publication is a team effort, and I must thank everyone on the Bookouture team, who worked so hard in the run up to publication day.

I am also very lucky to have on my side my agent, Jenny Brown of Jenny Brown Associates, who has always championed my work.

Special mention must be made of all the readers out there who have enjoyed reading an Ann O'Loughlin book, and have taken the trouble to write a review or have got in touch to say how much they loved the novels. To all of you dear readers, I say thanks a million for spreading the word, and making this author's day!

Ann

PUBLISHING TEAM

Turning a manuscript into a book requires the efforts of many people. The publishing team at Bookouture would like to acknowledge everyone who contributed to this publication.

Audio
Alba Proko
Sinead O'Connor
Melissa Tran

Commercial
Lauren Morrissette
Hannah Richmond
Imogen Allport

Cover design
Debbie Clement

Data and analysis
Mark Alder
Mohamed Bussuri

Editorial
Ruth Jones
Sinead O'Connor

Copyeditor
Jon Appleton

Proofreader
Liz Hurst

Marketing
Alex Crow
Melanie Price
Occy Carr
Ciara Rosney
Martyna Młynarska

Operations and distribution
Marina Valles
Stephanie Straub

Production
Hannah Snetsinger
Mandy Kullar
Jen Shannon
Ria Clare

Publicity
Kim Nash
Noelle Holten
Jess Readett
Sarah Hardy

Rights and contracts
Peta Nightingale
Richard King
Saidah Graham

Printed in Great Britain
by Amazon